The Lost Kingdom

written by

Jody Slyman

"The Lost Kingdom," by Jody Slyman. ISBN 978-1-60264-394-9.

Published 2009 by Virtualbookworm.com Publishing Inc., P.O. Box 9949, College Station, TX 77842, US. ©2009, Jody Slyman. All rights reserved. No part of this publication may be reproduced, stored in a retrieval system, or transmitted in any form or by any means, electronic, mechanical, recording or otherwise, without the prior written permission of Jody Slyman.

Manufactured in the United States of America.

This book is dedicated to some very special people:

To my brother, Michael Slyman, you're not only my brother, but my best friend. No matter what I've done in life, you've always been there with love and support. I can't ever thank you enough. I'll always be there for you no matter what. I love you bro.

To Stephanie Cross (Brookman), you are one of the best friends I've ever had in my life and I'm truly honored to know you. We've been through so much in life, the ups and the downs, but no matter what it has been, we've been there for each other. Thank you for always being there and being such a great friend. I will never forget it and I will always be there for you with all my love and support.

To my best little buddy, Brendan Brookman. It's been such a pleasure and an honor to see you grow from the time you were born until now. Remember to dream big cause you can do anything you want to in life. I believe in you and will always be there with my love and support.

To Marsha Pinkert, you mean so very much to me. In the time we've known each other, I've never been able to be so open and comfortable with someone as much as I am with you. You're a true friend and you will always hold a special place in my heart. No matter where life takes us, I will always be your friend and be there for you. I love you.

The Lost Kingdom

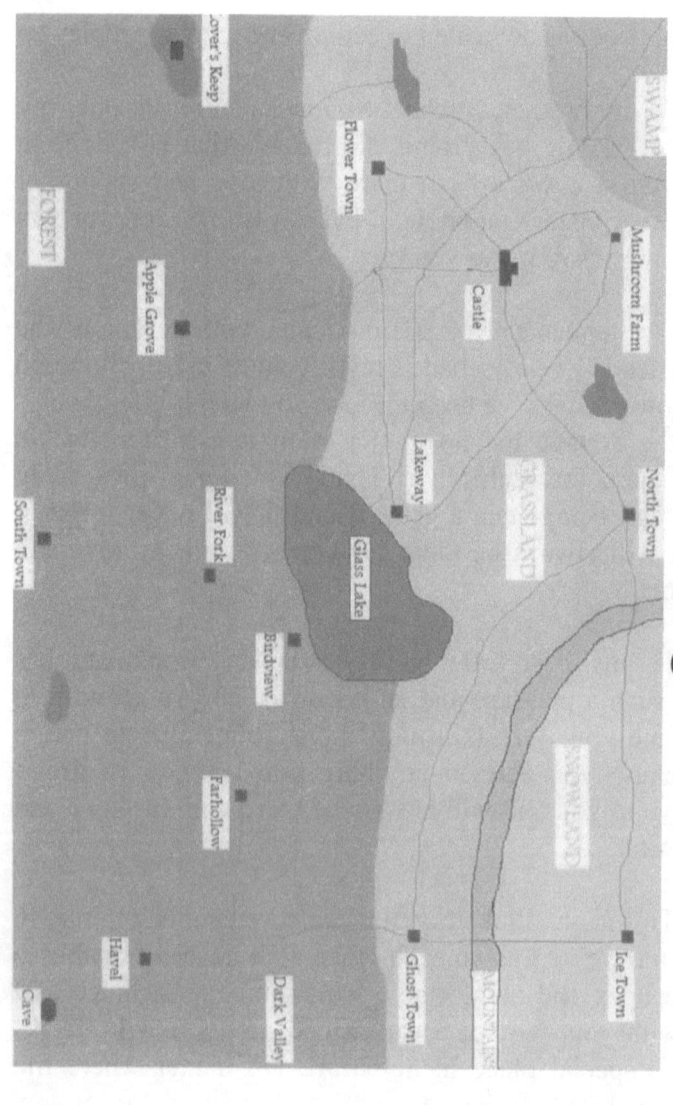

Introduction

I t is an overcast day in the city. The afternoon sun has not been able to break through the dark, gray clouds. The rain is now just a mist, but the ground shows the effects of the all day long rain. The smell of rain lingers in the air along with the usual smells of the city. The sound of cars driving along the rain soaked roads echo in the air.

A good looking Caucasian man in his mid-thirties that stands about 5'7" tall and weighing a fit 140 pounds is walking down one of the not so busy, rain soaked sidewalks in the older part of downtown. He has his light brown hair cut in a military style high and tight. He has blue-green eyes and a fairly nice build. He is wearing hiking shoes, faded blue jeans, brown belt, gray t-shirt and a hooded jacket.

The man walks into an old bookstore. When he opens the door, a bell over the door rings. The man looks at the numerous shelves lined with the used books.

An older man from behind the counter speaks, "How are you today?"

The younger man nods, "Good, a little wet. How are you?"

The older man smiles, "Not too bad young man. Can I help you with anything?"

The younger man shrugs, "Just going to look around some."

The older man nods and returns to his newspaper. The younger man walks down one of the isles. The younger man looks at the numerous books as if he is looking for a specific kind of book. He pulls a couple of different books from the shelf, but after reading the back of the books, he returns them to the shelf. The younger man continues to browse for another thirty minutes, but is unable to find anything that catches his eye.

As the younger man walks back by the counter, the older man speaks, "Couldn't find anything?"

The younger man sighs, "Not really."

The older man questions, "Looking for anything specific?"

The younger man nods, "I'm looking for a fantasy adventure or fairytale type story."

The older man's face gets a strange look. He glances around as if he is looking to see if anyone is watching them. The younger man appears a little puzzled by the older man's actions.

The older man speaks a little quieter, "I think I have just the book for you."

The younger man is unsure, but decides to check it out, "What is it?"

The older man reaches under the counter and pulls out an 8x10, leather bound book. The book appears to be old by the yellowing on the edges of the paper. The older man sets the book on the counter and slides it towards the younger man.

The older man speaks in almost a whisper, "This is a special book. It is an adventure that will draw you in and not let go."

The younger man looks at the cover of the book. The only words on the cover is the title and it reads, "The Lost Kingdom". The younger man glances over the cover and the spine of the book.

The younger man questions, "Who wrote it?"

The older man glances around again, "I don't know. No author's name is written anywhere."

The younger man thinks for a minute. He really

wants a good book to read and has spent all day looking for one without any success.

The younger man nods, "Okay. How much?"

The older man replies with a satisfied tone as if he is so grateful for the young man buying the book, "Ten dollars."

The younger man pulls out his wallet. He flips the wallet open to expose a picture of him in a Marine Corps Dress Blue uniform. Another picture is visible. It is of an absolutely beautiful Caucasian woman with dark brown, spiraling hair that hangs down past her shoulders. She has a very nice smile and attractive eyes. She looks to be in her late twenties. Also in the picture is a young Caucasian boy, about the age of six. The child has light colored hair and trim build.

The older man speaks, "That is a nice looking young woman and child."

The younger man smiles as he pulls out a twenty dollar bill, "Thanks, its my sister, Stephanie, and my nephew, Brendan."

The younger man hands the money to the older man.

The older man speaks while making change, "Marine Corps I see."

The younger man nods, "Oh yes."

The older man hands the change back, "Well, thank you for everything you've done."

The younger man nods, puts his money back in his wallet and returns his wallet to his pocket.

The younger man picks up the book, "You have a good day."

The older man nods, "You too, and take care of yourself."

The younger man appears a little puzzled by the response as he walks out of the bookstore. The young man walks about a mile down the city streets back to a ground level apartment complex. The young man walks up to one of the apartment doors and pulls out his keys. He unlocks the door and walks inside. He locks the door behind him and turns the lights on. He takes off his shoes and leaves them by the door. He looks around his decent sized apartment. He is in the living room where there is a couch, recliner, two end tables and a television on a console table.

The young man removes his jacket and lays it on the edge of the couch. He pulls his cell phone out of his pocket and sits down in his recliner with the book in his lap. He sets his cell phone on the end table and looks at the book. He starts to open the book, when his cell phone rings.

The young man answers his phone, "Hello."

A female voice comes on the line, "Hey Jody."

Jody smiles, "Steph, how are you doing?"

Stephanie replies, "I was just calling to see if you were able to get off work for Brendan's party. I can't believe my little boy is going to be seven."

Jody replies, "Yes I did so I'll definitely be there."

Jody and Stephanie visit for another ten minutes, then they both hang up. Jody puts his cell phone down and returns his attention to his new book. He hears thunder in the background as he opens the cover of the book. The first page has some kind of inscription on it. At the top of the page are the words: "read the following inscription out loud if you have an adventurous heart".

Jody looks puzzled, but he reads the inscription out loud, "For all those that do not fear a real adventure, look no further than these pages."

At that moment, a loud crash of thunder echoes through the apartment and the lights go out. Jody jumps in his chair as the sound gives him a quick scare. The apartment is nearly pitch black with all the lights out. Jody closes the book, sets it on the end table and gets up from his chair. He hears strange noises coming from outside his door.

Jody walks over, puts on his shoes and grabs his jacket. He puts on his jacket and unlocks his front door. He opens his door and a look of complete shock comes across his face. He was expecting to see the other apartment buildings and rain falling, but the scene he is looking at is nothing like that at all.

Jody blinks as he can't believe his eyes. He steps outside his front door, in complete shock of what he is seeing. He takes a couple steps and his front door suddenly slams closed behind him. Jody spins around in excitement. His face becomes even more puzzled at what he is looking at now. Instead of looking at the front door of his apartment, Jody is staring at the entrance to a cave in the side of a large hill.

Jody speaks as he just stares in disbelief at the entrance to the cave, "What in the world is going on?"

Chapter 1

T he dark clouds hang over the city as the smell of rain mixes with the other usual smells of the city. The large raindrops continue to fall into the spring afternoon as most people are preparing for the end of the work day. A two door car pulls onto the parking lot of the Junior High School and parks next to a red SUV. The woman from the picture in Jody's wallet, his sister, Stephanie, the most absolutely and unbelievably beautiful 30 year old woman, gets out of the driver's seat. She stands right at 5'7" and weighs a trim, incredible and near perfect 120 pounds that will get any man's attention. She has brown, wavy, almost spiraling hair that hangs down to her lower shoulder blades and captivating blue eyes. She is wearing faded, tight fitting blue jeans, a tight fitting brown, long sleeve pullover top with four buttons and the top three buttons are undone, casual brown flat soled sandals, a silver chain with silver St. Jude medallion necklace and a pair of small diamond earrings. Stephanie is holding the 8x10 leather bound book in her left hand that Jody had bought from the bookstore and an umbrella in her right hand.

Stephanie's seven year old son, Brendan, gets out of the back passenger's seat. He is about 4'4" tall and weighs a trim 56 pounds with short, light sandy brown hair and hazel eyes that change from light green to gray to blue. He is wearing blue and white tennis shoes, blue jeans and a camouflage "GAP" t-shirt. He gets under the umbrella with his mom. Stephanie uses her keychain to lock the car and the two of them walk up to the solid metal, windowless door of the school.

Stephanie hands the book to Brendan, opens the door and closes her umbrella. They go inside, walk down the hallway and into the first classroom on the right.

Standing next to the teacher's desk is a very beautiful and attractive, 23 year old Caucasian woman with a light complexion and some freckles. The young woman stands at 5'3" tall and has a petite, yet incredible looking 110 pound body that would turn any man's head. She has straight, strawberry blonde hair that hangs just to her shoulders and gorgeous green eyes that occasionally turn to a shade of blue. She is wearing black, square toed boots with a two inch heel that comes up to just below her knee, faded, tight fitting blue jeans which go down inside the boots, a tight fitting, lightweight, black v-neck top with long sleeves and a silver chain necklace with a pink stone in a heart shape.

Brendan runs over, tosses the book on the teacher's desk and hugs the young woman, "Hi Sherry."

Sherry hugs Brendan and smiles, "Hey there, how's my big man today?"

Brendan steps back, "Good."

Stephanie smiles at Brendan and Sherry, "Hey Sherry. How are you?"

Sherry gives a warm smile, "Pretty good. I've got everything ready for the book study group."

Stephanie hangs up her umbrella, "Thanks. You're by far the best teacher's aide I've had. You save me when I'm running late."

Sherry chuckles a little, "Thanks. It looks like everyone is running a little late."

Stephanie nods and sits down at her desk. Sherry sits down in a chair next to the desk and Brendan sits down in a chair next to Sherry. The three of them wait for everyone else to show up.

————————

About ten minutes later, a white car pulls onto the Junior High School parking lot and it parks next to Stephanie's car. A very cute 13 year old Caucasian girl gets out of the passenger's seat. She is about 4'9" tall and weighs about 75 pounds. She has short, straight blonde hair that hangs just below her ears and hazel eyes. She is wearing pink tennis shoes, blue jeans with a pink belt, a dark pink shirt with black trim around the neck and an outline of a skull and crossbones on the front made of clear stones, and a brown rope necklace with silver medallion.

An extremely beautiful and attractive, 30 year old Caucasian woman that no doubt gets plenty of attention from any man given her physical looks, gets out of the driver's seat and locks the doors. She stands 5'7" tall and weighs a most incredible and stunningly figured 160 pounds. She has straight, blonde hair that hangs down to the top of her shoulders and the most beautiful and captivating blue eyes. She is wearing blue and yellow tennis shoes, form fitting, faded blue jeans and a tight fitting gray, lightweight, long sleeve top. She is also wearing a pair of small diamond earrings and a silver chain with silver heart necklace that has the word "LOVE" on it.

The teenage girl and young woman run across the rain soaked parking lot to the unlocked door. Once inside, the two of them walk down the hallway and enter the classroom where Sherry, Stephanie and Brendan are waiting.

Brendan looks over to the door and immediately smiles at the young girl, "Hey Anna."

Anna smiles at Brendan, "Hi Brendan."

Brendan walks over and gives Anna a hug.

Stephanie looks at the young woman, "Hey Marsha. I take it the rain hasn't let up."

Marsha smiles and shakes her head, "Not even a little." She pauses, "Sorry we're a little late, my relief wasn't quite on time."

Marsha bends down and gives Brendan a hug, "How's my man today."

Brendan smiles as he hugs Marsha, "Good."

Sherry smiles, "It looks like the weather has everyone running a little behind."

Anna and Marsha take a seat by the desk and Brendan sits back down. Marsha looks at the book on the desk.

Stephanie looks at Marsha, "So, how's work going?"

Marsha nods, "It's good. I'm going to be moving from the cardiac unit to the emergency room soon."

Sherry nods, "That's cool."

Stephanie nods, "That'll be quite the change."

Marsha smiles, "Yea, but when I became an RN I was wanting to work in an emergency room."

Stephanie smiles, "That's good then."

Anna looks at the book on the desk, "What book do we have for the study group this time?"

Marsha speaks up, "It looks old." She pulls the book over in front of her and reads the title on the cover, "The Lost Kingdom. I've never heard of it."

Anna questions, "Where did you get it?"

Stephanie speaks a little more solemnly, "It was in Jody's things that we packed away last year when he disappeared. I've never even opened the book before."

Anna looks a little upset, "I'm sorry."

Stephanie gives a supportive smile, "It's okay."

Brendan looks at his mom, "Can we look at it?"

Stephanie smiles, "The others aren't here yet." She pauses and smiles at her son's interest in reading, "Well, I guess we can glance at it some while we wait."

Marsha slides the book over to Stephanie. Brendan stands up in his chair to get a better look as Anna stands up next to the desk. Stephanie opens the cover of the book as lightning flashes in the windows. The five of them look at the first page. At the top of the page are the words: "read the following inscription out loud if you have an adventurous heart". The five of them look at each other with a puzzled look.

Then, Anna smiles, "Should we read the inscription?"

Sherry shrugs, "Why not? We are all a little adventurous I would say."

Stephanie nods, "I guess it won't hurt anything."

The five of them all read the inscription at the same time, "For all those that do not fear a real adventure, look no further than these pages."

At that moment, lightning flashes in the windows followed by a deafening crash of thunder and all the lights go out covering the room in darkness. All five of them jump and let out different little screams as the sound scares them.

After taking a couple of breaths to slow down her racing heart, Stephanie speaks, "It's okay. The power just went out."

Anna chuckles as she catches her breath, "That scared me."

Sherry chuckles, "Yea it did."

Marsha chuckles and agrees, "Me too." She pauses, "But we've got Brendan here to protect us, right big guy?"

Brendan hops down from his chair, "Yea."

Anna speaks a little puzzled, "Hey, do you hear that?"

The others listen intently and they all hear what Anna is talking about. They can hear the faint sound of birds chirping.

Marsha questions, "What could that be?"

Stephanie shakes her head, "I don't know."

The five of them hear more faint animal sounds, then they each realize that they don't hear the rain or the storm anymore.

Marsha speaks up, "I think the storm stopped. I don't hear the rain or wind."

Sherry questions, "Should we go look?"

Stephanie replies, "Let's make our way to the door to the parking lot."

Stephanie takes Brendan's hand. The five of them make their way out of the dark classroom into the even darker hallway. A little confused by the noises and what is going on, Stephanie forgets her umbrella. The five of them make their way down the nearly pitch black hallway as the noises get louder. It takes a couple of minutes, but the five of them finally find the door to the parking lot and the noises are even louder and more distinct than ever.

Anna speaks up, "This is just too weird."

Stephanie sighs and pushes the solid door open. The five of them are nearly blinded by the sunlight in their faces. Once they start to get their eyes focused, they see something that none of them were expecting. All five of them just stare in shock and amazement.

Stephanie questions hoping she isn't going crazy, "Are you seeing what I'm seeing?"

Marsha nods in amazement, "Yea, but I don't believe it."

Sherry just stares, "What in the world?"

Stephanie and Brendan step through the doorway followed by Anna and Marsha, then Sherry. The five of them glance around, still in amazement. They find themselves not in the school parking lot, but in a very bright, plush forest. The five of them take a few more steps forward, looking all around in complete disbelief. Suddenly, the door behind them slams shut. The five of them turn around quickly as the noise startles them. Their faces are even more puzzled as they stare at the entrance of a cave in the side of a large hill. The same cave Jody stared at just one year ago.

Brendan questions a little nervously, "Mom?"

Stephanie just shakes her head and continues to stare, "Brendan, I don't know."

Chapter 2

A very pretty female elf with a light Hispanic complexion walks into a dark room lit with only candles. She stands at 4'11" tall and weighs a very attractive and well put together 140 pounds with dark brown hair with dark green highlights that hangs to her shoulders and captivating brown eyes. She looks to be in her mid-thirties even though she is nearly 200 years old. She is wearing black boots that come up to her mid-calf, tight fitting, royal blue with black trim pants, a form fitting, royal blue with black trim, long sleeve top, a black leather belt, a ruby amulet necklace and an emerald ring on her left hand. She is wearing a black cloak with the hood off. She has a two and a half foot long, gold handle with silver blade sword on her left hip. She is carrying a six foot long staff in her right hand that has an eagle claw on the end of it.

The room is about fifty feet by fifty feet with one wall lined with shelves. A table sits about twenty feet from the shelves. In the back of the room is a fire pit with a large caldron sitting on top of it. The shelves are lined with bottles and jars full of either liquid, herbs or body parts of animals. On the table is a nine inch dagger, a crystal ball and candles burning on each corner.

The female elf walks over to the table and gazes at the crystal ball. She seems very excited.

The female elf smiles at the crystal ball, "Can it be. Outland children are in the Kingdom."

She leans the staff against the table. She waves her

hands over the crystal ball and mumbles under her breath. A fog appears in the crystal ball. She continues to move her hands and mumble. The fog starts to clear and five images start to appear. A few more seconds pass and finally the images of Stephanie, Sherry, Marsha, Brendan and Anna appear in the crystal ball.

The female elf's eyes widen, "Two children." She moves her hands some more, "Where are they?"

The scene in the crystal ball changes to show Stephanie, Sherry, Marsha, Brendan and Anna in the forest not too far from the cave.

The female elf smiles again, "There you are."

She waves her hands some more and mumbles again. The image in the crystal ball changes to that of a Caucasian man's face. The man looks to be in his mid-thirties. He has short, spiky black hair and dark, powerful eyes. He has a two inch scar on his left cheek.

The man in the crystal ball speaks in a deep, powerful voice, "Queen Gabriela, what can I do for you?"

Gabriela smiles, "Choel, two children have entered the Kingdom. Come to the chamber and bring the horseshoes to summon the riders."

Choel bows his head, "Yes my Queen."

Gabriela moves her hands away from the crystal ball and Choel's face vanishes. Gabriela turns and walks over to the shelves.

Gabriela glances at the jars and bottles, "My dear children, I'll have you soon."

Gabriela grabs a dark green bottle, a blue jar and walks towards the caldron.

The most absolutely beautiful Hispanic female that stands around 4'11" tall with the most incredible 120 pound body is walking on a dirt road in the forest as the sun is halfway through the morning sky. She looks to be in her early twenties, even though she is nearly 175 years old, with straight dark brown hair with a few pink highlights that hangs to her shoulder blades and beautiful dark brown eyes. She is wearing brown leather boots that come up to her mid-calf, tight fitting, brown with pink trim pants, a tight fitting, brown with pink trim, sleeveless, low cut v-neck top, a brown leather belt and a brown cloak with the hood off. She has a two and a half foot long, silver handle with silver blade sword on her left hip. She is carrying a six foot wooden staff in her right hand that has a deep purple stone at the end of it. Sticking out just a little through her hair is her distinctive, pointy elf ears.

The woman suddenly stops and glances around as if she can sense or feel a presence around her. She looks around and sees a hollow tree stump filled with water next to the road. She walks over to the tree stump and stares down at the water.

She speaks in a calm, soothing voice as she holds her left hand over the tree stump, "It can't be."

The woman closes her eyes and takes a few deep breaths. The stone on her staff starts to glow as the image of Stephanie, Sherry, Marsha, Brendan and Anna in the forest appears in the water. The woman opens her eyes and stares at the image in the water in amazement.

The woman speaks a little shocked, "Outland children are in the Kingdom." She pauses, "Not far from here. I must get to them quickly."

The woman removes her hand and the image vanishes. She turns and starts walking into the forest at a fairly quick pace.

——— —— ——

Stephanie and the others are slowly wandering

amongst the forest trees as a soft breeze fills the crisp, clean air with the scent of leaves and a faint smell of spring water. Stephanie and the others stop near some underbrush in the forest.

Stephanie shakes her head, "This doesn't make any sense. We have walked all around this hill and all there is, is the cave." She pauses, "Where in the world did the school go?"

Sherry replies completely stunned, "I don't even know what to say."

Marsha lets out a sigh, "I don't know, I'm completely lost right now."

Then, the five of them hear what appears to be a female voice with a Texas accent, "You are in the Kingdom."

Stephanie looks at Marsha, "What was that?"

Marsha shakes her head, "I didn't say anything."

Stephanie and Marsha look at Sherry and Sherry shrugs, "It wasn't me."

They hear the voice again, "I said, you are in the Kingdom."

Brendan taps Stephanie, "Mom."

Stephanie, Sherry, Marsha and Anna look at Brendan. Brendan just stares and points over to the underbrush. Stephanie, Sherry, Marsha and Anna look over to where Brendan is pointing. They see a snow white, floppy eared rabbit by the underbrush.

The rabbit speaks, "Hello there. I'm Bailee."

The five of them just stare at the rabbit in amazement, not quite sure what to think.

Bailee speaks again, "You act as if you've never seen a talking rabbit before."

Stephanie speaks still staring at the rabbit, "Are you all seeing what I'm seeing?"

Marsha nods still staring, "Yea, but I don't believe it."

Sherry shakes her head, "Umm, yea."

Then, Anna surprises all of them, "You said we were in the Kingdom. What do you mean?"

Bailee replies, "This is the Kingdom of Prince Brian."

Stephanie glances at the others, then looks back at the rabbit, still not sure about what is happening.

Anna looks at Stephanie, "Do you think it's possible?"

Stephanie looks over to Anna, "What's that?"

Anna replies, "That we are in the story of 'The Lost Kingdom'?"

Marsha sighs, "Don't be silly Anna."

Sherry chuckles, "That's just not possible."

Bailee speaks again, "You're not safe here."

Stephanie looks back to the rabbit, "What?"

Bailee replies, "You're not safe here. You need to get as far away from the cave as you can."

Marsha questions, still not believing that she is talking to a rabbit, "Why?"

Bailee replies, "Because the evil, self-proclaimed Queen who controls this land, Gabriela, will send her dark riders after the children."

Marsha looks at Stephanie and the others with a very puzzled look.

Bailee speaks again, "You should head for the ferry on the river."

Anna looks at the rabbit and shakes her head, "We don't know where that's at."

Bailee replies, "I can take you, but we must hurry."

Brendan looks up at Stephanie, "Mom, I don't want to stay here."

Stephanie lets out a sigh and a slight nod, "Okay." She pauses and continues as if she can't believe what she is saying, "I guess we'll follow the talking rabbit."

Bailee starts to hop away, "This way, hurry."

Stephanie, Sherry and Marsha glance at each other with a quick, puzzling look, then the five of them start walking after the rabbit.

Chapter 3

G abriela stands by the large caldron. A fire burns under the caldron filling the air with smoke and the horrible smell of the stuff boiling in the caldron. She walks over to the table and takes the lid off of a dark blue jar. She reaches into the jar and pulls out what looks like a heart. She walks back over to the caldron and drops in the heart.

At that moment, the door opens and Choel walks in. He is a huge man standing every bit of 6'6" tall and weighs at least 260 pounds. He is dressed in pieces of black plate mail armor that covers his chest, arms and thighs. He has a five foot long, solid black sword on his left hip and he is carrying a four foot long, black shield in his left hand. He is carrying two horseshoes in his right hand.

Gabriela turns to the door, "Choel. Bring me the horseshoes."

Choel walks over next to the caldron and hands the two horseshoes to Gabriela. Gabriela takes one horseshoe and drops it into the caldron. The sound of the heavy horseshoe hitting the bottom of the metal caldron echoes through the room. Then, Gabriela takes the second horseshoe and drops it into the caldron. Again, the sound echoes through the room.

Gabriela speaks in a hollow tone, "We need to move back."

Choel walks back over by the door and Gabriela stands next to him. A couple seconds pass, then even with a fire burning in the room, the room starts to get cold. Choel begins to shiver from the cold filling the room. Gabriela just smiles at the caldron. Then, a cold rush of air blows through the room and the candles go out.

Gabriela smiles, "It's almost time. Don't look at the caldron Choel or you could be blinded."

Choel turns his head and closes his eyes. Gabriela closes her eyes as a dark red light starts to glow from the caldron. The dark red suddenly flashes to blue, then green. The room gets even colder and the smell in the room would make most people sick. Suddenly, a bright flash of golden light bursts from the caldron that makes one feel like they've looked directly into the sun, then the room goes dark.

Choel and Gabriela both open their eyes. They can't see very well at first, but they can make out the outlines of two people standing by the caldron. One figure is nearly 5'9" tall and weighs a trim 165 pounds. The second figure is a little shorter, around 5'7" tall and weighs around 155 pounds. Neither figure moves as Gabriela walks over to the table. She waves her hand over one of the candles and it starts to burn again filling the room with a little light. Choel can make out the figures better now. Both figures are Caucasian males.

The taller man is wearing black boots that come up to just below his knees. He is wearing form fitting, dark brown pants and a tight fitting, dark brown long sleeve top. He has a black leather belt holding a scabbard with a four foot long, solid black sword on his left hip and a solid black, foot long dagger on his right hip. He is also wearing a solid black, hooded cloak with the hood off at this time. He has short black hair and haunting hazel colored eyes.

The shorter man is wearing dark brown boots that come up to just below his knees. He is wearing form fitting, black pants and a tight fitting, black long sleeve top. He has a dark brown leather belt holding a scabbard with a four foot long, dark metallic gray sword on his left hip and a dark metallic gray, foot long dagger on his right hip. He is also wearing a dark brown, hooded cloak with the hood off at this time. He has short, blond hair and pure blue eyes.

Gabriela walks up to the two men and smiles at her magic.

Gabriela looks at the taller man, "Miclou." She turns her gaze to the shorter man, "Stecher." She pauses, "There are two outland children in the Kingdom. They came through the cave. Bring them to me and kill anyone who tries to stop you."

Miclou and Stecher bow their heads.

Gabriela looks over to Choel, "Show them to their horses."

Choel bows his head, "Yes my Queen."

Choel walks out of the room followed by Miclou and Stecher."

Gabriela watches them walk out of the room with an evil smile and speaks in a hauntingly evil tone, "Soon children, you'll be mine."

With the two men gone, the temperature in the room quickly rises again as Gabriela walks over to the table, grabs her staff and walks out of the room.

———————

As the sun has just passed through the warm, noon sky, the slight breeze blows the white clouds across the pure blue sky and the smell of the trees gets stronger as does the smell of fresh water. Stephanie and the others continue to follow the rabbit through the forest along a small trail.

Marsha shakes her head and chuckles as she walks, "I still can't believe this. We are in a fairytale story, following a talking rabbit because of an evil Queen."

Stephanie lets out a sigh, "Yea, it all seems so unreal right now."

Sherry chimes in, "I'm still at a loss for words."

Bailee responds while hopping, "It's very real."

Brendan looks up at Stephanie, "Mom, I'm getting tired."

Anna nods, "I could use a little rest too."

Bailee stops and turns to face the five of them, "We need to keep going. The dark riders are probably on their way already."

Stephanie shakes her head, "We just need a little break."

Bailee replies, "I guess we can take a short break."

Brendan and Anna sit down on the ground. Stephanie sits next to Brendan and Marsha sits next to Anna. Sherry sits by Stephanie and Brendan. Bailee hops over near the five of them. A couple minutes pass when they hear some movement in the forest around them.

Anna glances around, "What is that?"

Marsha quickly questions, "Is it those dark riders?"

Bailee replies, "No. The air would get cold if it was the riders."

The rustling gets louder as the five of them look around. Stephanie stands up and looks around to see if she can see what is making the noise. Sherry, Marsha, Anna and Brendan stand up and glance around. Suddenly, two large, gray wolves appear on the trail about twenty yards in front of the group.

Sherry glances around, "I don't like this at all."

Brendan speaks, "Mom, look."

Stephanie and the others spot the wolves.

Bailee speaks, "Oh no."

Marsha questions, "What do we do now?"

Stephanie replies while staring at the wolves, "Lets just slowly move back down the trail and maybe they will go away."

Anna slowly turns around and spots two more wolves about thirty feet behind them on the trail.

Anna's eyes widen, "There are two more."

Bailee speaks nervously, "They're here for the kids as well."

Stephanie replies, "What?"

One of the wolves moves closer as Bailee replies, "Wolves work for the evil Queen."

The closest wolf speaks in a deep, male voice with a German sounding accent, "Just give us the kids."

Marsha just stares, "The wolves talk too."

Bailee speaks again, a little more scared, "Most animals do here."

As the other three wolves move closer, the lead wolf speaks again, "No need for this to get messy. Just give us the children." The wolf pauses, "And the rabbit, we need a little snack for the long trip back."

Bailee's eyes get as round as two dinner plates. Stephanie and the others move closer together as the wolves are nearly to within ten yards of them. Suddenly, the two wolves that are behind them are hit by a fierce blast of concussive air. The wolves let out a cry as they fly about ten feet off the trail into the forest. The other two wolves stop moving and look left into the forest. Stephanie and the others are just frozen in place from what is happening. As if appearing out of thin air, the female elf that has been looking for them appears from the forest a couple of feet in front of Stephanie.

The female elf speaks to the wolves, "Get back."

The two wolves stop and the lead wolf speaks, "You should stay out of this Stefez. Gabriela will not approve."

Then, four men dressed in dark clothes and brown cloaks each carrying a three foot long sword, appear from the forest just behind the wolves.

Bailee's eyes widen again, "Bandits."

Then, everyone hears the thunder of horses getting closer. The bandits glance around.

The lead wolf speaks, "Get the children."

As the bandits start towards Stephanie and the others, three horses appear on the trail behind the group. The bandits stop in their tracks. Stephanie and the others are just frozen in place from everything that is going on around them.

On the first horse is a handsome Caucasian man looking to be in his mid-thirties and standing around 6'3" tall and weighing a fit 200 pounds with short, black hair and powerful blue eyes. He is wearing brown boots that come up to just below his knees, form fitting, purple pants with gold trim, a tight fitting, long sleeve purple with gold trim top covered by a purple with gold trim tunic and a brown leather belt. He is carrying a five foot long shiny silver sword with a golden handle on his left hip, a two foot long shiny silver with gold handle short sword on his right hip and he is holding a four foot shiny silver shield with purple emblem with his left hand.

On the second horse is a beautiful Caucasian female. The woman appears to be in her late twenties and is right at 5'9" tall and weighs an attractive and a very nicely figured 170 pounds. She has blue and orange streaked hair that hangs down just below her shoulder blades and beautiful brown eyes. She is wearing brown boots that come up to just below her knees, tight fitting, royal blue with yellow trim pants, a tight fitting, royal blue with yellow trim long sleeve top covered by a royal blue with yellow trim tunic and a brown leather belt. She has a four foot long, shiny silver sword with a gold handle on her left hip and a two foot, shiny silver with gold handle short sword on her right hip.

On the third horse is a very attractive Caucasian female. The woman appears to be in her mid-twenties and is 5'2" tall with a very nicely shaped 130 pound body.

She has straight, brown hair with dark purple streaks that hangs down to her shoulder blades and incredible blue eyes. She is wearing black boots that come up to just below her knees, tight fitting, dark gray pants, a tight fitting, dark gray long sleeve top covered by a dark gray with light blue trimmed tunic and a black leather belt. She is carrying a four foot long, dark metallic gray sword on her left hip, a two foot long, dark metallic gray short sword on her right hip and a six inch, dark metallic gray dagger on the back of her waist.

One of the bandits speaks, "It's Prince Brian."

Prince Brian draws his sword from his left hip and speaks with a powerful voice, "I would suggest you leave them alone."

The lead wolf speaks, "We'll meet again Prince Brian and Stefez, and the children will be ours."

The bandits and the wolves run off into the woods. Prince Brian and the two women dismount their horses. Stefez walks over to Prince Brian.

Stefez bows her head, "Prince Brian, it's my pleasure to see you." She looks at the taller woman, "Jennifer, I hope you're doing well."

Prince Brian smiles, "Looks like we got here just in time."

Jennifer puts her sword away, "I'm doing well."

The other woman speaks, "So, you're the elf, Stefez. I'm Jencent."

Stefez looks a little puzzled, "The mercenary. I would not have expected you to be with the Prince."

Prince Brian puts his sword away, "Every little bit helps."

Jencent puts away her sword, "I'll do anything if the pay is right."

Prince Brian looks over at Stephanie, Sherry, Marsha, Anna and Brendan. He is immediately captured by Stephanie's beauty. Stephanie just stares at Prince Brian, making an immediate connection.

Prince Brian finally breaks his gaze at Stephanie and looks at Stefez, "Outlander children, this changes everything now."

Jennifer sighs, "No doubt the dark riders have already been summoned and sent this way."

Stephanie finally speaks up, "Okay, what's going on here?"

Bailee hops over by Stefez, "We're okay now. Stefez found us."

Stefez smiles, "Of course I did." She pauses, "And just in time I see."

Marsha questions, still a little shocked, "Who are you?"

Stefez looks over to Marsha, "I'm Stefez. I live here in the forest."

Brendan notices Stefez's ears, "Your ears look funny."

Stefez smiles at Brendan, "I'm an elf." She pauses and looks at Stephanie, "I'll be happy to tell you what's going on, but we really should get moving along."

Bailee speaks up, "I was taking them to the ferry at the river."

Stefez nods, "That's a good idea."

Prince Brian walks up to Stephanie and smiles, "Hello. I'm Prince Brian." He motions to Jennifer, "This is my personal guard, Jennifer." He then motions to Jencent, "And this is Jencent."

Stephanie smiles and tries not to stare into Prince Brian's eyes, "I'm Stephanie." She motions to Marsha and Anna, "This is my friend, Marsha, and her little sister, Anna." She motions to Sherry, "This is my friend and teaching assistant, Sherry." She puts her hand on Brendan's head, "And this is my son, Brendan."

Prince Brian nods to the others, "It's an honor to meet all of you."

Stefez speaks up, "We really should be going."
Prince Brian nods, "Of course."
Stefez starts off north on the trail and the others follow.

———————

The slight breeze blows the leaves on the trees as the birds are chirping. It is a beautiful scene in the forest as a couple of squirrels run across the ground near the entrance of the cave where the others appeared. Then, the sound of two horses riding fast appear in the distance. The air starts to get colder as the squirrels stop moving and the birds stop chirping. The air gets even more cold as the birds fly off and the squirrels run off into the forest.

Then, as if appearing out of the forest like two ghosts, Stecher and Miclou ride up to the entrance of the cave, each one on a black horse. Knowing that they are too late, the two of them slowly ride around the entrance of the cave looking down at the ground.

After a few seconds, Stecher speaks in a ghostly voice, "I have them. This way."

Stecher starts off into the forest closely followed by Miclou.

Chapter 4

The breeze has almost disappeared along with the sun as Stefez and the others are still walking along the trail in the forest. Stefez stops on the trail next to a clearing in the forest.

Stefez turns to the others, "It will be dark soon. We should rest for the night."

Stephanie glances around, "Just here in the middle of the forest?"

Stefez smiles, "We'll be safe for the night. I'll have my friends watch over us. If all of you want to rest, I'll gather some fruit and berries to eat."

Stephanie, Sherry, Marsha, Anna and Brendan walk into the clearing. Stefez walks off in the opposite direction. Stephanie sits down and Brendan sits next to her. Marsha also sits down and Anna sits next to her. Sherry sits next to Stephanie and Brendan. Prince Brian, Jennifer and Jencent tie up their horses, then they too sit down in the clearing. Prince Brian sits near Stephanie. Jennifer sits close to Prince Brian. Jencent sits more by herself. Bailee hops over by Prince Brian. As they wait for Stefez to return, Prince Brian starts some conversation.

Prince Brian looks at Stephanie, obviously captured by her beauty, "You're from the outland. How long have you been in the Kingdom?"

Stephanie stares at Prince Brian unable to believe how drawn to him she is, "Just today. In fact, we're not really sure what's going on."

Prince Brian smiles at Stephanie, "So, what do you do in the outland?"

Stephanie can't help but return the smile, "I'm a teacher." She pauses, "So, you're a Prince."

Marsha and the others can tell that Prince Brian has taken an instant liking to Stephanie and that Stephanie has taken an instant liking to him.

Marsha speaks up, "So, what exactly is going on? I mean, we've heard about an evil Queen and dark riders. We've seen animals that talk and an elf that performs magic."

Sherry chimes in, "And something about being an outlander. Plus, Jennifer mentioned outlander children changing everything."

Before Prince Brian can answer, Stefez walks back up with a large brown pouch.

Anna questions, "Where did you get the bag from?"

Stefez smiles, "I made it."

Stefez sets her staff down. She walks over to Stephanie and reaches into the bag. She pulls out some red berries and an apple. She hands them to Stephanie. She reaches into the bag and pulls out more red berries and another apple and hands them to Sherry, then reaches into the bag and pulls out some more red berries and hands them to Brendan. Stefez walks over to Marsha, pulls out some red berries and a pear and hands them to her. She pulls out another pear and some more red berries and hands them to Anna. Stefez walks over to Bailee, reaches into the bag and pulls out a couple of carrots. She puts them on the ground next to the rabbit.

Stephanie and the others start to eat as Stefez reaches into the bag and pulls out a hand sized rock. She puts the rock in the middle of the clearing, walks over and picks up her staff. Everyone just watches Stefez. Stefez walks over to the rock and touches it with the stone on the end of her staff. She closes her eyes and mumbles under her breath. Everyone just continues to stare at Stefez and wonders what she is doing.

After a couple of seconds, Stefez removes her staff from the rock. The rock starts to glow a fire red, lighting up the clearing. Stephanie and the others are shocked at what they have just seen. Stefez sits down by Bailee, pulls an apple out of the bag and starts eating. With the bag now empty, the magical bag disappears.

Stephanie looks at Stefez, "So, can someone tell us what's going on?"

Stefez nods, "Yes, of course."

Marsha speaks up, "You can start with, where exactly are we?"

Bailee speaks up, "I told you. You're in the Kingdom of Prince Brian."

Prince Brian sighs, "I wish that were true. Fact is, that Gabriela is in control right now." He pauses, "My father use to rule the entire Kingdom, but some years ago Gabriela, who served my father, decided that she wanted to rule the Kingdom and started to build a secret army. After a few years, Gabriela finally left the castle with one of my father's Captains, Choel, and two of his Lieutenants, Brytil and Regas. Gabriela gathered her army and started for the castle."

Anna gets into the story, "What happened?"

Jennifer speaks up, "Gabriela couldn't defeat the King's army until one day, an outland child entered the Kingdom. Gabriela conjured her dark riders to capture the child." She pauses, "Once the child was captured and taken to Gabriela, she used the power of the child to help her defeat the King's army."

Prince Brian picks up the story while gazing at Stephanie, "My father was killed and my younger sister vanished. I barely escaped with Jennifer and a small, loyal group. We've been hiding out for a couple of years rebuilding the army to try and take back the Kingdom from Gabriela."

Anna looks at Stefez, "Couldn't you help them fight Gabriela? Your magical."

Stefez sighs, "Gabriela is very powerful, the most talented Elvin cleric that ever came along. We both grew up studying the magic of the light, but after a hundred years of training and during her time of serving the King, she was tempted by the dark magic. Her powers have grown ever since. I'm not too sure if I could defeat her."

Marsha nods, "Wow, you know her pretty well."

Stefez smiles, "I should, she's my older sister."

Everyone gets quiet at what Stefez just said.

Stephanie finally questions getting lost in Prince Brian's eyes, "So, what's the deal with children?"

Stefez explains, "In this Kingdom, outland children have a vast amount of magical power inside them. The outland children just don't know how to use the magic. Gabriela can use her torture spells to remove the magic from the outland children to give her great power."

Sherry questions, "So, what happens to the children?"

Stefez answers a bit more solemnly, "Unfortunately, the children die."

Everyone gets quiet at what Stefez just told them, then Marsha speaks up, "So, what's the deal with these dark riders?"

Stephanie, Sherry and Marsha notice that the mere mention of the dark riders makes, Stefez, Prince Brian, Jennifer and Jencent uncomfortable.

Stefez sighs, "They are pure evil. Many centuries ago, there were two great warriors that traveled the Kingdom, Miclou and Stecher. They got pleasure from creating death and chaos. Many tried to stop them, but they were the greatest warriors in the entire land." She pauses, "Finally, the King sent his entire army to find them and destroy them. Having been mortally wounded in battle, Miclou and Stecher hid out in a blacksmith shop.

As they were dying, they used the last of the magic potion they had to preserve their souls in two horseshoes."

Stephanie breaks her gaze at Prince Brian and gets a puzzled look, "What?"

Stefez nods, "Somehow Gabriela came into possession of the horseshoes and figured out the potion that combined with the horseshoes, can bring Miclou and Stecher back to life." She pauses, "However, they only exist until the next full moon rises in the sky, then their souls return to the horseshoes. That's why Gabriela has sent the wolves and bandits as well."

Sherry questions, "When is the next full moon?"

Stefez sighs, "It will be in thirty days."

Sherry, Marsha and Stephanie just shake their heads. Neither one can believe everything they are hearing.

Stephanie then asks the all important question, "So, how do we get home? We tried the cave again, but it didn't do anything."

Stefez explains, "The cave is only a one way portal into the Kingdom. You need the one way portal out of the Kingdom."

Marsha questions a little excited to hear that there is a way back home, "Where's it at?"

Bailee speaks up, "You're not going to like this."

Stefez shakes her head at Bailee and replies, "It's a well in the dungeon of the castle."

Sherry questions, "Why is that bad?"

Jencent finally speaks, "Because Gabriela and her army control the castle."

Brendan leans against Stephanie, "Mom, I'm tired."

Prince Brian smiles at Brendan, "We all should get some rest. Tomorrow will be another long day."

Stefez nods, "All of you go ahead and lay down. I will get someone to watch over us for the night."

Still in disbelief, Stephanie lays down on the ground. The plush, green grass has made the ground a little comfortable. Brendan curls up next to Stephanie and she puts her arm around him. Marsha lays down and Anna lays down right next to her. Sherry lays down close to Stephanie and Brendan. Prince Brian, Jennifer and Jencent all lay down. Before long, everyone drifts off to sleep as Stefez sits quietly.

———

Gabriela walks into the chamber where she conjured up Miclou and Stecher. The soft glow of the candles light up the dark room. She walks over to the table where her crystal ball is sitting. She waves her hand over the crystal ball and mumbles under her breath. After a few seconds, a gray mist appears in the crystal ball.

Gabriela continues to slowly move her hand and mumble. After a few more seconds, the face of Miclou appears in the crystal ball.

Gabriela speaks, "My wolves and bandits failed. How are you doing?"

Miclou replies in a hollow voice, "We found their trail from the cave and we're getting closer. We should have them by noon tomorrow."

Gabriela gives an evil smile, "Good." She pauses, "I can no longer see them so I have no doubt Stefez has found them and is using her magic to shield them from me."

Miclou replies uncaringly, "We'll have the children and if Stefez tries to interfere, she'll die."

Gabriela nods, "Very good. I'll look in on you tomorrow."

Miclou bows his head. Gabriela removes her hand from the crystal ball and the image disappears.

Gabriela smiles to herself, "Soon I'll have the children and then, I'll find and destroy Prince Brian."

Gabriela lets out an evil laugh as she turns and walks out of the room.

Chapter 5

A s the sun breaks across the morning horizon, the sound of two horses echo through the forest. The birds that had been chirping to celebrate a new day, are now quiet as the air starts to get colder. Then, through the morning haze, the two dark riders appear on the trail in the forest.

Miclou and Stecher slow their horses to a walk. The two ghostly figures look around the ground trying to find any clues as to where the outlanders have gone.

Miclou spots the bodies of the two wolves that Stefez saved the group from the day before, "Look, they're on this trail."

Stecher looks over and sees the wolves, "We should catch up to them by the time they reach Havel."

Miclou nods in agreement. The two dark riders start off at a faster pace along the trail.

The sun breaks across the morning horizon giving light to the dark of the forest. Stephanie opens her eyes and sees Brendan laying beside her, still asleep. She smiles at her son as she ever so gently sits up. She stretches her arms and yawns as Marsha and Sherry wake up. Marsha sits up and looks over to Stephanie. They both give the other a look as if to say, I was hoping it was all a dream. Sherry yawns, stretches and glances around.

Stefez smiles at the three women, "Good morning."

Stephanie smiles back, trying to get herself to wake up, "Good morning."

At that moment, Stefez looks over to the edge of the clearing behind Sherry, Stephanie and Marsha, "Thank you for watching over us last night."

Sherry, Stephanie and Marsha hear a deep male voice from behind them, "My pleasure."

Sherry, Stephanie and Marsha turn and see a huge brown bear just a mere ten feet from them. All of them get a very shocked look and slide back away from the bear. The movement wakes up Brendan and Anna.

Stefez speaks, "It's okay. Big Brown was just making sure nothing tried to harm us while we slept."

The bear wanders off into the forest, "Boy, you help some people and all they do is act like, look at the big scary bear. Oh no."

Brendan and Anna both stretch, trying to wake completely up. As the five of them try to get themselves awake and loosen up their bodies some from sleeping on the ground, Stefez stands up. Prince Brian and Jennifer walk up to Stefez.

Prince Brian speaks, "Jennifer and I must get to the Dark Valley and get the army ready. Jencent will stay with you. I told her that her sole mission is to protect the children."

Stefez nods, "Sounds good. For now we'll just go with the plan we talked about earlier."

Sherry, Stephanie and Marsha get up and walk over by Stefez.

Prince Brian looks at Marsha and Sherry, "It was nice meeting you."

Marsha nods, "Nice to meet you."

Sherry smiles, "Nice meeting you."

Prince Brian turns his caring gaze to Stephanie, "I must be going, but I pray that all of you make it okay and that we'll see each other again soon."

Stephanie smiles at Prince Brian, "I hope so."

Stephanie just stares as Prince Brian and Jennifer get on their horses and ride off into the forest.

Stefez speaks to the others, "We should be going."

Bailee comes hopping up to the others.

Stephanie questions, "Will we reach the river before the dark riders find us?"

Stefez shakes her head slightly, "I don't know. I'm sure Gabriela used her magic to send them from the castle to the cave where you appeared at."

Anna speaks up, "But your magic can stop them, right?"

Stefez sighs, "I'm afraid not. My magic can shield us from being seen by Gabriela so she can't just send her riders right to us, but they will no doubt be tracking us, plus, they are made from magic so I doubt I have spells that can hurt them. That's why I asked for help after all of you fell asleep last night."

Marsha questions, "Help, from who?"

Stefez picks up her staff, "There are two rangers that travel this forest, helping people that need it. I asked the wind to find them and ask them if they would help us. I had the wind tell them where we're at and where we're going."

The mention of the rangers catches Jencent's attention as she glances over to Stefez and the others.

Stephanie replies a little sarcastically, "You asked the wind to help you?"

Stefez nods, "Yes."

Bailee speaks up, "The wind can be very helpful in getting messages to others quickly."

Stefez takes a deep breath, taking in the morning air filled with the smell of leaves and fresh water, "We really need to get going. Hopefully the rangers will decide to help us and find us before the dark riders do."

Marsha chuckles, "Yea, lets hope for that."

Stephanie nods and Bailee starts to hop off down the trail. Stefez starts to walk off down the trail followed by Stephanie, Sherry, Marsha, Brendan and Anna. Jencent grabs the reigns of her horse and starts walking behind the group.

———————

As the mid-morning sun starts to warm the day in the forest, the sound of two horses riding hard fills the air. The pounding of the horse's hooves on the ground is thunderous. The once peaceful clearing in the forest where Stefez and the others slept, starts to fill with cold air as the sound of the horses slow to a gallop.

A few moments later, Miclou and Stecher ride into the clearing in the forest. They slow their horses down to a slow walk as the two dark riders look around the clearing. After just a few short moments, the two horses stop moving.

Stecher smiles as he sees the rock in the middle of the clearing, "This is where they camped."

Miclou nods, "It looks like two horses headed off into the forest and the rest of them took the trail heading towards the river."

Stecher looks over to Miclou, "We cannot let them make it to the river or we might lose them."

Miclou nods in agreement. The two dark riders turn their horses to the trail that Stefez and the others took earlier and ride off at a fast pace.

———————

As the warm sun nearly peaks at noon in the light blue sky dotted with white clouds, Stefez and the others clear the forest and see a village in the distance. The smell of fresh water mixed with the smell of stew and cooking meat fills the air all around them, making each of them think about how hungry they are.

Stefez smiles, "The village of Havel. We can get some water and food before catching the ferry."

Marsha sighs, "Good, I can use some water."

Stephanie chimes in, "And food."

Stefez replies, "We'll have to make it quick. The dark riders are no doubt closing in on us."

The group continues to walk towards the village as the smells in the air get stronger. As they get closer, they can start to make out the various wooden and grass huts as well as some gardens with fresh fruits and vegetables. As the group nears the edge of the village, they can see at least fifty different huts. They can hear the voices of the village people as well as the sounds of kids playing.

Marsha questions, "I hear children. If there are children here, why are Anna and Brendan so important?"

Stefez replies, "Because children born in the Kingdom do not have magical powers, just outland children."

The group enters the village from the south. They walk by a few small huts, some with fences and gardens and some without. The men are dressed in loose fitting pants and long sleeve, loose fitting shirts in various colors and the women are wearing dresses in varying colors. The younger boys are dressed like their fathers and the younger girls are dressed like their mothers. As the group passes by some of the huts, the villagers stop and stare at the outlanders. Stephanie and Marsha glance around because they are able to feel all the eyes looking at them.

Sherry speaks softly to Stefez, "Everyone is staring at us."

Stefez replies softly, "They're not use to seeing outlanders, especially children. They know that the outland children will bring the dark riders."

Stephanie replies softly, "So, they don't like us being

here?"

Stefez sighs, "Not really, but I have a friend that lives near the river and we can get water and food from her. Then, we'll get on the ferry."

The group continues through the village towards the river. They approach a hut with a small wooden fence around it. Stefez opens the gate on the fence. Jencent ties her horse to the fence. Stefez walks towards the hut and the others follow her. Suddenly, an African-American woman in her early twenties who is about 5'9" tall and weighs around 130 pounds with brown eyes and short, straight black hair walks out of the doorway. The woman is wearing brown sandals, a brown dress with a white undershirt top.

The woman smiles at her friend, "Stefez."

Stefez returns the warm smile, "Robin, good to see you."

Robin glances over to Stephanie and the others, "Outlanders?"

Stefez nods, "Yes. I'm trying to get them out of the Kingdom and I was hoping you might help us."

Robin gives another warm smile, "Of course. What can I do?"

Stefez replies, "I hate to ask, but some flasks of water and small bags of food would be of great help."

Robin replies with an upbeat tone, "It's my pleasure, come inside."

Everyone walks into the hut. In the middle of the room is a small table with two chairs. On the left wall is a bed and in the back right corner is a place to cook food. There is a large wooden chest next to the bed. Robin walks over to the chest while everyone waits near the door.

Robin opens the chest, "I have five flasks and small bags I can give you for the trip."

Stefez replies gratefully, "That would be so

wonderful. I thank you."

Robin pulls out five brown, soft leather, two quart flasks that have a long leather shoulder strap and five brown, soft leather pouches that could hold nearly a dozen apples that also has a long leather shoulder strap. She walks back over to Stefez and the others.

Robin smiles, "If you want to, take the bags out to the garden and fill them up, I'll fill the flasks with water from the well."

Stefez smiles, "Thank you Robin."

Robin hands Sherry, Marsha, Stephanie, Jencent and Stefez a bag. The five women sling the bags from their left shoulders to their right hips and walk out to the garden behind the hut followed by Anna, Brendan and Bailee. Robin walks across the small road to the village well.

Stefez, Stephanie, Sherry, Jencent and Marsha start to fill the bags with various fruits and vegetables.

Bailee speaks to Stefez, "Don't forget some nice carrots."

Stefez chuckles, "I wouldn't think of forgetting."

Anna speaks up, "This garden smells so wonderful."

Brendan smiles, "I'm ready to eat something."

As the five of them finish filling the bags with food, Robin walks up with the flasks.

Robin hands Sherry, Marsha, Stephanie, Jencent and Stefez a flask each, "Here you go."

Stefez gives a warm smile as she slings the flask from her left shoulder to her right hip, "Thank you so much for helping us Robin."

Stephanie gives her thanks also as she slings her flask from her right shoulder to her left hip, "I really appreciate you helping us."

Marsha chimes in also slinging her flask from her right shoulder to her left hip, "Absolutely, thank you so much."

Sherry slings her flask like the others, "Thank you so much."

Jencent nods as she slings her flask from her left shoulder to her right hip, "Thanks."

At that time, everyone hears the sound of two horses riding fast across the ground. The sound is thunderous and echoes through the village.

Bailee speaks nervously, "Do you think it's them?"

Brendan shivers a little, "I'm getting cold."

Brendan's words make the others realize that the air around them is getting colder. The sound of the horses grows louder as they can tell that the horses are getting closer to where they are.

A look of concern comes to Stefez's face, "It's the dark riders! We have to get to the river!" She turns to Robin, "Go inside and hide until they're gone."

Robin gives Stefez a quick hug, "Be safe."

Robin runs off to her hut.

Bailee quickly starts to hop away, "This way quick!"

Stefez speaks quickly, "It's not far to the river."

Stefez runs out of the garden to the dirt road that leads north out of town towards the river. Stephanie and the others quickly follow. In a hurry and knowing she doesn't have time, Jencent leaves her horse tied to Robin's fence. The air continues to get colder as the sound of the horses gets louder. In their excitement, Stefez and the others do not see the two cloaked figures running behind the hut across the road from Robin's hut. The two figures seem to be running the same way as Stefez and the others.

As the group passes the last hut at the northern end of the village, they can see the bridge and the small pier at the river ahead of them. The sound of the horses is deafening now and the air feels as if a winter storm is blowing in. Bailee is hopping as fast as she can as Stefez and the others are running as fast as they can without losing Brendan and Anna. Suddenly, Miclou and Stecher ride onto the road about fifty feet in front of Stefez and the others. Everyone quickly stops, realizing that they are blocked from the ferry by the two dark riders. As everyone tries to catch their breath, Miclou and Stecher slow their horses to a walk and start towards the group.

Miclou speaks in his loud, hollow voice, "Give us the children!"

Anna questions with fear in her voice, "What do we do now?"

The two dark riders get to within thirty feet as everyone shivers from the dropping air temperature.

Stecher draws his sword from his left hip with his right hand, "Give us the children, now!"

Stefez whispers to the others, "I'll distract them the best I can. You all run for the river."

Jencent replies softly, "Are you crazy."

The two dark riders are now just a mere twenty feet away. Stefez grips her staff with her left hand as she slowly moves her right hand towards the handle of her sword on her left hip.

Miclou draws his sword from his left hip with his right hand, "That would be a grave mistake, elf."

Suddenly, as if appearing out of thin air, one of the cloaked figures runs at the dark riders from their left and another cloaked figure runs at the dark riders from their right.

The figure on the left is a beautiful Hispanic female standing around 5'5" tall and weighing an attractively fit 150 pounds. She looks to be in her mid-twenties with straight black hair with dark red highlights that hangs to the top of her shoulder blades and dark brown, nearly black eyes. She is wearing black leather boots that come up to just below her knees, form fitting, dark blue pants, a tight fitting, long sleeve, dark blue with white trim top, a black leather belt and a dark green cloak with the hood on, concealing who she is. She has a four foot long, silver handle with silver blade sword on her left hip, a foot long silver handle with silver blade dagger on her right hip, a three foot long bow with quiver of ten arrows slung on her back, a two quart, leather flask of water slung from her left shoulder to her right hip and she is carrying a six foot long, wooden staff with both her hands.

The figure on the right is a Caucasian male standing around 5'7" tall and weighs a fit 140 pounds. He looks to be in his mid-thirties with very short, light brown hair and blue-green eyes. He is wearing brown leather boots that come up to just below his knees, form fitting, dark green with brown trim pants, a tight fitting long sleeve, dark green with brown trim top, a brown leather belt and a brown cloak with the hood on, concealing his identity. On his left hip, he carries the same kind of sword as the female and on his right hip, he carries the same kind of dagger. Strapped on his back is a two foot long, silver handle with silver blade short sword. He also has a six inch, silver handle with silver blade dagger in each one of his boots, a two quart, leather flask of water slung from his left shoulder to his right hip and he is also carrying a six foot long, wooden staff with both his hands.

Before anyone realizes the man and woman have appeared, the female extends her staff and hits Miclou in the chest, knocking him from his horse. As Stecher turns to see Miclou fall, he is hit in the chest by the man with the brown cloak on. Stecher falls from his horse and lands next to Miclou.

Without hesitation, Stefez yells, "Everyone run for the river!"

Stephanie, Sherry, Marsha, Anna, Brendan, Stefez, Jencent and Bailee head for the river. Close behind them is the man and woman who just helped them. Miclou and Stecher quickly get to their feet and start after Stephanie and the others on foot. As the group nears the river, they can see the twenty foot long pier close to the bridge. At the end of the pier is an older man dressed like the other villagers. He is sitting on twenty tree trunks tied together, all of which are about twenty five feet long.

The man sees Stephanie and the others running at him, then he sees the two cloaked figures about ten feet behind them. His eyes widen as the air starts to get colder and he sees the two dark riders running towards him about fifty feet behind the two cloaked figures. Stefez runs onto the pier. Jencent, Sherry, Stephanie, Marsha, Anna, Brendan and Bailee are right behind her. As the five women, two kids and Bailee reach the ferry, the two cloaked figures run onto the pier.

Stefez yells at the man in charge of the ferry, "Untie the rope!"

As the man starts to untie the rope holding the ferry against the pier, the two cloaked figures jump onto the ferry with Stefez and the others. As the rope falls into the water, the two cloaked figures push the ferry away from the pier with their staves. As the ferry catches the current of the river, Miclou and Stecher run onto the pier. Miclou and Stecher reach the end of the pier to see that the ferry is too far away for them to do anything about. The two dark riders just glare at the ferry, knowing that the children have slipped through their grasp.

Chapter 6

A s the warm sun passes the high noon point in the clear blue sky, Prince Brian and Jennifer are on their horses and have them at a slow walk east through the forest.

Prince Brian speaks to Jennifer, "When we reach the Dark Valley, we'll spend a short time training everyone together."

Jennifer replies, "Rein and our Captains should have the elves and our people ready. Hopefully the dwarves will be there so we can bring them into the battle strategy."

Prince Brian nods, "That would be a great help. I don't like having to move up the attack plans, but I feel we have no choice."

Jennifer sighs, "The outlander children being in the Kingdom really leaves us no choice."

Prince Brian nods in agreement, "Yes, I fear that if we don't move on Gabriela now, she may capture the children before we can get to the castle, then it would be too late."

Jennifer replies, "Hopefully Stefez and Jencent will be able to keep them safe and get them out of the Kingdom."

Prince Brian appears a little distracted, "I pray so. Whether they can get them out of the Kingdom, to just keep them safe until after we take back the castle would be good enough."

Jennifer smiles, "I'm sure the outlanders will be okay." She pauses, "So, what do you think of Stephanie my lord?"

Prince Brian doesn't look at Jennifer, but smiles, "She seems to be very nice. I would hope to see her again. Why do you ask Jennifer?"

Jennifer smiles, "It just appeared to me that she took a liking to you ..." She pauses, "And perhaps that you took a liking to her."

Prince Brian sighs, "She's very beautiful and yes, I was very much taken with her." He pauses, "But she's an outlander and I fear she would much prefer to go home than stay here with me."

Jennifer replies reassuringly, "You never know my lord, things have a way of working out."

Prince Brian smiles at the thought of Stephanie staying in the Kingdom. The two of them speed up their pace through the forest.

As the ferry moves down the river away from the pier and the dark riders, everyone breathes a sigh of relief. The just past high noon air gets warmer once again with the disappearance of the dark riders. The warm, soft breeze flows all around the group on the ferry and the smell of fresh water completely surrounds them.

As everyone catches their breath, Bailee speaks, "I'm so happy to see the two of you."

Stefez interjects, "Me too."

Jencent nods, "Most definitely, that was about to get very bad for us."

The female wearing the dark green cloak removes her hood to reveal her absolutely beautiful appearance, "We got the message not long after you sent it. We figured that since we were close, we would see for ourselves if it was true."

Stephanie finally catches her breath, "Well, thank

you so much for helping us."

The man with the brown cloak stands quite with his hood still on, just staring at Stephanie.

Stefez smiles and motions to the woman in the dark green cloak, "By the way, everyone, this is Shaun."

Before Stefez can continue, the man in the brown cloak speaks still staring at Stephanie, "I can't believe it's you."

The man removes the hood of his cloak to reveal his face. Stephanie and Brendan recognize the man immediately. A complete look of shock comes to their faces as they are now looking at someone they thought they would never see again. The two of them are looking at Jody.

Stefez appears puzzled, "Stephanie, you know Jody?"

Stephanie gets a huge smile on her face as her eyes start to tear up. She moves quickly, rocking the ferry back and forth as she throws her arms around Jody.

Stephanie can barely speak because she is so overjoyed, "I thought I'd never see you again." She pauses and sobs a little with joy, "I love you so much."

Jody hugs Stephanie and replies with a great happiness, "I love you too. I can't believe you're here."

Then, Jody feels Brendan hugging his leg. Jody looks down at his nephew and his smile gets even bigger. Stephanie moves back a little and Jody squats down and hugs Brendan.

Brendan just smiles and squeezes Jody, "I missed you so much Uncle Jody."

Jody gets a few tears in his eyes, "I missed you too big man."

Stefez and Shaun both speak at the same time, "Uncle Jody?"

Regaining his composure, Jody stands back up, "Yes. Stephanie is my sister and this big guy is my nephew." He pauses, "I entered the Kingdom a year ago, probably the same way they did."

Sherry, Marsha and Anna sit quietly, obviously not sure how to react to what is going on. The three of them have heard about Jody, but they've never met him before. Marsha stares at Jody, obviously taking an instant liking to what she sees.

Stephanie shakes her head, "I just can't believe it."

Shaun gently taps Jody on the shoulder, "You never said you had a sister and nephew."

Shaun holds out her hand to Stephanie, "Nice to meet you."

Stephanie shakes Shaun's hand, "It's really nice to meet you."

Shaun looks down at Brendan, "And this absolutely handsome man is your son."

Stephanie smiles, "Yes. His name's Brendan."

Shaun bends down, "It's nice to meet you Brendan." She smiles, "Do I get a hug too?"

Brendan smiles at Shaun, taking an instant liking to her. Brendan gives Shaun a big hug. Stephanie realizes that Sherry, Marsha and Anna have been quiet this whole time.

Stephanie motions to Anna, "Sorry everyone, this is one of my students, Anna." She motions to Marsha, "This is her big sister, Marsha." She then motions to Sherry, "And this is a friend of mine, Sherry."

Sherry raises her hand, "Hi there."

Anna gets a big smile, "Hi!"

Marsha is still quietly staring at Jody. Anna notices Marsha's look and gives her a nudge.

Marsha breaks her stare, "I'm sorry." She takes a moment to collect her thoughts, "Hi. It's nice to meet you both."

Shaun nods her head to the three of them, "It's nice to meet you."

Jody nods at Sherry, "Nice to meet you Sherry." He

turns to Anna and nods, "Nice to meet you Anna." He turns his head and gazes at Marsha, captured by her beauty, "Nice to meet you Marsha."

Everyone takes a seat to relax.

Shaun gets back to the business at hand, "So, what's the plan now? The dark riders won't give up that easy."

Stefez replies, "We've already seen Prince Brian so he knows about the outlanders. We talked and we think it's best if we make our way to the castle and try to get them out of the Kingdom." She pauses, "Prince Brian has decided to move up his attack on the castle."

Jody questions, "How did you plan on approaching the castle? If the dark riders are already involved, Gabriela no doubt has her army moving to cut off the route across Glass Lake."

Jencent chimes in, "And even if we sneak by her armies, I doubt we can make it all the way to the castle across the open grasslands without being seen."

Stefez nods, "I thought about that. I think that our best bet is to approach the castle from behind." She pauses, "From the northwest."

Shaun gets a puzzled look, "You mean, from the swamp."

Stefez nods in a positive response, "I don't think Gabriela will expect us to do that."

Bailee speaks up, "That's a long trip."

Jencent nods in agreement, "A very long trip indeed. Not to mention fairly dangerous."

The village man that is controlling the ferry just sits quietly, looking at everyone on the ferry and wondering what they are talking about.

Stefez sighs, "I know, but it's the safest way to go. We can figure out more details once we reach River Fork."

Jody nods, "Well, we should get as much rest as we can. We have a long walk ahead of us."

Shaun nods, "I agree."

Everyone makes room to lay down. Stephanie and Brendan lay next to Jody, still overcome with joy that they have been reunited. Everyone stares up at the crystal clear, blue sky as the warm breeze moves the white clouds slowly across the sky and fills the air with the smell of the trees of the forest and the fresh water of the river. It is such a serene moment that everyone forgets for the moment about the dark riders and everything else that is happening around them.

Gabriela walks into the chamber where she performs her magic. It is dimly lit from the candles as there are no windows to allow the afternoon sun in. She walks over to the table where the crystal ball is, apparently concerned about something. She leans her staff against the table.

Gabriela holds her left hand over the crystal ball, "Why have they not contacted me yet? They should have the children by now."

Gabriela slowly waves her hand over the crystal ball and mumbles under her breath. After a few seconds, the crystal ball gets cloudy. A few more seconds pass when Stecher's face finally appears in the crystal ball.

Gabriela questions, "What's going on? Where are the children?"

Stecher replies calmly, "We chased them into Havel. They escaped with some help. They're heading west on the river."

Gabriela's face changes to that of being upset with the news, "Very well." She pauses, "Take the road to Farhollow. I'll see what I can do to make them get off the river."

Stecher bows his head, "Yes my Queen."

Gabriela jerks her hand away from the crystal ball in

frustration. She walks over to the shelves. She grabs a clear glass jar full of water and another clear jar with a fish in it.

Gabriela turns and walks towards the caldron, "This may take a little time, but we shall see if they enjoy the river ride I'll give them."

Gabriela lets out a very evil sounding laugh that echoes through the dimly lit chamber.

Chapter 7

The morning sun breaks the dawn horizon casting light over the once dark forest and river. A strong breeze blows the early morning air around the ferry where Stefez and the others rested for the night. The ferry continues to float down the river as the village man steers the once calm, but now getting more rough water.

Stephanie wakes up as she feels the ferry rock back and forth in the rougher water. A couple moments later, Sherry and Marsha also wake up as the river gets harder to handle for the village man. Stephanie sits up and glances around. She sees that Stefez, Jencent, Shaun and Jody are already awake. Sherry and Marsha sit up as the ferry starts to rock even more than before.

Jody looks over to Stefez, "I don't remember the river being this bad here."

The village man speaks up, "It never has been before."

Stefez lets out a sigh, "It's not the river. I can sense that something else is at work."

At that time, Brendan and Anna both wake up as water splashes up on the ferry as it rocks back and forth at the mercy of the river. Stephanie wraps her arms around Brendan and holds him close to her.

Shaun glances around, "What do you mean?"

Stefez grips her staff tightly, "I mean, Gabriela has no doubt used some kind of magical spell to do this to the river." She pauses, "She obviously wants us off the river."

Jencent chimes in, "So the dark riders can catch us."

Marsha shakes her head, "What are we going to do?"

The village man does his best to steer the ferry, "It's getting really bad. I'm not going to be able to control the ferry much longer."

The once calm water is now running faster and the current has gotten much stronger causing the ferry to shake back and forth. Everyone holds on the best they can as the ferry is obviously about to lose control.

Jody points at the river ahead, "Look ahead."

The others look up the river and they can see that the river ahead of them has turned into full blown rough rapids with waves that rise up about five feet or more.

The village man speaks, "We'll never make it through that. We have to stop."

Stefez nods, "Okay, take us to the riverbank."

The village man struggles to move the ferry closer to the riverbank. Everyone holds on as the ferry cuts across the increasingly choppy water of the once serene river. Water continues to splash over the sides of the ferry as it gets closer to the riverbank. After what seems like a lifetime, the ferry comes out of the rough water and slides up on the soft dirt and mud of the riverbank. Jody, Stefez, Jencent and the village man hop off the ferry and pull it up on the riverbank until it sets firmly on the ground.

Jody helps Anna off the ferry as Stefez and Jencent walk a few feet towards the forest and look around. Shaun hops off the ferry as Jody helps Brendan off the ferry. Shaun walks over to Stefez and Jencent as Jody helps Stephanie off the ferry.

Stephanie warmly smiles at Jody, "Thanks."

Stephanie stands next to Brendan as Jody helps Sherry off the ferry.

Sherry smiles at Jody, "Thanks."

Then, Jody helps Marsha off the ferry.

Marsha smiles at Jody, "Thank you."

Jody returns the smile, "My pleasure."

Jody and Marsha walk over to Stephanie and the others.

Stephanie looks over to Stefez, "Okay, what now?"

Stefez glances around, "If I'm right, we should travel north. That will take us to a town."

The village man nods, "You're right. It will take you another day, but you will reach Farhollow if you travel north."

Shaun lets out a sigh, "Then, Farhollow it is." She looks at the village man, "What shall you do?"

Everyone hears Bailee's voice, "Don't forget me."

The village man smiles, "I'll wait until the river goes down, then continue on."

Stefez speaks up, "We should get going, it's a long walk."

Stephanie lets out a sigh, "Wonderful."

Jody smiles at Stephanie, then turns to Shaun, "We should give Stephanie, Marsha and Sherry a weapon. They might need it."

Shaun nods, "Good idea. We can also show them how to use them as we travel."

Jody walks over to Sherry and hands her his staff, "Here. You can use this to walk and fight if need be."

Sherry takes the staff, "Thanks, I think."

Stephanie chuckles slightly, "Are you serious?"

Jody smiles at Stephanie, "I know you can fight some, you've trained with me before."

Jody removes his short sword from his back and steps over to Stephanie, "Here, you take my sword."

Jody straps the sword around Stephanie's waist where the sword is on her left hip.

Stephanie just smiles at Jody, "Thanks. I'll try to remember some of the things you showed me before."

Jody smiles, "Trust me, it comes back quick."

Shaun walks over to Marsha, "Here, you should take my staff."

Marsha takes the staff from Shaun, "Thanks."

Jody replies, "We'll show you some stuff while we're traveling, just in case."

Marsha and Sherry both get the look of, I wonder if I can do this.

Stefez speaks up as Bailee finally gets off the ferry and hops over to the group, "Okay, lets get moving."

Bailee chimes in, "Off to Farhollow."

Stefez starts into the forest as the others walk closely behind her.

As the sun rises into the mid-morning sky, Gabriela walks into the throne room of the castle. It is a huge room, every bit of five hundred feet long by five hundred feet wide. In the past it has always been decorated with bright banners and flowers, but now it is dark and dreary looking. At one end of the room raised up ten steps is two large purple and gold chairs. Numerous windows on each side of the room let in the morning sun. Gabriela walks across the large room and up the stairs. She turns around and sits down in the chair on her right.

At that time, the large doors open and Choel walks into the throne room. Two small creatures with green wrinkled skin wearing rags for clothes pull the doors shut behind Choel. Choel walks powerfully across the room, up the steps and kneels in front of Gabriela.

Choel bows his head, "You wish to see me."

Gabriela nods, "Yes." As Choel looks up, Gabriela continues, "I have no doubt that Prince Brian will make his move on taking back the castle."

Choel questions, "What do you want me to do?"

Gabriela is silent for a moment, "I want you to send a small army to the village of Lakeway. I want Brytil to lead that army. Have Brytil send scouts across Glass Lake to the village of Birdview." She pauses, "Also, send scouts south to the crossroads near the forest and send more scouts east to camp on the road between the mountains and Glass Lake, halfway between North Town and Ghost Town. I want to make sure we can spot them when they move."

Choel bows his head, "It will be done my Queen."

Gabriela speaks up, "Also, as a precaution, I want Regas to get more of our army suited up and standing ready."

Choel replies in his powerfully deep voice, "Yes my Queen."

Gabriela motions with her left hand, "Very well. Go now and make sure it's done."

Choel replies, "Yes my Queen."

Choel stands up and turns around. He strides down the steps and back across the throne room. The two creatures open the doors as Choel walks out of the room.

As the doors are pulled closed, Gabriela speaks to herself, "This Kingdom is mine Prince Brian."

Gabriela sits back, closes her eyes and takes a deep breath.

———

As the soft breeze blows the white clouds across the mid-afternoon sky, Prince Brian and Jennifer ride over a hill covered by large trees. As they top the hill, they see the Dark Valley where their army awaits them. Spread throughout the large valley which is surrounded by hills and huge trees on all sides, are a couple hundred tents.

Numerous male and female humans are walking amongst the tents. Also walking around the camp are numerous male and female elves. Some of the male and female humans and elves are wearing various forms of armor and carrying swords with shields or bows and arrows along with swords. Some of the men and women are carrying long spears.

Some of the male and female humans are wearing loose fitting clothes in various colors of brown and green. A few fires are burning where some food is being cooked. Most of the humans and elves are practicing with their weapons.

Prince Brian and Jennifer ride into the camp. As the two of them pass by the different men and women, the men and women bow to Prince Brian. The two of them ride up to a large, very nice looking tent and stop. Prince Brian and Jennifer dismount and tie their horses to a tree next to the tent.

At that time, an incredibly beautiful female elf with a Hispanic complexion walks up. She appears to be in her mid-twenties even though she is actually close to 150 years old. She stands at 5'5" tall and weighs a most unbelievable 125 pounds. She has straight black hair with a few blonde highlights that hangs to her shoulder blades and dark brown, nearly black eyes. She is wearing brown leather boots that come up to just below her knees, tight fitting brown with dark green trim pants, a tight fitting brown with dark green trim, long sleeve top and a dark green cloak with the hood off. She is wearing a brown leather belt that holds a four foot long, silver handle with silver blade sword on her left hip and a foot long, silver handle with silver bladed dagger on her right hip. She has a three foot long wooden bow on her back with a quiver of ten arrows.

The female elf bows her head to Prince Brian, "It's good to see you made it back."

Prince Brian nods, "Thank you Rein."

Jennifer gets right to business, "Have the dwarves arrived yet?"

Rein shakes her head, "Not yet, but the training is coming along well. It shouldn't take but a week or two to mix the dwarves in when they get here."

Prince Brian sighs, "I'm afraid we don't have anywhere close to that long. We may have only a day or two, even a week may be too long."

Rein looks puzzled, "Why is that? A couple of weeks is a good prediction. Anything less would be taking a chance."

Jennifer speaks up, "We ran into five outlanders on our way here. Two of them are children."

Rein has a shocked look, "Outlander children?"

Prince Brian nods, "Yes, and Gabriela already knows they're in the Kingdom as well."

Rein lets out a sigh, "I see what you mean. Why didn't you bring them here?"

Prince Brian glances around, "We have enough to do and we don't need everyone knowing about them, it could make everyone think twice about fighting." He pauses, "Besides, they're with Stefez and she is taking them to the well to get them out of the Kingdom with the help of Jencent."

Rein nods, "So what now?"

Jennifer looks at Prince Brian, "Keep getting everything ready, right my lord?"

Prince Brian replies, "Lets go inside. I'll let you know about the plan Stefez and I have come up with."

Prince Brian, Jennifer and Rein walk into the tent.

Chapter 8

The warm sun starts into the mid-afternoon sky as the soft breeze fills the air with the smell of the fresh trees, leaves, grass and river water. Stefez and the others continue to slowly walk north through the forest each one snacking on a piece of fruit.

Stephanie speaks with some excitement, "I still can't believe you're here Jody."

Jody smiles at his sister, "It's all of you I can't believe is here."

Stephanie replies, "You've been gone for a year." She pauses, "We thought we'd never see you again."

Jody nods slightly, "When I first entered the Kingdom, Shaun found me. The two of us tried a couple of different times to get into the castle so I could get out of the Kingdom, but Gabriela's army was just too big to sneak pass." He pauses, then continues, "So, I decided to stay with Shaun and travel with her until Prince Brian regained control of the castle."

Marsha questions while trying not to stare at Jody, "So, will you go back with us when we reach the castle?"

Jody looks over and smiles at Marsha, "Of course I will." He pauses, "But the Kingdom is not that bad of a place. Wait until you see more of it. Sure, some things are bad, but for most part, it's a pretty amazing place."

Shaun chimes in, "It will be even better when Prince Brian is back in control."

Jody questions, "So Marsha, what are you going back to?"

Marsha replies, "I work as a Registered Nurse and take care of Anna."

Anna speaks up, "I think this is a really cool place."

Stephanie nods, "It's neat, but we don't belong here."

Anna replies, "What if we got stuck here?"

Brendan quickly speaks up, "That would be cool."

Jody replies with a smile, "We would make do the best we could."

Suddenly, Stefez stops walking. The others quickly stop behind her, wondering what is going on.

Stephanie questions, "What is it?"

Before Stefez can answer, they all notice that the ground is getting softer under their feet.

Stefez quickly speaks, "Everyone run, before the ground swallows us!"

Stefez starts to move fast as she slowly starts to sink into the ground. Stephanie grabs Brendan's hand and the two of them start to run as the ground gets softer. Sherry, Marsha and Anna quickly follow Stephanie and Brendan. Shaun runs fast and so does Jody. Bailee starts hopping as quickly as possible. Jencent also takes off fast.

The ground continues to get softer as everyone is slowly starting to sink. Each one does the best they can to run as the soft ground is making it harder. After about a hundred and fifty feet, Jody and Shaun are the first two to reach solid ground again. The others continue to run as their entire feet are covered now.

As Stefez and Jencent reach the solid ground, Jody heads back into the soft ground.

Shaun yells, "What are you doing!?"

Jody replies, "Stephanie and Brendan will never make it!"

Jody passes Sherry, Marsha and Anna on his way to Stephanie and Brendan. Sherry, Marsha and Anna get a few feet from Stefez and Shaun, but they are practically unable to move anymore.

Stefez extends her staff to Anna with her right hand, "Grab hold." She looks at Sherry, "Reach the staff over here."

Anna reaches out and grabs Stefez's staff. Sherry extends her staff and Stefez grabs it with her left hand.

Shaun yells to Marsha, "Reach the staff over here."

Marsha extends the staff she is carrying to Shaun. Stefez pulls hard on both staves. Shaun pulls hard on the staff. After a few seconds, Shaun and Stefez pull Sherry, Marsha and Anna out of the soft ground as Jody reaches Stephanie and Brendan.

Jody picks up Brendan, "Stephanie, go! I've got him."

Jody helps Stephanie get her feet moving as Bailee hops by them still on top of the ground. Stephanie moves as fast as she can to the others as Jody and Brendan are not far behind. Stephanie gets to the edge of the soft ground and Shaun and Jencent pull her onto the hard ground.

Jody and Brendan get closer to the edge as Jody's feet are completely covered now and he struggles to move his feet.

Just a mere fifteen feet from the others, Jody speaks to Brendan, "I'm going to set you down big man and you run as fast as you can to the others."

Brendan replies, "Okay."

Jody puts Brendan down and Brendan takes off running as fast as he can. Brendan reaches the others as Bailee hops up next to Stefez. Jody struggles to pull his feet up one at a time and continues to slowly move.

Stephanie speaks a little scared, "Jody!"

Stefez and Marsha extend their staves. Jody continues to struggle to move. He reaches out, but the two staves are just out of reach. He uses all his strength to take another couple steps in the soft ground and his hands grab hold of the two staves. Marsha and Stefez start pulling as Jody gets closer to the edge. Once he is close enough, Shaun grabs hold of Jody's left wrist and pulls him towards her with great force. Jody comes out of the soft ground as Shaun falls back onto the ground and Jody lands on top of her.

Jody smiles at Shaun, "Thanks partner."

Shaun smiles back, "Any time."

Jody gets to his feet and helps Shaun up to her feet.

Anna speaks up, "Well, that was fun."

Suddenly, a large, green vine from one of the trees wraps around Marsha's right ankle and more vines start towards the group.

Stefez speaks up, "Tangle vines. We have to get out of here."

Bailee hops off quickly. The vine pulls back and Marsha falls to the ground, but hangs on to the staff. Stefez, Jencent and Shaun start north quickly with Sherry, Stephanie, Brendan and Anna right behind them. Stefez, Jencent and Shaun draw their swords and start cutting the vines away when the vines get too close.

Jody draws his sword and rushes over to Marsha. With a quick swing, Jody cuts the vine just below Marsha's foot. Jody helps Marsha to her feet.

Marsha smiles, "Thanks."

Jody returns the smile, then he quickly pulls Marsha away with his left hand as his right hand moves his sword quickly and cuts away a vine that was heading for Marsha's back.

Jody quickly speaks, "Lets go."

Jody and Marsha quickly start after the others. Stefez, Jencent and Shaun continue to cut away vines as Sherry, Stephanie, Anna and Brendan avoid a few of the vines coming after them. After about fifty more yards, Stefez, Jencent and Shaun run into an opening in the forest and the vines vanish behind them. Sherry, Stephanie, Anna and Brendan rush into the opening next to Stefez, Jencent and Shaun. A few seconds later, Jody and Marsha run into the opening as Bailee hops up next to Stefez.

Stephanie smiles, "Wow, anymore surprises?"

Marsha shakes her head, "I really hope not."

Sherry chuckles, "I've had enough fun for awhile."

Stefez replies, "No, we should be okay now."

Anna speaks up, "I'm really tired now."

Brendan nods, "Me too."

Stefez nods, "We could camp in this clearing. Nothing should bother us." She pauses, "We can reach Farhollow before noon tomorrow."

Jody agrees, "That's a good idea. We could all use some rest."

Shaun speaks up, "Sounds good to me."

Jencent chimes in, "I could go for some rest."

Everyone finds a place to sit down as the sun gets lower in the sky. Everyone eats a piece of fruit, then prepares to sleep. Shaun lays down not far from Stefez. Marsha lays down and Anna lays down next to her. Jody lays down. Stephanie lays down next to Jody and Brendan lays down next to Stephanie. Sherry lays down close to Marsha and Anna. Jencent lays down not really close to the others. As the sun starts to set, everyone drifts off to sleep.

——— ———

In the hour just before dawn, Gabriela walks into her magic chamber. She waves her right hand as she walks in and the four candles on the table start to burn, casting light across the once dark room.

Gabriela walks over to the table where her crystal ball sits in the middle of the candles. She holds her right hand over the crystal ball as her left hand grips her staff. She starts to mumble under her breath.

The crystal ball starts to fill with a gray mist which

turns into a gray cloud. After a couple of more seconds, the cloudiness clears and the face of Stecher appears in the crystal ball.

Stecher speaks, "Yes my Queen."

Gabriela questions, "Where are you two at?"

Stecher replies in his hollow voice, "On the road to Farhollow. We'll reach the town by noon."

Gabriela smiles, "Excellent. I happen to know that the children are heading to Farhollow and should be there at that time."

Stecher inquires, "And how are you sure of that my Queen?"

Gabriela gives an evil smile, "You're not the only two I have after the children. I do have another helping me, and my animals." She pauses, "Contact me as soon as you have the children."

Stecher bows his head, "Yes my Queen."

Gabriela removes her hand from the crystal ball and Stecher's image vanishes. Gabriela turns and starts out of the room.

As she passes through the doorway, Gabriela speaks, "Soon children, you'll be mine."

Gabriela lets out an evil laugh.

The morning sun breaks across the horizon, bringing light to the forest. A cool morning breeze blows through the Dark Valley and Prince Brian's camp. Numerous birds are chirping in the early morning. Prince Brian walks out of his tent and stretches. He glances around at the camp. A couple of minutes pass, when Jennifer walks up.

Jennifer bows her head, "Good morning my lord."

Prince Brian smiles, "Good morning Jennifer."

Jennifer speaks while glancing around, "I have the

Captains getting everything ready so we can bring the dwarves into our battle plan and get some training together."

Prince Brian nods and questions, "Good. Have the dwarves arrived yet?"

Jennifer shakes her head, "Not yet, but they should be arriving at any time."

Then, the two of them hear the sound of hundreds of feet marching across the ground. They both know that it is the dwarf army. Prince Brian and Jennifer both look to the north towards the sound. A few moments later, they see about one hundred and fifty dwarves march over the northern hill into the Dark Valley. Everyone in the camp stops and takes notice of the dwarves. The elves are not overly happy to have to be fighting next to the dwarves, but they know that it is necessary in order to defeat Gabriela's army.

The dwarf army marches into the valley and they stop on the open field where the elves and humans have been training. Prince Brian and Jennifer walk over to where the dwarves have stopped. At the front of the dwarf army is a male dwarf with a dark skinned complexion that stands about 4'4" tall and weighs a stout 110 pounds. He has dark brown eyes, long black and gray hair with a black and gray beard. He is wearing brown boots, brown pants and a brown, long sleeve top. Covering his torso is a dark, metallic gray chest plate of armor. He is holding a three foot long battle axe in his hands.

Prince Brian walks up to the dwarf, "It's good to see you Ramaf."

Ramaf nods his head and speaks in a gruff voice, "And it's good to see you Prince Brian."

Jennifer speaks up, "You managed to raise more of an army than expected."

Ramaf smiles, "I managed about sixty more than I expected."

Prince Brian smiles, "Well, we happily welcome all the help."

At that time, Rein walks up and gives a slight nod to Ramaf, "Ramaf."

Ramaf nods in return, "Rein."

Everyone can feel the tension between Rein and Ramaf.

Prince Brian speaks up, "Jennifer has the Captains getting the army ready to train. We should get started. We have a lot to do and very little time." He looks at Jennifer, "I'll turn it over to you."

Jennifer bows her head, "Yes my lord."

Prince Brian walks off and Jennifer turns back to Ramaf and Rein.

Jennifer smiles, "Shall we get started."

Ramaf and Rein both nod.

Chapter 9

The warm sun is nearly in the noon sky. The warm breeze blows the smell of the forest all around Stefez and the others as they continue to walk north. Then, the forest opens up in front of them to reveal a small town in the distance. Everyone can now also smell the cooking of food mixed with the fresh tree and leaf smell.

Marsha closes her eyes and breathes in through her nose, "That smells so good."

Shaun smiles, "Farhollow."

Stefez nods, "We can stock up on food and water before heading west."

The group continues towards the small town. The smell of food gets stronger, but they can also start to hear the clanking of the metal in the blacksmith shops. Farhollow is much larger than Havel. Surrounding the small town are numerous huts with farms and gardens, but more towards the center of the town are wooden and stone buildings. A couple of taverns, a few blacksmith buildings and a few supply shops make up the center of the village along with a horse stable and barn. The people of Farhollow are dressed almost the same as those from Havel except there are more people in nicer looking clothes wandering the village.

As the group walks by the huts on the southern side of the village, Stefez speaks up, "We should get water from the well near the center of the town first, then food."

Jody replies, "We might not want to take too long. No doubt the dark riders will be headed here to look for us."

Jencent glances at Jody with her eyes narrowed. As the group passes the huts, the villagers take notice of Sherry, Stephanie, Marsha, Anna and Brendan, knowing they are outlanders that are not from the Kingdom.

Stephanie speaks as the group continues on, "Everyone is staring at us again."

Shaun replies, "You better get use to that. They know you're outlanders and they know that you'll bring the dark riders."

Marsha sighs, "So, we won't get a warm reception in any town."

Jody nods, "Don't count on it."

Sherry lets out a sigh, "Wonderful."

Jencent chimes in, "Everyone fears Gabriela and her army and they definitely fear the dark riders."

The group walks by the large barn and horse stables to find themselves on a dirt road that circles around a fairly large well in the center of town. They see a tavern off to their right, a blacksmith shop across the circle and a supply shop off to their left. The group waits for a horse drawn wagon to pass in front of them, then they walk up to the well. Villagers are wandering all around the group and taking notice of the outlanders.

Jody fills Marsha's flask, Sherry's flask then Stephanie's flask. He fills his flask next, then Stefez's flask and Jencent's flask. Finally, Jody fills Shaun's flask as the villagers continue to go about their daily routine around them.

Anna questions, "Do we have time to eat?"

Brendan speaks up, "I'm really hungry."

Jody shrugs, "What do you think?"

Jencent speaks up, "I would think so. Also, we could use a good meal every chance we get."

Stefez is quiet for a second, "I guess we can get something to eat at the tavern."

Bailee speaks up, "I'll wait outside for you. Just make sure you bring me something good to eat."

Shaun smiles, "We wouldn't dare forget."

The group walks over to the two story, stone building that has a wooden sign hanging over the door that reads, "Tom's Tavern". Jody opens the door and everyone steps inside. The group looks at the large, open room in front of them. It has about fifty tables, a third of which are filled with villagers. Everyone stops what they are doing when they see the outlanders standing by the doorway.

Marsha speaks quietly, "This is awkward."

The group hears a man's voice, "We don't serve outlanders here!"

The group notices the man standing behind the bar on the left side of the room as the one who just yelled at them.

Stephanie speaks to the others, "Maybe we should just go."

At that time, another man's voice fills the now quiet room, "They're with me!"

The man behind the bar immediately changes his tune, "I'm sorry. I didn't know." He looks over to Jody and the others, "Please, come on in."

Stefez whispers to the others, "Back right corner table."

As the group starts across the room, all the villagers return to their meals. Everyone in the group sees the table that Stefez was talking about and they see a man sitting at the table facing the door. It is a nice looking Caucasian man that appears to be about 37 years old with short, black, wavy hair and hazel eyes. He has a stout 6' tall 215 pound build. He is wearing brown leather boots that come up to just below his knees, form fitting royal blue with red trim pants, and a tight fitting, royal blue with red trim, long sleeve top covered by a royal blue with red trim tunic. Around his waist is a brown leather belt with a five foot long, gold handle with silver bladed sword on his right hip and a foot long, gold handle with silver bladed dagger on his left hip. He also has a two quart water flask and a small brown leather bag for food slung from his right shoulder to his left hip.

The group reaches the table and they all stop. The man looks at Stefez, smiles and nods.

Stefez shakes her head, "Michael."

Michael motions with his left hand, "Stefez, please, grab some chairs and have a seat."

Stefez and the others grab some chairs and sit down around the table with Michael.

———

As the noon sun beats down on the plush, green grasslands, the warm breeze is filled with the pungent odor of decomposing bodies. The villagers of Lakeway all stop as they can smell the coming of Gabriela's army. Lakeway is a village about the same size and layout of Farhollow. It sits on the northern bank of a huge, crystal clear blue lake known as Glass Lake. The sound of a hundred and twenty soldier's marching feet echo in the air as Gabriela's army draws closer to the village.

Then, the evil army comes into view of the villagers of Lakeway. The army is made up of humans and elves brought back from the dead by Gabriela. Their decomposed skin is covered by pieces of dark metallic plate mail armor. The elves carry swords along with bows and arrows. Some of the humans carry swords and shields while others carry spears. Mixed amongst the humans and elves are the grotesque looking, green skinned trolls. The trolls also wear pieces of dark metallic armor and the trolls carry merely a sword.

At the front of the army is Brytil, a Caucasian man standing nearly 5'6" tall and weighing a very stout 200 pounds. He looks to be in his late twenties and is bald with brown eyes. He has pieces of shiny silver armor covering his chest, arms and thighs. He is wearing a four foot long, gold handle with silver bladed sword on his left hip. He is carrying a three foot long, shiny silver shield in his left hand. He cries out orders to the army as the army moves into the village. A group of twenty trolls move through the village to the bank of Glass Lake. As the rest of the army settles into the village, the twenty trolls get in four small canoes and start across the river for the village of Birdview on the far bank.

At the same time, miles to the northeast of Lakeway where the dirt road divides the few miles between Glass Lake and the huge mountain range that hides the snow lands from the rest of the Kingdom, a group of ten trolls set up a small camp on the side of the road halfway between North Town and Ghost Town.

Also at this time, miles south of the castle just before the beautiful grasslands run into the plush forest where four dirt roads intersect, another ten trolls set up camp at the intersection.

At all three locations, the creatures of Gabriela's army sit and wait for either Prince Brian or the outlanders.

———

As the sun starts into the afternoon sky, Michael, Stefez and the others walk out of the tavern where they ate their lunch. A couple wagons pass by them as other villagers go about their daily business.

Marsha smiles, "That was some good food."

Stephanie nods in agreement, "Yes it was."

Stefez speaks up, "Lets head to the supply shop on the other side of the circle."

As the group starts for the supply shop, Stefez questions Michael, "So, why didn't you stay with Prince

Brian?"

Michael sighs, "I just lost the will to fight."

Stefez questions, "What about Rein?"

Michael smiles at the name, "She decided to stay and as much as I cared for her, I couldn't. Besides, it's not easy for the Elf Queen to explain to her people why she is with a human."

The group walks up to the fruit stands outside the supply shop and start to gather some fruit.

Michael speaks up, "So, with outlanders in the Kingdom, I guess Prince Brian will move to attack the castle now."

Stefez nods, "That's what we're planning on."

As the group continues to gather some fruit, the sound of two horses riding hard echoes across the town circle and the air starts to get colder. Everyone's face shows the look of worry as they all know what is going on. They know that the dark riders have found them. Everyone turns around to see the dark riders sitting on their horses just across the circle from them.

Stefez's eyes widen, "Run!"

Michael yells out, "This way!"

Michael runs into the supply shop followed by everyone else as Miclou and Stecher ride towards them. Bailee hops as fast as she can to stay with the group. As Michael and the others dart through the supply shop, Miclou heads around the left side of the shop and Stecher heads around the right side, knowing the group will head for the back door of the supply shop. As the group exits out the back of the shop onto the dirt road, Stecher appears on their right and Miclou on their left. Miclou and Stecher both draw their swords and slowly start riding towards the group.

Stephanie speaks trying to slow down her breathing, "What now?"

Jody, Shaun and Jencent draw their swords getting

ready for the fight of their lives.

Michael draws his sword, "We'll have a better chance of losing them if we can get by the one on the left."

Miclou's voice echoes down the road, "Give us the children!"

Stecher's voice closely follows, "Drop your swords and we'll spare your lives!"

Stefez whispers, "Okay, we rush the one on the left."

Michael gives a slight smile, "Lets do it."

The group turns towards Miclou and charges at him. Michael, Jody, Shaun and Jencent lead the way with Stefez right behind them. Just behind Stefez is Sherry, Stephanie, Marsha, Anna and Brendan. Bailee is hopping along side Stefez. Stecher picks up his pace as he closes in from behind the group. Most people would be a little fearful of the group coming at them, but Miclou just smiles, knowing he finally gets to fight.

As the group gets closer to Miclou, Stefez starts to mumble under her breath and the stone on her staff starts to glow. As the group gets to within ten feet of Miclou, a strong vortex of wind sends dirt from the road up at Miclou. Jody moves to the right of the horse and brings his sword at Miclou. Miclou squints as the dirt hits him in the face, but he brings his sword over quick and deflects Jody's cut. At that time, Shaun comes across the left side of the horse and swings at Miclou. As if unaffected by the dirt, Miclou moves with incredible speed and his sword comes back across the deflects Shaun's sword away as Michael starts up on right side of the horse. Miclou brings his sword back across his body and knocks Michael's sword away. Jencent runs by without swinging her sword as another large amount of dirt flies up and distracts Miclou. Before Miclou can get his vision back, Stefez and the others run by him.

As the group rushes out to the road near the barn and

horse stables, Stecher rides up next to Miclou and the dirt starts to settle. The group runs into the front of the barn as the two dark riders start after them.

Stecher yells, "I'll go around back if you take the front!"

Miclou nods and the two dark riders start towards the large front and back doors of the barn. Michael and the others stop just inside the front of the barn and close the doors behind them. A few feet in front of them are two wagons full of loose hay with a horse tied to the front of each wagon.

Stefez speaks up, "They're going to trap us in here."

Marsha speaks up, "What now?"

Then, everyone hears a horse stop at the front of the barn. The group starts for the back of the barn, when they hear another horse ride up to the back of the barn.

Sherry speaks nervously, "We're trapped."

Jody looks around and sees the ladder that leads up to the loft of the barn, "I have an idea."

Bailee quickly replies, "I'm all ears."

Jody glances over to the wagons, "Hide under the hay on the wagon."

Stefez quickly speaks, "We all can't fit on one wagon."

Shaun speaks up, "Then some of us will get on one and some on the other."

Stefez, Michael, Shaun, Jencent, Stephanie, Marsha, Sherry, Anna, Brendan and Bailee start for the wagons as Jody rushes over to the ladder. In front of the barn, Miclou dismounts from his horse. In back of the barn, Stecher dismounts from his horse.

Michael runs up to the wagon on the right, "Lets go."

Jody slides the ladder in the dirt a couple feet to make it look like they climbed the ladder, then he runs for the wagons. Michael grabs Bailee and tosses the rabbit in the back of the right wagon. Stephanie helps Brendan into the back of the left wagon.

Stefez speaks up, "Faster."

Stephanie climbs in the back of the left wagon with Brendan. Sherry climbs into the back of the left wagon with Stephanie and Brendan. Stefez jumps in the back of the right wagon. As Jody runs up to the wagons, Jencent quickly grabs Anna by the arm and puts her in the back of the right wagon. Jencent climbs in the right wagon. Shaun jumps in the back of the right wagon. Michael quickly climbs in the right wagon with Stefez, Shaun, Jencent, Anna and Bailee.

Marsha starts to move towards the right wagon, "I can't leave Anna."

Jody grabs Marsha's hand, "There's not enough room in that wagon." Jody guides Marsha into the left wagon, "Hurry, we're out of time."

Jody gets in the back of the left wagon with Sherry, Stephanie, Marsha and Brendan. As Miclou and Stecher slowly approach the doors, careful not to get ambushed, everyone buries themselves under the hay in the wagons.

As the front and back doors start to open, Jody whispers loud enough for Stefez and the others to hear him, "Stay ready in case they find us."

Then a silence falls over the barn as Miclou steps into the front of the barn and Stecher steps into the back of the barn. The air in the barn slowly gets colder. Miclou and Stecher slowly move towards each other, glancing all around. Miclou gets closer to the wagons as Stecher slowly walks towards the ladder that Jody slid. As Miclou starts between the two wagons, he hears something behind him back by the door and he spins around quickly with his sword at the ready. Two male villagers stop in their tracks just inside the front doors when they see Miclou. Miclou ignores the two men, turns back around and starts walking towards the back of the wagons. Everyone lays as still as they can, breathing as lightly as possible. Miclou turns to his right and is now standing at the back of the wagon where Jody, Sherry, Stephanie, Marsha and Brendan are hiding.

Jody grips the handle of his sword tighter as Miclou raises up his sword as if he is going to stab the hay.

Suddenly, Stecher speaks up, "Over here Miclou."

Miclou turns, lowering his sword as he sees Stecher standing by the ladder. Miclou starts over to Stecher as the two villagers walk slowly into the barn towards the wagons.

Miclou stops next to Stecher, "What is it?"

Stecher points at the base of the ladder with his sword, "Look."

Miclou looks at the ground to see the slide marks in the dirt as the one villager gets in the seat of one wagon and the second villager gets in the seat of the other wagon.

Miclou looks up at the loft and smiles, "We have them trapped."

Stecher starts to climb the ladder as Miclou is close behind him. As the two dark riders climb, the two wagons ride out the front of the barn. As the wagons get to the road, Stephanie sneezes. Miclou and Stecher both stop climbing and start looking around. The two dark riders start back down the ladder, glancing around as if they are unsure where the noise exactly came from.

Then, the wagon with Stefez, Shaun, Michael, Jencent, Anna and Bailee turns east on the road as the wagon with Jody, Sherry, Stephanie, Marsha and Brendan turns west on the road and start away from each other.

Anna can barely see through the hay, "They're headed away from us."

Stefez whispers, "Stay still. We can't risk the dark riders seeing us."

As the two dark riders walk towards the front of the barn, the two wagons speed up to a faster trot.

Jody whispers as he sees the other wagon moving away from them, "We have to get back to the others."

As Jody starts to move, he suddenly stops as he sees Miclou and Stecher walk out of the front of the barn.

Jody quickly whispers, "No one move, it's them."

Miclou and Stecher glance right and left as more wagons pull onto the dirt road. In a few moments, the two wagons lose sight of each other. Miclou and Stecher turn and walk back into the barn.

Anna whispers knowing she has been separated from Marsha, "What now? We lost the others."

Michael whispers, "We stay completely still in case they start after us."

On the back of the other wagon, Marsha whispers knowing she has lost Anna, "We lost the others, didn't we?"

Jody whispers in return, "Yes, but we have to remain still. We can't risk getting out of the wagon and alerting others to our presence."

As Miclou and Stecher finish searching the barn and return to their horses, the wagon with Stefez and the others heads east out of the village and the wagon with Jody an the others heads west out of the village.

Chapter 10

G abriela walks into her chamber where her cauldron and crystal ball are. The four candles on the table light up the room. Gabriela walks over and leans her staff against the table. Gabriela closes her eyes, moves her right hand over the crystal ball and mumbles under her breath. The crystal ball gets cloudy as Gabriela continues to slowly move her hand and mumble. After a few more seconds, the face of Stecher appears in the crystal ball.

Stecher speaks, "Yes my Queen?"

Gabriela opens her eyes and replies with enthusiastic hope, "Do you have the children?"

Stecher responds in an indifferent tone, "No. We chased them in Farhollow, but they slipped away. We are still searching the town."

Gabriela sighs, "Very well, keep looking." She pauses, "I'll send word to my animals to look for them as well. If they are spotted, I'll contact you. Send me word if you find them."

Stecher bows his head, "Yes my Queen."

Gabriela removes her hand from the crystal ball and Stecher's image disappears. Gabriela grabs her staff with her right hand.

As Gabriela walks out of the chamber, she speaks, "You will not keep getting lucky my dear children."

———

With a soft breeze in the air and the town of

Farhollow and the dark riders a distant memory, the wagon carrying Michael, Stefez, Shaun, Jencent, Anna and Bailee continues along the dirt road. The man driving the wagon is still completely unaware of the additional passengers in the back. Once the group feels it is safe, Michael pops out from under the hay. The man driving the wagon is completely surprised and pulls the wagon to a quick stop. Stefez, Shaun, Jencent, Anna and Bailee pop out from under the hay.

The village man in shock, "Who are you?"

Stefez replies in a calm voice, "Don't be afraid. We have no intentions of harming you."

Anna sounds a little scared and dejected, "We've lost the others."

Michael looks at the village man, "It's okay, we just need a ride away from Farhollow."

Stefez chimes in, "We're trying to help Prince Brian against Gabriela. We need your help."

The village man smiles, "Anything to help Prince Brian. Sit back and relax."

The village man starts the wagon on down the road again as the sun moves into the mid-afternoon sky.

The wagon carrying Jody, Sherry, Marsha, Stephanie and Brendan continues along the dirt road heading west from Farhollow. The village man is unaware of the passengers in the back. Once the group is certain that they are far away from the dark riders, Jody pops out from under the hay, startling the village man driving the wagon. As the village man pulls the wagon to a stop, Sherry, Marsha, Stephanie and Brendan pop out from under the hay.

The village man looks at Jody, "The ranger." He looks at the others, "Outlanders."

Jody smiles, "We need your help."

Marsha sighs and looks sad, "We lost the others."

Jody glances at Marsha, "I know it's upsetting about losing Anna, but we have to keep moving west."

The village man questions, "What can I do for you?"

Jody turns back to the villager, "All we need is a ride and to get as far away from Farhollow as possible."

The village man smiles, "Well then, just sit back and relax."

The village man starts the wagon moving again as the sun enters the mid-afternoon sky.

The air is still as the sun gets lower in the sky. The wagon carrying Stefez and the others continues along the dirt road.

Anna looks at Stefez, "So, what are we going to do about finding the others?"

Stefez sighs, "Nothing right now. We can't afford to retrace our route."

Michael nods, "All we can do is continue on as I'm sure they will do the same."

Anna speaks a little depressed, "But you once said that Gabriela could send the dark riders to our location if not for your magic. If they're spotted, can't she do that?"

Stefez smiles, "No. My spell still protects them. I placed the protection in Sherry, Marsha and Stephanie's necklaces while you all slept." She pauses, "Just like I did with your necklace. As long as you are within a hundred feet of your necklace and they are the same with theirs, all of you are protected."

Anna sighs and looks down, "I don't like being away from Marsha."

Stefez tries to sound reassuring, "I know, but we have to keep moving and I'm sure she will be safe with Jody.

Besides, we have put some distance between us and the dark riders and I'm sure they have too."

Michael glances around as if he heard something, "It still doesn't stop Gabriela of learning our location in other ways."

Anna looks at Michael, "What do you mean?"

Jencent replies, "If we're spotted by any creature that is helping Gabriela, they can inform her of our location. Then she can tell the dark riders."

Anna yawns, "Wonderful."

Stefez smiles and glances around, "We probably should find a place to rest for the night."

The village man speaks up, "Not far ahead is a clearing I usually rest at."

Michael nods, "Good, we should get some rest. Tomorrow is another long day."

As the wagon continues on down the road, five wolves emerge from the woods onto the road.

One wolf speaks in a Russian accent, "We need to contact Queen Gabriela and tell her of the outlander child we just saw."

The wolves run back into the forest as the wagon disappears around a bend in the road.

———————

As the sun draws closer to the evening horizon, the wagon carrying Jody and the others continues on the dirt road heading west.

Marsha is the first to speak, a little dejected, "What are we going to do about finding the others?"

Jody shakes his head and speaks as caringly as he can, "Nothing for now. We can't afford to backtrack and risk running into the dark riders."

Marsha questions, "So, what are we going to do? I can't let anything happen to Anna."

Jody replies, "Well, first we'll camp for the night, then continue on to River Fork tomorrow." He pauses, "We know that the goal is to get to the castle. So we just keep going that way until we hear something from Stefez. I'm sure she'll send a message bird or the wind to let us know what is going on." He gazes at Marsha and tries to reassure her with a smile, "I know you're worried about Anna, but I know Stefez will make sure she stays safe. Plus Shaun and Michael are with them."

Marsha can't help but gaze at Jody, "It's just that I'm responsible for her. I've taken care of her ever since our parents passed away and this place is so different."

Jody gives a reassuring smile and stares at Marsha, "It's different, but despite Gabriela and the dark riders, it really is a wonderful place with some very wonderful people."

Marsha stays lost in Jody's eyes, "Thanks."

Brendan leans back against Stephanie, "I'm tired mom."

Jody looks over at Brendan and smiles. Stephanie looks at Brendan, then looks at Jody and smiles. Jody continues to smile as he looks up at Stephanie.

Stephanie lets out a sigh, "Me too little man."

Jody speaks to the village man driving the wagon, "We should find a place to rest for the night."

The village man replies, "There's a spot no too far ahead where I usually stop."

Marsha tries to take her mind off of losing Anna while she continues to gaze at Jody, "So, what do you think about the Kingdom, since you've been here longer?"

Jody is still captured by Marsha, "I really like it here. It's an incredible place." He pauses as his heart beats a little faster, "And it's gotten even better these last couple of days."

Brendan yawns, "I like it too."

Marsha glances at Brendan, then looks back at Jody. Marsha smiles at Jody and winks. Jody and Marsha share a gaze into each others eyes, neither sure why they have taken such a quick liking to the other. Suddenly, the sound of crows breaks the silence. Jody breaks his stare and starts looking around.

Stephanie questions, "What is it?"

Sherry looks a little worried, "Something wrong?"

Jody replies still looking around, "Crows."

Marsha glances around, "What about them?"

Jody continues to look around, "Crows work for Gabriela. If they spot us, they'll tell her where we're at."

Stephanie looks around, but is unable to see anything. Jody keeps a watchful eye out. As the wagon continues on, six crows watch from their perch high in one of the trees.

One of the crows speaks in a raspy voice, "We must let Queen Gabriela know of the outlanders."

The crows fly off as the wagon continues on down the dirt road.

———————

As the sun has completely set over the Kingdom, Gabriela walks into the chamber where her crystal ball is. She walks over to the table and leans her staff against the table. She holds her right hand over the crystal ball and mumbles under her breath. After a few seconds, the images of the wolves appear in the crystal ball.

Gabriela questions, "What do you have for me?"

The lead wolf replies, "Queen Gabriela, we have spotted one of the outlanders, a child."

Gabriela questions again, "Where?"

The lead wolf replies, "One the road that heads east from Farhollow. They have stopped for the night."

Gabriela smiles, "Good, stay with them if you can."

Gabriela closes her eyes and mumbles again. The image in the crystal ball changes to the crows.

Gabriela opens her eyes and questions, "You have something for me?"

The lead crow replies, "Yes Queen Gabriela. We have spotted three outland women and an outland child headed west towards River Fork from Farhollow."

Gabriela's eyes narrow, "Interesting, they've split up." She pauses, "Very good. Try to stay with them."

Gabriela closes her eyes again and mumbles under her breath. After a few seconds, the face of Miclou appears in the crystal ball.

Miclou speaks, "Yes Queen Gabriela."

Gabriela opens her eyes and questions, "Where are the two of you?"

Miclou replies, "In Farhollow, we've searched the entire town."

Gabriela speaks, "I've been contacted by the animals. They've spotted the outlanders."

Miclou questions, "Where are they my Queen?"

Gabriela replies, "They've split up for some reason. One child is on the road headed east and the others are on the road west to River Fork." She pauses, "Miclou, you head east, send Stecher west after the others."

Miclou bows his head, "Yes Queen Gabriela."

Gabriela removes her hand from the crystal ball and the images fade away.

Gabriela grabs her staff, "Time is running out for you my dear children."

Chapter 11

As the soft breeze blows the cool morning air, the sun breaks the horizon, casting light on the once dark forest. Stefez wakes up and glances around the clearing in the forest where the group camped for the night. Stefez sees Michael, Shaun, Anna, the village man and Bailee. Stefez doesn't see Jencent with the others.

As Stefez stretches, the others start to wake up. Stefez stands up and breathes in the morning air. Michael stands up and also notices that Jencent is not there. Shaun and Anna both sit up and stretch.

Michael looks around, "Where's Jencent?"

Stefez shakes her head, "I don't know. She wasn't here when I woke up."

Shaun glances around as the village man gets up and walks over to the wagon. Anna stands up and walks over by Stefez. At that time, Stefez, Shaun, Michael and Anna hear movement in the forest. Stefez readies her staff. Shaun and Michael draw their swords.

Stefez speaks to Anna, "Stay behind us."

After a couple of seconds, Jencent walks into the clearing from the forest. Stefez relaxes as Michael and Shaun put their swords away.

Michael speaks to Jencent, "Where did you go?"

Jencent replies without looking at Michael, "I don't like sleeping in a clearing. Besides, I cleaned up a little and didn't want to wake everyone."

Stefez speaks up, "With the dark riders after us, you should let one of us know if you're going off by yourself, just to be safe."

Jencent just nods, then changes the subject, "So, what now?"

Anna questions, "Are we going to try and find the others?"

Shaun shakes her head, "I don't think we should. It would still be too dangerous to head back towards Farhollow."

Jencent speaks up, "So we just keep heading east? That takes us away from the castle."

Stefez sighs, "For now, that's what we must do. In fact, I think we should head to the Dark Valley."

Jencent looks puzzled, "Why is that? It is nearly at the eastern most part of the Kingdom."

Stefez is unsure if she should tell why, but decides she needs to in order to convince the others.

Stefez replies, "That's where Prince Brian and his army is hiding out." She pauses, "I would've figured that you would've known since you were traveling with him."

Jencent shakes her head slightly, "He picked me up in South Town. He didn't say where we were going."

Michael nods, "We would be safe there until we can get word to the others."

Jencent agrees, "That's true."

Stefez speaks up, "Then we head to the Dark Valley." She looks at Anna who looks sad, "Don't worry Anna, the others are going to be just fine. I'll send a message bird to them once we reach the Dark Valley."

The village man speaks up, "I can take you as far as the fork in the road, but then I must turn north to Ghost Town."

Stefez nods, "We'd be greatly in your debt. Thank you."

Shaun, Stefez, Anna and Jencent climb into the back of the wagon. Michael puts Bailee in the back of the wagon, then he climbs in. The village man gets in the driver's seat of the wagon and starts heading east down the dirt road.

———————

As the morning sun casts it's light on the forest and the soft breeze blows the smell of trees and leaves through the warming air, Jody and Sherry are both standing in the clearing where they camped for the night, watching the village man get the wagon ready.

Sherry glances around, "So, what do you think?"

Jody sighs, "I'm thinking we keep heading to River Fork."

Jody and Sherry look over as they hear Marsha, Stephanie and Brendan getting up.

The village man speaks as Stephanie, Marsha and Brendan walk over to Jody and Sherry, "I'm almost ready."

Stephanie yawns and stretches, "So, what are we going to do now?"

Jody smiles, "We're going to keep going west. We should reach River Fork by evening."

Marsha stretches, "What about the others?"

Jody sighs, "I'm sure Stefez will send us a message bird soon to let us know how they're doing. Until then, we just keep going." Jody smiles at Marsha, "I'm sure they are fine."

Marsha returns the warm smile, "Thanks."

Stephanie speaks as Brendan leans against her, "What do we do after we reach River Fork?"

Jody replies, "I'm not sure. We can either head north to Birdview or keep heading west to Apple Grove." He pauses, "We can figure out what we want to do once we get to River Fork. We don't want to get too far ahead of ourselves, things around here can change in a hurry."

Sherry chuckles, "Boy have we seen that already."

The village man climbs up in the seat of the wagon, "Everything's ready if you are."

Jody and the others gather up their things and walk over to the wagon. Jody picks up Brendan and puts him in the back of the wagon. Jody helps Sherry climb in the back of the wagon next. Jody helps Stephanie into the back of the wagon, then he helps Marsha into the back of the wagon.

Marsha smiles at Jody, "Thank you."

Jody climbs into the back of the wagon, "My pleasure."

Stephanie smiles at Jody, knowing that he has taken a liking to Marsha. Jody looks over and sees the smile on Stephanie's face. Jody smiles at his sister, knowing why she is smiling at him. Everyone leans back as the wagon starts off down the dirt road.

As the sun nearly reaches the noon sky and the warm breeze slightly blows the fresh leaf and tree smell all around the forest, the wagon carrying Stefez, Michael, Jencent, Shaun, Anna and Bailee stops at a fork in the dirt road. One fork of the road heads north and one fork of the road heads south. Stefez, Shaun, Michael and Jencent climb out of the back of the wagon. Michael helps Anna out of the wagon, then helps Bailee out of the wagon.

Stefez speaks to the village man, "Thanks for your help."

The village man nods, "My pleasure. Good luck to you all."

The wagon heads off to the north.

Anna questions, "What now?"

Stefez replies, "We head east into the forest."

At that moment, Stefez and the others hear the thundering sound of a horse riding fast towards them. The air starts to get colder. Stefez looks at the others and their faces say it all. Everyone looks back down the dirt road they just traveled and they see the dark rider, Miclou, heading straight at them.

Michael draws his sword, "Quick, into the forest!"

Jencent and Shaun draw their swords and run into the forest. Stefez and Anna run into the forest. Bailee hops as fast as she can to keep up with the others. Michael runs into the forest right behind the others. Miclou slows his horse as he reaches the edge of the forest. Miclou draws his sword and rides into the forest after the group.

Stefez and the others are running hard, but Miclou closes in on them. As Miclou draws closer, he slides off his horse and lands on his feet running. Stefez and the others are only fifty yards ahead of the dark rider. Stefez and the others clear some trees and quickly stop. The group is standing at the edge of a large ravine that is about a hundred feet wide and near two hundred feet deep.

Anna tries to catch her breath, "What now?"

Stefez glances around and sees a wooden plank, rope bridge about fifty feet to their right, "Over there, the bridge."

Stefez and the others run fast for the bridge as Miclou closes in fast. As Bailee starts hopping across the bridge followed by Anna. Miclou catches up to the group. Michael and Shaun turn to face Miclou as Stefez, Jencent, Anna and Bailee keep going towards the bridge. Michael cuts his sword in at Miclou, but the dark rider moves fast and knocks the sword away. Shaun brings her sword in fast at Miclou. Miclou spins left and the sword misses. Miclou brings his sword around Shaun towards Michael. Michael brings his sword up just in time to stop the deadly blow. Miclou quickly withdraws his sword and ducks as if he knows what is behind him and Shaun's sword narrowly misses the dark rider.

Jencent runs onto the bridge as Stefez, Bailee and

Anna reach the far side of the ravine. Stefez, Anna and Bailee stop and turn back to the others to see what is happening.

Miclou does a forward roll as Michael brings his sword down at him. As Michael's sword hits the ground where Miclou was at, Miclou rolls to his feet. Miclou spins towards Michael and sweeps Michael's feet out from under him. Michael lands hard on his back. Miclou raises his sword, but Shaun comes moving in fast with her sword. Miclou brings his sword around with uncanny speed and blocks Shaun's sword.

Miclou spins around behind Shaun and drives his elbow into her back, sending her stumbling forward. Michael quickly gets back to his feet and cuts his sword in at Miclou. Miclou quickly blocks Michael's sword.

As the two swords meet, Michael yells to Shaun, "Get to the bridge!"

Jencent reaches the other side of the ravine and stops next to Stefez, Anna and Bailee. Shaun runs onto the bridge.

Miclou stares coldly at Michael as their swords are still together, "You have no chance of winning."

Miclou feels Michael start to push forward. Miclou steps to the side and Michael's momentum causes him to stumble past Miclou. Michael catches his balance and runs for the bridge. Stefez points her staff at a tree near Miclou and starts to mumble under her breath. The stone on the end of her staff starts to glow. As Miclou starts after Michael, he quickly stops as a small tree crashes to the ground in front of him. Michael runs onto the bridge as Shaun makes it to the far side of the ravine and stops next to the others. Miclou hops over the tree and starts for the bridge.

Stefez yells, "He's still coming!"

Michael looks back and sees Miclou nearing the bridge. Michael knows the only thing he can do to keep the dark rider from chasing them. Michael stops and wraps his right arm around one of the ropes. Michael brings his sword across and cuts the ropes holding the bridge up. The bridge breaks. Michael holds on tight as he falls towards the far edge of the ravine. Miclou stops at the edge of the bridge and just watches.

Stefez yells, "Michael!"

Michael crashes into the side of the ravine, but hangs on to the bridge and his sword. Michael puts his sword away and starts to climb up the bridge to the others. Michael makes it to the edge of the ravine and soon climbs over the edge and finds himself next to Stefez and the others. Michael gets to his feet. Stefez and the others look across the ravine at Miclou. Miclou just turns and starts back towards his horse.

Stefez looks at Michael, "You okay?"

Michael nods, "Yea."

Shaun chuckles, "That was crazy, but it worked."

Michael smiles, "It was the only thing that came to mind at the time."

Stefez lets out a sigh of relief, "Well, we're safe for now, but he won't give up that easy."

Bailee chimes in, "Lets get some distance between us and him."

Shaun nods, "Yea, cause I don't feel like facing him again any time soon. He's good."

Michael nods, "Me too." He looks at Jencent, "We could've used some help back there."

Jencent replies coldly, "I gave Prince Brian my word to take care of and stay with the children at all times. That's what I intend on doing."

Stefez speaks up, "It's all okay now so lets get moving. We should reach the Dark Valley by sunset."

Stefez and the others start walking east into the forest.

Chapter 12

The wagon carrying Jody and the others continues to travel west along the dirt road through the forest. As the sun gets lower in the evening sky, the warm breeze blows the smell of trees and leaves around the wagon, then the air suddenly fills with the smell of food being prepared. Jody and the others look ahead from the back of the wagon as the wagon leaves the forest and crosses over a river on a wooden bridge. Stephanie and the others see a huge town just ahead, much larger than any town they have seen yet. All the buildings are made of stone. Most of the buildings are one story, some are two stories and a few are even three stories tall.

As the wagon rolls off the bridge and passes a few wooden huts just outside the town, Jody smiles, "River Fork."

Marsha closes her eyes and breathes in through her nose, "It smells so wonderful."

The wagon continues on as the dirt road changes into a stone road. Stephanie and the others see numerous people walking around the town. They are dressed nicer than the people that they saw in Farhollow and Havel. Their clothes are made of brighter and more alive colors. The wagon passes a couple of buildings, then stops at a barn and horse stables.

The village man turns to the others, "This is my stop. I'm happy I could help you."

Jody nods and smiles, "We definitely appreciate the help."

Jody gets out of the back of the wagon. Jody helps Brendan out of the wagon first. Jody helps Sherry out of the back of the wagon, then he helps Stephanie out of the wagon. Finally, Jody helps Marsha out of the wagon.

Stephanie questions, "What now?"

Jody glances around, "I think we should find a tavern where we can get something to eat and get some rest."

Marsha looks around, "This town is huge compared to the others."

Stephanie sighs, "They're not going to like us here either, are they?"

Jody shakes his head slightly, "Not really, but not nearly as much like the other towns. We should be okay for the night." He pauses and looks around, "Lets head towards the center of town and see what we can find."

Jody starts walking. Stephanie takes Brendan's hand and the two of them start walking behind Jody. Sherry and Marsha follow right behind Stephanie and Brendan. Some of the townspeople take notice of the group, but most just go about their business. As the group gets closer to the center of town, the smell of wonderfully cooked food gets stronger. The air also fills with the sounds of upbeat medieval period music.

Marsha looks at Jody, "This is an amazing town."

Stephanie smiles, "Seeing these people and now the music, it's like a movie."

Jody nods, "I told you this place was quite amazing." He pauses, "Lets try that tavern over there. It doesn't look to busy from out here."

Jody and the others walk towards a large, two story, stone building. A wooden sign hangs over the door reading, "Bill's Place". Jody opens the wooden door and steps inside. Stephanie and the others walk in behind him. They find themselves in a large open room with about twenty tables. Along the right side of the room is a bar and a large cauldron hangs over a burning fire in the back of the room. Only three tables have people sitting at them and no one takes notice of Jody and the others.

Jody lowers his voice, "Lets go sit down."

Jody and the others walk into the room and over to the first table along the left side of the room away from the other patrons. Jody sits down facing the door. Sherry sits across from Jody. Stephanie sits next to Jody on his right. Brendan sits between Stephanie and Sherry on Stephanie's right. Marsha sits between Jody and Sherry on Jody's left.

Stephanie speaks up, "Well, at least no one has yelled at us yet."

Jody smiles, "Shaun and I have a good reputation here in River Fork. We helped the town awhile back with a problem."

Marsha questions, "What kind of problem?"

Jody looks at Marsha and gazes into her eyes, "Four trolls use to come into town every night and take things. We happened through the town and they asked us to help." Jody pauses and smiles, "We got rid of the trolls."

Stephanie sighs, "Now we have trolls too."

Jody finally breaks his gaze at Marsha and looks at Stephanie and smiles, "You're going to find that this place is right out of a fairytale story and everything in it."

At that time, a younger woman wearing a brown dress and sandals walks up to the table, "One of the rangers, its good to see you again."

Jody nods, "Thank you."

The woman looks at Stephanie, Sherry, Marsha and Brendan, "Outlanders?"

Jody nods, "Yes. We're helping Prince Brian and Stefez by trying to get them out of the Kingdom."

Stephanie looks at Jody and breaks a smile at the sound of Prince Brian's name.

Jody speaks again, "We won't cause any trouble. We just need some food and a place to sleep."

The woman is quiet for a moment, then finally replies, "We don't normally serve outlanders here." She pauses and smiles, "But since they're with you, its okay. What can I get you?"

Jody smiles, "Five bowls of that wonderful smelling stew, four cups of ale and one cup of milk."

The woman smiles, "I'll be right back."

As the woman walks off, Marsha speaks up, "I'm glad you're welcome here. We stand out so bad we would never make it on our own."

Jody looks over to Marsha, "If we have time in the morning, we'll see about getting the three of you some clothes so you won't stand out."

Marsha smiles and gazes at Jody, "That would definitely help."

Brendan slightly bounces in his chair, "I'm hungry."

Stephanie and the others look at Brendan and smile. The young woman walks back up with the five bowls of stew and sets them on the table. Everyone starts eating as the woman walks off and quickly returns with the drinks.

Jody questions the young woman, "May we stay here for the night?"

The young woman glances around to make sure no one can hear her, "Sure. I have a room with two beds you can have."

Jody smiles, "Thank you so much."

The woman smiles and walks off.

Brendan eats some of the stew, "This is good."

The others smile at Brendan and start eating.

As the warm breeze softly blows the smells of the forest and the sun is nearly on the evening horizon, Stefez and the others continue their way through the forest towards the Dark Valley.

Stefez speaks to the others as the group nears the top of a tree covered hill, "Just over this hill."

When Stefez and the others reach the top of the hill, they clear the last of the trees. Before them the forest opens up into the Dark Valley. The group sees the camp of Prince Brian. Stefez and the others notice numerous humans, elves and dwarves wandering the camp.

Stefez speaks to the others, "Lets find Prince Brian, then we can get some rest."

Stefez starts down the hill into the Dark Valley followed by the rest of the group. As they enter the camp, the humans, elves and dwarves take notice of the group, especially Anna.

Bailee speaks while hopping next to Stefez, "Well, no more keeping the outlanders a secret."

Jencent nods slightly, "True. It might cause a problem with some of them wanting to fight against Gabriela now."

Michael chimes in, "I don't know. It might actually encourage them to fight, knowing that they must defeat Gabriela before she gets the outlander child."

The group walks through the camp towards Prince Brian's tent. Stefez and the others can feel all the eyes watching them and hear the whispers of the humans, elves and dwarves. As Stefez and the others clear the last tent before Prince Brian's tent, they hear a familiar voice.

Jennifer calls out, "Stefez!"

Stefez and the others stop and look to their right. They see Jennifer walking towards them. Stefez smiles and gives a quick nod to Jennifer as she walks up.

Jennifer glances at the group, "I didn't expect to see you here."

Hearing Jennifer outside, Prince Brian walks out of his tent and sees the group. Prince Brian starts towards the group with a smile, but as he reaches the group, he loses his smile when he sees that some of the outlanders are missing.

Stefez bows her head, "My lord."

Prince Brian glances around, "Stefez. This is a surprise." He pauses, "Where are the others?"

Stefez replies, "The dark riders caught up to us in Farhollow where we picked up Michael."

Jennifer notices the instant look of concern on Prince Brian's face, knowing he is thinking about Stephanie and Brendan.

Stefez continues, "We escaped on separate wagons, but last we saw them, they were headed west as we were heading east." She pauses, "I don't know since then."

Jencent speaks up, "One dark rider caught up to us at the fork in the road. So I'm guessing the other dark rider was sent after them."

Michael speaks up, "They should've reached River Fork by now."

Prince Brian glances over to Michael, "It's good to see you again."

Michael bows his head, "Good to see you too my lord."

Jennifer speaks up, "Rein will be surprised to see you."

Michael smiles at the name, "I'm sure she will."

Prince Brian speaks up as a few humans in the camp start lighting torches due to the sun setting, "We will have time to talk things over in the morning." He turns to Jennifer, "Get them set up in a tent. I'm sure they could use some rest."

Stefez bows her head, "Thank you my lord."

Prince Brian walks back into his tent with a sad look on his face. Stefez and the others look around and notice numerous people watching them.

Jennifer speaks up, "Follow me."

Stefez puts her arm around Anna and everyone follows Jennifer.

Jody and the others walk down the hallway of the second story in the tavern where they ate. They reach a wooden door at the end of the hallway and stop. Jody opens the door and everyone walks into the room. It is a small room that has a desk with a wash basin on it, two beds and a small table between the two beds with a burning candle on it.

Marsha smiles, "Not the Hilton, but definitely better than sleeping on the ground."

Jody nods, "We won't have much time to sleep, but at least it'll be more comfortable."

Stephanie looks over at Jody, "Is it that late?"

Jody sighs, "That late and we have to also figure that the dark riders know where we are so we can't stay still too long. It won't take them long to catch up to us."

Sherry smiles, "I'll take any rest in a real bed right now."

Jody removes his cloak and his weapons, "Well, lets get some rest." He pauses, "Steph, why don't you, Brendan and me take the bed near the door and Sherry and Marsha will take the bed by the wall."

Stephanie nods and removes her sword, "Sounds good to me."

Jody puts his weapons and cloak down and lays down in the first bed. Stephanie climbs into bed and lays next to Jody while Brendan climbs into bed and lays next to Stephanie. Marsha climbs into the second bed. Sherry climbs into the second bed next to Marsha. Jody is laying on his side and looks over to see Marsha laying on her side looking at him. Marsha smiles at Jody.

Jody smiles, licks his finger and thumb and reaches over to the candle, "Good night everyone."

Jody puts the candle out and darkness covers the

room. Jody rolls over, puts his arm around Stephanie and places his hand on Brendan's shoulder.

———————

The stars light up the clear sky over the town of River Fork. The cool, predawn breeze continues to blow through the town. If it wasn't for a few people still walking the streets, the town would look empty. It is the normal way that River Fork looks in the hour before sunrise, however, this morning will be a little different.

The sound of a horse riding on the torch lit, stone street thunderously echoes through the town. As a homeless patron wanders the street, he starts to shiver as the air gets colder around him. The man glances around hearing the horse get closer to him. The sound of the horse suddenly stops as the man nears the corner of a two story, stone building. The man steps around the corner of the building and stops immediately.

Just a mere ten feet from him and a couple of torches burning in the background, the man can make out the image sitting on the horse in front of him. The man shivers from the cold air and his eyes show that of paralyzing fear as the man knows he is looking at one of the legendary dark riders.

Stecher slowly moves his horse towards the man. The man continues to just stand there as Stecher stops next to him.

Stecher looks down at the man, "I'm looking for some outlanders. Have you seen them?"

The man is quiet, still overcome with fear.

Stecher speaks again in his hollow voice, "I'll let you live if you tell me."

The man finally finds the ability to speak, "They arrived last night and headed towards the center of town. I don't know if they're still here."

Stecher replies, "Very good. I would suggest you not telling anyone about me."

Stecher slowly takes his horse around the corner of the building, leaving the fearful man standing there.

Chapter 13

In the cool, early morning, Jody and the others come walking down the stairs in the tavern where they spent the night. The smell of wonderfully cooked food fills the air. The group sees the young woman from the night before. She is walking around the tavern getting the place ready to open for the day.

Stephanie speaks to Jody, "So what now?"

The young woman walks over to the group, "Good morning."

Jody nods, "Good morning."

The young woman glances around, "Just thought you should know. Word came in that some of Gabriela's army is waiting in Birdview."

Jody nods again, "Thank you, for everything."

The woman smiles and walks off.

Jody turns to the others, "I guess that answers our question. Looks like we'll head west to Apple Grove. Now, lets see if we can find a shop open to maybe get you all some clothes."

Marsha smiles, "Yea, so we won't stand out quite so much."

Jody and the others walk over to the front door. Jody opens the door and steps outside into the bright morning sun. The others step out behind him and the cool breeze softly blows across their faces.

Stephanie closes her eyes for a second and breathes in the fresh air, "I can't believe how clean and fresh it is here."

At that moment, the serene moment is broken by a couple of screams in the distance. Jody and the others look off to their left to see where the screams came from. Suddenly, the air starts to get colder as they hear the sound of a horse slowly riding towards them on the stone road.

Sherry gets a worried look, "Oh no."

Then, Stecher emerges from behind a building a mere two hundred feet from Jody and the others. Stephanie, Sherry and Marsha get a look of fear on their faces.

Marsha speaks with fear in her voice, "They found us."

Jody yells, "Run!"

Jody and the others quickly run in the opposite direction from where the dark rider is at. Stecher flips his reigns and starts riding fast after Jody and the others. Jody turns the corner with the others right behind him. Jody sees a three story building just up the road that appears to be open.

Jody yells while running, "Head for that tall building!"

The sound of the horse gets louder as Stecher turns the corner and starts to close in on the group. The air continues to get colder as Jody and the others near the wooden front door of the building which has a canvas canopy over it. Stecher closes in fast as Jody stops at the front door of the building and pushes the door open. Sherry, Stephanie, Marsha and Brendan run inside. As Stecher slows his horse down, Jody steps inside and closes the door. Jody and the others find themselves in a large room with some furniture and other goods. Jody sees a desk near the front door where they are standing.

Jody looks at the others, "Quick, help me move this desk in front of the door."

Jody grabs the desk. Sherry, Marsha and Stephanie also grab the desk. Even Brendan helps push on the desk.

As the group slides the heavy wooden desk in front of the door, Stecher stops his horse in front of the building and dismounts. Stecher ties his horse to one of the poles holding up the canopy over the front door and walks towards the door.

Jody and the others quickly make their way through the first floor of the shop, but they are unable to find a back door to the place. Stecher pushes on the front door to find that it is blocked. Stecher pushes a little harder, but is still unable to move the door. Stecher quickly starts around towards the back of the building.

Jody questions, "Do you see the back way out?"

Sherry shakes her head, "I don't see it."

Jody looks at the others, "How about you two?"

Stephanie sighs, "Nope."

Marsha shakes her head, "Me either."

At that time, the shopkeeper, a middle aged man, walks up to the group. He has a surprised look when he sees Sherry, Stephanie, Marsha and Brendan.

The shopkeeper speaks to them, "Outlanders."

Jody questions, "Do you have a back door? We can't seem to find it."

The shopkeeper smiles, "Its one of the things we sell here. It's a hidden door."

Jody smiles, "It would be a great help if you showed us where it's at."

The shopkeeper starts to walk towards the back, "Follow me."

Jody and the others follow the shopkeeper. Stecher hurries around to the back of the building, but he is unable to find the back door as well. Stecher draws his sword and slowly scans the back of the building.

The shopkeeper leads the group to a small, iron ring on the back wall, "See here, this is the handle and the wood is made to look like stones. Neat, huh?"

Jody nods, "Really nice, thank you."

Jody grabs the iron ring and turns it. Jody pushes the door open and takes a step outside. As the rest of the group starts to move, Jody stops quickly when he sees Stecher standing only twenty-five feet away.

Stephanie bumps into Jody, "What is it?"

Jody replies while moving back, "Its him."

Everyone moves back into the shop and Jody closes the door. Stecher rushes towards where the hidden back door is at.

The shopkeeper smiles, "Its okay, there is no outside handle."

In the heat of the moment, no one in the group thinks about the front door where they came into the shop.

Jody glances around and sees the stairs leading up, "Quick, upstairs."

Jody and the others rush towards the stairs. Stecher stops where he knows the door is at, but he is unable to find a handle. Stecher steps back and kicks the door with great force. The door creaks, but doesn't give in. Jody and the others reach the second floor and look around. They see a window over by the front side of the building.

Jody motions with his hand, "Since I completely forgot the front door while downstairs, quick, over to the window."

Stecher steps back and kicks the door again. This time the door cracks some, but doesn't open yet. Jody stops at the window and looks out. He sees the canopy that covers the front door just below them about ten feet and numerous townspeople starting to wander the streets.

Jody opens the window, "Okay, we jump down to the canopy and then get back down to the street."

Marsha looks at Jody like he's lost his mind, "Yea right. I'll take the front door."

Jody replies, "Too late, he might already be inside. It's this or fight the dark rider."

Sherry steps up to the window, "That's an easy

decision for me."

Sherry takes a deep breath to gather herself and tosses the staff out the window first. As the staff lands on the road, Sherry jumps out the window and lands on the canopy. She slides to the edge of the canopy, then drops to the road. Sherry quickly picks up her staff.

Jody looks at the others, "See, nothing to it." He pauses, "Steph, you go next. I'll send Brendan after you."

Stephanie chuckles slightly, "Oh boy."

Stephanie steps over to the window. She closes her eyes, holds the sword against her left leg and jumps. Stephanie lands on the canopy. She slides over to the edge and drops off the canopy to the road. Stephanie takes a deep breath and stands next to Sherry.

Stecher steps back and kicks the door again. One of the pieces of wood cracks this time. Jody and Marsha hear the echo of the door in the distance.

Jody looks at Brendan, "Okay big man, you ready."

Brendan smiles, "Yea!"

Jody helps Brendan out the window and Brendan jumps down to the canopy. He slides over to the edge. Stephanie and Sherry catch Brendan as he drops off the canopy. Marsha steps over to the window and tosses her staff out.

Marsha takes a deep breath, "Okay."

Marsha jumps out the window and lands on the canopy. She slides over to the edge and drops off the canopy to the road. Marsha grabs her staff and stands with the others. Jody holds his sword against his left leg and jumps out the window. He lands on the canopy as Stecher kicks the door again and the door gives in and opens in a crash. Jody slides over to the edge of the canopy and drops to the road.

Brendan is slightly bouncing, "That was fun."

Jody smiles, "Boy was it big guy." He glances around, "Lets get out of town, fast."

Jody and the others run off westward down the road that heads out of River Fork. Stecher runs up to the second floor and sees the open window. Stecher runs over to the open window and looks out. The dark rider sees the different townspeople walking along the streets, but no signs of Jody and the others.

─── ─ ── ──

The warm noontime sun shines down on the Dark Valley where Stefez and the others have spent the morning. The soft breeze blows the wonderful smell of stew and fresh cooked meat through the camp. Michael and Rein are walking amongst some of the tents heading towards Prince Brian's tent.

Rein speaks while they walk, "Its good to see you again Michael."

Michael breaks a slight smile, "Its really good to see you too." He pauses, "Look, I'm sorry for leaving, especially the way I did."

Rein replies softly, "Its all in the past. I know why you did what you did." She looks at Michael, "It didn't make me feel any different about you. I still care for you just as much as I did then. Besides, I knew we would be together again one day."

Michael looks at Rein, "I was hoping we would be." He pauses, "But we are going to have to be moving out soon. This is far from over. We have to get the outlanders out of the Kingdom."

Rein stops with Michael at the front of Prince Brian's tent, "I know, but once its over and Gabriela is defeated, we'll be together again."

Michael smiles at Rein, "I look forward to that day."

Michael and Rein walk inside Prince Brian's tent. Prince Brian is sitting across from the entrance to the tent. Jennifer is sitting next to Prince Brian on his right. Stefez is sitting next to Prince Brian on his left. Anna is sitting next to Stefez. Shaun is sitting next to Anna. Jencent is sitting next to Jennifer. Ramaf is sitting next to Jencent. Rein and Michael sit down across from Prince Brian. Bailee is in the corner of the tent.

Prince Brian speaks up, "Okay, now that we're all here, lets talk about how to approach Gabriela."

Jennifer nods, "We're going to have to move on the castle soon. If the dark riders do manage to capture the children before we reach the castle, we won't have a chance."

Ramaf sighs, "Its risky. We haven't had much time to train together."

Rein nods, "I agree its risky, but I also understand that we don't really have any other choice."

Michael chimes in, "We have to do something fast cause we don't even know what happened to the others. They may have already been captured or killed."

Stefez can see the sadness on Prince Brian's face at the sound of something happening to Stephanie, "I'll send a message bird to find them and tell them about whatever plan we come up with. They can send the bird back to let us know how they are doing."

Prince Brian speaks up trying to hide his concern, "This is what I'm thinking. Our scouts have told us that Gabriela has lookouts in Birdview and a small army in Lakeway." He pauses, "We take our army straight at Birdview, then cross Glass Lake to Lakeway. That will no doubt draw Gabriela's attention to us."

Stefez nods seeing where Prince Brian's plan is going, "And if we can make her armies focus on you, then we can move around behind the castle and approach it from behind. While they are occupied with you, we can sneak into the castle from the north."

Michael speaks up, "That is a long trip, plus, we need to eventually link up with the other group."

Shaun, Anna, and Jencent just sit quietly listening to the others.

Stefez speaks up again, "I can have the message bird tell them to meet us in Mushroom Farm."

Jennifer nods, "Once all of you get there, we can use a message bird to coordinate our attack on the castle so that all of you can sneak into the castle from the north while we attack from the southeast."

Rein speaks up, "You know, that just might work."

Prince Brian nods, "Its going to have to, we don't have much time and this is the most direct way to attack the castle."

Michael chimes in, "Well, I'm definitely in."

Rein smiles at Michael's enthusiasm towards getting back involved with the fight against Gabriela.

Jencent finally speaks, "Not to bring everyone down, but this all depends on avoiding the dark riders and keeping the children from being captured. Not to mention, Gabriela will no doubt ask for other creatures to help her."

Ramaf nods, "She has a point."

Stefez speaks up, "We'll just have to do our best not to let that happen." She pauses, "They will have to kill me before they take Anna."

Michael chimes in quickly, "Me too. I'll protect her to my last breath if it comes to that."

Jencent smiles, "I'm getting paid either way so I'm in."

Shaun finally speaks up, "I'll do everything I can to keep her safe too."

Prince Brian lets out a sigh, "Then that's the plan." He pauses as he thinks about Stephanie, "Send the message bird. I hope it finds them okay."

Shaun looks at Prince Brian, "I'm sure they're okay my lord. Jody is a very capable fighter. One of the best I've ever seen."

Stefez stands up, "We'll go ahead and rest here today

and head out at dawn tomorrow." Anna stands up and Stefez takes her hand, "Come on Anna, lets go send the message bird."

Stefez and Anna walk out of the tent. Stefez holds up her right hand and a bright green and yellow bird the size of a cardinal lands on her hand.

Stefez speaks to the bird, "Find the ranger, Jody. He should be near River Fork by now and tell him that we are all okay. We have a plan on getting them out of the Kingdom and we need for them to meet us in Mushroom Farm as soon as they can get there."

The bird replies in a high pitched, chirpy voice, "As you wish."

The bird flies off heading west out of the Dark Valley.

Chapter 14

As the sun starts to set over the Kingdom, Gabriela walks into her magic chamber. The candles burning on the table cast a dim light across the room. Gabriela walks over and leans her staff against the table.

Gabriela holds her right hand over the crystal ball on the table, "Still nothing from them."

Gabriela closes her eyes and starts to mumble under her breath. The crystal ball starts to get cloudy. Gabriela continues to mumble under her breath and after a couple more seconds, Miclou's face appears in the crystal ball.

Miclou speaks in his hollow voice, "Yes my Queen?"

Gabriela opens her eyes and questions, "How does it go?"

Miclou replies, "I've chased them into the forest, but they've escaped. I'm still trying to pick up their trail again."

Gabriela replies a little disappointed, "Very well. Keep me posted on how it goes."

Miclou bows his head, "Yes my Queen."

Gabriela closes her eyes again and starts to mumble under her breath. After a few seconds, Stecher's face appears in the crystal ball.

Stecher speaks in a haunting voice, "Yes my Queen?"

Gabriela opens her eyes and questions, "Miclou is still trying to find the group he is after, how are you doing?"

Stecher replies, "I caught up to them in River Fork, but they managed to escape. I'm still trying to pick up their trail."

Gabriela sighs, "Very well. Keep me posted."

Stecher bows his head, "Yes my Queen."

Gabriela closes her eyes again as Stecher's image vanishes from the crystal ball, "I can't believe they continue to get this lucky, but that will soon change."

Gabriela mumbles under her breath as the crystal ball gets cloudy again. After a few more seconds, the image of the moon and stars in the sky over the Kingdom appears in the crystal ball.

Gabriela opens her eyes and speaks in a voice that echoes through the room, the crystal ball and the Kingdom only heard by those she wants to hear the message, "To all my creatures, outlander children are in the Kingdom. I will give the best estate in the Kingdom to whoever brings me the children."

Gabriela removes her hand from the crystal ball and the image vanishes. Gabriela grabs her staff.

Gabriela speaks as she walks out of the room, "Lets see how long your luck continues now my dear children."

———

The cool morning breeze blows the fresh smell of trees and leaves through the Dark Valley. As the sun clears the morning horizon, Stefez, Anna, Michael, Jencent, Shaun and Bailee prepare to leave Prince Brian's camp. Numerous elves, dwarves and humans are also gathering their belongings and preparing to leave.

Stefez looks at the others, "We'll head north to Ghost Town."

At that time, Prince Brian, Jennifer and Rein walk up to Stefez and the others.

Prince Brian looks at Stefez, "I see you all are ready."

Stefez bows her head, "Yes my lord. The earlier start we can get, the better."

Jennifer speaks up, "All of you be safe on your journey." She looks over to Prince Brian, "I'll see the rest of the army is getting ready."

Prince Brian nods and Jennifer walks off.

Rein looks over to Michael, "Be safe. I await the day I'll see you again."

Michael smiles at Rein, "You be safe as well." He steps closer to Rein, "I too await that day."

Rein and Michael hug each other and Rein steps back.

Rein looks at Prince Brian, "I'll go help Jennifer get the army ready my lord."

Rein smiles at Stefez and the others, then walks off.

Prince Brian looks at Stefez again, "I'll pray you have a safe journey. If you need to let us know anything, send us a message bird." He pauses and gets a sadder look on his face, "And if you hear from the others, let me know how they're doing."

Stefez smiles, "I will my lord. Good luck and all of you be safe. Hopefully, we'll be seeing you again soon, in the castle."

Prince Brian nods his head, turns and walks off.

Stefez turns to the others, "Everyone have everything?"

Shaun nods, "I'm ready to go."

Michael replies, "I'm as ready as I'll ever be."

Jencent nods, "I'm ready."

Bailee speaks up, "I'm ready too."

Anna just lets out a slight smile, still bothered by being separated from Marsha and the others.

Stefez smiles, "Then, shall we go."

Stefez and the others start to walk north out of the Dark Valley and back into the forest.

The warm afternoon sun shines down on Jody and the others who are walking down a dirt road in the forest. The soft breeze blows the fresh smells of the forest all around the group.

Stephanie questions as they walk, "About how much further to Apple Grove?"

Jody thinks for a second, then replies, "We'll have to sleep in the forest tonight. We should reach it by late morning tomorrow."

Brendan speaks up, "We get to camp again, cool."

Marsha smiles about Brendan's reaction, then looks over at Jody, "So Jody, what did you do before you were a hero in a fairytale story?"

Jody looks over at Marsha, once again captured by her gaze, "Well, after my time in the Marine Corps, I was working as a security guard for an armored car company and teaching hand-to-hand combat in my spare time."

Marsha just gazes at Jody and smiles, unsure why she has fallen so quickly for him, "What did you do in the Marines?"

Jody's heart beats faster and he smiles knowing that he has fallen for Marsha, "I was an infantry rifleman."

Brendan looks up at Stephanie, "I miss Anna. I wish she was here."

Stephanie nods slightly, "I know. I miss her too."

Jody sees the expression change on Marsha's face to concern and sadness. Jody moves over next to Marsha as they all continue walking.

Jody places his hand on Marsha's shoulder, "Don't worry. I know Anna is okay. Stefez, Shaun and Michael won't let anything happen to her."

Marsha smiles at Jody, "Thanks." She pauses, "Its just that I was an only child for so long, then Anna can along. Then mom and dad passed away a few years back and I started taking care of her. She's all I've got left."

Jody reassures Marsha again, "Everything will work

out, you'll see."

Marsha smiles at Jody again as her heart beats a little faster looking into his eyes and feeling his hand upon her shoulder. At that time, the group approaches a fork in the road. One fork of the road continues west and the other fork turns to the south. The group stops for a second.

Stephanie questions, "So, which way do we take?"

Jody replies after taking a drink of water, "We keep heading west. The other road leads to South Town."

Everyone hears the sound of a bird loudly chirping. Jody lets his hand slide off Marsha's shoulder as he looks up into the sky. Marsha turns to look up into the sky and her hand brushes along Jody's hand. Jody glances back at Marsha and the two of them smile at each other. The bird that Stefez sent from the Dark Valley descends on Jody and the others.

Sherry points at the bird, "Look."

Stephanie sees the bird, "Its coming at us."

Brendan sounds a little worried as he squeezes Stephanie's hand, "Mom."

Jody holds up his right hand, "Its okay everyone. Its a message bird."

The bird gracefully lands on Jody's hand.

Jody looks at the bird, "What can I do for you?"

The bird replies, "I have a message from Stefez."

Marsha gets a little worried waiting to hear what the bird has to say.

The bird continues, "They are okay. They met with Prince Brian in the Dark Valley. They said to keep going and they will meet up with you in Mushroom Farm. Prince Brian is going to take his army and attack the castle from the southeast to get Gabriela's attention."

Stephanie smiles and her heart speeds up each time she hears Prince Brian's name. Marsha's face shows the look of relief about finding out that Anna is okay.

Jody speaks to the bird, "Thank you. Find Stefez and

let her know that we are okay and that we are almost to Apple Grove. Tell her we'll try to get to Mushroom Farm as fast as we can."

The bird replies, "Okay."

The bird flies off.

Jody looks over to Marsha, "Feel a little better."

Marsha smiles at Jody, "Yea, that helps."

Jody smiles and winks at Marsha. Jody takes a drink of water.

Sherry speaks up, "Well, that's good news."

Jody smiles, "Yes it is. Shall we continue."

Stephanie smiles, "Why not."

Jody and the others starting walking again taking the dirt road heading off to the west.

———

As the warm noon sun is high in the clear blue sky, Miclou is slowly walking his horse through the forest. He is looking over the ground closely to try and find traces of Stefez and the others. He continues to look around the ground and before Miclou realizes it, he finds himself standing on the northern hill of the now empty Dark Valley.

Miclou scans the area. He can tell that a large army was camping in the Dark Valley and by all the tracks in the ground, he can tell that the army has not been gone too long. He slowly looks over the hillside and before long, Miclou finds what he is looking for in the grass and soft dirt of the forest ground. He sees the smaller footprints of Anna next to the four different footprints of Stefez, Shaun, Jencent and Michael.

Miclou speaks to himself, "Heading north are we. No doubt to Ghost Town."

Miclou gets on his horse and starts riding north keeping an eye on the trail left by Stefez and the others.

As the noon sun bears down on the town of River Fork, Stecher has spent the last day looking around the town trying to find Jody and the others who disappeared on him the day before.

Stecher stops his horse next to a couple of shopkeepers who are visiting with each other by one of their fruit stands. The two shopkeepers shiver from the cold air as they stare up at the dark rider in complete fear.

Stecher speaks in a cold, evil voice, "I'm looking for some outlanders. Have you seen them?"

The two shopkeepers look at each other. The two men know that if they don't help the dark rider, Stecher might kill them.

Finally, the shopkeeper on the left speaks up, "I saw them heading out of town yesterday with a ranger."

Stecher smiles, "And which way would that be?"

The shopkeeper swallows hard, "They took the road heading to Apple Grove."

Stecher turns his horse, "Very good, you just saved your lives."

Stecher rides off on his horse.

Chapter 15

As the evening sun gets lower in the sky and the warm breeze gently blows through the forest, Stefez, Shaun, Jencent, Michael, Anna and Bailee continue on towards Ghost Town. The plush forest starts to get less and less dense as the trees are starting to get less abundant.

Anna speaks while walking, "Are we getting close yet?"

Stefez replies with a smile, "We're about to the edge of the forest. We should reach Ghost Town by early night."

Anna replies with a sigh, "Good. I'm getting a little tired."

Shaun takes a drink of water, "It has been a long day today."

Bailee suddenly stops, "Did you see that?"

Stefez quickly stops and looks over at Bailee, "What did you see?"

Michael, Shaun, Jencent and Anna stop walking and start looking around.

Bailee hops closer to Stefez, "I could swear I saw that tree move it's limbs on it's own."

Stefez, Shaun, Michael, Jencent and Anna look around at the tall trees around them. The trees are all about twenty feet tall each with at least seven limbs covered with leaves. Then, a tree not more than ten feet from the group moves one of it's limbs a couple of feet as if it was an arm.

Anna quickly speaks as her eyes widen, "I saw that!"

Stefez continues to glance around, "I think we should get out of here. The edge of the forest is less than a mile."

Bailee starts to hop away heading north, "Sounds good to me."

Michael looks over towards Bailee and quickly speaks, "Wait."

Before Bailee can stop, a small net made of vines just big enough to catch a rabbit or squirrel flies up from the ground catching Bailee in it's web. The net flies up and stops about six feet off the ground. Bailee frantically kicks her legs trying to get out of the trap.

Bailee speaks fearfully, "Someone get me out of this!"

Michael starts to walk towards Bailee, "Now who would set a trap here. The people of Ghost Town are not hunters."

Suddenly, two of the trees near Michael each swing a branch quickly pulling a vine across the ground towards Michael's feet.

Shaun quickly yells, "Look out!"

The vine hits Michael at the ankles and pulls his feet from under him. Michael falls forward and lands on the ground with a thud.

Stefez quickly moves next to Anna, "Anna, stay close to me."

Suddenly, as if appearing out of thin air, fifty pixies, six inch tall humans with wings wearing leather clothing and carrying little bows and arrows, fly out from behind the trees surrounding Stefez and the others. Jencent steps over next to Anna and Stefez trying keep herself between the pixies and Anna.

As the pixies get closer and start shooting arrows, Shaun draws her sword, "Pixies, lets get out of here."

Michael scrambles to his feet as a couple of the little arrows hit him in the arm. Being so small, Michael doesn't even notice the arrows. Shaun rushes over to

Bailee who is still stuck in the trap. As Shaun starts to swing her sword at the vine holding the trap in the air, a tree limb comes at her from behind. Michael pulls Shaun out of the way just in time for the limb to miss hitting her in the back of the head. As more tiny arrows fill the air, Stefez taps her staff on the ground and mumbles under her breath. The wind around them starts to pick up and the pixies start having trouble staying in the air.

Stefez grabs Anna's hand, "Lets go!"

Stefez, Anna and Jencent start running north. Shaun quickly cuts the trap down from the tree. When Bailee lands on the ground, the trap opens and Bailee takes off hopping north. Shaun puts her sword away. This time, two tree limbs come at Shaun and Michael. Shaun and Michael avoid the tree limbs and take off running after Stefez and the others.

Stefez and the others keep running as the living trees and the pixies disappear behind them. The group keeps running and before they know it, they run out of the forest into a new scene. They find themselves in open grasslands. The grass is plush and bright green. The warm evening breeze blows across the small rolling hills. Stefez and the others finally stop.

As Stefez catches her breath, "That was exciting."

Bailee replies sarcastically, "Exciting for you. I was the one in the trap."

Michael, Shaun, Jencent and Anna chuckle at the rabbit.

Stefez smiles, "True." She pauses, "Shall we continue. It's not much further now to Ghost Town."

The others just smile at Stefez and everyone starts walking north again.

The warm, evening sun is getting lower in the sky as

the shadows of the trees get longer across the ground. The warm breeze continues to blow the fresh smells all around Jody, Sherry, Stephanie, Marsha and Brendan who continue to walk along the dirt road heading towards Apple Grove. The sounds of the birds chirping completes the so real, but seemingly fairytale land like scene.

Marsha questions while they walk, "Is there any chance we will reach Apple Grove by tonight?"

Jody replies, "No, we'll have to stay the night in the forest."

Stephanie sighs, "Wonderful."

Jody smiles, "We'll be okay." He looks at Brendan, "Another night of camping, right big guy."

Brendan replies a little excited, "Yea."

Marsha, Stephanie and Sherry chuckle at Brendan's excitement. All of a sudden, Jody stops and glances around.

Marsha stops and looks puzzled, "What is it?"

Jody continues to glance around, "Listen."

Stephanie looks around, "I don't hear anything."

Jody nods, "Exactly. All the birds stopped chirping all of a sudden."

Sherry gets a sickened look on her face, "Do you smell that?"

The soft breeze that once carried the fresh smells of the forest, now carries a very pungent and sickening odor.

Stephanie covers her nose, "Oh my goodness."

Brendan holds his nose, "That stinks."

Marsha gets a sickened look, "What is that?"

At that time, Jody looks left as he hears movement in the forest just off the road.

Jody draws his sword, "Get ready"

Stephanie questions as the noise gets closer, "What?"

Jody replies, "Its trolls. Marsha, you, Stephanie and Sherry stay close to Brendan and get ready for a fight."

Marsha and Sherry move close together keeping

Brendan between them. The two outland ladies hold their staves ready in preparation of the chance they might have to fight something for the first time. Stephanie draws her sword and gets ready, hoping she will remember how to fight. The sound in the forest gets even closer.

Brendan catches movement in the forest, "I saw something."

Jody readies his sword, "I would say four." He pauses, "Here they come."

Then, four trolls emerge from the forest onto the road near Jody. The trolls are all around five and a half feet tall with grotesque deformities that distort their faces. Their skin is green and wrinkled. The troll's teeth are yellowed and look like the teeth of a warthog. Each troll has on ragged clothing and are barefooted and they each carry a three foot long, wooden club.

One troll speaks with a snarl, "Get the child for Gabriela."

One troll runs at Jody and the other three trolls run at Sherry, Marsha and Stephanie. The troll running at Jody swings it's club at Jody's head. Jody ducks under the club and throws his shoulder into the troll sending the troll crashing to the ground from being off-balance. Jody quickly takes the moment to move over towards Sherry, Marsha, Stephanie and Brendan.

As the three trolls get closer to Sherry, Marsha, Stephanie and Brendan, one of them stops when he sees Jody closing in. The troll turns to face Jody while the other two trolls close in on Sherry, Marsha and Stephanie who block the two troll's path to Brendan.

Stephanie steps a few feet away from Marsha and Sherry, hoping to draw one of the troll's away from Brendan. It works as one of the two trolls starts towards her and the other troll continue on towards Sherry and Marsha who block the path to Brendan.

The troll that Jody knocked down gets back to it's

feet and starts towards Jody from behind. The troll in front of Jody swings it's club down at Jody's head. Jody steps to his left as the club misses him. Jody cuts his sword into the back of the troll's legs. The sword knocks the troll's legs out from under it and the troll crashes to the ground on his back.

Marsha yells at Jody, "Jody, behind you!"

Jody turns around in time to see the other troll's club coming at his head from the right. Jody ducks under the club at the last second, slides to his left and kicks the troll in the stomach with his right leg. The troll doubles over in pain from the hard kick.

The troll swings it's club down at Marsha. Marsha raises the staff up and manages to stop the club from hitting her in the head. Sherry jabs her staff at the troll and the end of the staff strikes the troll in the side of the head. The troll turns and swings it's club at Sherry. Sherry holds out her staff and manages to block the troll's club, but the force of the blow makes her take a step back.

The troll swings it's club at Stephanie. Everything seems to come back to Stephanie as she raises her sword and blocks the club. Stephanie pulls her sword back and swings at the troll's head. The troll brings it's club up and stops the sword. The troll moves closer trying to push Stephanie back. Stephanie takes a step back with her right foot, then sends her right foot forward delivering a solid kick to the groin area of the troll. The troll's eyes get as round as two small dinner plates. The troll falls to it's knees. Stephanie steps in and delivers a blow to the troll in the side of the head with the flat side of her sword. The troll drops it's club and falls to the ground.

The troll that had his legs cut by Jody remains on the ground as the other troll moves in and swings it's club at Jody's head. Jody stops the club with his sword. Jody spins left and brings his sword around at the troll's head. The troll ducks under the sword and brings it's club across at Jody's shins. Jody jumps up in the air as the club goes under his feet. As Jody comes back down, he slams the handle of his sword into the top of the trolls head. The troll drops to his knees and drops it's club. As Jody steps back, the troll falls face first to the ground. Jody turns to Sherry and Marsha.

The troll swings it's club down at Marsha's head. Marsha raises her staff again and barely manages to block the dangerous blow. Sherry just takes a fairly wild swing at the troll and her staff connects to the troll's groin area. The troll's eyes widen in shock. The troll drops it's club and falls to it's knees. Marsha takes the opening and swings her staff as hard as she can. The staff slams into the side of the troll's head sending the troll the rest of the way to the ground. Marsha and Sherry both take some deep breaths trying to collect themselves.

Jody steps up to the three women with a big smile on his face, "Nice work. I like it."

Stephanie lets out a little chuckle, "It was the first thing that came to mind. Kick him where it counts."

Sherry smiles and chuckles, "I was just swinging."

Marsha chuckles also, "Me too."

Brendan hops around and throws a couple of little punches in the air, "Yea, we showed them."

Stephanie and the others laugh at Brendan.

Jody finally stops laughing, "We should get going. It's going to be dark soon."

Jody and Stephanie put their swords away. The group takes one last look at the trolls, then starts walking westward down the dirt road.

Chapter 16

As the sun drops behind the evening horizon giving way to the moon and stars which shine brightly in the clear night sky, Prince Brian and his army start to setup camp for the night. Prince Brian dismounts from his horse and ties it to a tree. Jennifer, Rein and Ramaf also dismount and tie their horses to a tree.

Prince Brian walks a few feet from his horse and closes his eyes. He lets the soft breeze blow across his face and his mind wanders to Stephanie, the outlander he has taken such a liking to. Jennifer, Rein and Ramaf walk up to Prince Brian.

Jennifer speaks to Prince Brian, "Everything okay my lord?"

Prince Brian opens his eyes and looks over at Jennifer, "Yes. I was just thinking."

Jennifer smiles knowing who he was thinking about, "I'm sure they're fine my lord."

Prince Brian smiles and nods, "Yes, I'm sure they are." He pauses, "How goes the camp?"

Ramaf speaks first, "My people are just about to bed down."

Rein nods in agreement, "So are the elves my lord."

Prince Brian nods, "Good. Make sure we have plenty of guards for the night. Also, I want to make sure we get started just after dawn. We still have a long way to Birdview."

Jennifer nods, "Yes my lord." She pauses, "And how should we handle Birdview?"

Prince Brian replies, "I was thinking that most likely Gabriela will only have a small scout group in Birdview."

Rein speaks up, "So if we attack with a small group, then we might be able to take Birdview without the rest of her army knowing."

Prince Brian nods, "That's what I was thinking."

Ramaf speaks up, "That way also, we don't have to show the true number of our army in the first battle."

Jennifer replies, "Keeping our numbers a secret for as long as we can, I like it."

Prince Brian sighs, "Then we'll go with that plan unless something comes up tomorrow and we have to change the plan." He pauses, "Each of you pick out five of your best to join us in the attack on Birdview. That should cover it."

Jennifer bows her head, "Yes my lord."

Rein bows her head, "It will be done my lord."

Ramaf also bows his head, "I'll have them ready my lord."

Prince Brian smiles, "Very well then. Lets get some rest."

Jennifer, Rein and Ramaf all bow their heads once again and walk off. Prince Brian turns back around and closes his eyes as he pictures Stephanie's face once again.

———————

As the cool night breeze blows across the open grasslands, Stefez and the others see the soft glow of torches in the distance and the outline of a fairly large town. Ghost Town is a little smaller than River Fork, but it is laid out nearly the same. The town is surrounded by huts and homes made of mud and wood. The buildings in the town are made of stone. Most of the buildings are one story, but some of the buildings are two stories tall and a couple are even three stories tall. However, the town is much older and more worn down than River Fork.

As the group walks past some of the huts just outside of the town, Stefez speaks, "Its fairly late. We should find a place to rest for the night."

Anna speaks up, "Sounds good to me, I'm tired."

Michael chimes in as the group passes the last hut and starts into town and the dirt road becomes a stone road, "Sleep will be good, but we need to get an early start. I'm sure the dark rider has picked up our trail again."

Shaun speaks up, "And I don't feel like facing him again."

The group passes by the first couple of stone buildings. A few townspeople are walking the streets which are lit up by torches along the roads. The people of Ghost Town pay little mind to the group and especially the outland child.

Stefez motions to a building just up the road, "Lets try that tavern."

Stefez and the others continue along the road, keeping their eyes open just in case another surprise comes along. They reach the wooden front door of the tavern. Stefez opens the door and everyone walks inside. The room has twenty tables with chairs and a bar along the left side of the room. In the back of the room is a large caldron, but there is no fire beneath it. In the back, right of the room is the stairs that lead up to the second story.

Michael looks around, "This will work just fine."

Then, a man's voice calls out from the top of the stairs, "Can I help you?"

Stefez and the others see a middle aged man walk down the stairs dressed in fairly nice clothes. Stefez starts to walk towards the man. Michael, Shaun, Jencent, Anna and Bailee stay by the front door.

Stefez bows her head, "Yes. We are in need of a place to stay for the night."

The man looks at Michael and the others, then back at Stefez.

The man speaks, "You're that magical elf that helps Prince Brian?"

Stefez glances around and replies softly, "Yes."

The man stares at Stefez for a minute, then smiles, "I thought so. I have a room you and your friends can use for the night, no charge."

Stefez replies thankfully, "Thank you so much."

The man nods, "It's the last door on the left."

Stefez nods to the man and the man walks off towards the bar. Stefez motions for the others to join her. Stefez walks up the stairs followed by the others.

———

As the moon shines bright in the clear night sky and the cool night breeze gently makes it's way along the dirt road, Jody, Stephanie, Sherry, Marsha and Brendan continue walking west towards Apple Grove.

Brendan speaks with a tired look, "Mom, I'm tired."

Stephanie sighs, "Me too little man."

Sherry looks at Jody, "Should we go ahead and stop for the night?"

Jody stops walking and looks around, "This is as good a place as any." He pauses, "Lets just move into the forest so no one can see us."

Marsha stops and speaks up, "Sounds good to me."

Jody walks off the road to his left and the others follow right behind him. The five of them walk about a hundred feet into the forest until they find an opening big enough for the five of them to sleep. The bright moon casts enough light in the forest that Jody and the others can still see fairly well.

Jody stops in the small clearing, "This should work."

Stephanie stops in the clearing, "Anything will work

right now."

Brendan, Sherry and Marsha stop next to Stephanie.

Jody looks around as if thinking, then speaks, "I don't think we need to have someone up, we should be safe enough for the few hours."

Stephanie nods in agreement, "That sounds okay with me."

Stephanie lays down near the left edge of the clearing. Brendan lays down and curls up against Stephanie. Sherry lays down on the right edge of the clearing. Jody is standing about ten feet from Stephanie and Brendan and about twenty feet from Sherry. Jody removes his gear and weapons and places them on the ground. Marsha walks over to Jody. Jody looks at Marsha and smiles as he gazes into her eyes.

Marsha gazes at Jody and whispers to him, "Can I lay down with you?" She pauses, "Its just, well, …"

Jody gives Marsha a warm smile and whispers back, "I understand and of course you can. I would really like that."

Marsha warmly smiles and winks at Jody, "Thanks."

Jody lays down on his left side. Marsha lays down on her left side and snuggles up against Jody. Jody puts his right arm around Marsha.

Marsha takes hold of Jody's right hand and whispers, "I could get use to this."

Jody smiles and whispers back, "So could I."

In no time, Sherry, Stephanie, Brendan, Jody and Marsha drift off to sleep.

———

In the dark of the night, Gabriela walks into her magical chamber where the candles burning on the table cast a soft glow over the room. Gabriela walks over and leans her staff against the table.

Gabriela speaks to herself as she holds her right hand over the crystal ball, "I can't believe the children haven't been captured yet."

Gabriela closes her eyes and mumbles under her breath. After nearly a minute, the crystal ball becomes cloudy. In a few more seconds, the face of Stecher appears in the crystal ball.

Gabriela opens her eyes and questions, "How does it go?"

Stecher replies in a cold tone, "I caught up to them in River Fork, but they slipped away heading towards Apple Grove. I'm on their trail right now."

Gabriela replies a little disgusted, "Very well. Keep after them. Their luck will eventually run out."

Stecher bows his head, "Yes my Queen."

Gabriela closes her eyes and mumbles again. In a few seconds, the image in the crystal ball changes to the face of Miclou.

Gabriela opens her eyes and questions, "How is it going?"

Miclou replies in his hauntingly hollow tone, "I picked up their trail again in the forest near Dark Valley. It looks like their headed to Ghost Town. I'm still on their trail."

Gabriela sighs, "Very well."

Miclou speaks again, "One more thing my Queen."

Gabriela questions, "What is it?"

Miclou replies, "A large army, no doubt Prince Brian, was camped in the Dark Valley. It appears that they are moving west towards Farhollow and Birdview."

Gabriela's eyes narrow, "So, with the children in the Kingdom, Prince Brian is making his move." She pauses, "Good work, keep after the children."

Miclou bows his head, "Yes my Queen."

Gabriela removes her hand from the crystal ball and Miclou's image disappears.

Gabriela grabs her staff, "Making your move are you Prince Brian." She turns and starts towards the door, "This Kingdom is mine."

Chapter 17

As the morning sun breaks across the horizon lighting up the once dark Ghost Town, Stefez, Shaun, Michael, Jencent, Anna and Bailee exit the front door of the tavern where they stayed the all to short night. The cool morning breeze blows around them and the smell of food lingers in the air.

Stefez breathes in the crisp morning air, "Looks like its going to be a nice day."

Michael smiles, "Especially if we can avoid any trouble."

Bailee chimes in, "Any day without trouble is a good day."

Anna stands next to Stefez, "What are we going to do now?"

At that time, the bird that Stefez sent to Jody and the others, and that Jody sent back, chirps loud getting Stefez's attention.

Stefez looks up and sees the bird, "Looks like we got a response."

Stefez holds up her hand and the bird gently lands on it.

Stefez questions the bird, "So, what do you have for us?"

The bird replies in it's high pitched chirping voice, "Jody and the others are doing okay. They are almost to Apple Grove and said they would try and meet up with you in Mushroom Farm."

Anna sighs in relief, "I'm so happy Marsha and the

others are okay."

Michael chimes in, "Looks like all we need to do is get some supplies and get started."

Jencent speaks up, "I can see a supply shop just up the road."

The bird speaks again, "You should not take the road to North Town."

Stefez questions, "Why not?"

The bird replies, "Gabriela has a small lookout group waiting by the road about halfway. I saw them as I was flying back to find you."

Shaun speaks up, "That makes things a little more difficult."

Stefez nods to the bird, "Thank you. I'll call if I need you again."

The bird flies off and Anna questions, "So what do we do?"

Stefez speaks up, "Well, we gather some supplies like Michael mentioned." She pauses, "Then, as I see it, we have to head north towards Ice Town on the other side of the mountains. That's the only way we can avoid being seen."

Shaun speaks up, "That's a long trip."

Michael nods, "Not to mention, dangerous and cold."

Bailee speaks up, "Wonderful."

Stefez smiles, "We really don't have much choice." She pauses, "First lets get the supplies."

Stefez and the others start walking up the road towards the supply shop Jencent pointed out earlier.

———

As the sun shines bright in the clear blue, mid-morning sky, Miclou slows his horse down to a slow trot as he passes by the huts just outside of Ghost Town. The townspeople stop working in their gardens and shiver from the cold air when they see the dark rider slowly passing by their huts. Miclou continues on until the huts give way to the stone buildings of Ghost Town and the dirt road turns into a stone road. The sound of the horse's hooves echo through the streets which are getting busier with townspeople going about their day.

As Miclou slows his horse down to a walk, the different townspeople stop what they are doing and watch as the dark rider passes by them. Miclou sees the first tavern along the road and starts towards it. The same man who helped Stefez and the others is sweeping around the outside of the front door. The man shivers as Miclou approaches. The man stops sweeping when he hears Miclou's horse stop behind him. The man turns around and his eyes widen in fear when he sees the dark rider.

Miclou speaks in his hollow voice, "I'm only going to ask once. Have you seen a small group of travelers which included an outlander child?"

The man swallows to clear his throat, then replies fearfully, "Yes, they stayed here last night and left a couple hours ago."

Miclou questions, "Do you know if they are still in town?"

The man shivers from the cold, "I'm not sure. Maybe, they didn't have many supplies so they might be getting some."

Miclou grabs the reigns of his horse, turns and slowly starts down the road towards the middle of town.

———————

The warm mid-morning breeze blows along the dirt road in the forest and the soft white clouds slowly move across the blue sky. Jody and the others continue to walk west along the dirt road. The normal forest trees start to give way to small, more beautiful apple trees as the smell of fresh apples fills the warm morning air. Jody and Brendan are about twenty feet in front of Sherry, Marsha and Stephanie.

As they walk, Stephanie speaks softly to Marsha, "So, when I woke up this morning I saw you were sleeping comfortably."

Marsha breaks a smile at the thoughts of sleeping in Jody's arms, "It was quite wonderful. I don't know why I've been so quickly attracted to Jody. Its just, I feel this connection to him." She pauses, "I hope you don't mind."

Stephanie smiles, "Of course I don't mind. It would be really cool if the two of you ended up together." She looks at Sherry, "What do you think?"

Sherry chuckles, "Jody is awesome. I think it would be really cool too. He seems like a great man and deserves someone good."

Stephanie, Sherry and Marsha chuckle which catches Jody's attention.

Jody looks back at the girls, "What are you ladies laughing about?"

Stephanie smiles, "Nothing, just girl talk."

Marsha smiles and winks at Jody causing Jody to smile back at Marsha.

Jody shakes his head, "Oh boy. Just no embarrassing stories."

Sherry smiles, "Oh yes, we need to hear some of those."

Jody shakes his head and looks down at Brendan, "Lets collect some apples. Oh, and some advice, stay single little man."

Brendan bounces towards to side of the road, "Yea, girls are yucky."

Sherry, Stephanie and Marsha laugh at Brendan as Jody follows Brendan over to the side of the road which has opened up to a village. The village is about twice the size of Havel. The huts are all made of grass and wood.

Apple trees surround the village and grow throughout the village as well. Numerous villagers, dressed like the villagers from Havel and Farhollow, go about their daily farming and gardening. Many teenage kids are carrying baskets and collecting up as many apples as they can carry.

Stephanie stops next to Brendan, "Wow, look at this place."

Jody steps next to Stephanie, "Apple Grove. You can see why it got that name."

Marsha stops next to Jody, "It smells fantastic."

Jody holds out an apple to Marsha, "Here you go beautiful."

Marsha stares into Jody's eyes, "Thanks honey."

Marsha runs her hand over Jody's hand as she takes the apple from him. Jody smiles at Marsha.

Jody finally turns to the others, "We can get some more fruits and vegetables from one of the food stands and get some water from their well." He pauses, "We don't want to take too long though. No doubt the dark rider is still chasing us."

Stephanie speaks up, "I can't wait until we're rid of him."

Marsha chimes in, "Me too."

Sherry nods in agreement, "Yea, he's a real pain in the butt."

Brendan jumps around and swings his arms, "I'll take care of him."

Sherry, Marsha and Stephanie chuckle at Brendan.

Jody smiles and pats Brendan on the head, "I bet you would big man." Jody motions to the others, "Lets go."

Jody starts walking into the village closely followed by Stephanie, Brendan, Marsha and Sherry.

As the sun peaks in the warm, noon sky, Prince Brian and his army continues to make their way through the forest towards Birdview. As Prince Brian slowly rides on his horse, he closes his eyes and breathes in the fresh, warm air. He pictures Stephanie's face and hopes that she is okay. He wishes he could have stayed with her, but knows that he is doing what he has to do.

Jennifer rides up next to Prince Brian, "My lord, is everything okay?"

Prince Brian opens his eyes and looks at Jennifer, "Yes. I was just thinking about Stephanie."

Jennifer smiles, "You really like her, don't you my lord?"

Prince Brian smiles, "Yes I do. I don't know why, but I just connected with her from when I first saw her."

Rein rides up next to Prince Brian and replies having heard what he said, "That's how it works when you meet the right person." She pauses and thinks of Michael, "That's how it was when Michael and I met."

Prince Brian sighs, "I just hope nothing happens to her, or the others for that matter. I just feel like we abandoned them."

Jennifer shakes her head, "They're going to be okay. We made the best plan we could. We couldn't have foreseen that they would have gotten split up because of the dark riders."

Rein nods, "We are doing what we must to ensure their safety. The more we can make Gabriela focus on us, the less she can focus on finding them." She pauses, "With her army concentrating on us, she has to rely on the dark riders and random creatures to help her find the children. That gives them a better chance of making it."

Prince Brian nods, "I know, but I still can't help but worry about them." He pauses, "Especially Stephanie and Brendan."

Jennifer smiles, "That's because you care about

them."

Prince Brian nods and decides to get back to business, "So Jennifer, how long until we reach Birdview?"

Jennifer replies, "We should reach Birdview by early evening."

Prince Brian questions again, "And do we have the ones selected to help us take Birdview?"

Rein nods, "I have my five picked out and ready my lord."

Jennifer nods, "I have five picked out too. I know Ramaf has his five ready as well my lord."

Prince Brian sighs and smiles, "Good. Go ahead and check on everyone and let me know if there are any problems."

Jennifer and Rein bow their heads, turn their horses and ride off. Prince Brian closes his eyes again and pictures the face of the woman he has taken such a liking to, he pictures Stephanie and smiles.

Chapter 18

A s the sun is peaked in the warm noon sky, Stefez and the others are walking north along one of the streets in Ghost Town. They can hear festive music in the distance as they get closer to the center of town.

Anna speaks up, "I can't believe how much this place is like a movie."

Shaun looks at Anna, "A what?"

Anna smiles, "Oh yea, I forgot. You all don't know what that is, sorry."

Stefez chuckles slightly, "We have our food and water, but since we have to head north, we should get Anna, Michael and Jencent a cloak so they can stay warm when we reach the snow lands on the other side of the mountains."

Shaun nods, "Good idea. Plus, a cloak will help conceal that Anna is an outlander."

Bailee speaks up, "If it helps us avoid trouble, I'm all for it." She pauses, "Sorry Anna."

Anna smiles at Bailee, "Its okay. I won't mind avoiding trouble either."

At that time, the group passes a three story, stone building and the town opens up into a large, crowded square. It is six square blocks and has numerous open sided tents with various merchants selling their goods. The merchant tents are made of a heavy canvas and are fairly large being held up with a main, wooden pole in the center of the tent and smaller wooden poles holding up the corners. The people of Ghost Town are walking amongst the tents shopping for whatever they need. In the center of the square is a wooden stage where a medieval band is playing festive music.

Anna just stares at everything, "Wow, this place is amazing."

Stefez smiles, "Lets find a place to get you all a cloak. Then we'll get on the road north."

Michael glances around, "I think I see a tent that might have what we need."

The group starts to make it's way through the crowd towards a clothing tent. A few of the townspeople take notice of Anna, but everyone continues to go about their business. Stefez and the others walk up to the tent where numerous cloaks are hanging. Michael looks at a couple of cloaks, then picks out a dark blue cloak and tries it on. Jencent picks out a black cloak and tries it on. Anna looks at a few cloaks as Stefez talks to the male shopkeeper. Anna finally finds a light gray cloak in her size and puts it on. Stefez walks back up to the others.

Stefez questions, "Did everyone find what they needed?"

Anna nods, "Yea, but how are we able to afford all this?"

Stefez smiles, "Its taken care of. It helps to know people."

At that time, the group hears the thunderous sound of a horse in the distance and the air starts to get colder. They all look at each other knowing that the dark rider has found them. A few screams in the background confirm what they each were thinking.

Shaun glances around, "The dark rider has found us."

Michael looks around, "Do you see him?"

The sound of the horse stops as the townspeople start running all around. The air continues to get colder.

Jencent shakes her head, "I don't see him."

Then, they all hear the hollow voice of Miclou

through the crowd, "Give me the child and I'll let you live!"

Stefez and the others look in the direction of the voice and see Miclou standing by the tent just fifty feet from where they are at. Miclou has his sword in his right hand.

Anna softly questions, "What now?"

Michael, Shaun and Jencent all draw their swords. Stefez takes Anna's hand and glances around quickly trying to come up with a plan of escape. Any normal person would be timid in facing three armed opponents, but Miclou gives a slight smile and takes a few steps towards Stefez and the others.

Miclou speaks again, "You're making this difficult."

Michael grips his sword tight, "He doesn't seem too afraid of us."

Jencent replies while taking a step back, "Because he knows how good he is."

Michael, Shaun and Jencent each take a couple steps back which brings them closer to the center of the tent as Miclou takes a few more steps closer.

Miclou speaks again, "Last chance to save your lives."

Stefez whispers to the others, "Lets see if we can trap him under the tent so we can escape."

Shaun sighs and whispers back, "Ok."

Suddenly, Miclou charges at Stefez and the others. Jencent immediately moves to Miclou's right and Shaun moves to Miclou's left. Michael stands his ground as Miclou comes straight at him. Stefez pulls Anna behind her and Bailee hops around behind Stefez. Jencent and Shaun both swing their swords at Miclou as he gets close. A second later, Michael thrusts his sword in Miclou's direction. With uncanny reflexes, Miclou leans just enough to his left and Jencent's sword narrowly misses. At almost the exact moment, Miclou also ducks down and

Shaun's sword just goes over the top of his head. Seeing Michael's sword coming straight at him, Miclou brings his sword across and knocks Michael's sword aside.

Without missing a step, Miclou hops into the air and brings his right knee up. Miclou's right knee slams into Michael's body sending him tumbling backwards over a table. Miclou lands on his feet and turns back to Jencent and Shaun. Miclou quickly draws his dagger with his left hand. Now on his right, Shaun quickly comes in at Miclou with her sword. Miclou spins right and brings his dagger across his body. Miclou stops Shaun's sword with his dagger and continues to spin. Jencent sees Miclou's sword now coming right at her head.

Jencent brings her sword up at the last second, barely stopping the deadly blow from the dark rider. As if having eyes in the back of his head, Miclou ducks down as Shaun's sword misses his head and slams into Jencent's sword. Miclou quickly spins and uses his right leg to sweep Shaun's feet out from under her. Shaun crashes to the ground. Moving fast, Jencent swings her sword down at Miclou who is still in a low squat. Miclou dives forward and Jencent's sword narrowly misses.

Stefez yells, "Now Michael!"

Michael throws his body weight into the wooden pole holding up the middle of the tent. The pole dislodges and the middle of the tent starts to collapse. Bailee takes off hopping like a flash. Shaun does a back roll and returns to her feet as Jencent runs by her. Stefez and Anna take off running in the same direction Bailee is hopping. Shaun turns and starts running. As Miclou rolls to his feet, Michael falls in behind Shaun who is right behind Jencent and only a few feet behind Stefez, Anna and Bailee. Miclou turns to see Stefez and the others running away. Miclou starts to run as the center of the tent lands on his head. As Michael, the last one, runs out from under the tent, he cuts down the corner pole holding the tent up.

The heavy canvas tent collapses on the dark rider, trapping Miclou underneath it. Bailee, Stefez, Anna, Jencent, Shaun and Michael don't even slow down as they run north out of the town square through all the commotion of the townspeople also running to get as far away from the dark rider as they can.

A minute or two later, Miclou finally cuts his way out from under the tent. Miclou looks around and all he can see are the townspeople running every different direction, but no sign of Stefez and the others. As Miclou slowly walks back to where he tied up his horse, Stefez and the others head north out of Ghost Town.

Stefez and the others look north as they slow down to a walk and see the mountains in the distance. The mountains look enormous with their peaks reaching up into the sky beyond the clouds. The group can see what appears to be snowcaps as the peaks of the mountains disappear into the clouds.

Bailee speaks up, "That was close."

Stefez catches her breath, "Yes it was."

Jencent speaks up, "We got lucky again, but our luck won't last forever."

Shaun chuckles slightly, "I don't even want to think about having to face him without a chance of escape." She pauses, "He's really good."

Michael nods in agreement, "One of the best ever, but I think if we fight together we just might be able to beat him. All of us are really good too."

Stefez smiles, "Lets just hope we don't have to find out."

Bailee chimes in, "Amen to that."

Anna looks a little gloomy, "What about the others though?"

Michael questions, "What do you mean Anna?"

Anna replies, "There were two dark riders, but only one is after us. The other one must be after them." She pauses, "How could they possible fight him off with only Jody knowing how to fight?"

Shaun smiles, "Jody is an extremely good fighter with and without weapons. Plus, he will be showing the others some things on how to fight."

Jencent speaks up, "Anna is right. Its really just Jody against a dark rider. He might be real good, but lets be realistic, can he hold his own one on one?"

Michael nods, "Yea, that's not too promising."

Shaun speaks with confidence, "I think he'll do fine."

Stefez nods, "I think he will cause it's his sister and nephew at stake. I don't think he'll let them down and he'll find a way to keep them safe."

Anna sighs, "I hope so."

Stefez places her hand on Anna's shoulder, "It will be fine, you'll see."

The talking dies down as the group continues walking towards the mountains in the distance.

The warm sun has just passed the high noon sky as the smell of fresh apples fills the air. Jody and the others are walking through the village of Apple Grove. The villagers take notice of the outlanders, especially Brendan, knowing that the dark riders will surely follow. None of the villagers say anything out of respect for the ranger who has helped them in the past.

Jody places the last apple in Stephanie's food pouch, "Well, that does it for food and water."

Stephanie questions, "So, what now?"

Sherry chimes in, "How do we get to Mushroom Farm?"

Jody glances around, "We take the road north." He pauses, "Less than a mile we'll reach the river. If there is a ferry there, it will be faster to take it than walk."

Marsha speaks up, "I hope so. I'm getting tired of walking."

Jody looks over and smiles at Marsha, "It does take some getting use to." He breaks his stare, "Shall we go."

Jody and the others start walking north on the road out of Apple Grove. As the group passes by the last hut and start back into the forest, the familiar sound of a thunderous horse echoes out. Everyone stops for a second and looks at each other as the air starts to get colder.

Stephanie's eyes widen, "Oh no!"

Sherry glances around, "It's him!"

Jody draws his sword, "Quick, to the river!"

Marsha and Sherry start running as fast as they can along the road. Stephanie takes Brendan's hand and the two of them run as fast as they can behind Marsha and Sherry. Jody glances back towards the village and sees the blurry image of Stecher riding towards them. Jody turns and runs north.

The sound of the horse gets louder as Marsha and Sherry see a stone bridge ahead of them. The stone bridge is twenty five feet wide with a two foot ledge on each side of it to keep anything from sliding off into the river and raises into a ten foot arch over the river that runs east and west under it.

Jody yells while running, "The pier is on the right! See if there is a ferry!"

Marsha and Sherry run towards the right of the bridge as Brendan trips and falls on the road losing his grip on Stephanie's hand. Stephanie stops and turns back to Brendan. Stephanie sees Jody running at her and a few hundred feet behind him is the dark rider.

Jody yells, "I've got him! Get to the river!"

Stephanie turns and starts running again. Marsha and Sherry reach the pier and see a ferry, the same size as the one they were on before, tied to the end of the pier. The two women glance around and do not see anyone around the ferry.

Marsha quickly speaks, "Lets get on the ferry and get ready to untie it."

Marsha and Sherry run down the pier to the ferry. Jody picks up Brendan and the two of them start running as Stephanie reaches the pier. Stephanie stops at the pier and looks back. She sees Jody and Brendan getting closer, but she sees the dark rider nearly on top of them.

Stephanie yells as Stecher draws his sword, "Look out behind you!"

Jody stops, ducks and pulls Brendan close. Stecher's sword narrowly misses Jody's head. Stecher slides to his left, drops from his horse and lands on his feet. Jody looks at the dark rider who is now between him and the pier.

Jody yells to Stephanie, "Get on the ferry if its there!"

Stephanie turns and runs towards Marsha and Sherry who are waiting on the ferry. Stecher pays no attention to the women as what he is looking for is now only being blocked by Jody.

Jody whispers to Brendan, "Do your best to stay a few feet behind me, okay big guy."

Brendan replies, "Okay Uncle Jody."

Stecher starts to slowly walk towards Jody and Brendan, "Just give me the child and I'll let you live."

Jody swallows and shakes his head, "I don't think so."

Stecher lets out a hollow sigh, "Have it your way then."

Stecher quickly lunges towards Jody. Jody steps to his right and brings his sword across in front of him and knocks Stecher's sword away. Jody brings his sword back across as fast as he can at Stecher. Stecher moves with incredible speed and blocks Jody's sword.

Jody speaks while holding his sword in place, "Brendan, run for the bridge."

Brendan starts to run. Stecher steps back and moves fast towards the bridge. Jody rushes after Stecher and Brendan. As Brendan reaches the right edge of the bridge, Stecher jumps in front of him, cutting Brendan off from the pier. Stecher reaches out to grab Brendan as Jody runs up and thrusts his sword at Stecher. Stecher hops back out of the way, spins in a circle and brings his sword around at Jody. Jody grabs Brendan and pulls him back as he brings his sword up and blocks Stecher's sword.

Jody sees the women on the ferry and yells, "Untie the ferry!" He lets go of Brendan, "Get up to the middle of the bridge big man."

Brendan starts onto the bridge as Marsha, Sherry and Stephanie work on untying the ropes. Stecher steps in and brings his sword at Jody from the left. Jody moves as fast as he can and barely blocks the deadly sword. Jody shuffles back and disengages his sword. Staying on the attack, Stecher moves forward and cuts his sword in at Jody's head. Jody again moves fast and barely blocks the sword. Jody again shuffles back which continues to move him towards where Brendan is waiting at the middle of the bridge ten feet over the river.

Marsha, Sherry and Stephanie get the last rope undone and the current of the river starts to move the ferry towards the bridge. Stephanie gets a scared look knowing that Brendan is still up on the bridge.

Stephanie yells to Jody, "We're moving!"

Jody glances over and sees the ferry starting to pick up speed in the river as it heads for the bridge. Stecher moves in and cuts in at Jody's head again. Jody moves quick and blocks the sword. Stecher quickly steps in and throws a kick with his right leg. The foot slams into Jody's stomach knocking him backwards. Stecher steps in and swings down at Jody who is bent over at the waist. Jody quickly steps to his left as the sword narrowly misses. Jody throws his body into Stecher, knocking

Stecher away a few feet.

Jody yells to Brendan as the ferry starts under the bridge, "Get on the ledge big man!"

Jody steps up and swings his sword at Stecher. Stecher moves fast and blocks the would be deadly blow. Stecher quickly withdraws his sword and thrusts it in at Jody. Jody quickly knocks the sword up and returns the favor by kicking Stecher in the stomach. As Stecher stumbles back a few feet, Jody turns and runs over to the edge of the bridge where Brendan is standing. Jody hops up on the ledge next to Brendan as the ferry starts out from under the bridge, just now under where Jody and Brendan are standing. Stecher regains his balance and starts towards Jody and Brendan.

Jody speaks, "Brendan, jump."

Brendan jumps off the side of the bridge as Jody puts his sword away. Brendan lands safely in the middle of the ferry. Stecher closes in on Jody quickly. As Jody jumps from the side of the bridge, Stecher swings his sword at Jody's back. The sword narrowly misses as Jody lands safely on the very back of the ferry next to the steering rudder. Stecher looks over the edge of the bridge as the river's current moves the ferry away. Stecher puts his sword away knowing that the ferry is too far for him to reach. The ferry picks up speed as Stecher turns and walks back towards his horse.

On the ferry, Jody lays on his back and looks up at the blue sky, "That was close."

Marsha speaks up, "That was incredible."

Sherry nods, "Amazing."

Stephanie shakes her head, "I would say, scary."

Brendan smiles and speaks up as Jody sits up, "That was fun."

Jody smiles at his nephew and grabs the steering rudder, "It was kind of fun wasn't it."

Stephanie sighs and smiles, "Your crazy bro."

Sherry speaks up, "You held your own against him."

Jody shakes his head, "I got lucky. He underestimated me since I was alone. He won't do that again." He sighs, "Lets hope we don't have to find out with a next time."

Marsha gazes at Jody, "So, what do we do now? I'm sure he'll start after us again."

Jody gazes back at Marsha, "I'm sure he will, but the river will keep us ahead of him since he'll have to make his way through the dense forest."

Stephanie questions, "So, we just keep floating?"

Jody breaks his gaze and nods, "We'll stay on the river until it gets dark. Then, we'll stop and camp on the bank of the river for the night." He pauses and smiles, "For now, we relax."

The ferry continues along the clear blue river as Jody and the others breath a sigh of relief as they know the dark rider is getting further behind them.

Chapter 19

A s the sun gets lower towards the evening horizon, Prince Brian and Jennifer stop their horses on the road just a mile from the village of Birdview and about two hundred yards ahead of the rest of the army.

Prince Brian looks over at Jennifer, "Go tell the others to set up camp in the forest. Have them also start making as many boats and rafts as they can for when we need to cross Glass Lake." He pauses, "Have Rein and Ramaf get their five soldiers, get our five soldiers and meet me back here."

Jennifer bows her head, "Yes my lord."

Jennifer turns and rides back towards the main army behind them. Prince Brian dismounts from his horse and walks his horse just off the road to the north and into the forest about a hundred feet. He ties his horse to a tree and waits for Jennifer and the others. As Prince Brian waits, he closes his eyes, lets the soft breeze blow across his face and pictures Stephanie's face in his mind. As he thinks about her beautiful eyes and perfect smile, he smiles to himself.

Prince Brian is unsure how much time has passed when Jennifer, Rein, Ramaf and their soldiers walk up to where he is waiting. The five dwarves that Ramaf have with him are all dressed in brown, dark brown or black clothes and boots. Each dwarf has a dark metallic chest plate of armor and a dark metallic, open faced helmet. Three of the dwarves are carrying battle axes and the other two dwarves are carrying short swords. The five elves that Rein brought with her are all dressed in green, dark green and brown clothes and boots. Each elf has a shiny silver chest plate of armor, a medium length sword and a bow with quiver of ten arrows. The five humans that Jennifer brought are each dressed in royal blue clothes and tunic with brown boots. Each human is wearing a medium length sword and carrying a medium length shield.

Prince Brian turns to Jennifer and the others, "Is the camp getting ready?"

Jennifer nods, "Yes my lord."

Prince Brian nods, "Our scout told us earlier of twenty trolls in the village." He looks at Ramaf, "You and your men ready?"

Ramaf smiles, "Ready to defeat some trolls."

Prince Brian looks over to Rein, "Are you and your men ready?"

Rein nods slowly, "Yes my lord."

Prince Brian looks at Jennifer, "How about you and our men?"

Jennifer replies, "We're ready my lord."

Prince Brian unties his horse, "We're about a mile from Birdview. We'll make are way through the forest to the village. We must strike quickly before they can signal what is happening."

Everyone bows their heads as Prince Brian gets on his horse. Prince Brian starts to slowly ride west towards Birdview as Jennifer and the others walk behind him.

As the sun nears the evening horizon, the once warm breeze now gets colder as Stefez and the others near the base of the huge mountain range that seems to go on forever both east and west. The mountains reach up into the sky and disappear into the clouds as the once rolling hills and grasslands have given way to more and more underbrush and pine trees. The group stops walking as the road ahead of them goes straight into the mountains.

Stefez looks around at the others, "I think we should stop for the night."

Shaun questions, "Even with the dark rider after us?"

Stefez nods slightly, "I think we're safe for now. It should take him some time to pick up our trail again." She pauses, "Besides, I don't think it's a good idea to start into the mountains right before nightfall."

Bailee speaks up, "That sounds good to me."

Anna replies in a tired voice, "Yea, I'm getting pretty tired."

Jencent nods, "Yea, not knowing the weather, it would be best to travel in the daytime."

Shaun nods in agreement, "That's true."

Michael glances around, "We should move off the road and find a place to camp." He spots a group of pine trees, "I see a good spot."

Michael starts walking towards the group of pine trees and the others follow him. Michael stops at the group of ten pine trees about a hundred feet from the road. The pine trees are fairly tall and their lower branches are about four feet above the ground.

Michael looks back at the others, "This should provide us with enough cover for the night."

Shaun nods in agreement, "Looks good to me. It will definitely keep any of Gabriela's creatures from accidentally spotting us."

Jencent glances at Shaun, then replies, "I'm with Anna. I'm just ready to get a little rest."

Stefez ducks down to make sure none of the branches hit her, "Then its settled." She starts to walk under the pine trees, "Lets go."

Anna follows right behind her as Bailee hops beside Anna. Shaun is the next to follow Stefez, then Jencent starts after Shaun. Michael looks back towards the road, then looks around the area to see if anyone or anything is watching them. Once he's sure its clear, Michael ducks down and follows the others into the pine trees.

———————

As the sun is nearing the evening horizon, the current has slowed considerably on the river where the ferry with Jody and the others continues to float. The warm evening air blows softly across the water. Everyone sits quietly on the ferry. Brendan is laying against Stephanie and he is trying to stay awake.

Jody glances at the others, then looks ahead and sees a fork in the river, "It's getting late, we should stop for the night."

Stephanie nods in agreement, "Yea, Brendan is pretty much out and I'm getting tired too."

Marsha speaks up, "I could go for some rest."

Sherry smiles, "Me too."

Jody looks at Sherry and Marsha, "Use your staves to push us towards the bank while I steer."

Jody steers with the rudder while Sherry and Marsha use their staves to push the ferry over to the bank of the river. The ferry gently slides up on the shallow edge of the riverbank. Jody hops off the ferry. Jody helps Marsha off the ferry.

Marsha gazes and smiles briefly at Jody, "Thank you."

Jody smiles at Marsha, "My pleasure."

Jody helps Sherry off the ferry next. Stephanie gently picks up Brendan who is now asleep and walks over to the edge of the ferry. Stephanie passes Brendan over to Marsha. Jody helps Stephanie off the ferry. Marsha passes Brendan back to Stephanie.

Jody grabs the ferry, "Help me pull it up on the

ground."

Marsha and Sherry set their staves down and grab the ferry with Jody. The three of them pull the edge of the ferry a few feet onto the solid ground.

Jody nods, "That will work."

Sherry and Marsha grab their staves again. Jody starts walking into the forest as Marsha, Sherry and Stephanie, still carrying Brendan, follow. Jody walks about fifty feet and finds a small opening in the forest.

Jody looks at the others, "This should work for the night."

Marsha sighs, "Anything will work for me right now."

Sherry smiles, "Me too. I didn't realize how tired I was."

Marsha and Sherry both sit down and put their staves down.

Stephanie steps over next to Marsha, "Can you watch Brendan for a few minutes? I'm going to wash up at the riverbank."

Marsha nods, "Sure."

Stephanie kneels down and gently places Brendan down next to Marsha and Sherry. Stephanie stands back up and starts walking towards the river. Jody can tell something is wrong with Stephanie.

Jody looks at Marsha and Sherry, "I'll be right back."

Sherry nods, "Okay."

Jody walks after Stephanie back towards the river. Stephanie is standing at the riverbank with a few tears running down her cheeks.

Jody walks up next to Stephanie, "What's wrong Steph?"

Stephanie sniffles and wipes her cheeks, "I'm scared." She sniffles again, "I'm scared something will happen to Brendan and I can't protect him."

Jody steps closer to Stephanie, "I promise you,

nothing will happen to him. I'll die before I let that happen."

Stephanie turns to face Jody, "I know you would." She pauses and slightly smiles, "Thank you so much Jody."

Jody reaches out and pulls Stephanie into a hug, "He's my nephew and you're my sister. Of course I'll do everything I can to keep you safe." He hugs Stephanie tight, "I love the two of you."

Stephanie hugs Jody tight and places her head on his shoulder, "I love you too. I don't know what I'd do without you here."

Jody doesn't say anything and just keeps hugging Stephanie, letting her hug all her worries away with him.

After a minute or two, Jody leans back, "Shall we get back to the others and get some rest."

Stephanie smiles at Jody, "Yea." She pauses, "Thank you."

Jody kisses Stephanie on the forehead, "Of course sweetheart."

Stephanie takes Jody's hand and the two of them start walking back to the clearing where Marsha, Sherry and Brendan are resting at.

———————

The evening sun is just above the western horizon as the warm, gentle breeze carries the fresh smell of the crisp, clean water from Glass Lake through the small village of Birdview. The village of Birdview is about the same size of Havel with all the huts made from wood. All the huts are built into the tall trees making them appear to be an actual part of the forest about thirty feet above the ground. Connecting the huts are numerous wood and rope bridges. Wood and rope ladders hang down in numerous locations around the small village leading up into the trees to various wooden platforms that help connect all the bridges, platforms and huts.

Prince Brian, Jennifer, who now has a white, bone horn slung from her left shoulder to her right hip, and their five soldiers are hiding in the forest just on the eastern edge of Birdview. Rein and her five elves have made their way around Birdview and are hiding in the forest on the western edge of the village. Ramaf and his five dwarves are hiding in the forest on the southern edge of Birdview.

In the middle of the village are four small tents. In the middle of the tents a small fire is burning with a pig roasting over the fire. Sitting around the fire are the twenty trolls that have been waiting in Birdview. The smell of the roasting pig fills the air along with the horrible smell of the trolls.

Prince Brian sighs and looks at Jennifer, "The others should be ready. Sound the attack."

Jennifer grabs the horn and places it to her lips. Jennifer blows hard into the horn and the deep echo of the horn sounds loud through the forest.

Rein draws her sword and looks at her elves when she hears the horn, "Lets go."

Rein and her elves with their swords drawn run into Birdview heading towards the middle of the village.

Ramaf grips his axe tight and looks at his dwarves when he hears the horn, "Lets go!"

Ramaf and his dwarves with weapons ready run into Birdview heading towards the middle of the village.

Prince Brian draws his sword and nods at Jennifer, "Lets go."

Jennifer draws her sword and looks at the five soldiers, "With the Prince."

Prince Brian runs into Birdview heading towards the middle of the village with Jennifer and the others right behind him.

The trolls look at each other when they hear the sound of the horn. Knowing that the horn is that of Prince Brian, the twenty trolls stand up and grab their swords preparing for battle. As the trolls glance around, Rein and her elves, Ramaf and his dwarves, and Prince Brian and the others close in on the trolls.

Rein and her five elves rush into the opening where the trolls are at. As the trolls start towards the elves, Prince Brian and the humans rush into the opening. Seven trolls start for Rein and the other thirteen start for Prince Brian. Ramaf and his dwarves are getting closer to the opening where the battle is about to begin.

Two trolls run at Rein as she prepares for the fight. The other five trolls run at the other five elves. Three trolls run at Prince Brian, three trolls run at Jennifer and the other five trolls run at the five human soldiers.

Rein ducks under the first sword and cuts her sword in at the second troll. The second troll blocks the deadly blow, but Rein snaps her right leg out and kicks the second troll in the stomach. As the second troll staggers back, the first troll turns back to Rein and swings it's sword again. Rein blocks the sword and shuffles away from the two trolls a few feet.

The first troll to reach Prince Brian swings it's sword at his head. Prince Brian blocks the sword with his shield as the second troll steps in and swings at Prince Brian. Prince Brian raises his sword and blocks the second sword. Prince Brian steps into the trolls and using all his strength, pushes the two trolls away as the third troll steps up and swings at Prince Brian. Prince Brian ducks under the sword and steps back away a few feet from the three trolls.

The first troll runs up and swings at Jennifer. Jennifer blocks the troll's sword with her short sword in her left hand. The second troll steps in and swings it's sword at Jennifer. Jennifer ducks under the sword and kicks the first troll in the stomach causing the first troll to stumble backwards. The third troll runs up and swings at Jennifer's head. Jennifer blocks with her medium sword in her right hand. The second troll brings it's sword back across at Jennifer. Jennifer pushes the third troll away, blocks the second troll's sword again with her short sword and drops to one knee. Jennifer thrusts her medium sword upward into the second troll's neck and head. Jennifer removes her sword and turns back to the other two trolls.

As the five humans and the five elves fight the other ten trolls, Ramaf and his five dwarves run into the opening. Now seeing the dwarves, One troll facing Prince Brian runs at Ramaf, two trolls that were fighting the humans and one troll that was fighting the elves run at the five dwarves with Ramaf.

As the five elves fight the four trolls, the first troll comes at Rein again. Rein blocks the sword with her sword and spins to her left. The move is so fast that the second troll never sees Rein's sword. Rein strikes the second troll in the neck sending the second troll to the ground. The first troll turns around and swings at Rein's head. Rein drops to a knee and cuts her sword across the front of the first troll's legs. As the first troll bends over from the cut to it's legs, Rein stands up bringing the handle of her sword up into the first troll's head. The powerful blow sends the first troll to the ground and it lays motionless.

The first troll moves at Prince Brian and swings it's sword. Prince Brian ducks under the sword. Prince Brian lungs into the first troll with his shield sending the troll back a few feet. The second troll comes at Prince Brian with it's sword. Prince Brian brings his sword around and knocks the troll's sword away. Prince Brian brings his shield across and with a powerful blow to the second troll's head, the second troll crashes to the ground and doesn't move. The first troll steps back in and swings at

Prince Brian. Prince Brian blocks the sword with his shield and brings his sword across. Prince Brian's sword strikes the first troll in the stomach causing the first troll to double over. Prince Brian moves his sword fast and brings it around into the back of the first troll's neck. The first troll falls face first to the ground and lays motionless.

As the five elves fight the four trolls, one elf falls and two trolls fall. While the five humans fight the three trolls, two humans fall and one troll falls. As the five dwarves fight the three trolls, one dwarf falls and one troll falls.

As those fights continue, the first troll comes at Jennifer and swings it's sword at her head. Jennifer ducks and kicks the first troll in the stomach sending the first troll a few feet back. Jennifer brings her medium sword around at the second troll standing there. The second troll ducks under the sword and thrusts it's sword at Jennifer. Jennifer continues to turn right and brings her short sword across and knocks the second troll's sword away. Jennifer continues into a spin and brings her medium sword back around. This time Jennifer's medium sword strikes the second troll in the side of the head sending the second troll to the ground. As the second troll lays motionless, the first troll comes back in and swings at Jennifer. Jennifer blocks the sword with her medium sword and brings her short sword over and down removing the first troll's hand that holds it's sword. Jennifer steps in and strikes the first troll in the face with the handle of her medium sword and the first troll crashes to the ground and doesn't move.

The troll swings it's sword down at Ramaf. Ramaf knocks the sword away with the handle of his axe and brings his battle axe around at the troll. The troll steps back as the axe barely misses. The troll steps in and thrusts it's sword at Ramaf. Ramaf moves to his left with amazing speed for a dwarf and brings his battle axe into the troll's right knee. As the troll bends forward, Ramaf brings his battle axe up into the troll's face. The troll's head snaps back and the troll falls to the ground and stops moving.

As Ramaf, Rein, Jennifer and Prince Brian defeat the trolls they were facing, the remaining trolls fall to the elves, dwarves and humans. When the last troll finally falls, everyone stops and looks around at the small battlefield.

Prince Brian puts his sword away and catches his breath, "What did we lose?"

Ramaf replies first, "I lost one dwarf."

Rein puts her sword away, "I lost one elf."

Jennifer puts both her swords away, "We lost two my lord."

Prince Brian sighs, "Not what I would like to have seen, but very well." He looks at Jennifer, "Return to the camp and bring twenty of our soldiers back to camp in Birdview for the night. That should be plenty until morning when we can move the rest of the camp here."

Jennifer bows her head, "Yes my lord."

Jennifer turns and hurries off to the east back towards the camp about a mile away as the sun drops off the horizon and night rises over the Kingdom.

Chapter 20

With the moon high in the night sky over the Kingdom, Gabriela walks into her magic chamber where the four candles on the table cast a dim light over the room. Gabriela walks over to the table.

Gabriela leans her staff against the table, "Why have they not contacted me yet?"

Gabriela closes her eyes, holds her hand over the crystal ball and starts to mumble under her breath. The crystal ball gets cloudy. After a few more seconds, Miclou's face appears in the crystal ball.

Gabriela opens her eyes and questions the dark rider, "Have you captured the child yet?"

Miclou answers with his hollow voice, "No my Queen. They escaped from me in Ghost Town and I haven't picked up their trail yet."

Gabriela replies, "My scouts on the road to North Town hasn't seen them so they may have headed north towards Ice Town."

Miclou bows his head, "I shall try that direction my Queen."

Gabriela replies, "Very well, contact me when you have the child."

Gabriela closes her eyes and mumbles again. After a few seconds, Stecher's face appears in the crystal ball.

Gabriela opens her eyes and questions, "Do you have the child?"

Stecher replies in his cold, evil tone, "No my Queen. They escaped on the river just outside of Apple Grove. I haven't picked up their trail yet."

Gabriela sighs, "They will most likely take the river towards Flower Town. Keep trying to pick up their trail and I'll have my scouts at the crossroads send a couple of soldiers into Flower Town in case they show up, they can contact me."

Stecher bows his head, "Very well my Queen."

Gabriela replies, "Contact me when you capture the child."

As Stecher bows his head, Gabriela closes her eyes and mumbles once again. After a minute, Choel's face appears in the crystal ball.

Gabriela opens her eyes and questions, "Do we have any news about Prince Brian and his army?"

Choel replies, "I have just received word that Prince Brian along with a small group of elves and dwarves defeated our army and are now in Birdview."

Gabriela's eyes narrow, "So, the humans, elves and dwarves have teamed up against me." She pauses, "Do we know how large their army is?"

Choel shakes his head, "Only about twenty attacked Birdview. The true size of their army is still unknown my Queen."

Gabriela nods slightly, "Make sure Brytil in Lakeway knows about this. No doubt Prince Brian will try to cross Glass Lake and capture Lakeway next."

Choel bows his head, "Yes my Queen. Any word about the children?"

Gabriela sighs, "They still elude us. Carry out my orders."

Choel bows his head, "Yes my Queen."

Gabriela removes her hand and the crystal ball returns to it's clear, normal state.

Gabriela grabs her staff, "So Prince Brian, I didn't expect you to come straight at the castle. What are you planning?"

Gabriela exits the room, thinking of her next move.

As the sun breaks across the morning horizon giving birth to a new day in the Kingdom, Prince Brian is standing on the shore of Glass Lake looking northwest towards Lakeview. He closes his eyes and lets the cool breeze blow the smell of the fresh water all around him. He pictures Stephanie's face in his mind and he smiles. His heart starts to beat a little faster as he envisions a possible life in the Kingdom with Stephanie. He doesn't want to see Stephanie sad, but he hopes that something will happen to keep her in the Kingdom. Prince Brian can't help but smile at the thought of ruling the Kingdom with Stephanie by his side. A few more moments pass, then Jennifer, Rein and Ramaf walk up next to Prince Brian.

Jennifer questions, "Everything okay my lord?"

Prince Brian opens his eyes, "Yes. I'm fine."

Rein looks across the lake, "My scout told me 50 trolls, 25 undead elves and 25 undead humans wait for us in Lakeway. They are being lead by Brytil."

Ramaf nods, "No doubt they will try to fire arrows into us as we near the shore."

Prince Brian nods, "We'll divide up evenly so we can have enough shields in each boat and on each raft."

Jennifer nods in agreement, "So, when do you want to begin the attack my lord?"

Rein speaks, "With the sun in the east, it gives us an advantage as they'll be looking into the sun if we attack in the morning."

Prince Brian nods his head in approval, "My thoughts exactly." He looks at the others, "Have the boats and rafts brought up with the army. We'll start the attack as soon as everyone is here."

Jennifer bows her head, "Yes my lord."

Jennifer, Rein and Ramaf turn and hurry off. Prince Brian turns back to the lake, closes his eyes and smiles as he pictures Stephanie's beautiful face once again.

———————

As the sun starts to rise over the morning horizon and the soft breeze blows through the forest, Jody opens his eyes from the short, yet restful sleep he just had. Laying next to him is Stephanie and next to her is Brendan, both still sleeping. Jody gently rolls over. He sees Marsha laying right behind him and Sherry next to her, both still asleep.

Jody stands up ever so gently as to not wake the others. He grabs his weapons and straps them back on. Jody kneels down and wakes up Stephanie. Stephanie opens her eyes and glances around. She smiles at Jody as Jody moves over and wakes up Marsha next. Stephanie sits up and stretches as Marsha wakes up.

Marsha smiles at Jody, "Good morning. I could get use to waking up this way."

Jody returns the smile, "Good morning beautiful."

Stephanie gently wakes up Brendan as Marsha wakes up Sherry. Jody stands up and glances around the area. Stephanie stands up and straps her sword around her waist. Marsha stands up and grabs her staff as Sherry sits up and stretches.

Stephanie questions, "What now Jody?"

Jody glances around as if he heard something, "We'll get back on the river."

Marsha looks over at Jody, "Which fork in the river are we going to take?"

Jody glances around some more, "The right one. It'll take us north." He pauses, "Do you hear that?"

Sherry stands up and grabs her staff, "Hear what?"

Jody looks over at Stephanie, "Something is in the forest near us. Get Brendan and get back to the ferry." He looks at Marsha and Sherry, "You two also."

At that time, they all hear some movement in the forest just to their south.

Sherry quickly questions, "More trolls?"

Marsha questions, "The dark rider?"

Jody shakes his head, "No. We'd smell the trolls and the air is too warm for the dark rider. It could be bandits or gypsies."

Stephanie takes Brendan's hand, "How bad is that?"

Jody glances around and draws his sword, "They both work for Gabriela." He looks at the ladies, "To the ferry."

At that moment, three human men and one human woman rush out of the trees right at Jody and the others. The men are of average size each wearing various brown and green clothing and carrying a medium length sword. The woman is a little shorter than the men. She is wearing brown and green robes with sandals, some elaborate gold jewelry and is carrying a staff.

Jody hollers to the others, "Gypsies! Everyone get to the ferry and get it in the water!"

The woman gypsy yells, "Get the child for Gabriela!"

Stephanie and Brendan run as fast as they can for the ferry at the river. Right behind them is Marsha and Sherry. Jody starts backing up as fast as he can without taking his eyes off the gypsies which are getting closer with every passing second. In their rush, Jody leaves his cloak and water flask behind. Sherry, Marsha and Stephanie each forget their water flasks and food pouches.

Stephanie, Brendan, Marsha and Sherry reach the ferry. Jody is only thirty feet away and the gypsies are almost on top of him now.

Stephanie yells to Brendan, "Brendan, get on the ferry!"

Brendan hops on the ferry as Stephanie, Marsha and Sherry grab the ferry to push it into the river. However, the male gypsies have caught up to Jody who is only twenty feet away from the ferry.

The first male gypsy swings his sword at Jody's head. Jody ducks under the sword and swings his sword at the second male gypsy. The second male gypsy brings his sword up and blocks Jody's sword. The third male gypsy starts around the other two trying to get to Brendan. Jody quickly spins away from the second male gypsy and brings his sword at the third male gypsy. The third male gypsy just barely brings his sword up in time to stop the deadly blow. The first male gypsy steps up and thrusts his sword at Jody as the second male gypsy starts for the ferry.

Jody steps to the side as the sword narrowly misses and Jody kicks the first male gypsy in the front of his right knee. The knee buckles and the first male gypsy falls to the ground screaming in pain.

Jody yells to Stephanie and the others, "Watch out!"

The gypsy woman stops and points her staff towards Jody and starts to mumble under her breath as the third male gypsy swings his sword at Jody's head. Jody blocks the sword and kicks the third male gypsy in the stomach. The third male gypsy staggers back.

Sherry, hearing Jody, turns around in time to see the second male gypsy coming at them. Sherry grabs her staff with both hands and brings it up as the second male gypsy swings down at her. Sherry blocks the sword as Marsha turns around and swings her staff at the second male gypsy's knees. The staff strikes the second male gypsy in the left knee causing him to bend to his left side. Stephanie turns and pushes the second male gypsy as hard as she can in his right shoulder. The second male gypsy, being off-balance from the blow to his knee and already leaning to his left, staggers to his left, loses his footing and falls into the river, losing his sword. Stephanie, Sherry and Marsha turn back to the ferry and start sliding it into the river.

Jody, now with his back to the female gypsy, thrusts his sword in at the third male gypsy in front of him. The third male gypsy blocks the sword to the side and spins in a circle. Jody hears the woman behind him and feels the air getting heavier. Jody drops to his right knee and grabs the dagger in his left boot with his left hand. As the third male gypsy finishes his spin and brings his sword around where he thought Jody would be, he is hit in the chest with a violent blast of air formed in a small vortex from the female gypsy's staff.

The third male gypsy is knocked off his feet and crashes to the ground. Jody quickly turns and throws the dagger in his left hand at the female gypsy. The female gypsy moves her staff quickly in front of her and the dagger sticks in the staff, but breaks her concentration on her magic.

Stephanie yells, "Jody!"

Jody looks over and sees the ferry slide into the water. Jody takes off running fast as the female gypsy pulls the dagger out of her staff. The female gypsy watches as Jody leaps from the bank of the river onto the ferry. The female gypsy drops the dagger on the ground as Jody and the others head up the right fork in the river.

Chapter 21

A s the sun nears the mid-morning sky and the warm breeze blows the crisp, fresh water smell across Glass Lake, twenty five boats and twenty five rafts are closing in on the shore of the lake near Lakeway. The boats and rafts are filled with humans, elves and dwarves ready for their first major battle. Prince Brian is in the lead boat with four human soldiers. In the boat just to his right and a little behind him is Jennifer with four human soldiers. In the boat just to Prince Brian's left and a little behind him is Rein and four elves. In the boat directly behind Prince Brian is Ramaf and four dwarves. All the other boats and rafts are each carrying five either dwarves, elves or humans totaling the size of Prince Brian's army at two hundred and fifty soldiers crossing Glass Lake. On each boat and raft, the first, third and fifth person is carrying a shield while the second and fourth person is paddling.

Brytil, holding his medium sword in his right hand and his shield in his left, looks out across Glass Lake from the shore and sees the boats come into sight. Brytil's eyes widen as he was not ready for the numbers he is seeing.

Brytil looks at a troll next to him, "Have the army move here to the beach. We will try to stop them before they can all land on the shore."

The troll, who is wearing a dull metallic chest plate of armor and carrying a medium sword, runs off back to Lakeway to get the rest of the army and bring them to the shore.

Prince Brian looks across the pure blue water of

Glass Lake and sees the far shore. As the boats and rafts get closer to the bank, Prince Brian sees Gabriela's army start to mass on the beach.

Prince Brian yells as loud as he can to Jennifer, Rein and Ramaf, "They've spotted us! Prepare for incoming arrows! Pass the word!"

On the beach waiting for Prince Brian and the others is now fifty trolls all dressed in brown clothes with a dark metallic chest plate of armor and carrying a medium sword. Also waiting with the trolls are twenty five decomposed, undead human soldiers each wearing brown clothes covered by pieces of armor that protect their chest, arms and legs. Ten undead humans are carrying a medium sword and a shield while the other fifteen are carrying six foot spears. The last group is twenty five decomposed, undead elves each wearing brown and green clothes covered by pieces of armor that protect their chest, arms and legs. Each undead elf has a medium sword and is carrying a bow with ten arrows.

Brytil yells, "Elves to the front! Prepare to fire arrows!"

The twenty five undead elves step up to about twenty yards from the water and prepare their bows and arrows.

Brytil yells, "Fire!"

The undead elves draw back their bows and send twenty five deadly arrows into the air heading towards Glass Lake and Prince Brian's incoming army.

Prince Brian yells, "Arrows! Raise shields!"

Prince Brian raises his shield along with the other two humans in his boat. Jennifer and the two humans in her boat raise their shields. Rein and her two elves also raise their shields. Ramaf and his dwarves raise their shields. Seeing Prince Brian and the others, all the other boats and rafts follow the same direction and raise their shields to protect themselves from the arrows.

The deadly arrows fall from the sky heading towards

Prince Brian and the others. Prince Brian hears and feels an arrow bounce off his shield that would have otherwise struck him in the chest. The rest of the arrows bounce off various other shields or land harmlessly in the water around Prince Brian's army. The boats and rafts continue to close in on the beach where Gabriela's army waits.

Brytil yells again, "Fire arrows at will!"

The undead elves draw back their bows and fill the sky with arrows again. Before those arrows reach Prince Brian's army, the undead elves fire another round of arrows into the air, then grab more arrows and continue to fire as fast as they can.

Prince Brian and the others keep their shields raised to protect themselves from the deadly arrows. This time as the arrows bounce off the shields and land in the water around the boats and rafts, a couple of arrows hit their mark. A human and an elf are both struck by an arrow and fall from their rafts into the water. As the arrows from the undead elves continue to fly, Prince Brian and the others are getting ever so close to the shoreline now.

Prince Brian, with shield and sword in hand, yells, "Be ready to disembark!"

Jennifer, Rein and Ramaf repeat the orders to the other boats and rafts as they are all merely fifty yards from the shoreline now.

Brytil turns to his army and yells, "Prepare for battle!"

As the undead elves prepare to fire more arrows, the undead humans and trolls ready their weapons and start to move towards the water and the incoming army.

———

As the mid-morning sun shines down on the huge mountains that reach up into the sky with their snowcap peaks seeming to disappear into the clouds, the now cooler breeze blows the fresh smell of the pine trees and snow all around Stefez and the others was they walk along the road that winds north through the mountains. The landscape is covered with green shrubs and pine trees. Large rock columns also dot the land around the road.

Shaun speaks up, "The temperature is dropping."

Stefez nods in agreement, "Yea, we're getting higher into the mountains and closer to the snow lands."

Michael interjects, "You know, this is going to make it harder for us to tell when the dark rider is close with the air already cold."

Jencent nods, "That's very true."

Bailee chimes in, "Great. That's all we need now, not being able to know when the dark rider finds us."

The others chuckle at Bailee's comment.

Anna questions, "So, will we make it out of the mountains before the sun goes down?"

Stefez shakes her head, "Only if the weather stays perfect, which I doubt it will with the temperature changing this much already."

Suddenly, the ground shakes as if something extremely heavy just fell. Everyone stops and glances around.

Anna is the first to question, "What in the world was that?"

Then, the ground shakes again and the sound is closer.

Jencent shakes her head, "I don't know, but it was closer that time."

The ground shakes again as the sound has gotten even closer to the group.

Michael glances around, "Whatever it is, it's moving towards us."

Bailee questions, "You mean something is walking towards us causing the ground to shake like that?"

Shaun speaks up as the ground shakes again, "Whatever it is, it can't be good."

Stefez continues to glance around, "I think I might know what it could be."

Bailee quickly replies with fear in her voice, "Please share."

Stefez speaks as the ground shakes again, "It could be a stone golem."

Michael, Shaun and Jencent just look at Stefez.

Anna questions, "Is that bad?"

Jencent nods, "If it is, no doubt it will be working for Gabriela."

Shaun glances around, "Which means it's coming for Anna."

This time when the ground shakes, everyone looks north up the road and what Stefez mentioned has come true. A twelve foot tall, humanoid creature made of solid rock with black eyes, two holes for a nose and a mouth steps out from behind the pine trees onto the road. The stone golem has three fingers on each hand and his feet are solid, not having any toes.

Bailee's eyes widen, "Oh no!"

Stefez steps in front of Anna, "It's the stone golem."

Michael draws his sword, "What now?"

Shaun draws her sword also, "It's blocking our path."

Jencent draws her sword, "This is great."

Stefez glances over at the others, "We have to find a way to get by it. It's big, but slow. If we get by it, we can lose it."

Anna finally speaks, still in awe, "I'm going to guess that its harder than it sounds."

The stone golem reaches over and picks up a small boulder that weighs every bit of 750 pounds. The stone golem turns and throws the boulder at Stefez and the others. Stefez grabs Anna's hand and quickly pulls her out of the way of the path of the boulder. Bailee hops off quickly to avoid the huge rock. Michael, Shaun and Jencent all scatter out of the way of the massive boulder. The boulder lands on the road where the group was standing and the ground shakes from the impact.

The stone golem speaks in a deep, gravelly voice, "Give me the child!"

The stone golem reaches over and picks up a large piece of wood from the ground. The makeshift club is a tree branch that is about eight feet long and two inches in diameter. The stone golem turns back to Stefez and the others.

The stone golem speaks again, "I must have the child!"

Michael takes a deep breath and charges at the stone golem. Shaun grips her sword tight and runs towards the stone golem right behind Michael. Jencent sighs, shakes her head and runs towards the stone golem.

Stefez looks at Anna, "Stay close to me."

Anna nods, "Okay."

As Michael gets close to the stone golem, the stone golem swings the club at Michael. Michael ducks under the club and swings his sword at the stone golem's body. Shaun sees the club coming at her that Michael just ducked under. Knowing she doesn't have much time to react, Shaun raises her sword up to block the club. The club slams into Shaun's sword and the incredibly powerful blow sends Shaun stumbling off to the side of the road and unable to get her balance, Shaun falls to the ground. Michael's sword finds the mark and strikes the stone golem square in the chest area. However, the sword only chips a piece of the rock off the stone golem seeming to leave the stone golem unharmed.

As the stone golem looks down at Michael, Jencent runs up and swings her sword at the stone golem. The stone golem sees Jencent's sword and ignores it as if knowing the sword will do no damage. As Jencent's sword bounces off the stone golem merely chipping a small piece of rock from it's left arm, the stone golem swings the club at Michael. Michael brings his sword up and the powerful blow from the club as it strikes his sword sends Michael stumbling backwards about ten feet, but he remains on his feet.

With the stone golem's attention squarely on Michael, Jencent and Shaun, Stefez takes the time to come up with a spell to help them escape. Stefez grips her staff with both hands and mumbles under her breath. The stone on the end of Stefez's staff starts to glow.

Shaun gets back to her feet and tries to run around behind the stone golem. The stone golem sees Shaun and steps over, blocking her path, and the stone golem swings the club again. This time Shaun ducks under the club and strikes the stone golem in the right leg. The sword harmlessly bounces off leaving just a small chip mark on the stone golem. At the same time, Jencent's sword strikes the stone golem in the left arm, but again, the sword just bounces away.

Michael starts back towards the stone golem when he sees Stefez running straight at the stone golem. Michael can tell be the glowing stone on Stefez's staff that she is prepared to cast a spell.

Michael yells at Shaun and Jencent, "Get out of the way!"

Shaun and Jencent both look over to see Stefez running at the stone golem with Anna about ten feet behind her. Shaun and Jencent move quickly away from the stone golem. The stone golem turns to see Stefez running in it's direction. The stone golem raises the club ready to deliver a massive, crushing blow to the elf.

Stefez suddenly stops ten feet from the stone golem, drives the stone on her staff to the ground and yells, "Ground wave!"

Suddenly the ground sends a few ripples, each about

a foot high, straight at the stone golem. The ground looks like a pool of water right after someone throws a large rock into it. The ground waves slam into the stone golem's feet. The stone golem tries hard not to lose it's balance, but after the third wave, the stone golem tips backwards and crashes to the ground. The ground shakes from the massive impact.

Stefez raises her staff and yells, "Now run!"

Stefez and Anna quickly runs by the stone golem before it can start to move. Michael, Shaun and Jencent waste no time and take off running right behind Stefez and Anna. Bailee comes hopping out of the bushes from the side of the road and quickly catches up to Stefez and the others.

By the time the stone golem gets to it's feet again, Stefez and the others have disappeared up the road.

Chapter 22

As a deadly arrow from an undead elf bounces off Prince Brian's shield and falls harmlessly into the shallow water, Prince Brian stands up and prepares to jump off the boat as it is nearly to the shore. Prince Brian sees the undead humans and trolls running towards where him and the others are preparing to land. The undead elves draw back their bows one more time and send a last volley of deadly arrows at Prince Brian's army. A dwarf and an elf are both struck by an arrow and fall into the lake. The undead elves put their bows away, draw their swords and start towards Prince Brian's army.

The boat with Prince Brian on it slides into the soft sand of the shoreline. Prince Brian, with sword and shield in hand, leaps from the front of the boat. As he lands on his feet in the soft sand, the boat with Jennifer, Rein and Ramaf slide into the soft, sandy shoreline. Jennifer, with sword in hand, but leaving her shield behind, jumps from the boat to the shore. Rein, also with sword in hand, but leaving her shield behind, leaps from her boat to the shore. Ramaf drops his shield and grabs his battle axe, then leaps from his boat to the shore.

As the undead humans, undead elves and trolls continue towards Prince Brian and the others, the soldiers from the already landed boats start to climb onto the shore. Prince Brian looks at Jennifer, Rein and Ramaf and smiles, then turns back to Gabriela's army, yells loud and charges at them. Jennifer yells and charges after Prince Brian as more boats slide into the sand and offload. Rein and Ramaf yell loud and charge forward. More and more boats and rafts slide to a stop and the soldiers unload. Before Brytil realizes it, Prince Brian, Jennifer, Rein and Ramaf are being followed by nearly their whole army, all yelling and charging right at his army. The undead humans, undead elves and trolls stop running and prepare for battle.

Prince Brian runs up to an undead human that is carrying a sword and shield. Jennifer runs up on Prince Brian's right. Rein runs up on Prince Brian's left and Ramaf runs up on Rein's left. The rest of Prince Brian's army charges up on both sides of him and the battle erupts as the humans, elves and dwarves charge into the undead humans, undead elves and trolls.

Prince Brian swings his sword at the undead human. The undead human blocks with his shield and swings his sword back at Prince Brian. Prince Brian blocks with his shield, pulls his sword back and thrusts in at the undead human. The undead human moves fast and barely blocks Prince Brian's sword. Prince Brian quickly spins right and brings his shield around. The undead human tries to move his shield across, but its too late as Prince Brian slams his shield into the undead human's body. Prince Brian quickly cuts in with his sword and this time his sword finds it's mark as the undead human falls to the sand.

Another undead human steps up and swings at Prince Brian. Prince Brian deflects the sword with his shield and moves past the undead human as Prince Brian's eyes see Brytil. Before the undead human can turn back to Prince Brian, one of Prince Brian's human soldiers steps up and engages the undead human freeing Prince Brian to continue on towards Brytil.

As the sound of clanking swords, shields and spears echoes across the beach, Jennifer quickly steps up to an undead human and brings her sword in fast. The undead human brings his shield across and just barely blocks

Jennifer's sword. The undead human thrusts in quick with his sword. Jennifer spins around the sword and while spinning, Jennifer draws her short sword from her right hip with her left hand. As she stops her spin, Jennifer blocks a second undead human's sword with her short sword that would have struck her in the head. Jennifer quickly thrusts her medium sword in at the second undead human and the sword finds it's mark.

As Jennifer pulls her sword back, she turns back to face the first undead human and sees the first undead human's sword coming at her head. Jennifer ducks under the sword and brings her medium sword across at the first undead human. The first undead human blocks the sword with his shield, but Jennifer quickly pushes the shield away with her medium sword and cuts in with her short sword. This time the first undead human moves too slow and Jennifer's short sword sends the first undead human to the sand next to the other undead human.

Rein steps up to an undead elf and swings her sword in from the left. The undead elf moves fast and barely blocks Rein's sword. The undead elf brings his sword around quickly at Rein. Rein steps back and brings her sword across and blocks the deadly blow. Rein throws her left leg out and kicks the undead elf back as a troll steps up and swings it's sword at Rein. Rein brings her sword up and stops the troll's sword. The undead elf steps back up and thrusts his sword at Rein. Rein spins left around the sword and brings her sword around at the undead elf's back.

The strike is true and the undead elf falls to the sand as the troll steps back up and swings it's sword in again at Rein. Rein brings her sword across quickly and barely manages to knock the troll's sword away. Rein quickly counters with a cut from her own sword, but the troll manages to bring it's sword back and block the deadly blow. Rein quickly withdraws her sword as the troll prepares another swing. Before the troll's sword can reach Rein, Rein thrusts her sword in and the sword finds the target. Rein pulls her sword back as the troll falls to the sand to join the other fallen.

As more and more of Gabriela's army falls at the hands of Prince Brian's army, two trolls come at Ramaf who has made his way fairly deep into Gabriela's army. The first troll brings it's sword down at Ramaf. Ramaf steps to the side as the sword narrowly misses. The second troll steps in and swings it's sword at Ramaf. Ramaf brings his battle axe across and stops the sword. Ramaf pushes the sword away and brings his battle axe back across at the first troll. The first troll blocks the battle axe with it's sword. The second troll steps in and brings it's sword down at the back of Ramaf's head.

As Ramaf turns to see the sword coming down at him, Prince Brian steps over and blocks the second troll's sword with his sword. Ramaf gives Prince Brian a quick nod of thanks and Prince Brian gives Ramaf a quick smile. Prince Brian pushes the second troll's sword away at the same time Ramaf pushes the first troll's sword away.

The first troll brings it's sword down at Ramaf. Ramaf steps to the side and the sword misses. Ramaf brings the handle of his battle axe around and strike's the first troll in the side of it's right knee. As the first troll reacts to the blow to it's knee, Ramaf brings his battle axe blade over and down. The battle axe knocks the sword from the first troll's hand. Before the first troll can react, Ramaf spins around the first troll and his battle axe slams into the first troll's back sending the troll crashing into the sand.

Prince Brian steps in and blocks the second troll's sword with his sword. Prince Brian uses his shield and body and slams into the second troll, knocking the second troll off-balance. Prince Brian quickly cuts in with his sword. The second troll barely manages to block the sword while still off-balance. Prince Brian moves fast and brings his shield across, knocking the second troll's sword out of the way. Prince Brian seizes the moment and cuts in with his sword again. The blow to the second troll's neck sends the second troll to the sand next to the first troll that just fell.

Ramaf looks at Prince Brian, "Fine work my lord."

Prince Brian smiles, then catches sight of Brytil sending an elf to the sand, "I'll see you when it's over my friend."

As the battle rages on and the sun starts to get closer to the noon sky, Ramaf looks for his next opponent as Prince Brian continues to fight his way towards Brytil.

As the sun gets closer to the noon sky, the warm breeze blows the smell of the fresh water and the forest trees all around the ferry that Jody and the others are slowly riding down the gentle current of the river. Sherry is sitting at the front of the ferry keeping a look out. Marsha and Brendan are laying in the middle of the ferry taking a nap. Jody is sitting at the back, steering the ferry down the river. Stephanie is sitting next to Jody staring off into the clear, blue sky which is dotted by soft white clouds. Stephanie closes her eyes for a moment, pictures Prince Brian's face and smiles.

Jody looks at Stephanie, "So, who or what are you thinking about?"

Stephanie opens her eyes and looks over at Jody, "Oh, nothing really."

Jody slightly smiles at Stephanie, "Really?"

Stephanie finally breaks a smile, "What?"

Jody replies, "I thought you might be thinking about a certain someone."

Stephanie tries to give a puzzled look as if she doesn't know what Jody is talking about, "Who?"

Jody gives Stephanie a sarcastic look, "I don't know, maybe, Prince Brian."

Stephanie instantly smiles at the name and her heart beats a little faster, "What makes you think that?"

Jody smiles, "I don't know. The gazing at the sky, then the smile after you closed your eyes."

Stephanie slightly chuckles, "I can't get him off my mind, even with everything else going on." She pauses, "What do you think about him?"

Jody shrugs, "I've never met him. All I know about him is what I've heard from others and from what I've heard, he seems like a great man. He is honorable, courageous and very caring seems to be what everyone mentions first." He pauses, "So, what do you think about him since you got to meet him?"

Stephanie smiles, "Well, he does seem very thoughtful and caring. Plus, it doesn't hurt that he is very handsome." She pauses and her voice gets a little down, "But what would he see in me? I'm an outlander teacher and a single mom. He could have anyone in the Kingdom."

Jody shakes his head at Stephanie, "Oh come on sis. First, you're extremely, drop dead beautiful. Plus, just a few moments with you and he'll see that your inner beauty far surpasses your outer beauty which says a lot. You're very loving and caring, you're just a wonderful person. Any man would be lucky to have you" He pauses, "And Prince Brian would be crazy not to want you."

Stephanie smiles at Jody, "Thanks bro." She pauses, "But ..."

Jody nods, "We're looking at going back home and leaving the Kingdom."

Stephanie just nods, but says nothing.

Jody places his hand on Stephanie's shoulder, "You

can't think about that. No telling what's going to happen and everything will work out the way it's suppose to."

Stephanie smiles at Jody, "Thanks. You're the best." She pauses, "So, what about you?"

Jody gets a puzzled look, "What about me?"

Stephanie gives Jody a sarcastic look like he gave her earlier, "Huh, you and Marsha maybe?"

Jody smiles, "We were talking about you. When did this become about me?"

Stephanie shakes her head, "Oh please, its so obvious."

Jody chuckles slightly, "I don't know. She's beautiful and seems like a very wonderful lady." He pauses, "I'm just drawn to her for some reason."

Stephanie replies, "She is a wonderful person and it's obvious she's so very much into you."

Jody sighs, "You think so?"

Stephanie nods, "Oh yea."

Jody smiles and glances at Marsha, "I just wish I could ease her mind about Anna."

Stephanie smiles, "Always thinking of others." She pauses, "Well, just like you look out for your little sister, I look out for my big brother and I sure do approve of her for you."

Jody lets out a nice little laugh, "Thank you."

Stephanie leans over and gives Jody a kiss on the cheek, "Anytime bro."

Sherry turns and looks back at Jody and Stephanie, "Hey, there's a fork in the river coming up."

Stephanie looks at Jody, "Which way?"

Jody replies, "We need to take the left fork. It will take us to a town called, Lover's Keep. We can get some supplies there since we lost ours when the gypsies attacked us."

Sherry nods, "True. I'm sure everyone is getting as hungry as I am."

Stephanie looks at Jody again, "Lover's Keep?"

Jody smiles, "You'll like this town."

Stephanie nods and looks back up at the sky and white clouds. Stephanie closes her eyes and pictures Prince Brian's face as the name, Lover's Keep, echoes through her mind. Sherry turns back around and watches the river as Jody steers the ferry down the left fork in the river.

Chapter 23

A s the bright, warm sun crosses into the clear, blue afternoon sky, the battle for Lakeway continues. Prince Brian's army has clearly taken the upper hand as the last of the undead humans, undead elves and trolls are completely surrounded by the humans, dwarves and elves of Prince Brian's army. As the sound of metal clanking on metal echoes across the beach, Prince Brian makes his way to Brytil. Brytil sees Prince Brian break free from the battle and start his way. Brytil readies himself for battle. Ramaf, Rein and Jennifer break away from the battle and watch as Prince Brian and Brytil prepare to decide the fate of Lakeway with a one-on-one battle.

Prince Brian charges at Brytil and thrusts his sword in. Brytil moves fast and brings his shield across, deflecting Prince Brian's sword away. Brytil brings his sword around and cuts in at Prince Brian from the left. Prince Brian brings his shield up and blocks the deadly sword. Prince Brian steps forward behind his shield and pushes forward. The powerful shove sends Brytil back a few steps. Prince Brian steps forward and swings his sword down at Brytil. Brytil raises his shield and blocks Prince Brian's blow.

Brytil pushes Prince Brian's sword away and thrusts his sword in at Prince Brian's chest. Prince Brian brings his shield across and knocks the sword away. Prince Brian continues into a spin and brings his sword around at Brytil. Brytil tries to bring his shield over, but he's too late as Prince Brian's sword strikes Brytil's right thigh causing blood to run down Brytil's right leg. Jennifer, Rein and Ramaf all smile.

Brytil steps back and Prince Brian moves in quick with his sword cutting in from the right. Brytil moves fast and just barely manages to stop the deadly sword with his shield. Prince Brian brings his shield over and knocks Brytil's shield out of the way. Prince Brian quickly follows with a kick as his right foot slams into Brytil's stomach. Brytil staggers back and slips on the loose sand. Without hesitation, Prince Brian steps in and cuts down at Brytil. Being off-balance, Brytil is unable to bring his shield or sword up to protect himself. Prince Brian's sword strikes a deadly blow to the base of Brytil's neck on the left side.

As Brytil drops to his knees, Prince Brian delivers the final blow as his sword strikes Brytil in the right side of the neck this time. Prince Brian steps back as the man who once served his father falls face first into the sand.

Jennifer lets out a yell, "Yes!"

Prince Brian turns to see the battle ending as the last of Gabriela's army falls to the sand. As the humans, elves and dwarves start to celebrate their victory, Jennifer, Rein and Ramaf walk up to Prince Brian.

Jennifer bows her head to Prince Brian, "Well done my lord."

Ramaf glances around and smiles, "Victory is ours."

Prince Brian nods, "For now, but we don't have time to celebrate. No doubt Gabriela will be upset and the next army we face won't be so small."

Rein nods in agreement, "Very true my lord."

Jennifer questions, "What now my lord?"

Prince Brian glances around, "Send half the army back to help bring everyone else across the lake. We'll move into Lakeway and start setting up camp." He pauses, "I want everyone across and camp completed by nightfall."

Jennifer bows her head, "It will be done my lord."

As Jennifer walks off, Prince Brian looks at Ramaf and Rein, "Count our losses and get back to me with the numbers."

Rein and Ramaf both bow their heads and walk off. Prince Brian puts his sword away and lets out a deep sigh. Prince Brian looks to the sky and closes his eyes. He takes in a breath of fresh air and allows himself a slight smile.

As the sun starts to get near the evening horizon, Jody and the others continue the slow ferry ride towards Lover's Keep. Jody continues to steer the ferry along the river. Marsha is now sitting next to Jody. Stephanie, Sherry and Brendan are sitting near the front of the ferry, watching the river ahead. As the soft breeze blows the smell of the trees and fresh water around the ferry, another scent catches the breeze. The smell of roses and baking pastries fills the air now.

Jody smiles, "We're almost there."

Marsha looks at Jody and smiles, "Oh my God, that smells so good."

Stephanie looks back at Jody, "Wow, it smells amazing."

Brendan smiles and speaks up, "I'm really hungry."

Sherry smiles at Brendan, "Me too little man."

Jody points with his left hand, "Look."

Everyone turns and looks ahead of the ferry. Just a few hundred yards ahead, the river opens up into a very large lake about one third the size of Glass Lake. At the entrance to the lake is a huge, ivory colored, stone archway that extends up thirty feet over the mouth of the river. However, its not just the lake and amazing archway that captures everyone's attention. It's also Lover's Keep, the huge town seemingly built as part of the lake. Lover's

Keep is twice the size of River Fork and Ghost Town and is the largest town in the Kingdom except for the castle. It is an incredibly beautiful town. All the buildings are made of ivory looking stone. Banners of bright red, green, blue, yellow and pink hang all around the town.

Men and women of all ages are walking the streets of the town. Children of all ages are also running and playing all over the town. Everyone is dressed in very nice clothes of the same bright and alive colors as the banners hanging around the town. Everyone seems so happy as if completely unaware of the Kingdom being under the control of Gabriela or the looming war and the summoning of the dark riders.

Stephanie just stares at the incredibly beautiful town, "It's beautiful."

Sherry also just stares, "It's built right into the lake."

Marsha can't help but stare also, "I can't believe what I'm seeing."

Jody just smiles at all their reactions, "I told you this place was amazing." He pauses, "We will tie up the ferry on the pier, then we can find a place to eat and stay for the night."

Brendan starts to bounce in excitement, "Yea."

Jody, Stephanie, Sherry and Marsha all laugh at Brendan. Sherry, Stephanie and Brendan continue to stare as the ferry passes under the archway and enters the lake.

Marsha casts a loving gaze at Jody, "Lover's Keep. It's so beautiful."

Jody returns the loving gaze, "Even more so with you here."

Marsha smiles and starts to lean towards Jody as if to kiss him. Jody holds his breath as Marsha's lips get closer to his.

Suddenly, Brendan turns around and speaks, "Uncle Jody, do they have ice cream here?"

Marsha and Jody quickly separate before Sherry and

Stephanie also turn around. Marsha and Jody smile at each other about the near kiss.

Jody looks over at Brendan, "You bet they do big man." He pauses, "I think we need some, don't you?"

Brendan gets a big smile and bounces some more, "Yea!"

Everyone laughs at Brendan's reaction again. Jody continues to steer the ferry towards the long pier just a couple hundred yards ahead of them.

As the evening sun is starting to set, the cold, mountain breeze has gotten worse and snow has started to fall as Stefez and the others continue to walk along the road through the mountains. The dimming light of the day and the increasing snowfall is making the road harder to see for Stefez and the others who all have their cloaks wrapped around them with their hoods on trying to protect themselves from the worsening weather.

Shaun speaks as the wind picks up, "We're going to have to stop. The weather is getting worse."

Michael chimes in, "It's getting too dangerous to keep going."

Jencent nods, "We're going to lose sight of the road soon."

Stefez stops and glances around, "You're right, lets find a place to get out of this weather and get some rest."

Bailee chimes in as her voice shivers from the cold, "Sounds good to me."

Anna agrees, "Me too. I'm tired and really cold."

Stefez peers through the falling snow to try and find a suitable place for them to rest for the night. Michael, Shaun and Jencent also look around.

Stefez shakes her head, "I can't see that well. Anna and Bailee come with me." She pauses, "Lets spread out and see if we can find something."

Stefez, Anna and Bailee head off to the left of the road. Michael, Shaun and Jencent all head off in different directions. Everyone walks around slowly to see if they can find any shelter to protect them from the weather for the night.

After a few minutes, Shaun yells to the others, "Over here! I found a cave!"

Stefez, Anna and Bailee turn and start to make their way in the direction of Shaun's voice as the weather grows worse by the minute. Michael hears Shaun and starts in her direction along with Jencent who quickly finds Michael in the worsening weather. Shaun yells again so the others can continue to try and find her. A few moments pass, then Michael and Jencent walk up to Shaun.

Shaun yells a couple more times so Stefez and the others can find them. A couple minutes and a couple more yells, Stefez, Anna and Bailee meet up with Shaun, Michael and Jencent.

Shaun points to the eight foot around entrance to a cave, "We can rest in there for the night."

Anna speaks up, "I'll take anything right now."

Stefez glances around as the ground is completely covered in snow and the road is nearly invisible now.

Stefez nods, "I don't think we have a choice. It'll have to do."

Michael draws his sword and starts into the cave first. Shaun draws her sword and follows Michael. Jencent, Stefez and Anna start into the cave.

Bailee hops next to Stefez, "Please, no bears."

Stefez and the others chuckle as they make their way into the cave and out of the bad weather.

Chapter 24

With the sun now set and the moon and stars shining brightly in the night sky, the soft glow of torches light up the streets of Lover's Keep. The wonderful smell of roses and baked pastries still fills the air as Jody and the others are walking down a fairly busy road towards the middle of town. The people of Lover's Keep continue on with whatever they are doing, not really taking notice of Stephanie, Sherry, Marsha and Brendan.

Stephanie looks over at Jody while they walk, "This place is simply amazing."

Sherry nods, "I can't believe that the people seem to not care that we're outlanders."

Marsha glances around at the beauty of the town, "It's like they have no worries here about everything else going on."

Jody smiles as he holds Brendan's hand, "That's because they're not worried about all the things going on. This town has been pretty much left unchanged by everything going on." He notices the next door is an entrance to a tavern, "Lets stop in here and get something to eat."

Brendan smiles, "Yea."

Everyone smiles at Brendan as they walk up to the wooden door that has a heart carved into it. Jody opens the door and steps inside. The smell of the food being made fills the air and the sound of soft music echoes through the room. Numerous townspeople are sitting at some of the tables enjoying their meals and the music.

Jody spots an open table in the corner and starts walking towards it. Stephanie and the others follow, just amazed at the whole scene inside the tavern. Jody sits down with his back to the wall. Brendan sits down next to Jody on his left as Stephanie sits down next to Brendan. Marsha sits down on Jody's right and Sherry sits down between Marsha and Stephanie.

Marsha looks around the room, "I still can't believe this place."

Jody smiles at Marsha, "This place is what everyone thinks of when they think of a fairytale."

Sherry nods, "You got that right."

At that time, a nicely dressed woman in her thirties walks up to the table.

The woman speaks, "Lovely evening. I'm Kristen, what can I get for you."

Jody looks at Brendan, "You ready for food and desert big guy."

Brendan smiles and starts to bounce in his chair, "Uh huh."

Everyone smiles at Brendan.

Jody looks at Kristen, "Five stews, four ales and one milk." He pauses and glances at Brendan, "And after that, ice cream."

Brendan's eyes widen with joy, "Yea, ice cream!"

Kristen smiles at Brendan, "Boy, you must really like ice cream." She looks back at Jody, "Will the five of you need a room for the night?"

Jody nods, "Yes, if you have one available."

Kristen smiles, "Of course, you can take the last room on the right." She pauses, "I'll be right back."

Jody smiles, "Thank you."

Kristen walks off.

Stephanie looks over at Jody, "How can we afford all of this?"

Jody smiles at Stephanie, "It's free. Everything in this

town is free."

Sherry gets an amazed look, "What?"

Marsha chimes in, "Are you serious?"

Jody nods, "Oh yes. The town is built over a magical water pocket on the bottom of the lake where a magical water lily lives that the original founders of the town saved. To show it's gratitude, the water lily furnishes the town with everything they need."

At that time, Kristen and another young woman walk up and place the food and drinks on the table. The two women walk off.

Stephanie chuckles, "Okay, that's about as fairytale as it can get."

Jody laughs at Stephanie's response, "It's a magical, fairytale land that you're now in." He pauses, "Where all things are possible."

Brendan speaks while in between bites, "I like it here."

Everyone smiles at Brendan and the talking dies down as everyone eats. After a few minutes, everyone is done eating. Kristen and the other woman walk back up a minute later with five bowls of ice cream.

Brendan's eyes widen as he picks up his spoon, "Yea!"

Jody and the others eat their ice cream and enjoy the music being played by the three men in the far corner of the tavern.

Once everyone is done, Jody speaks up, "We should get upstairs and get some rest."

Sherry nods, "Sounds good to me."

Stephanie smiles, "I can definitely use some rest."

Jody and the others get up from the table and make their way over to the stairs.

In the darkness of the night, Gabriela walks into her magic chamber where the soft glow of the candles cast some light in the room. Gabriela walks over and leans her staff against the table. She closes her eyes, holds her right hand over the crystal ball and starts to mumble under her breath. A few moments pass, then Stecher's face appears in the crystal ball.

Gabriela opens her eyes and questions, "Have you found them?"

Stecher replies in his cold voice, "No my Queen. I haven't picked up their trail again. I'm going to follow the river until I reach the lake near Flower Town. I should be able to pick up their trail by then."

Gabriela nods, "Very well. Let me know if you find them."

Stecher bows his head, "Yes my Queen."

Gabriela closes her eyes and mumbles again. The crystal ball goes cloudy, then the face of Miclou appears.

Gabriela opens her eyes and questions, "Have you found them?"

Miclou replies in his hollow voice, "No my Queen. I searched all of Ghost Town and couldn't find them. I've just started on the road towards the mountains."

Gabriela nods, "Very well. Contact me if you find them."

Miclou bows his head, "Yes my Queen."

Gabriela removes her hand from the crystal ball and the image fades away. Gabriela grabs her staff when Choel walks into the chamber.

Gabriela turns and looks at Choel, "Anything new?"

Choel sighs, "Prince Brian crossed Glass Lake with his army. He defeated our army and took back Lakeway. Brytil was killed in the battle my Queen."

Gabriela's face changes to a look of anger, "That's not exactly the news I was looking for Choel."

Choel replies, "Regas already has the army in the

castle gathering."

Gabriela nods, "Good. Make sure everyone is prepared and the defenses are put into place. I'm going to think about our next move."

Choel bows his head, "It will be done my Queen."

Choel turns and walks out of the room.

Gabriela grinds her staff with her right hand, "This Kingdom is mine Prince Brian."

The soft breeze blows the smell of the fresh water from Glass Lake along the shoreline that saw so much death earlier in the day. The clear night sky allows the stars and quarter moon to reflect brightly off the surface of the water. As the rest of the army is resting, Prince Brian walks quietly across the sand and stops about twenty feet from the water.

Prince Brian closes his eyes and breathes in the crisp, fresh air. He pictures the face of the woman who has completely captured his heart, he pictures Stephanie's face. Prince Brian smiles as he thinks about the incredible woman who he only hopes has the same feelings for him. He can't figure out why Stephanie instantly captured his heart, but he just knows she is the right one for him. The thought of her leaving the Kingdom brings a sad look to his face.

Jennifer walks up a few feet behind Prince Brian, "My lord, is everything okay?"

Prince Brian opens his eyes, "Yes."

Jennifer can tell what is on Prince Brian's mind, "You're thinking of Stephanie again."

Prince Brian smiles and turns to Jennifer, "Yes. I don't know why, but she has completely captured my heart."

Jennifer lets out a sigh, "I've never been good at the

whole love thing. I've been raised to be a personal warrior for the royal family." She pauses, "But I do believe in true love and in love at first sight."

Prince Brian nods, "So do I." He pauses, "And I just feel that she is the one. The one I want for my Queen when we recapture the Kingdom."

Jennifer nods, "Perhaps it will happen. Anything is possible my lord, especially if it is fate."

Prince Brian sighs, "I truly hope so." He pauses and gets a more sad tone, "I just hope Stephanie and her son are okay."

Jennifer replies confidently, "I'm sure they are my lord." She pauses, "Its getting late my lord, we should get some rest."

Prince Brian nods and looks back at Glass Lake, "Yes, of course. I'll be there in a minute."

Jennifer bows her head and walks off. Prince Brian closes his eyes, pictures Stephanie's face again and a big smile comes to his face.

In the middle of the cold, dark night, Anna is standing by herself at the entrance to the cave where they took shelter earlier. Anna wraps herself up in her cloak and peers out into the night. She can see the ground and the pine trees covered with snow. Anna shivers from the cold as a sad look comes to her face.

Anna whispers to herself, unaware that Stefez has walked up behind her, "I miss you Marsha. I hope you're okay."

Stefez speaks in a calm, soothing voice, "I'm sure she is Anna. I'm sure they all are."

Anna turns around a little surprised, "Stefez! I didn't know you were up."

Stefez walks up next to Anna and peers out into the

night, "I couldn't sleep either." She pauses, "Besides, I had a spell cast to warn me if you went a certain distance away from me. Just in case."

Anna smiles at Stefez, "That's cool." She looks back out into the night, "I still can't believe this place."

Stefez places her left hand on Anna's shoulder, "I'm sure this is a lot for you to take in at this time, but when the journey is over and Prince Brian is back in control, you'll see just how wonderful the Kingdom really is."

Anna sighs, "I can't wait."

Stefez smiles, "We should get some more rest. It's a long trip ahead of us, but we should reach the snow lands tomorrow."

Anna nods, "Yea."

Anna and Stefez turn around and start back to where the others are sleeping.

———————

As Jody lays sleeping in the bed he is sharing with Stephanie and Brendan, a soft breeze blows across his face. Jody opens his eyes knowing that the balcony doors have been opened. He can tell by the temperature in the air that it is not the dark rider. Jody gently slides his right arm from around Stephanie and Brendan and rolls over.

With the clear night sky allowing the stars and moonlight to shine bright, Jody can see Marsha standing out on the balcony. Jody ever so gently gets out of bed and quietly walks over to the balcony doors.

Jody whispers to Marsha, "Hey, are you okay?"

Marsha turns around and wipes a tear from her cheek, "Yea. I was just thinking about Anna."

Jody walks up next to Marsha, "I'm sure she's alright."

Marsha sighs, "I just can't help but worry about her."

Jody reaches his right hand around Marsha and places

it on her right shoulder, "Everything is going to be okay, you'll see."

Marsha turns and places her head on Jody's shoulder as she wraps her arms around him, "I'm just so scared. She's all the family I have left."

A few tears run down Marsha's cheeks.

Jody hugs Marsha tight, "Before you know it, you'll be seeing her again and all this will be a bad memory."

Marsha squeezes Jody tight, "I'm sure you're right."

Jody gently runs his hands up and down Marsha's back. Marsha also runs her hands up and down Jody's back.

After a minute, Marsha whispers to Jody, "You know, it's not all going to be a bad memory."

Jody whispers back, "What do you mean?"

Marsha leans back and gazes into Jody's eyes, "I met you." She pauses as her heart beats faster, "I've fallen for you Jody. I think I'm in love with you."

Jody gazes into Marsha's eyes and smiles, "I think I've fallen in love with you too."

With the stars and moon shining bright, the soft sound of music in the distance and the smell of fresh roses and crisp, clean water in the air, the moment becomes too much for Jody and Marsha. Jody closes his eyes and leans in towards Marsha. Marsha closes her eyes and holds her breath. Their lips finally meet as Jody and Marsha embrace and share a passionate, loving and lingering kiss. After a few moments, Jody and Marsha both lean back and smile at each other as they gaze into the other's eyes.

Jody clears his throat and continues to smile at Marsha, "We should get back to sleep. It'll be a long day tomorrow."

Marsha quickly licks her lips, "Yea." She pauses, "I'll be able to sleep better now."

Jody slides his arms from around Marsha and takes her right hand with his left, "Me too."

Jody and Marsha walk back into the room. Marsha gently climbs back into the bed she is sharing with Sherry as Jody gently climbs back into the bed he is sharing with his sister and nephew.

Chapter 25

As the sun shines bright from the clear blue, mid-morning sky, Jennifer, Rein and Ramaf are walking through the camp towards Prince Brian's tent. Prince Brian is sitting in his tent waiting for everyone else to arrive. He closes his eyes and pictures Stephanie's face again, hoping that she is okay. His heart is saddened at the thought of her leaving the Kingdom when they recapture the castle from Gabriela.

Prince Brian opens his eyes when he hears Jennifer's voice from outside his tent, "My lord!"

Prince Brian yells, "Come in!"

Jennifer, Rein and Ramaf walk into the tent and sit down making a small circle with Prince Brian.

Prince Brian questions, "How is the army doing?"

Jennifer replies with a smile, "They're in a relatively optimistic mood my lord. Seems they are looking forward to the next battle."

Rein questions, "What have you been thinking of doing next my lord?"

Prince Brian replies, "We need to take our time heading towards the castle. I don't want to just rush at Gabriela to find out we've fallen into a trap."

Ramaf nods, "Is it a good idea to slow down? What if the children are captured?"

Prince Brian sighs at that thought, "It's a chance we must take." He pauses, "I have no doubt that Gabriela will send a part of her army to meet us in battle as we move towards the castle."

Jennifer nods, "And no doubt with Brytil dead, she will have Regas leading the next army and it will be a much larger army at that."

Rein nods in agreement, "I'm sure of it."

Ramaf questions, "I wonder why she doesn't send her whole army with Choel? He is their Captain."

Prince Brian replies, "Gabriela will no doubt keep at least half her army in the castle along with Choel. She will figure it is better for her to defend than to risk an all out attack."

Jennifer nods, "That's what I would do. Plus, it buys her more time for her dark riders to try to capture the children."

Prince Brian nods with a sad look on his face, "Exactly." He pauses, "Today we will let the army rest. Send scouts towards the castle to see if they can get any information on what Gabriela might be doing."

Jennifer bows her head, "Yes my lord."

Prince Brian smiles, "Now, if you all don't mind, I need some time to myself."

Jennifer, Rein and Ramaf all stand up. They each bow their head and walk out of the tent. Prince Brian lets out a long sigh as he returns his mind to thinking about the woman he has fallen in love with, as he thinks about Stephanie.

With the mid-morning sun shining in the clear blue sky that is dotted by a few soft white clouds and the soft breeze blows the fresh smell of flowers and warm baked pastries all around the streets of Lover's Keep, Jody and the others are walking around the middle of town looking for a supply shop. Many of the townspeople are out and about the town enjoying the beautiful day along with the festive music being played by a group of locals.

The local shopkeepers are calling out to the different people as they pass by trying to get them into their shops.

Stephanie glances around while holding Brendan's hand, "I still can't believe this place."

Brendan smiles, "Yea, it's great here."

Sherry nods, "Now, if we were going to get stuck someplace, this would be the place to get stuck at."

Marsha gently brushes Jody's hand with her hand, "I know I like it here."

Jody looks at Marsha and smiles, "Me too."

At that time, a middle aged man steps out in front of Jody and the others, "Excuse me. I can't help but notice that your outlanders."

Jody nods, "Yes. We're heading to the castle."

The shopkeeper smiles, "Well, a trip that long, you're going to need some food and water, and perhaps other things."

Jody replies, "That's what we're looking for actually."

The shopkeeper smiles, "Then it's your lucky day. I carry all kinds of supplies and a few magical artifacts."

Jody smiles, "We'll start with food and water."

The shopkeeper turns around, "Follow me then."

Jody and the others follow the shopkeeper inside the two story building. The first room opens up into a large room full of furniture with beautiful wood carving designs and silver design trim.

Stephanie smiles, "Wow, I would like some of this stuff in my place. It's beautiful."

The shopkeeper smiles, "Thank you young lady."

The shopkeeper sees a young couple looking at a dresser and a bed, "I need to help this young couple. My supplies are in the back room, please, help yourself."

Jody bows his head, "Thank you."

The shopkeeper walks off. As Jody and the others make their way to the back room, Stephanie takes notice of a full body mirror. The mirror is six feet tall and four feet wide. The mirror's glass is crystal clear. The trim around the mirror is beautiful silver with very elaborate designs. The mirror is no doubt something that would catch anyone's attention with it's beauty and craftsmanship.

Jody and the others walk into the back room to see water flasks and food pouches hanging along the wall and numerous wooden crates full of fresh fruit and vegetables.

Sherry smiles, "It smells wonderful in here."

Jody smiles as he grabs a two quart flask full of water for each of them, "Yes it does. Here are the flasks."

Marsha, Sherry and Stephanie each take a flask and sling it over their shoulder. Jody then grabs four empty pouches and hands one to Stephanie, Marsha and Sherry. Each one of them grabs different pieces of fruit and puts them in their pouches until all the pouches are full.

Jody looks around, "That should be everything we need. We should be getting back to the ferry."

Sherry, Marsha, Stephanie and Brendan follow Jody back into the main room. Stephanie sees the beautiful mirror again and feels a drawing to it.

Stephanie stops, "Look at that mirror over there."

Jody and the others stop and look over to where Stephanie is looking. They see the mirror Stephanie is talking about.

Marsha's eyes widen, "It's beautiful."

At that time, the shopkeeper walks back up, "I see you've noticed my mirror."

Stephanie nods, "It's beautiful."

The shopkeeper smiles, "It's magical."

Sherry looks at the shopkeeper, "What?"

The shopkeeper looks at the group, "Would you like to see?"

Stephanie looks at Jody, "What do you think?"

Jody smiles knowing his sister really likes the mirror,

"Sure, we can take a quick look at it."

Jody and the others follow the shopkeeper over to the mirror. The mirror is even more beautiful up close. Everyone notices what appears to be strange carvings all around the trim of the mirror.

Jody gets a puzzled look, "The carvings, dwarves and Elvin languages?"

The shopkeeper smiles, "Yes. You speak it?"

Jody shakes his head, "No, I just recognize it."

The shopkeeper explains, "This mirror was made for the very first King of this Kingdom. He was unable to find a Queen so the dwarves and elves combined their skills and created this mirror." He pauses, "It's called, True Loves Mirror."

Marsha chuckles, "What?"

The shopkeeper smiles, "It was smuggled out of the castle and brought here just before Gabriela took over." He pauses, "Would you like to try it?"

Sherry smiles, "You're not serious right?"

The shopkeeper smiles, "All you do is step in front of the mirror and close your eyes. You must empty your mind of all thought and when you open your eyes, the image of your true love will appear in the mirror. However, the one looking is the only one that can see the image. The rest of us will just see your reflection."

Marsha shakes her head, "That's crazy."

The shopkeeper smiles again, "So, like to try?"

Sherry shakes her head, "I'm okay."

Marsha glances at Jody, "I don't think I need to."

Jody glances at Marsha and smiles, then looks over at Stephanie, "How about it Steph?"

Stephanie chuckles, "Yea right."

Marsha smiles, "Oh come on, what's it going to hurt."

Stephanie lets out a sigh, "Okay, I'll try it. It better not show me some troll or something."

Jody and the others chuckle as Stephanie steps in front of the mirror and everyone sees her reflection. Stephanie closes her eyes and concentrates on removing all thoughts from her mind. The others just watch. After a minute passes, Stephanie opens her eyes.

A complete look of shock crosses Stephanie's face as she stares at the image in the mirror. She can't believe that the image in the mirror is that of Prince Brian. Jody and the others can tell by the look on Stephanie's face that the mirror must have worked even though all they see is Stephanie's reflection. Stephanie steps out from in front of the mirror quickly.

Sherry questions, "So, did it work?"

Stephanie can't find the words to reply.

Jody smiles, "I would say by her reaction that it worked."

Marsha smiles, "So, who did it show?"

Stephanie still can't speak and continues to stare.

The shopkeeper smiles, "That often happens the first time someone experiences magic on a personal level."

Jody glances around, "Well, we should be getting back to the ferry."

The shopkeeper smiles, "Good luck on your journey."

Jody takes Brendan's hand. Sherry, Marsha and Stephanie, who is still in a little shock, follow Jody and Brendan out of the supply shop. Jody and the others make their way through the incredible town of Lover's Keep back towards the pier where their ferry waits.

Chapter 26

As the sun shines down from the clear, mid-afternoon sky and the cool breeze blows the smell of fresh pine and snow along the road, Stefez and the others clear the top of a hill they were walking up and they see the end of the mountains giving way to the snow lands. The road heads down at a mildly steep angle with rocks and pine trees along each side for about half a mile, then the road flattens out as the rocks all but disappear and all that's left is snow covered ground dotted by underbrush and pine trees. The road is still visible for most part even with the ground being mostly covered with snow.

Stefez sighs, "The snow lands. Hopefully the road be clear enough for us to be able to follow it all the way to Ice Town."

Michael smiles, "Yea, because this is not the land to get lost in."

Bailee chimes in, "Yes, getting lost, bad."

Stefez and the others chuckle at Bailee, then they hear some rustling in the trees around them. Everyone stops and starts to look around.

Anna quickly questions, "What is it?"

Jencent glances in each direction, "Whatever it is, its on both sides of the road."

Michael grabs the handle of his sword, "If I was a betting man, I would say that its not good."

Shaun grabs the handle of her sword as she glances around, "I'd say that would be a safe bet."

The rustling gets louder, then everyone hears some

growling.

Stefez glances over at the others, "Wolves."

Bailee's eyes widen, "Great."

Michael, Shaun and Jencent draw their swords. Stefez takes her staff with both hands.

Stefez steps over next to Anna, "Stay close to me Anna."

Anna glances around, "Okay."

At that moment, three wolves and two mountain lions appear from the left side of the road and three wolves and two mountain lions appear from the right side of the road. Michael steps over by Stefez and the two of them turn and face the wolves and mountain lions on the left. Jencent and Shaun step over and face the wolves and mountain lions on the right. Bailee and Anna stand in the middle of the road between Stefez, Michael, Jencent and Shaun. Anna and Bailee glance left and right to try to keep an eye on all the wolves and mountain lions. Suddenly, the wolves and mountain lions on both side charge the group.

The three wolves move at Michael as the two mountain lions head at Stefez. Stefez starts to mumble under her breath as the mountain lions close in. The other three wolves start at Shaun as the other two mountain lions start for Jencent.

The first wolf charges and leaps at Michael. Michael steps to his right and brings his sword up. As his sword strikes the first wolf in the back legs, the second wolf charges and leaps at him. Michael pulls his sword back quickly and leaps to the right as the second wolf just misses him. As the first wolf lets out a cry of pain and lands on the ground without the use of it's back legs, the third wolf charges at Michael. Michael brings his sword around at the third wolf, but the wolf jumps out of the way as the second wolf lands behind Michael and sees Anna and Bailee.

Bailee's eyes get completely round in shock, "This is

bad Anna."

Michael hears Bailee behind him. Michael holds his sword at the third wolf with his left hand and draws his dagger with his right hand. Michael glances back and throws his dagger at the second wolf. The dagger sticks in the second wolf's back near it's back legs. The second wolf lets out a painful cry. The third wolf, thinking it has an opening, leaps up at Michael. Michael quickly looks back at the third wolf, drops down and rolls to his back. As the third wolf gets above Michael, Michael thrusts his sword up into the third wolf's stomach. The third wolf lands on the ground next to Michael's head.

As the first mountain lion charges in and leaps at Stefez, she lets go of her staff with her right hand but still holding the staff with her left hand, spins to her left and draws her sword with her right hand. As the first mountain lion lands on the ground behind Stefez, the second mountain lion closes in, but doesn't see that Stefez has already completed her spin and is waiting on the second mountain lion with her staff ready. Stefez points her staff at the second mountain lion which is closing in on her.

Stefez speaks with authority in her voice, "Sky fire!"

A bolt of lightning shoots out of Stefez's staff. The bolt of lightning hits the second mountain lion with a thunderous clap. The second mountain lion flies back, slams into a large rock on the side of the road, falls to the ground and stops moving. The first mountain lion charges at Stefez, but Stefez has already turned back around and she sees the first mountain lion charging at her. As the first mountain lion leaps at Stefez, Stefez steps to the left and brings her sword across. The sword leaves a decent, but nonfatal cut along the first mountain lion's right side. As the first mountain lion lands, Stefez turns to face the first mountain lion again.

As the first wolf closes in on Shaun, Shaun holds her

sword with her right hand and draws her dagger with her left hand. The first wolf leaps at Shaun. Shaun quickly steps to her right and thrusts her dagger back at the first wolf. The dagger drives deep into the first wolf's left side. Shaun lets go of the dagger and the first wolf falls to the ground as the second wolf charges in at her. Shaun brings her sword across at the second wolf, but the second wolf jumps out of the way of the sword.

At that time, the third wolf charges by the second wolf and leaps in at Shaun. Shaun steps to her left and cuts upward with her sword. The sword cuts deep across the third wolves belly. The third wolf falls to the ground and lays motionless next to the first wolf which lays motionless with Shaun's dagger buried in it's side. Shaun turns back to face the second wolf.

The first mountain lion charges in and leaps at Jencent. Jencent steps to her left and swings her sword down with her right hand as she draws her short sword with her left hand. The sword strikes the first mountain lion in the back, breaking the first mountain lion's spine. The first mountain lion cries out in pain then crashes to the ground and stops moving. Thinking it has an opening, the second mountain lion charges in at Jencent. Jencent sees the second mountain lion out of the corner of her eye. As the second mountain lion prepares to jump up on Jencent, Jencent drops to her right knee and thrusts her short sword straight at the second mountain lion. The short sword pierces the second mountain lion's chest sending the second mountain lion straight to the ground.

Michael walks towards the second wolf which is unable to use it's back legs due to the dagger Michael threw at it. Michael thrusts his sword down and finishes off the wolf. Michael glances around and sees that the fight is pretty much over. The last wolf facing Shaun and the last mountain lion facing Stefez realize they have no chance and they run off into the trees.

Stefez glances around, "Is everyone okay?"

Michael quickly replies, "I'm good."

Jencent gives a quick nod, "Good."

Shaun puts her sword away, "I'm fine."

Anna smiles and looks down at Bailee, "Bailee and I are okay."

Michael retrieves his dagger and puts his sword and dagger away. Jencent puts her two swords away. Shaun retrieves her dagger and puts it away. Stefez puts her sword away.

Anna chuckles, "That was amazing Stefez. You hit that thing with a bolt of lightning."

Bailee chimes in, "Yea, that mountain lion never saw it coming."

The others smile at what Bailee just said.

Then, Jencent speaks up, "Two got away so you know what that means."

Stefez nods, "They'll tell Gabriela where we're at."

Shaun speaks up, "Which means the dark rider will be back on our trail."

Michael lets out a sigh, "Then we should get moving and put as much distance between us and him as we can."

Everyone takes one last look around, then Stefez and the others start walking north as they leave the mountains behind and enter the snow lands.

As the sun closes in on the evening horizon and the warm breeze blows gently across the river stirring up the smells of fresh water and the trees and leaves of the forest, Jody and the others continue to float north through the forest along the river. Jody is sitting at the back of the ferry steering it along the river. Stephanie and Brendan are sitting in the middle of the ferry. Sherry is sitting at the front of the ferry and Marsha is sitting at the back next to Jody.

Stephanie looks back at Jody, "About where are we?"

Jody thinks for a second, "We got back on the main river from Lover's Keep awhile back so we should be nearing the edge of the forest."

Marsha gazes at Jody with a smile, "What's beyond the forest?"

Jody returns the gaze at Marsha, "The Kingdom opens up into green grass and rolling hills. We shouldn't have to worry about going to Flower Town with the supplies we have. We can continue on to a smaller lake west of Flower Town."

Sherry looks back, "Flower Town?"

Jody smiles, "Yea. It's about the same size as Farhollow, but the entire town is surrounded by fields of flowers, from sunflowers to roses to honeysuckle vines."

Marsha nods slightly, "Wow, I bet it's real pretty and smells nice around that town."

Jody nods and smiles at Marsha, "It is very pretty, but nothing like Lover's Keep."

Sherry looks ahead and speaks, "I think I can see the edge of the forest."

Jody breaks his gaze at Marsha and looks up the river. He sees the trees start to thin out and become less abundant.

Jody nods, "That would be the edge of the forest."

At that moment, the ferry rocks side to side lifting up about three feet as a good size wave moves under the ferry. Everyone grabs a hold of the ferry and looks around with a slightly shocked look.

Stephanie looks back at Jody who is scanning the water around the ferry, "What was that?"

Jody scans the water closely, "I really hope it wasn't a Henom fish."

Marsha looks at Jody, "Is that bad?"

Jody nods as he scans the water, "It's a very large

fish that somehow survives in the shallow water of the river." He pauses, "Unfortunately, it will attack anything moving in the water."

Sherry looks around the water, "Wonderful."

Jody looks back over his shoulder and he sees a five foot long, greenish blue fin sticking up about two feet out of the water.

Jody yells to the others, "Everyone hang on!"

The razor sharp fin of the Henom fish wedges between two of the logs tied together just where Jody and Marsha are sitting. Marsha moves to her right and Jody moves to his left as the fin slides through the ropes holding the logs together. The Henom moves the entire length of the ferry cutting the ropes at both ends. The ferry starts to separate into two pieces. Marsha, Stephanie and Brendan are on one half of the ferry and Jody and Sherry are on the other half of the ferry.

The half with Marsha, Stephanie and Brendan starts to spin slowly out of control since the rudder of the ferry is on the other half with Jody and Sherry. The half with Jody and Sherry starts to move ahead of the half with Marsha, Stephanie and Brendan.

Jody yells to Stephanie, "You won't be able to stay on the part of the ferry much longer before it flips over! You need to quickly get off and get to the bank of the river closest to you!"

Stephanie yells back, "What about you two?!"

Jody yells, "I can still steer us to the bank and we'll make enough motion to try and keep the Henom distracted!"

The piece of ferry with Marsha, Stephanie and Brendan lifts up. Marsha grips her staff tight as Stephanie grabs Brendan's hand. The piece of ferry finally loses all control and flips over sending Marsha, Stephanie and Brendan into the river.

Jody sees the fin of the Henom fish starting back their

way. Jody raises the rudder of the piece of ferry him and Sherry are on and slaps it up and down in the water to try and draw the Henom to them. As Marsha, Stephanie and Brendan struggle towards the east bank of the river, the Henom fish starts towards Jody and Sherry.

As the Henom fish passes under Jody and Sherry, the ferry starts to rock back and forth. Jody feels the rudder shake in his hand, then feels it break off as the Henom fish bites the rudder in half.

Jody shakes his head, "This is not good." He pauses, "Sherry, we're going to flip over!"

Sherry manages to grab her staff as the piece of ferry spins, then rolls over sending Jody and Sherry into the river. Jody quickly emerges and grabs Sherry's hand helping her to the surface. The distraction was enough as Marsha, Stephanie and Brendan hurry out of the river onto the east bank.

Jody and Sherry quickly make their way towards the east bank where Marsha, Stephanie and Brendan are waiting. The Henom fish being so large, slowly makes it's way down the river to a spot where it manages to turn around.

Jody and Sherry move quickly and get about twenty feet from the river bank, when the fin of the Henom fish comes into view.

Marsha yells, "It's coming back! Hurry!"

Jody and Sherry reach a point where they can put their feet down and start running through the water as fast as they can. With the Henom fish just fifty yards away and closing fast, Jody and Sherry are just ten feet from the bank. Jody and Sherry rush out of the water and up next to Stephanie, Marsha and Brendan as the Henom fish swims by.

Stephanie shakes her head, "That was too close."

Jody lets out a sigh, "Well, it got close enough to still hurt us in a couple of ways."

Marsha questions, "What's wrong?"

Jody grabs his food pouch and lifts it up, "I managed to keep everything on me, but most of my food fell out of my pouch."

Stephanie, Marsha and Sherry each check their food pouches and discover the same thing.

Sherry just shakes her head, "Great, what do we do now?"

Jody looks around, "I think it would be best if we just camped here at the edge of the forest for the night and dry out. We'll have to go to Flower Town and get more food."

Stephanie questions, "You said a couple of ways it hurt us, what's the second?"

Jody lets out a sigh, "The fish saw us so now it can tell Gabriela where we're at. Which means the dark rider can pick up our trail again or even catch up to us in Flower Town."

Marsha shakes her head, "Oh this really bites."

Jody looks over at Marsha and can't help but smile, "Yea it does, but we'll manage somehow."

Marsha returns the smile and Jody continues, "Well, lets gather up some wood and get a small fire started. Then, we can eat, dry out and get a little rest."

Jody and the others start walking around and gathering up some firewood.

Chapter 27

The temperature has dropped as the sun is just above the evening horizon. The cold breeze blows the fresh smell of snow and pine all around Stefez and the others as they continue north along the road which is getting harder to see as the sunlight starts to fade.

Stefez looks over at the others, "We're going to have to stop for the night. Its too dangerous to travel at night, we might lose sight of the road and wander off into the snow lands."

Bailee replies, "Yea, lets not do that."

Michael stops and looks around, "I think I see something that might work."

Shaun glances around, "What is it?"

Michael points at a grove of pine trees, "Over there, we can make camp in those pine trees and burn some of the pine wood for the night to help keep warm."

Jencent nods, "Sound good to me. Definitely better than getting lost."

Stefez looks over to where Michael pointed, "That will work. Lets make sure we mark our way from the edge of the road to the trees that way we won't have a problem finding the road in the morning if the weather turns on us tonight."

Michael nods, "Okay. All of you head for the trees. I'll mark a trail behind you."

Stefez and the others start walking towards the trees as Michael pulls out his sword. Michael slowly cuts along the ground through the snow as he makes his way towards the trees. Stefez and the others reach the grove of trees and make their way into the middle of the trees. A minute later, Michael makes his way into the middle of the trees where Stefez and the others are at.

Michael puts his sword away, "I'm going to use some long branches to mark the path I made if you all want to get a fire going."

Stefez nods, "Okay."

Michael picks up five good pine tree branches that had fallen on the ground and walks back out of the grove of trees. Jencent, Shaun and Anna gather up some smaller branches and pile them in the middle of the opening in the middle of the pine trees. Stefez walks over to the pile of limbs and starts mumbling under her breath. A few seconds pass, then Stefez touches the stone on her staff to the pile of limbs and the limbs catch fire. Stefez, Anna, Jencent, Shaun and Bailee sit and wait around the warm fire for Michael to return.

A few minutes pass, then Michael walks back into the camp area. Michael sits down between Jencent and Shaun.

Anna questions between bites of her apple, "How far to Ice Town?"

Stefez replies after taking a bite of her fruit, "We should reach Ice Town by noon unless the weather gets bad."

Shaun speaks up, "We need to let the others know that we're okay and that we're still planning to meet up in Mushroom Farm."

Stefez nods, "I'll send a message to them tomorrow to let them know we're okay and to wait for us if they get there first."

Anna looks a little sad, "I hope they're okay."

Michael speaks up, "I'm sure they're fine. Trust me, we would know about it if Gabriela had captured the child."

Jencent questions, "And how would we know that?"

Stefez replies, "I would be able to feel the torture spells and the influx of magic into the Kingdom as she pulls it out of the child. Its very powerful magic."

Shaun nods interestingly, "Well, I guess that's helpful."

Jencent replies, "Very interesting."

Stefez finishes her fruit, "We should get some rest, it's going to be another long day tomorrow."

Anna wraps her cloak around her, "I can't wait."

Everyone makes themselves as comfortable as they can in the cold and lay down to try and get some sleep.

In the darkness of the night with the half moon high in the night sky filled with stars, Gabriela walks into her magic chamber that is lit up by the soft glow of candles. She walks over to the table where the candles and crystal ball are sitting. She leans her staff against the table and holds her left hand over the crystal ball. Gabriela closes her eyes and starts to mumble under her breath. After a few seconds, the face of Miclou appears in the crystal ball.

Miclou questions in his cold voice, "Yes my Queen?"

Gabriela opens her eyes and replies with her own questions, "Where are you? Have you found the child yet?"

Miclou sighs, "After searching all of Ghost Town, I'm on the road north just about to the mountains. I haven't found them yet and I'm not sure they headed this way."

Gabriela replies, "I heard from my animals. They are in the snow lands right now getting close to Ice Town." She pauses, "So, if the weather stays good, you should be able to reach them in the next day or two."

Miclou quickly nods, "I will travel with utmost haste."

Gabriela smiles, "Good, let me know when you catch them."

Miclou bows his head, "Yes my Queen."

Gabriela closes her eyes and mumbles under her breath again. After a few seconds, the face of Stecher appears in the crystal ball.

Stecher questions in his cold, evil tone, "Yes my Queen?"

Gabriela opens her eyes and replies with her questions again, "Have you found the child yet? Where are you?"

Stecher replies coldly, "I haven't picked up their trail yet. I'm in the forest heading slowly north towards Flower Town."

Gabriela smiles, "Good. I heard from one of my animals that they are by the river at the edge of the forest. You should be able to catch up to them in the next day or two."

Stecher lets out an evil smile, "I'll travel with great haste then."

Gabriela smiles, "Good, let me know when you have them."

Stecher bows his head, "Yes my Queen."

Gabriela removes her hand and the image in the crystal ball disappears.

Gabriela grabs her staff and turns towards the door, "Now to figure out what to do with you Prince Brian."

Gabriela walks out of the room.

As the sun breaks across the morning horizon casting a beautiful reflection off the clear, blue water of Glass Lake, Prince Brian is waiting in his tent for the others to arrive. As he waits, Prince Brian thinks of the battle that he knows will be coming soon. He also thinks about the woman who has completely taken over his heart, he thinks of Stephanie.

A few more minutes pass, then Prince Brian hears Jennifer's voice from outside his tent, "My lord!"

Prince Brian yells, "Come in!"

Jennifer, Rein and Ramaf walk into the tent. The three of them sit down forming a circle with Prince Brian.

Jennifer questions, "So, what is the plan my lord?"

Prince Brian returns his thoughts to the matter at hand, "Lets go ahead and get the army ready to move." He pauses, "We will proceed slowly."

Rein questions, "How far shall we move today?"

Prince Brian replies, "Lets make sure to cover about one third the distance from here to the castle. Then we can setup camp for the night."

Ramaf nods, "My dwarves are already packed and ready to move."

Rein smiles and nods having gained a lot of respect for the dwarves, "So are the elves my lord."

Jennifer chimes in, "We are just about ready. All we need to do is pack up the tents, then we'll be ready to move my lord."

Prince Brian smiles at the responses and how well they each know the way he thinks, "Very good." He looks at Jennifer, "Have them pack up everything, then come get me. They can pack up my tent last. After that, we will get moving."

Jennifer bows her head, "Yes my lord."

Prince Brian looks at Rein and Ramaf, "While Jennifer see to that, each of you pick out two scouts and send them northeast to scout out our route towards the castle."

Rein bows her head, "Yes my lord."

Ramaf bows his head, "It will be done."

Prince Brian nods, "Okay. That's all."

Jennifer, Rein and Ramaf stand up and walk out of the tent. Prince Brian returns his thoughts to the looming battle, but he finds that the thoughts of Stephanie keep intruding which he doesn't seem to mind.

Chapter 28

As the sun peaks in the clear blue sky, the cool breeze blows the fresh smell of snow all around as Stefez and the others continue north on the road towards Ice Town. Before too long, Ice Town comes into view. It is a fairly large town, about the same size as River Fork as far as population. However, the town is more spread out given the fact that all of the buildings are only one story tall. The buildings are either made of stone from the mountains or, very few, are made out of ice blocks.

The people of Ice Town are dressed in fairly nice clothes, except most of them are wearing cloaks or parkas made from animal fur. Ice sculptures are located all throughout the town. Adults are walking around the town going about their daily business as most of the children are playing.

As the group nears the outskirts of Ice Town, Stefez speaks up, "First thing we need to do is get some food and water."

Anna questions, "Are we going to stay here for the night or continue on?"

Jencent speaks up, "Staying here would be the safest thing to do."

Shaun nods, "That is the safest, but I'm sure the dark rider is closing in on us since he doesn't have to stop and rest."

Michael chimes in, "It may be more dangerous, but we really should press on towards North Town. We can get quite a ways before having to stop for the night."

As the group passes by the first few buildings, Bailee speaks up with a sarcastic tone, "Why is it always something dangerous?"

Stefez chuckles slightly, "We can't make things too easy now can we?" She pauses, "Michael's right, we'll continue on after we get some supplies."

The group continues down the main road towards the center of town. Numerous people stop and take notice of the group. Anna keeps her cloak wrapped around her with the hood on so she won't be recognized as an outlander. The people of Ice Town knows there is something different about Stefez and the others, but they are unaware of Anna.

Shaun speaks up as the group enters the town square in the middle of Ice Town which has a large ice sculpture water fountain in the middle of the square, "I think I see a supply shop across the square."

Everyone looks across the square and sees the shop Shaun is talking about. The group starts through the crowd of people heading towards the supply shop.

With the sun in the noon sky that is dotted by pure, white clouds and the warm breeze blowing the incredible smell of fresh flowers across the plush, green rolling hills, Jody and the others continue walking over a small hill and Flower Town comes into view. Flower Town is about the same size as Farhollow. The town is surrounded by fields of sunflowers, roses and honeysuckle vines which fills the air with an amazing aroma.

The town is built mainly out of wood with a few stone buildings, all one story tall. The colors that decorate Flower Town are much more bright and alive than all the other towns except for Lover's Keep. The people are dressed in really nice outfits made from the same bright and alive colors as the banners around town. Most adults are going about their daily business as the children are playing.

Jody and the others start through a field of sunflowers where the sunflowers are about four feet tall.

Marsha speaks up, "These sunflowers are huge."

Jody smiles and replies, "Yea, everything here is a little different." He pauses, "We need to make this fast and find a supply shop that's not in the middle of town."

Stephanie questions, "Why is that?"

Jody sighs, "No doubt the dark rider is back on our trail and closing in on us. Also, this town is the closest town to the castle. It won't be hard for anyone to get word to Gabriela quickly about seeing us."

Marsha nods, "Good points." She pauses and smiles, "Lets try not to get noticed."

Sherry chuckles, "I'm definitely with Marsha on that one."

Jody chuckles slightly, "I don't blame you all for that." He pauses, "In fact, it would probably be best if I take the pouches into the town by myself while all of you wait outside of town for me."

Stephanie smiles, "Anything to keep us from getting noticed."

Stephanie removes her food pouch and hands it to Jody. Marsha and Sherry both do the same.

Jody slings the pouches over his shoulder, "Okay, I won't be long. Just hide down in the sunflowers. Once I get back, we'll head towards the small lake due west."

Stephanie and the others sit down in the field of sunflowers as Jody continues on towards Flower Town.

With the sun starting into the early afternoon sky over the snow lands, Stefez and the others have their supplies and are walking along the road heading west out of Ice Town.

Shaun questions, "How far do you think we'll make it by nightfall?"

Stefez glances around as they walk by the last couple of buildings heading out of town, "If the weather stays nice like this, we should be able to get nearly halfway to the mountains."

Anna just sighs, "More mountains?"

Bailee chimes in, "I hear you girl. Short legs like mine make it rough hopping through mountains."

Everyone gets a good laugh at Bailee's words. Stefez looks around some more and Michael notices what Stefez is doing.

Michael questions, "Stefez, is everything okay? You keep glancing around like you're looking for something."

Stefez notices a group of pine trees, "And I found what I was needing."

The others look to the north and see the grove of pine trees Stefez is looking at.

Shaun questions, "Okay, and you needed those for what?"

Stefez looks at the others, "Just wait here. I'm going to go and send a message on the wind to let Jody and the others know where we're at and that we're still planning to meet in Mushroom Farm."

Anna questions, "Why can't you just do that here?"

Stefez smiles, "It's a complicated thing, plus, the wind likes to keep things private."

Anna nods, "Oh, okay."

Stefez smiles, "You all just relax. I'll only take a few minutes."

Stefez walks off towards the pine trees as the rest of the group moves off to the side of the road and waits.

As the sun shines down on the sunflower field where Stephanie and the others are waiting, the three woman start to get a little nervous about Jody being gone for as long as he has.

Stephanie whispers to the others, "I hate not having Jody here."

Sherry nods and whispers, "Me too. It's like I just expect the dark rider guy to show up now."

Marsha sighs and whispers, "I don't even want to think about that."

Stephanie can tell that Marsha and Sherry are worried so she tries to change the subject, "So Marsha, what's up with you and Jody?"

Marsha tries not to smile, but can't help it, "What do you mean?"

Sherry whispers, "Please girl."

Marsha shakes her head and whispers, "I really think I'm in love with him." She pauses, "We kissed on the balcony of our room in Lover's Keep when all of you were asleep."

Stephanie's eyes widen and she smiles, "What?"

Sherry smiles, "You kidding? How was it?"

Marsha licks her lips and smiles big, "It was amazing. I didn't want it to end."

Stephanie smiles, "That's so cool."

Then, all of them hear footsteps approaching.

Brendan looks at Stephanie, "Mom?"

Stephanie reaches over and grabs the handle of her sword, "I don't know honey. I hope it's Jody."

The footsteps get closer, but they are moving around like whatever or whoever it is, is looking for someone or something. Stephanie and the others hold their breath and try to be as quiet as possible.

Finally, Stephanie and the others hear Jody's voice, "Steph, where are you?"

Stephanie lets out the breath she was holding, "Over here!"

Stephanie stands up and sees Jody about twenty feet away. Jody walks over as Marsha, Sherry and Brendan stand up.

Jody starts passing the food pouches back, "Well, the shopkeeper looked at me funny for having so many pouches, but didn't say anything."

Sherry slings the pouch over her shoulder, "So, what now?"

Jody glances around to make sure no one is watching, "We'll head west towards the lake. We can camp there for the night."

Brendan smiles, "Cool."

Everyone smiles and chuckles at Brendan's youthful enthusiasm. Then, Jody and the others start walking west.

Chapter 29

A s the sun gets lower in the evening sky, Prince Brian and his army continues to move slowly northwest towards the castle. Prince Brian is riding at the front of the army. He looks around at the landscape, then he looks up at the sky to see where the sun is at. Prince Brian stops his horse and holds up his right hand. Jennifer, Rein and Ramaf who are about thirty feet behind Prince Brian, ride up next to him.

Jennifer questions, "Something wrong my lord?"

Prince Brian looks over at Jennifer, "Nothing wrong. We'll stop here and setup camp for the night." He pauses, "I'm guessing we made it about a third of the way to the castle."

Rein nods, "That's about what I figure my lord."

Prince Brian glances around, "Jennifer, see to it that camp is setup. Rein, send a couple scouts out to make sure no one is around the area. Ramaf, get a guard detail setup for the night."

Jennifer, Rein and Ramaf bow their heads and ride off. Prince Brian dismounts and stands next to his horse. He looks around at the rolling green hills and closes his eyes. He lets the warm, soft breeze gently blow across his face as he breathes in deeply. He pictures Stephanie's face and wonders how she is doing. He smiles at the thoughts of the women he has totally fallen for. Prince Brian is unsure how long he has been standing there with his eyes closed, but he starts to hear the noises of camp being set up. Prince Brian opens his eyes, takes his horse, turns around and starts walking back towards his army and his camp.

As the sun gets closer to the evening horizon, the breeze across the snow lands has picked up and the temperature has started to drop. Stefez and the others continue to walk west along the road heading towards the mountains and eventually North Town.

Anna speaks up as she holds the cloak closed around her, "I'm starting to get cold."

Shaun nods and speaks up, "The temperature is going to get even worse as the sun sets."

Michael chimes in, "We should probably find a place to stop for the night."

Stefez stops walking and glances around. She sees a few different small groups of pine trees and rocks.

Stefez sighs, "This is as good a place as any. Lets move over to a group of trees and get a fire started."

Bailee speaks up, "A campfire sounds great right about now. I like warmth."

The others smile at Bailee. Stefez starts walking over to a group of trees about fifty feet from the road. Everyone follows her. The group weaves their way into the trees until they find an opening suitable for a camp. They gather up some branches and start a campfire in the middle of the clearing. Everyone sits down and grabs something to eat.

After a minute, Stefez speaks up, "When we reach the mountains, I think it would be best if we take the ice caverns instead of the road through the mountains."

Jencent looks at Stefez, "Are you sure? People get lost in the ice caverns all the time."

Stefez sighs, "It might be a little more dangerous, but it's a lot faster than taking the road through the mountains and time is starting to work against us."

Shaun questions, "How is that?"

Stefez replies after taking a bite of fruit, "If we take too long to get to Mushroom Farm and the others get there and have to wait awhile on us. The dark rider might catch up to them and they won't have anywhere to escape to."

Michael nods in agreement, "I see what you're saying and you're right."

Bailee speaks up, "Something dangerous always has to come up. I'll be happy when Prince Brian is back in control of the Kingdom."

Stefez, Shaun, Michael and Anna chuckle at Bailee as Jencent just sits quietly and shakes her head slightly.

Stefez finishes her fruit, "Well, we better get some rest. Another long walk waits for us tomorrow."

Anna lays back, "I can't wait."

Everyone else finishes up eating and gets as comfortable as they can for another cold night in the snow lands.

Jody and the others continue to walk west as the sun is nearly set. The warm breeze blows the smell of the fresh water of the lake all around them.

Jody smiles, "The lake should be just over this next hill."

Marsha smiles, "Good, I'm ready to take a break from walking."

Brendan sighs, "Me too. I'm tired."

Jody smiles at Brendan, "You want a piggy back ride the rest of the way big man?"

Brendan smiles, "Yea Uncle Jody."

Stephanie chuckles and shakes her head. Brendan walks over and climbs on Jody's back. Jody stands back up, looks at Stephanie and smiles.

Jody speaks up, "Alright, hang on big man."

Marsha just gazes at Jody and smiles unable to help how she feels for him. It only takes a few minutes, then the group tops the hill and sees the lake about a hundred yards in front of them.

Sherry lets out an exhausted sigh, "That's a wonderful sight."

The others chuckle and Jody speaks up, "You ready to run big man."

Brendan gets a big smile, "Yea!"

Jody sprints off towards the lake. Stephanie smiles and shakes her head at the two boys. Marsha gazes at Jody and smiles. Sherry lets out a slight chuckle.

Marsha speaks to Stephanie and Sherry, "He's so wonderful."

Stephanie nods in agreement, "He's the best and definitely one of a kind."

Jody and Brendan reach the lake and stop. Jody lets Brendan down and the two of them wait for the women to arrive. Jody gathers up some small pieces of wood laying around and starts working on a fire as Stephanie, Sherry and Marsha arrive.

Brendan looks at his mom, "That was fun."

Stephanie smiles at her son as Sherry and Marsha let out a good laugh. It doesn't take Jody long to get a small fire going. Jody sits down by the fire and pulls out a piece of fruit.

Jody looks at Brendan, "Here you go big guy."

Brendan grabs the fruit and sits next to Jody. Marsha sits down on the other side of Jody and pulls out a piece of fruit. Stephanie sits next to Brendan and Sherry sits next to Marsha. Everyone starts eating.

After a couple minutes, Stephanie questions, "So, what's the plan for tomorrow?"

Jody takes a drink and replies, "We'll head north now

towards the swamp."

Sherry looks at Jody, "Swamp?"

Jody smiles and nods, "Oh yea." He pauses, "And it's about as fun as it sounds."

Marsha shakes her head, "Wonderful."

Jody looks over at Marsha and smiles, "Yea, but it's the safest way to get to Mushroom Farm without getting seen."

Stephanie speaks up, "Well, I'll take anything over that and having to deal with that dark rider guy."

Sherry chimes in, "Me too."

Everyone finishes eating.

Brendan looks at Stephanie, "I'm tired mom."

Stephanie nods, "Me too big guy. Why don't you lay down."

Brendan lays down next to Stephanie. Sherry is the next to make herself comfortable.

Stephanie looks at Jody and whispers, "Thank you for everything."

Jody gets a puzzled look, but smiles at his sister. Stephanie lays down and puts her arm around Brendan. Jody lays on his back and looks up at the now dark sky filling with stars. Marsha lays down next to Jody, rolls over next to him and puts her right arm across his chest.

Marsha whispers to Jody, "You don't mind do you."

Jody looks at Marsha and gazes into her eyes, "Definitely not. In fact, I was kind of hoping to lay with you."

Marsha closes her eyes, "Umm, that's what I was hoping for too."

Jody closes his eyes. It doesn't take long for everyone to drift off to sleep.

In the darkness of the night, Gabriela sits in the

throne room that is lit up by a row of candles on each side of the room. The large doors open and Choel walks into the throne room. He walks across the large room and up the ten steps to where Gabriela is sitting in one of the throne chairs.

Choel kneels, "You wanted to see me my Queen?"

Gabriela nods, "Yes. How is it going with the army?"

Choel looks up at Gabriela, "The army is suited up and armed. They are ready for battle. Regas has made sure of it."

Gabriela smiles, "Good. My dark riders are back on the trails of the children. Our scouts have told us where Prince Brian is at. I want to send half of the army in the castle southeast towards Prince Brian. I want Regas to lead that army."

Choel nods, "I'll see to it my Queen."

Gabriela continues, "I want you to have the rest of the army ready in case Regas fails and Prince Brian continues on to the castle."

Choel bows his head, "It will be done my Queen."

Gabriela smiles, "Good. Have Regas and the army ready tomorrow. I'll address them myself." She pauses, "You can go now."

Choel bows his head, "Yes my Queen."

Choel stands up and walks back down the stairs and across the room. Once Choel exit's the room, Gabriela looks over and stares out one of the large open windows of the throne room.

Gabriela speaks while staring at the night sky, "Soon you will be mine children and soon Prince Brian you will be defeated." She pauses, "This is my Kingdom."

Chapter 30

As the sun peaks in the high noon sky, the cool breeze blows gently across the snow lands. The fresh smell of pine fills the air. Stefez and the others continue to walk west along the road towards the mountains.

As they walk, Anna questions, "So, will the wind tell us about the others like the message birds do?"

Stefez shakes her head, "It will if they send us a reply."

Shaun knows Anna is worried, "I'm sure Marsha and the others are okay."

Anna sighs, "I know. It's just …" She pauses, "Marsha is all the family I've got. Our parents died five years ago and Marsha has pretty much raised me since."

Michael nods and tries to sound reassuring, "I know Jody will take care of them."

Jencent finally speaks up, "Everyone has a lot to lose right now. We just have to stay focused on the task at hand."

Bailee chimes in, "It's going to work out, you'll see Anna."

Michael finally shows some emotion, "I sure hope so too. Having seen Rein definitely makes me want to be with her again." He pauses, "They have quite a battle ahead of them against Gabriela's army."

Stefez nods, "They sure do, but Prince Brian knows what he's doing. Plus, Rein is a very capable fighter. You don't get to be Queen of the elves without being a great leader and warrior."

Michael smiles, "Boy is that right."

Anna looks at Stefez, "What about you Stefez? What do you have to lose out of all this?"

Stefez sighs, "Gabriela is my sister and what she did ruined my family's name and standing with the elves and humans. Helping to restore Prince Brian to the throne will help restore my family's name." She pauses, "Not to mention bringing peace to the Kingdom."

Anna looks over at Shaun, "How about you Shaun?"

Shaun smiles, "I've been a ranger my whole life, living off the land and traveling the Kingdom. However, the Kingdom was a safer place before Gabriela took control. Plus, Gabriela knows that the rangers are against her and many joined Prince Brian's army." She pauses, "Our people can return to our natural way of life with Prince Brian back in control of the Kingdom."

Anna smiles and looks at Jencent, "What about you Jencent?"

Jencent is quiet for a few seconds, then replies, "I don't really have much to lose. Being a mercenary is beneficial no matter who is in control."

Anna lets out a sigh and looks down at Bailee, "I bet even you have something to lose, don't you Bailee?"

Bailee replies quickly, "More than you know. It's just that I can't tell you." She pauses, "I'm sorry Anna."

Anna smiles, "Oh, that's okay Bailee."

Jencent just shakes her head wondering what a rabbit could possibly have to lose.

Stefez speaks up while glancing around, "Lets take a short break and eat. We should reach the mountains and the entrance to the ice caverns by sunset."

Bailee chimes in, "A carrot sounds good to me."

Everyone chuckles at Bailee's response as they move off to the side of the road.

The warm breeze blows across the rolling hills as the noon sun shines down from the clear, blue sky dotted by a few puffy, white clouds. Jody and the others continue walking north towards the swamp.

While walking Stephanie questions, "So, will we reach the swamp today?"

Jody nods, "Yea. We'll stop at the edge of the swamp and camp for the night." He pauses, "Hopefully we'll hear something from the others soon."

Marsha walks up next to Jody and takes his left hand with her right hand, "I hope so."

Jody reassuringly squeezes Marsha's hand, "I'm sure Anna is just fine."

Marsha smiles at Jody, "Thanks."

Stephanie speaks up, "I hope Prince Brian is okay. This plan really depends on them."

Sherry looks over at Stephanie and smiles, "I'm sure you're not just worried about the plan, are you?"

Stephanie tries not to smile, "What do you mean?"

Jody shakes his head, "Come on now. We all know how much you like Prince Brian."

Stephanie gets a little embarrassed, "Sure, I like him a lot."

Jody looks at Stephanie, "So, he was the one you saw in the true love mirror in Lover's Keep, isn't he?"

Stephanie smiles, but doesn't say anything.

Marsha smiles at Stephanie, "Shut up. He totally is the one you saw in the mirror."

Stephanie finally nods, "Yea. It was him." She pauses, "But it's just a silly mirror."

Jody shakes his head, "Oh no, it's a magical mirror and magic is very precise."

Stephanie takes a deep breath, "But that doesn't mean he loves me."

Sherry speaks up, "Yea right. How could he not?

You're such an awesome person and beautiful at that."

Stephanie smiles, "Thanks."

Suddenly, the wind starts to pick up. Jody stops walking. Stephanie and the others stop and look around as the wind is blowing extremely hard now and starts to create a vortex around them.

Brendan looks at Stephanie, "Mom, what is it?"

Stephanie shakes her head, "I don't know Brendan."

Jody can tell the others are worried, "It's okay. We're about to get a message from the wind."

Marsha looks at Jody, "Huh?"

Jody nods, "Stefez must have sent us a message."

The vortex of wind gets closer around them and the wind makes a howling sound. After a few more seconds, the vortex stops and the face of an older man appears in front of them. The face is about three feet tall and has flowing hair and a beard with a mustache. The face appears transparent.

The wind speaks in a powerfully deep voice, "I have a message from Stefez."

Jody bows his head, "Please, may I have the message master wind?"

The wind speak again, "Stefez and the others are okay. They still wish to meet up in Mushroom Farm. They are still in the snow lands traveling west."

Jody bows his head, "Thank you master wind. May I send a message back to them?"

The wind replies, "Yes. What is the message?"

Jody speaks, "Let them know that we're okay and nearly to the swamp. We'll meet them in Mushroom Farm and wait for them there if we arrive before them."

The wind replies, "It will be done."

Jody bows his head, "Thank you master wind."

The face starts to disappear and the vortex returns. After a few seconds of the vortex and strong winds, the wind goes calm once again.

Jody looks at the others, "Well, that's good news."

Stephanie, Sherry and Marsha are just staring at where the face of the wind was at, not able to believe what they just saw.

Brendan finally speaks up, "That was cool!"

Jody smiles and nods, "It sure is big man."

Stephanie finally speaks up, "Wow, that was amazing."

Marsha shakes her head, "I still can't believe what I just saw."

Sherry chuckles, "This place is just crazy."

Jody chuckles at their responses, "Well, now we know they're okay and soon they'll know the same about us." He pauses, "We should get moving again."

Stephanie, Sherry and Marsha just nod. The group starts walking north towards the swamp again.

The sun starts to pass through the evening sky casting shadows across the castle. The tall castle walls are made of thick six foot by six foot ivory colored stones and reach up thirty feet high. In each of the corners of the castle wall are forty foot tall, round towers. Along the south wall is a large, twenty foot high by twenty foot wide wooden set of doors. Through the doors in the front of the castle is a very large, open courtyard which once was beautifully covered in trees, bushes and flowers, but is now dominated by vines and overgrowth. In the back of the castle is a large horse stables and open field where the army of Gabriela is waiting. The castle is a massive structure made of ivory colored stone once decorated in bright banners and colors, but now has a dreary look about it. The hill the castle sits atop is twice as tall as all the other hills around. Surrounding the castle and the hill it sits atop is a town larger than any other in the Kingdom.

Choel is standing at the front of the large army of trolls, decomposing elves and decomposing humans. Standing next to Choel is another man. The man has a light Hispanic complexion and stands about 5'10" tall and weighs a stout 175 pounds. He looks to be in his mid-thirties. He is bald with brown eyes. He has pieces of shiny armor covering his chest, arms and thighs. He is wearing a four foot long, gold handle with shiny silver bladed sword on his left hip and is carrying a three foot long, shiny silver shield in his left hand.

Gabriela walks up to Choel, "Is the army ready?" She looks at the other man, "And are you ready Regas?"

Choel bows his head, "The army is ready my Queen."

Regas bows his head, "I am ready too my Queen."

Gabriela nods her head, "Good. Our scouts tell me that Prince Brian has set up camp. Regas, I want you to take half of our army and leave the castle at first light traveling southeast." She pauses, "If Prince Brian breaks camp at dawn, you should meet him about halfway between here and Lakeway."

Regas bows his head, "Yes my Queen."

Gabriela looks at Choel, "I want you to have the rest of the army ready and waiting here in the castle."

Choel bows his head, "Yes my Queen."

Gabriela smiles, "Good. Choel, let me know first thing in the morning when Regas has left the castle."

Choel bows his head again, "Yes my Queen."

Gabriela smiles, turns and walks off. Choel and Regas turn back to the army to get everything ready for the next day.

Chapter 31

As the sun sets over Prince Brian's camp, Jennifer, Rein and Ramaf make their way towards Prince Brian's tent. Prince Brian is sitting in his tent waiting for the others to arrive. As he sits, he thinks of the battle that lays ahead. He is almost certain Gabriela will send another smaller army after them before they reach the castle. He also thinks about what it's going to take once they reach the castle and how hard it will be to break through the castle defenses.

Prince Brian also has something else on his mind. Its something that always seems to be there in the back of his mind and usually finds it's way into his main thoughts. He thinks about Stephanie. He hopes that she is okay. He smiles as he thinks about her and the chance of seeing her again when all the battles are over.

Prince Brian hears Jennifer's voice, "My lord, its us!"

Prince Brian replies, "Come in!"

Jennifer, Rein and Ramaf walk into the tent. Jennifer and the others sit down to make a circle.

Prince Brian questions, "Have the scouts reported anything important?"

Rein shakes her head, "No my lord. No signs of Gabriela's army."

Prince Brian nods, "Good. We should be able to get a good night's rest then."

Jennifer questions, "What is the plan now my lord?"

Prince Brian sighs, "We will break camp at dawn. As the camp is being packed up to move, we'll take the army ahead to the northwest towards the castle."

Ramaf questions, "How far do you think we can make it tomorrow?"

Prince Brian smiles, "If I was going to guess, I would think Gabriela will send part of her army towards us. No doubt with her animal spies she knows where we're at."

Jennifer questions, "How many soldiers do you want to take with us and how many will stay with the camp?"

Prince Brian replies, "We'll take all the soldiers. We're at the point now that victory is more important than protecting the camp. We can't afford not to win and to do so, we'll need every soldier we have to fight."

Rein nods, "So, from here on, each battle will either take us one step closer to regaining the Kingdom or Gabriela will stay in control forever."

Ramaf nods in agreement, "Risky, but I see Prince Brian's point. It's too risky to split up the army now and especially this close to the castle."

Prince Brian smiles at the trust they show in him, "Go ahead and let the army and the others know what the plan is for tomorrow." He pauses, "I'll see you all just before dawn."

Jennifer, Rein and Ramaf all bow their heads. The three of them stand up and walk out of the tent. Prince Brian lets out a sigh, closes his eyes and smiles as he returns to the thoughts of Stephanie.

With the sun nearly set, the temperature dropping by the minute and the cold breeze starting to pick up, Stefez and the others have left the main road and started looking for the entrance into the ice caverns. They have left the snow lands and started into the mountain range again. Once again, large rocks and pine trees dot the landscape as the huge mountains stretch high into the sky.

Anna questions while hugging her cloak around her, "How much further?"

Stefez looks around, "Not very far. Maybe a couple hundred more yards."

Bailee chimes in, "Good. I'm starting to freeze."

Anna agrees, "Me too."

The group continues along, then the entrance to the ice caverns comes into view. It is a cave entrance about ten feet high and eight feet wide that leads straight into the side of the mountains. The group walks up to the entrance to the ice caverns. Michael draws his sword and walks into the entrance first. Shaun draws her sword and follows Michael. Stefez, Anna and Bailee are next into the entrance. Finally, Jencent draws her sword, looks around and walks into the entrance.

Now out of the cold breeze, they all can feel it getting a little warmer. The group walks about a hundred yards into the cavern and it opens up into a large, sixty foot by sixty foot chamber. The rock walls and ceiling of the chamber is dotted with large ice sickles.

Michael looks over at Stefez, "What do you think?"

Stefez nods her head, "This will do for the night. We can get some rest and get a fresh start tomorrow."

Bailee speaks up, "That sounds good to me."

Shaun puts her sword away, "What are we going to do for a fire? I don't see any wood laying around."

Stefez glances around, "Lets get a good sized rock and place it in the middle of the chamber. I can make it glow with one of my spells." She pauses, "It won't be as warm, but it'll have to do for the night."

Michael walks around and finds a rock. He places it in the middle of the chamber. Stefez walks over to the rock and touches the stone on the end of her staff to the rock. As Stefez mumbles under her breath, Michael, Shaun, Jencent and Anna all sit down around the rock. After a few seconds, Stefez removes her staff and the rock starts to glow a dull, fire red. The chamber starts to warm up a little, but not much.

Stefez sits down and grabs a piece of fruit, "It should take us a little over a day to get through the ice caverns. We should reach North Town by nightfall on the second day."

Jencent speaks up, "Given we don't get lost in the ice caverns."

Bailee speaks up, "Lets think positive, okay."

Shaun chuckles at Bailee, "I'm not worried about getting lost. I'm more concerned with the dark rider catching up to us."

Michael finishes his fruit, "If he was after us, he is probably on the main road. We did a good job of concealing our tracks when we left the road and started towards the caverns. He may not find us."

Bailee chimes in, "See, positive thinking. I like it."

Everyone chuckles at Bailee.

Jencent finishes eating, "Maybe we threw him off, but the dark rider is very good at tracking."

Stefez nods and looks at Jencent, "True. We need to keep are senses open just in case he finds us."

Anna finishes eating, "Well, I think its time for me to get some rest. I'm really tired."

Stefez smiles at Anna, "Me too."

Everyone lays down and gets as comfortable as they can. Bailee hops over next to Anna. Anna opens her cloak and lets Bailee get inside her cloak to help stay warm. It doesn't take long for everyone to fall asleep, everyone except Jencent.

———

The sun has nearly set and the warm breeze has all but stopped as Jody and the others continue walking north towards the swamp.

Sherry questions, "How much further would you say it is?"

Jody glances around, "Not much." He pauses, "Can you smell that?"

Stephanie, Sherry and Marsha catch the smell Jody is talking about. The fresh smell of grass and flowers has given way to mucky water and rotting mushrooms.

Marsha looks over at Jody, "I take it that's the swamp."

Jody nods, "Oh yes."

Stephanie shakes her head, "We have to smell that the entire time we're traveling to Mushroom Farm?"

Jody nods and sighs, "Unfortunately, that's what we get to smell the next two days or so."

Stephanie chuckles sarcastically, "Wonderful."

Then, everyone sees the beginning of the swamp just ahead of them. They can see the weeping willow trees as the sun is just about to disappear.

Jody speaks up, "Lets go ahead and stop here for the night. The swamp is no place to try and travel through at night."

Sherry stops and glances around, "Sounds good to me."

Jody looks at Brendan, "How you doing big guy?"

Brendan smiles, "I'm tired Uncle Jody."

Jody smiles back, "Me too." He pauses, "It's pretty warm tonight. I don't think we need a fire. Besides, this close to the castle and still in the open grasslands, a fire can be seen for a long ways."

Stephanie sits down and grabs a piece of fruit, "Yea, the less attention the better."

Brendan sits down next to Stephanie and grabs a piece of fruit. Sherry sits down and starts eating. Jody and Marsha sit down next to each other and also start eating. Everyone is quiet for a few minutes until they are finished eating.

Stephanie lets out a long tiring sigh, "I think it's time to stretch out."

Sherry chuckles, "I whole heartedly agree."

Stephanie lays down and tries to get comfortable, "I can't wait until I have a comfortable bed to sleep in."

Marsha jokes with Stephanie, "A comfortable bed, with a comfortable person in it?"

Stephanie chuckles, "Marsha."

Sherry chimes in, "Hey, nothing wrong with having an extra comfortable pillow so to speak."

Stephanie laughs, "You guys are crazy."

Marsha, Jody and Sherry get a nice laugh. Brendan lays down next to Stephanie. Sherry lays down and does her best to get comfortable. Marsha lays down and rolls over to her left side, trying to get comfortable. Jody lays down and moves up against Marsha's back.

Jody slides his right arm around Marsha's waist, "You don't mind do you?"

Marsha snuggles against Jody, "Heck no."

Marsha takes Jody's right hand with her right hand.

Jody kisses Marsha on the cheek, "Goodnight beautiful."

Marsha just smiles, "Sweet dreams."

Before too long, everyone drifts off to sleep.

———————

In the darkness of the midnight hour, Gabriela walks into her magic chamber as the small, emerald ring on her left hand is softly glowing.

Gabriela walks over to the table, "Someone is trying to contact me." She leans her staff against the table, "I hope this is good news."

Gabriela closes her eyes, holds her right hand over the crystal ball and starts to mumble under her breath. The crystal ball gets cloudy, but no image appears.

Gabriela opens her eyes, "This is difficult. No doubt some sort of magic is trying to conceal who this is."

Gabriela closes her eyes again. She concentrates even harder and begins to mumble under her breath. The crystal ball continues to get cloudy and after another few seconds, the image of the person trying to contact Gabriela appears in the crystal ball. It is the face of Jencent.

Gabriela opens her eyes and smiles, "I was wondering when I was going to hear from you."

Jencent glances around, "I don't have much time. They keep a close eye on me and Stefez is using magic to shield us."

Gabriela nods, "I figured as much. What do you have?"

Jencent replies in a whisper, "Tell Miclou that we left the main road and are just inside the entrance to the ice caverns." She pauses and glances around, "We are planning to meet the other group in Mushroom Farm. As far as I know, Stefez hasn't changed the plan without us knowing."

Gabriela nods, "I see. Prince Brian attacks from the southeast so they can sneak into the castle from the northwest."

Jencent nods, "Yes. I'll try to contact you again if something changes." She glances around as if she heard something, "I have to go."

Gabriela gives a quick nod and removes her hand from the crystal ball. Gabriela smiles as she grabs her staff.

Gabriela turns and starts towards the door, "I will have you soon enough my children."

Gabriela lets out a laugh as she walks out of the magic chamber.

Chapter 32

J ust before the sun breaks the morning horizon, the temperature is still very cold, but being in the chamber leading into the ice caverns, Stefez and the others are unable to feel the breeze. However, with the temperature already cold, the group is unable to also feel the approach of someone they were hoping wouldn't find them.

As the group gathers up their things, Shaun speaks up, "I didn't notice last night, but there are three different tunnels leading out of the chamber."

Bailee speaks up, "Great, which one do we take?"

Stefez smiles, "Don't worry. I've been through the ice caverns before."

Then, they all hear Miclou's voice from the entrance into the chamber, "And you may live long enough to travel them again if you give me the child!"

Stefez and the others turn to the entrance of the chamber with a shocked look on their faces, not wanting to believe that the dark rider found them. Miclou stands at the entrance to the chamber like a ghostly apparition with his sword in his right hand.

Anna speaks up, "So much for losing him by leaving the road."

Michael draws his sword, "Any ideas?"

Shaun draws her sword, "We better come up with something quick."

Miclou slowly shakes his head, "That would be a grave mistake. Hand over the child and I shall let you live."

Jencent draws her sword, "Tell me you have a plan Stefez?"

Miclou takes a step towards the group.

Stefez takes Anna's hand and pulls Anna behind her, "Stay behind me Anna."

Bailee speaks up, "I hope the plan is more than that."

Stefez glances around as Miclou takes another step closer, "Umm, run middle tunnel!"

Without hesitation, Stefez and Anna take off running into the middle tunnel. Bailee hops as fast as she can right behind Stefez and Anna. Jencent and Shaun take off as fast as they can with Michael right behind them. Miclou sprints after them and slowly starts to gain on the group.

Jencent yells while running, "Okay, what now?!"

Stefez yells back, "Just keep running and don't lose me or you'll get lost!"

Bailee chimes in while hopping fast, "Great!"

The eight foot tall by six foot wide tunnel with ice sickles hanging from the ceiling continues straight for about two hundred feet then opens up into another large chamber covered in ice. The footing gets slippery as the group runs into the large chamber.

Stefez yells as she starts across the chamber towards another tunnel on the far side, "Watch your footing!"

Halfway across the chamber, Michael hits a patch of ice and loses control of his balance. Michael falls and slides across the ground still heading towards the tunnel the others are nearly at.

Shaun stops and looks back, "Michael!"

Shaun puts her sword away and grabs her bow from her back and draws an arrow as Michael gets back to his feet. Michael starts running again right at Shaun who draws her bow back and aims at the far tunnel the group came running out of.

Shaun yells, "Duck!"

As Miclou runs into the chamber, Shaun releases her

arrow. Michael ducks low just in time as the arrow flies past his head straight at Miclou. Miclou sees the arrow flying at him and brings his sword up fast as he leans to his left. Miclou cuts the arrow from the air, but in doing so he loses his balance on the icy ground and wipes out.

As Miclou looks up and starts to get to his feet, he sees the group run into the tunnel on the far side of the chamber. Miclou quickly gets to his feet and starts after the group again. The tunnel goes on for another six hundred feet, bends to the left and goes on for another two hundred feet, then opens up into another large chamber covered in ice. On the far side of the chamber is four tunnels.

Stefez starts across the chamber as carefully and fast as she can, "Second tunnel from the left!"

Anna stays right behind Stefez and Bailee is right behind Anna. Jencent is still a few feet behind Anna and Bailee. Shaun is about twenty feet behind Jencent and Michael is ten feet behind Shaun. Jencent puts her sword away so she can run faster. As Shaun enters the chamber, she slings her bow back across her back.

As Stefez, Anna, Bailee and Jencent get nearly to the other side of the chamber, Shaun who is halfway, slips on a patch of ice and falls to her knees. Keeping control of her body, Shaun slides on her knees towards the tunnel the others are running for. Michael catches up to Shaun and grabs her left arm with his right hand. Shaun hops up as Michael pulls up on her arm and Shaun lands on her feet. Stefez and the others start into the tunnel with Shaun and Michael not far behind.

As Michael and Shaun start into the tunnel, Miclou enters the chamber and sees which tunnel Shaun and Michael run into. Miclou starts his way across the chamber after the group that has managed to keep a lead on the dark rider. The tunnel goes straight for three hundred feet, then starts to slope downwards. Stefez slows up and comes to a stop. Anna, Bailee and Jencent stops right behind Stefez.

Jencent quickly speaks while catching her breath, "Why are we stopped?"

Stefez taps her staff on the ground and mumbles under her breath. The stone on the end of her staff starts to glow and lights up the tunnel as Shaun and Michael come running up and slide to a stop next to the others. Everyone now sees why Stefez stopped. The tunnel drops off in front of them at a downward, sixty degree angle. In the wall of the tunnel is an iron ring with a rope tied to it. The rope heads off down the slope in the tunnel.

Anna quickly questions, "What now?"

Shaun looks back, "He's getting closer."

Stefez grabs the rope, "We'll use this to make our way down the slope. At the bottom, the tunnel breaks off into three tunnels. If you slip off the rope and slide down, make sure you get into the right tunnel."

Stefez grabs the rope and starts making her way down the slope. Anna grabs the rope and starts down after Stefez. Jencent starts down the rope next. Shaun picks up Bailee and puts the rabbit in her food pouch, then starts down the rope. Michael, still with his sword in his left hand, grabs the rope, then looks back. Michael sees the outline of Miclou closing in fast, no more than a hundred feet away.

Michael shakes his head, "He's too close! Everyone hold on and get ready to slide!"

Michael swings his sword down, cutting the rope loose at the iron ring. Michael turns to the tunnel and dives feet first down the icy slope. Stefez and the others feel the rope get cut loose and they all start to pick up speed quickly as they start to slide down the icy slope. The screams from everyone fills the tunnel as Miclou reaches the top of the slope.

Miclou puts his sword away, "They are crazy."

Miclou squats down and pushes himself down the icy slope after the others. Stefez sees the branch of tunnels coming up fast as she has managed to keep control of herself.

Stefez reaches her staff back to Anna, "Grab my staff!"

Anna reaches, but misses the staff as the branch of tunnels are coming up fast. Anna tries again and manages to get the staff. As the icy slope opens up into a small chamber, Stefez manipulates her body weight and manages to direct herself towards the right tunnel. Anna holds onto the staff tight and she and Stefez slide into the right tunnel and continue on.

Jencent sees the small chamber ahead and pulls out the dagger from the back of her waist. As Jencent slides into the chamber, she places the dagger into the icy ground and manages to direct herself into the right tunnel. Shaun is the next one to close in on the chamber. Shaun pulls her dagger from her right hip as she slides into the chamber. Shaun uses her dagger to also change her direction and she slides into the right tunnel. Michael is right behind Shaun as he slides into the chamber. He uses his sword in his left hand to change his direction and he slides into the right tunnel right behind Shaun.

Miclou closes in on the chamber fast as the screams of Stefez and the others continue to echo through the ice caverns. Miclou sees the chamber ahead, but he is going faster than he expected. Miclou quickly pulls his dagger as he slides into the chamber. He places his dagger into the icy ground and tries to change his direction. Miclou sees that it's too late and he pulls his dagger up. Miclou slides into the middle tunnel, just barely missing the rock and ice wall that separates the tunnels.

As the sun breaks across the morning horizon, the warm breeze blows across the grasslands. Prince Brian walks over to his horse and unties it from the pole of his tent. Prince Brian mounts up and starts to ride slowly north out of the camp which is being taken down by the noncombatants made up of humans and elves living with Prince Brian. Prince Brian gets about a hundred yards north of the camp and he sees Jennifer, Rein and Ramaf sitting on their horses at the front of his army.

The army is made up of a hundred and fifty humans, a hundred elves and a hundred dwarves, each dressed and ready for battle. Prince Brian rides up to Jennifer, Rein and Ramaf.

Jennifer bows her head, "Good morning my lord."

Prince Brian nods, "Good morning. I see everything is ready."

Rein smiles, "Of course my lord." She pauses, "The camp should be traveling about two miles behind the army by the time they get everything packed up."

Prince Brian gives a smile of approval, "Very good." He looks at Jennifer, "Shall we get moving."

Jennifer raises the bone horn to her mouth and blows. The horn sounds loud and the army prepares to move. Prince Brian, Jennifer, Rein and Ramaf start their horses towards the northwest. The army, moving together as one big unit, starts walking behind Prince Brian and the others.

As the sun breaks the morning horizon and brings light to the dark and dreary castle, Choel walks into the throne room where Gabriela waits. Choel walks across the room and up the steps to the throne.

Choel kneels in front of Gabriela, "I bring news my Queen."

Gabriela motions with her left hand, "Continue."

Choel looks at Gabriela, "Regas and his army has left the castle heading southeast towards Lakeway."

Gabriela questions, "Any news from our scouts about Prince Brian?"

Choel replies, "No my Queen."

Gabriela nods, "Very well. Let me know as soon as we know anything about Regas finding Prince Brian."

Choel bows his head, "Yes my Queen."

Choel stands up, turns around and walks off.

Chapter 33

With the new morning sun casting light over the edge of the swamp and the warm breeze blowing the not so good smells of the swamp across the land, Jody and the others are getting ready for the day of traveling the swamp that lays ahead.

Jody speaks as everyone is nearly ready, "We need to do our best to stay on the trails. The swamp is full of dangers, mainly quicksand."

Stephanie shakes her head and chuckles, "It's never easy is it?"

Sherry lighthearted laughs, "We can't have anything easy. What fun is there in that?"

Marsha chimes in, "Hey, I wouldn't mind an easy day." She pauses and laughs, "Just one will do."

Jody laughs, "You three are crazy."

Everyone is too busy talking, joking and laughing that they don't realize that the air is getting colder. They don't realize it until Brendan says something.

Brendan hugs his arms around himself, "Its getting cold mom."

Jody's expression immediately changes to that of worry when he realizes Brendan is right. The air around them is getting colder.

Marsha shakes her head, "Please tell me it's not him."

Then, the sound of a horse's hooves pounding the ground echo across the land.

Jody looks at the others, "Quick, run for the swamp!"

Marsha and Sherry take off running towards the swamp. Stephanie takes Brendan's hand and the two of them start running after Marsha and Sherry. Jody looks to the south and sees Stecher ride over a hill about five hundred yards away. Jody turns and runs after the others. As Stecher closes in fast to only three hundred yards away, Stephanie and the others run into the swamp.

Stephanie looks at Jody, "Which way?"

Jody glances around and sees a small trail leading north, "This way."

Jody starts off quickly down the trail with the others right behind him as Stecher continues to close in on the edge of the swamp. As Jody and the others run along the trail, they do their best to avoid all the low hanging vines that hang from the weeping willow trees.

Stecher draws his sword from his hip as he slows down and enters the swamp. All the extra vines and trees make Stecher slow down quite a bit. The dark rider starts along the trail after Jody and the others using his sword to cut the vines and overgrown branches out of his way. Even with the vines and branches in his way, Stecher is still able to travel faster than Jody and the others.

Brendan starts to slow down, "Mom, I'm getting tired."

Jody slows down and looks around.

Stephanie slows down to a walk next to Brendan, "Brendan, we can't stop or he'll catch us."

Marsha shakes her head, "We'll never out run him. There has to be something we can do."

Sherry looks around, "With what? We surely can't fight him."

Jody nods while glancing around, "I have an idea. It's going to take some teamwork."

Stephanie looks over at Jody, "Whatever it is, I trust you."

Marsha nods, "Me too."

Sherry smiles, "Lets do it."

Jody draws his sword and cuts down a couple of long vines, "Okay, this is what we're going to do. Sherry and Marsha, you take one vine. Stephanie and I will take the other vine." He pauses, "Brendan, stay with me big guy."

As Jody quickly explains what the plan is, Stecher closes in fast along the trail. Stecher continues to swing his sword cutting away the vines and tree branches. Stecher slows to a quick trot, when all of a sudden, Jody and Stephanie pull the vine tight from each side of the trail. The vine comes up right in front of Stecher about chest level. Stecher brings his sword up fast and just barely cuts the vine in time, but at the same time, Sherry and Marsha pull their vine tight from each side of the trail. This time the vine only comes up to the knees of Stecher's horse.

Moving as fast as he is and with the first vine distracting him, Stecher never sees the second vine come up in front of his horse's knees. The horse rides into the vine. The vine holds and the horse topples forward, throwing Stecher over the head of the horse. Stecher crashes hard on the ground and rolls off the trail into a murky pond of disgusting swamp water.

Jody yells to the others, "Now, run!"

Jody leaps from his hiding place. As Stephanie, Sherry and Marsha take off running. Brendan climbs on Jody's back and Jody runs after the others. After fifty yards, the trail splits into three different trails.

Stephanie and the others stop at the fork. Jody runs up and stops next to the others.

Jody looks back, "He'll expect us to take the right fork since it heads more towards the castle, but we'll take the left just to lose him."

Jody and the others take off quickly down the left trail. During this time, Stecher climbs out of the nasty pond and walks back over to the trail. He looks around for a minute and finally finds his sword. Stecher picks up his sword and puts it away. He walks over to where his horse is now standing. The dark rider checks over his horse and once he is sure the horse is okay, he mounts up.

Stecher starts off down the trail, now well behind Jody and the others. Stecher soon reaches the fork in the trail. He looks around the ground some, but after a minute and knowing he is falling further behind, he decides to go with his gut feeling and rides off down the right trail.

———————

As the sun peaks in the noon sky which is clear blue dotted with puffy, white clouds, Prince Brian and his army continues northwest towards the castle. The soft breeze blows gently across the serene looking grasslands and to any onlooker, they would not know about the terrible battles that have torn apart the Kingdom.

Jennifer rides up next to Prince Brian, "I would say that we are nearly halfway to the castle my lord."

Prince Brian nods, "That's what I figure as well."

Rein rides up next to Prince Brian, "I'm a little worried. Our scouts have not returned my lord."

Ramaf rides up next to the others, "Word has been passed that the camp is moving about three miles behind us."

Prince Brian nods, "Good." He pauses, "The scouts disappearing worries me as well."

Then, the breeze carries a very pungent and recognizable odor all around Prince Brian and the others. It is the odor of decomposing bodies and the easily noticeable, troll smell.

Jennifer starts to look around, "Can you smell that?"

Ramaf coughs a little, "How could someone not smell that?"

Rein glances around, "With the smell that powerful,

it is a large number."

Prince Brian nods, "No doubt we are closing in on Gabriela's army." He pauses, "Form the army into battle lines."

Jennifer, Rein and Ramaf give a quick nod and ride back to the army which is a hundred yards behind them. Prince Brian continues on up the hill and when he tops the rolling hill, he sees the source of the foul smell. Prince Brian stops his horse as he stares at Gabriela's army which is already positioned in it's battle formation about five hundred yards in front of him.

Gabriela's army is made up of a hundred trolls, seventy five decomposing humans and seventy five decomposing elves. All are dressed in pieces of plate armor covering their chest, arms and thighs. The trolls are carrying swords. The undead humans are carrying swords and shields or long pikes. The undead elves are carrying bows with arrows and swords. Standing at the front of the army is Regas. Laying at Regas' feet is a human and an elf, the scouts from Prince Brian's army.

Prince Brian slowly starts down the side of the hill as Jennifer, Rein and Ramaf start over the hill behind him. Right behind Jennifer, Rein and Ramaf is Prince Brian's army. Prince Brian stops and gets off his horse. Jennifer, Rein and Ramaf ride up next to Prince Brian and dismount. Two young boys run up out of the army, grab the four horses and run for the back of the army. A few seconds later, Prince Brian's army stops in it's battle formation right behind him, Jennifer, Rein and Ramaf.

Prince Brian looks at the others, "Looks like we have a slight advantage in numbers."

Rein nods, "No doubt Gabriela didn't send all of her army."

Ramaf grinds his battle axe with his hands, "Well, what are we waiting for."

Prince Brian smiles, looks over at Jennifer and nods.

Jennifer raises the bone horn to her mouth and blows. The horn echoes across the battlefield as Prince Brian draws his sword and starts in a slow jog right at Gabriela's army. Jennifer puts the horn away, draws her sword and starts after Prince Brian. Rein draws her sword and starts after Jennifer and Prince Brian.

Ramaf starts to run, "Here we go."

The rest of Prince Brian's army lets out some battle screams and starts running after their leaders. Regas smiles, draws his sword and grips his shield tight. Regas holds his sword up and yells. Regas lowers his sword and starts running at Prince Brian's army. The rest of Gabriela's army lets out some battle cries and runs after their leader.

The once serene and peaceful landscape has now given way to two large armies on a massive collision course which might decide the fate of the Kingdom.

Unable to see that the sun is in the early afternoon sky and not knowing that a major battle for control of the Kingdom has begun, Stefez and the others continue walking through the tunnels and chambers that make up the ice caverns.

Bailee speaks up, "How awesome would it be if the dark rider gets lost?"

Anna chimes in, "It sure wouldn't hurt my feelings."

Stefez glances around, "Unfortunately, if he made it into the middle tunnel, he will link back up with where we're heading, he'll just be way behind us."

Bailee lets out a sigh, "You didn't have to rain on our parade so quickly."

Stefez, Anna, Shaun and Michael all let out a nice laugh. Jencent glances around to try and see if she can find any distinguishing marks to tell where they are at.

Shaun speaks up, "I can't believe he found us. We covered are tracks really well."

Jencent looks over at the others, "He's an excellent tracker."

Michael speaks up, "Who knows? We may have been spotted by an animal or something and not even known it."

Stefez nods, "In this land, there is no telling how he found us so easily." She pauses, "We just need to make sure we keep up a good pace and stay way ahead of him."

Michael nods in agreement, "Very true. One of these times we may have to stand and face him and I wouldn't want to do that in these tunnels. The narrow tunnels will negate our number advantage."

Shaun chuckles, "Something tells me that having the numbers wouldn't matter."

Jencent nods, "Yea, I'm thinking that too."

At that time, the group walks into another large chamber with five tunnels branching off on the far side of the chamber.

Anna looks at Stefez, "Which way now?"

Stefez is quiet for a minute as she and the others stop walking. Stefez glances at the tunnels.

Bailee speaks up, "Please, tell me you haven't forgot the way?"

Stefez finally breaks a smile, "Oh no, just wanted to see if any of you would panic if it looked like I forgot."

Bailee replies with wide eyes, "That's just mean Stefez."

Stefez and the others get a good laugh at Bailee.

Stefez points with her staff, "The second tunnel from the right."

Stefez and the others walk across the chamber and into the tunnel she had just pointed at.

Chapter 34

As the sun starts into the afternoon sky, the once serene land has given way to a massive battle for control of the Kingdom. The clanking of swords, pikes, shields and armor echoes across the land. The battle is still very much up for grabs, but Prince Brian's army has started to take an upper hand as they have suffered far fewer losses than Gabriela's army.

Ramaf has pushed his way into Gabriela's army a little ways and finds himself facing a troll. Ramaf steps up and brings his battle axe around from the right. The troll brings it's sword across and manages to block the axe. The troll pushes the axe away and swings it's sword down at Ramaf. Ramaf hops to the left and the sword narrowly misses.

Ramaf brings his battle axe around over his head and swings in at the troll from the left. The troll steps back and the axe misses. The troll steps back in, but before the troll can swing it's sword, Ramaf continues into a spin and brings his battle axe around again. This time the battle axe finds it's mark and strikes the troll just above the right knee. The troll cries out in pain and falls to it's back, losing grip of it's sword. Ramaf wastes no time bringing his battle axe over and down, finishing off the troll.

As Ramaf looks for his next fight, Rein squares off against a troll and an undead elf. The troll steps in and brings it's sword in at Rein from the left as the undead elf brings it's sword in at Rein from the right. Rein hops back and both swords barely miss. Rein spins to her left and cuts her sword in at the troll. The troll brings it's sword back across and just manages to block Rein's sword. Rein pushes the troll back as the undead elf steps forward and thrusts it's sword in at Rein's chest. Rein steps to the left and knocks the sword away with her sword. Rein quickly snaps out her right leg and kicks the troll in the gut causing the troll to stagger backwards.

Rein spins around and drops to her right knee as the undead elf spins around. The undead elf's sword goes over Rein's head, but Rein's sword strikes the undead elf hard in the chest sending the undead elf crashing to the ground and out of the fight. Rein quickly stands up and turns as the troll comes back in and swings it's sword in at Rein from the right. Rein stops the sword with her sword. Rein spins her sword in a tight circle and knocks the troll's sword up. Now with the troll's sword out of the way, Rein thrusts her sword in. The sword finds it's mark and the troll falls on the battlefield next to the undead elf.

Jennifer steps up to a troll and an undead human with her sword in her right hand and her short sword in her left hand. The troll brings it's sword in from the right and the undead human thrusts it's pike in at Jennifer's chest. Jennifer steps to the right and blocks the sword with her sword as she knocks the pike away with her short sword. Jennifer pushes the troll back a step and brings her short sword across at the troll. The troll manages to block the short sword.

The undead human pulls it's pike back and thrusts in at Jennifer again. Jennifer brings her sword across and knocks the pike away as she steps back from the troll. The troll steps in and swings it's sword down at Jennifer's head. Jennifer raises her sword and blocks the troll's sword as the undead human thrusts it's pike in once again. This time Jennifer redirects the pike with her short sword and the pike stabs into the troll.

As the undead human pulls the pike back, the troll falls to the ground. Jennifer turns and swings her sword down at the undead human. The undead human knocks the sword away with it's pike, but the undead human is too slow as Jennifer thrusts her short sword in. The undead human tries to bring the pike up to knock the short sword away, but Jennifer's short sword drives deep into the undead human just above it's chest plate. Jennifer withdraws her short sword and looks for her next fight.

As Prince Brian pushes his way through the ongoing battle which has turned in favor of his army, an undead human with a sword steps in front of him and swings it's sword in from the left. Prince Brian brings his shield over and blocks the sword. Prince Brian brings his sword around and cuts in at the undead human. The undead human steps back and just manages to block the sword. Prince Brian brings his shield across and knocks the undead human's sword to the side.

At that time, a troll steps up and thrusts it's sword in at Prince Brian from the right. Prince Brian catches the troll out of the corner of his eye and brings his sword across. Prince Brian knocks the troll's sword away at the last second. The undead human swings it's sword in again. Prince Brian brings his shield across and knocks the sword away. The troll quickly brings it's sword around at Prince Brian.

Prince Brian moves fast and brings his sword around and stops the troll's sword. Prince Brian steps in at the troll and brings his shield across. The edge of the shield smashes into the troll's head, splitting the troll's head wide open. The troll falls to the ground as the undead human thrusts it's sword in at Prince Brian. Prince Brian moves fast and manages to knock the sword away with his sword. Prince Brian steps forward and uses his weight and shield to knock the undead human backwards off-balance. Prince Brian sees his opening and swings his sword in at a downward angle. The sword finds it's mark and chops into the undead human's exposed neck.

Prince Brian steps back as the undead human falls to the ground. Prince Brian glances around to see how the battle is going and notices that his army has taken the upper hand. Prince Brian also sees Regas sending an elf to the ground. Prince Brian starts towards Regas.

———————

With the sun in the mid-afternoon sky and the pungent smells of the swamp being carried all around by the gentle breeze, Jody and the others continue walking along the trail through the swamp.

Stephanie speaks while walking, "This smell is killing me."

Sherry chimes in, "Yea, I definitely can't get use to it. It feels like it's soaking into my skin."

Marsha chuckles, "I'm going to have to bathe for a month to get all this smell off my body."

Jody looks over, gazes at Marsha and smiles, "I could go for that."

Marsha looks at Jody with wide eyes, "Jody!"

Jody chuckles, "What?"

Stephanie and Sherry let out a good laugh at Marsha's shocked response to what Jody said.

Marsha can't keep from laughing and shakes her head while her face starts to turn reddish colored, "Oh my God, I'm so embarrassed."

Sherry laughs at Marsha, "Why you turning so red there Marsha?"

Stephanie laughs, "Wow, bright red girl."

Marsha continues to laugh and fans her face with her hand as she looks away, "Oh my God. You all are killing me, stop."

Jody laughs some more, "Wow, I was just agreeing

with you. Your mind went completely in another direction." He pauses and smiles, "Not that I minded what you were thinking about."

Marsha looks at Jody with another shocked look as she laughs and her face is bright red now, "Oh my God. Stop, I can't breath." She tries to catch her breath, "Poor Marsha."

Stephanie, Sherry and Jody laugh at Marsha's response and bright red face. Brendan laughs along, but only because everyone else is laughing. The group walks around a bend in the trail and the trail forks off in front of them, one heading to the left and one heading to the right. Everyone stops walking as the laughing finally dies down and Marsha's face turns back to its normal color.

Sherry, still chuckling, looks at Jody and smiles, "So, which way sweetie?"

Jody motions with his head and smiles, "The right trail, beautiful."

The group starts walking again and heads off down the right trail.

With the sun beating down from the mid-afternoon sky, the battle between Prince Brian's army and Gabriela's army continues, though it is only now a matter of time as Prince Brian's army has complete control of the battlefield and Gabriela's army has dwindled down to nearly nothing.

Ramaf faces off against another troll. The troll steps up and cuts it's sword down at Ramaf. Ramaf raises his battle axe and blocks the sword. Ramaf brings his sword around in a small circle and cuts his axe in at the troll's knees. The troll brings it's sword down and blocks the battle axe. Ramaf slides his battle axe forward and hooks the sword with the head of his battle axe. Ramaf jerks his battle axe hard and pulls the sword out of the troll's hands.

Ramaf thrusts his battle axe forward and it slams into the troll's stomach. The troll doubles over in pain. Ramaf brings his battle axe over and down and the powerful blow to the troll's back sends the troll face first to the ground ending the fight. Ramaf glances around and sees Prince Brian closing in on Regas. Ramaf starts towards Prince Brian.

Rein squares off against an undead human with a shield and sword. Rein steps in and brings her sword at the undead human from the right. The undead human brings it's shield over and blocks the sword. The undead human thrusts it's sword in at Rein. Rein steps to the side and knocks the sword away with her sword. The undead human steps in and swings it's sword at Rein's head. Rein ducks under the sword and brings her sword across. The undead human manages to bring it's shield down and just barely blocks Rein's sword.

Rein quickly spins while still in a low crouch and sweeps the feet out from under the undead human. The undead human crashes to it's back and loses it's shield and sword. Rein reverses her grip on her sword and brings her sword down into the undead human, finishing the fight. Rein removes her sword and looks around. She sees Prince Brian closing in on Regas and starts in that direction.

Jennifer faces off against an undead elf carrying a sword. The undead elf steps in and swings it's sword at Jennifer. Jennifer brings her short sword across and knocks the sword away. Jennifer brings her sword across behind her short sword at the undead elf's head. The undead elf ducks under the sword and it narrowly misses. The undead elf thrusts it's sword in at Jennifer.

Jennifer brings her short sword back quickly and knocks the sword away. Jennifer continues into a spin and brings her sword around at the now exposed back of the undead elf. The sword strikes the undead elf in the back of the neck. The undead elf falls face first to the ground, ending the fight. Jennifer looks around and sees that the battle is nearly over now. She also sees Prince Brian and Regas preparing to face off. Jennifer makes her way towards Prince Brian.

Prince Brian stands facing Regas, both holding their sword and shield at the ready. Jennifer, Rein and Ramaf stop about twenty feet away and prepare to watch what will be the final fight of the battle. As Prince Brian and Regas prepare to fight, two trolls break away from the battle and start back northwest in the direction of the castle.

Regas moves in fast and brings his sword around from the right. Prince Brian brings his shield over and blocks the sword. Prince Brian quickly thrusts his sword in at Regas. Regas brings his shield across and knocks the sword away. Regas continues into a spin and brings his sword around at Prince Brian's head. Prince Brian moves fast and brings his shield back over and blocks the sword. Prince Brian brings his sword around and cuts in at Regas' knees.

Regas hops back out of the way and the sword just barely misses. Regas steps back in and thrusts his sword in at Prince Brian. Prince Brian brings his shield over and knocks away the sword. This time Prince Brian continues into a spin and brings his sword around at Regas' head. Regas manages to bring his shield up and blocks the deadly sword blow.

Regas and Prince Brian both step back and look at each other, realizing their skill level is practically the same. Regas gives a quick nod, then steps back in and brings his sword down at Prince Brian. Prince Brian brings his shield up and blocks the sword. Prince Brian thrusts his sword in at Regas. Regas brings his shield over and knocks the sword away. Prince Brian allows the momentum of his sword to carry him in a circle. Regas brings his shield up expecting Prince Brian's sword. This time as Prince Brian finishes his spin, he brings his shield around and slams his shield into Regas' shield.

The larger and more powerful Prince Brian knocks Regas backwards off-balance when their shields slam together. Prince Brian seizes the opening and cuts his sword across at Regas' legs. Regas tries to bring his shield down, but is unable to block or avoid the sword this time and the sword strikes hard into the front of both his legs. With his shield now down by his legs, Regas' upper body is exposed and Prince Brian moves fast to take advantage. Prince Brian brings his sword up, over and down. Prince Brian's sword finds home and strikes a deadly blow to Regas' neck.

Regas falls to his knees and drops his sword. Prince Brian kicks Regas in the chest and Regas falls backwards to the ground, ending the fight and the battle. Prince Brian looks around and sees that his army has captured victory. Prince Brian sees Jennifer, Rein and Ramaf.

Prince Brian walks over to Jennifer, Rein and Ramaf, "Good to see you all made it my friends."

Jennifer nods, "Good to see you made it my lord."

Rein puts her sword away, "What now my lord?"

Prince Brian puts his sword away, "Enough for today." He pauses, "Jennifer, go ahead and go back to the camp that's following us and bring them up here. We'll setup camp here for the night."

Jennifer puts her swords away, "Yes my lord."

Jennifer bows her head and hurries off.

Prince Brian looks at Rein and Ramaf, "Take count of our loses and prepare the field for the arrival of our camp."

Rein and Ramaf both bow their head and hurry off. Prince Brian looks around at the battlefield littered with bodies. He looks up at the sky and closes his eyes. He takes a deep breath and allows himself to enjoy the victory for a moment.

Chapter 35

After starting the day being chased by the dark rider and the rest of the day spent walking the ice caverns, Stefez and the others have stopped in a large chamber that has ice formed on the ceiling and walls. Everyone is sitting around a glowing rock and eating some fruit.

Bailee questions after finishing munching on her carrot, "So, do you think the dark rider will catch up to us?"

Stefez takes a drink of water, "I'm not sure. We should be quite a ways ahead of him."

Anna finishes her apple, "Are we going to get out of the ice caverns tomorrow?"

Stefez nods, "We should be out of the caverns by mid-morning, but definitely no later than noon."

Shaun smiles, "Good. I'm ready to see some sunlight again."

Michael nods in agreement, "Me too."

Jencent sits quietly and glances around every so often as the others talk.

Stefez finishes her apple, "We'll have to stop in North Town and get a few supplies."

Shaun finishes eating, "I was thinking that too."

Michael finishes his fruit, "We'll have to be careful not to draw attention to ourselves. North Town is not far from the castle."

Shaun nods in agreement, "Yea, we don't need any attention, that's for sure. Especially getting that close to Mushroom Farm and meeting up with the others."

Bailee chimes in, "I'm all for avoiding anything that might result in a negative outcome."

The others chuckle at Bailee's response.

Stefez sighs and stretches, "We should try and get some rest. Another long day awaits us."

Anna smiles and lays back, "How fun."

Everyone gets as comfortable as they can and tries their best to get some rest.

As the sun gets lower towards the evening horizon, Prince Brian watches as his people have nearly completed setting up camp. As he waits for the rest of the camp to be completed, Prince Brian walks into his tent and waits for the others to arrive. Prince Brian sits down in his tent and closes his eyes. His thoughts drift to Stephanie and he wonders if she is still okay. He smiles to himself as he pictures Stephanie's face and her smile. He only hopes that things will work out and he thinks about what things could be like if she stayed in the Kingdom.

Prince Brian opens his eyes when he hears Jennifer's voice, "My lord!"

Prince Brian replies, "Come on in!"

Jennifer, Rein and Ramaf walk into Prince Brian's tent. Prince Brian nods to them, but still appears to be slightly distracted by the thoughts of Stephanie. Jennifer can tell by the look on Prince Brian's face that something is on his mind. Jennifer, Rein and Ramaf sit down.

Jennifer questions, "Is everything okay my lord?"

Prince Brian breaks his stare and replies, "Yes, of course." He pauses, "So, how is it going on the camp?"

Jennifer replies, "It will be done before sunset."

Prince Brian nods, "Good. What of our loses and how many soldiers do we have left?"

Ramaf replies, "They are resting now. We have one

hundred and eighteen humans, eighty one elves and seventy six dwarves left."

Prince Brian nods, "Okay."

Rein questions, "So, what's the plan for tomorrow my lord?"

Prince Brian sighs, "We'll rest the army tomorrow. I'll also come up with our next move after getting some rest tonight." He pauses, "Make sure everything gets finished and setup a guard rotation for the night."

Jennifer, Rein and Ramaf bow their heads and stand up. Rein walks out of the tent followed by Ramaf. Jennifer gets to the entrance of the tent and turns back to Prince Brian.

Jennifer sighs, "My lord, may I say something?"

Prince Brian nods, "Of course Jennifer."

Jennifer replies, "All due respect, we need your mind here with us and I know what you're worried about." She pauses and smiles, "Why don't you send a message bird to see if Stephanie's okay?"

Prince Brian smiles, "You know me too well Jennifer." He pauses and nods, "I'm okay though, my mind is focused on what's next."

Jennifer bows her head, "Goodnight my lord."

Jennifer walks out of the tent. Prince Brian stands up and thinks for a second about what Jennifer suggested. Prince Brian walks out of his tent and looks around at the camp and his people. He walks around to the opposite side of the tent so no one can see him. Prince Brian softly whistles a tune and holds up his right hand. A few seconds later, a small, brightly colored bird lands on his hand.

The bird speaks in a chirpy voice, "How can I help you?"

Prince Brian smiles, "I need you to take a message to an outlander woman."

The bird replies, "Tell me what she looks like and the

message my lord."

Prince Brian leans in close and whispers to the message bird. After a minute, Prince Brian leans back away from the message bird.

The bird replies, "No problem my lord, I know right where that person is at. Many of us have seen her."

Prince Brian raises his right hand and the message bird flies off.

———— ———

As the sun touches the evening horizon, Jody and the others continue walking along one of the trails through the swamp. The breeze is all but gone along with the sun and the heavy, mushroom smelling air hangs all around.

Jody speaks while walking, "Its going to be dark soon. We better find a place to sleep for the night."

Sherry speaks up, "I could go for some food and rest."

Brendan smiles, "Me too."

At that time, they walk around a bend in the trail and they see a small clearing off on the right side of the trail.

Stephanie looks over at Jody, "What about that little clearing there?"

Jody stops and glances around, "Yea, I think this will work for the night."

The five of them walk off the trail and into the clearing. Jody removes his equipment and weapons and sits down. Marsha lays her staff down, removes her equipment and sits down next to Jody on his left. Stephanie removes her sword and equipment and sits down next to Jody on his right. Brendan sits down next to Stephanie. Sherry lays her staff down, removes her equipment and sits down between Brendan and Marsha. Everyone gets a piece of fruit and starts eating.

Marsha questions between bites, "So, how much

further until we make it out of this swamp?"

Jody finishes a bite, "I would guess another day and a half."

Stephanie looks over at Jody, "You're kidding."

Jody shakes his head, "I'm afraid not. We had to take the longer trail in order to lose the dark rider or we would have been out of the swamp tomorrow."

Sherry finishes a bite, "Great. Another reason to hate that guy."

Jody chuckles, "Yea, he's definitely off the Christmas card list."

Brendan looks at Jody, "Is there Christmas here Uncle Jody?"

Jody looks at Brendan and smiles, "Actually, there is a day like Christmas here in the Kingdom. They celebrate the birthday of the very first King of the Kingdom just like we do Christmas." He pauses, "And its not too far off."

Brendan's eyes get wide, "Cool!"

Stephanie smiles at Brendan's reaction, "I would've never guessed that."

Sherry finishes eating, "Is there anything else here like where we came from?"

Jody finishes his fruit, "There are also three festival weeks in the Kingdom. The elves, dwarves and humans each have a different week where they hold a festival somewhere in the Kingdom and everyone is invited to go and celebrate with them." He pauses, "Its kind of like what we would consider a state fair without fancy rides."

Marsha finishes eating, "That's really neat."

Brendan finishes eating and looks at Stephanie, "I'm tired mom."

Stephanie finishes her fruit, "Me too Brendan. I think its time to get some rest."

Sherry nods, "I'm down for that."

Stephanie lays down and tries to get comfortable.

Brendan lays down next to Stephanie and she puts her arm around him. Sherry lays down a few feet from Brendan and Stephanie. Jody lays down on his left side and tries to get comfortable. Marsha lays down on her right side facing Jody. Jody and Marsha slide together and place their arms around each other.

Marsha smiles and gazes into Jody's eyes, "Good night sweetheart."

Jody returns the smile, "Good night beautiful."

Jody and Marsha lean close and share a nice, loving kiss, then they nestle in and quickly join the others sleeping.

———————

As the sun breaks the morning horizon casting light on a new day in the Kingdom, Gabriela walks into the magic chamber. She walks over and leans her staff against the table. She holds her hand over the crystal ball, closes her eyes and starts to mumble under her breath. The crystal ball gets cloudy, then after a few more seconds, Miclou's face appears in the crystal ball.

Gabriela opens her eyes and questions, "Do you have the child?"

Miclou replies in a haunting voice, "No my Queen. They escaped into the ice caverns. I'm still trying to pick up their trail again."

Gabriela sighs, "Very well. The plan may change. I'll contact you when I've made up my mind. Until then, keep after them."

Miclou bows his head, "Yes my Queen."

Gabriela closes her eyes and starts to mumble under her breath again. After a few seconds, Stecher's face appears in the crystal ball.

Gabriela opens her eyes and questions, "How is it going? Do you have the child yet?"

Stecher replies in a cold, evil tone, "No my Queen. They escaped and I lost them in the swamp. I'm still trying to pick up their trail again."

Gabriela sighs, "Very well. Like I told Miclou, the plan may change. I'll contact you when I've decided what to do. Until then, keep after them."

Stecher bows his head, "Yes my Queen."

Gabriela removes her hand from the crystal ball and Stecher's image vanishes. As Gabriela grabs her staff, Choel walks into the magic chamber. Gabriela turns and looks at Choel.

Gabriela questions, "What is it?"

Choel bows his head, "I just received word my Queen. Our army was defeated and Regas was killed in battle."

Gabriela sighs and shakes her head, "This is not going as originally planned." She pauses, "Make sure the army is ready, I'll talk with you later about what to do."

Choel bows his head and walks off.

Gabriela turns back to the table, "What to do now?"

Chapter 36

N ot able to tell what time of day it is, Stefez and the others continue walking along through the ice caverns. The group passes through a smaller chamber and into another tunnel. As they walk along the tunnel, they notice that the walls and ceiling is no longer covered with ice. Everyone also notices that the temperature is getting much warmer.

Stefez smiles, "I think we're close to the exit."

Bailee chimes in, "Thank goodness. I can't take much more of this."

The others chuckle as they continue on and as they round a bend in the tunnel, they see a bright light about two hundred yards ahead of them. Everyone smiles as they know that they are looking at the exit of the caverns and the sunlight.

Shaun smiles, "The exit."

Michael also smiles, "Another good thing is that I'm sure we found our way out before the dark rider. We can put some distance between us and him."

Jencent nods as they continue to walk, "That sounds good to me."

The group continues to walk towards the end of the tunnel. As they get closer, they can feel the warmth and they can also start to feel the soft breeze. The group reaches the end of the tunnel and stop. The sun is shining down from the mid-morning sky. Everyone narrows their eyes as they try to adjust to the sunlight.

The group walks out of the tunnel and find

themselves back in the plush, green rolling hills of the grasslands as the tunnel exits out the side of a fairly large hill. Everyone looks back and sees the mountains behind them.

Anna smiles, "I'm glad that's over."

Bailee speaks up, "Me too Anna."

Stefez, Shaun, Michael and Jencent glance around and start to try and figure out exactly where they are at.

Michael looks at Stefez, "What do you think?"

Stefez glances around some more, "If I'm right, we walk straight west and we'll pick up the road again heading to North Town."

Shaun nods in agreement, "I believe you're right." She pauses, "And we should be able to reach North Town by nightfall."

Anna smiles, "You mean, a real bed to rest in tonight."

Stefez smiles and nods at Anna, "Absolutely. We just have to make sure no one recognizes us."

Michael nods, "I think we can manage that."

Stefez sighs, "Well, shall we continue on."

Bailee chimes in, "Off to North Town."

Everyone smiles and the group starts walking west across the rolling, emerald green hills.

———————

With the sun beating down from the noon sky and the slow moving breeze carrying the horrible smells of the swamp all around, Jody and the others turn onto another trail now heading east through the swamp.

Jody speaks while walking, "Well, we picked up the east trail so we are heading towards Mushroom farm now."

Sherry questions, "How far would you say it is?"

Jody thinks for a second, "We still have the rest of

today and nearly the entire day tomorrow."

Marsha shakes her head, "That really sucks."

Jody smiles, "Yea. The swamp is not nearly as big as the forest or grasslands, but its so much slower to travel because of all the winding in the trails given there are no roads to travel on."

Stephanie speaks up, "I'll sure be happy when we're out of here."

Marsha, Sherry and Jody nod in agreement. The group hears a chirpy bird overhead. Everyone stops and looks around to see if they can find the source of the noise.

After a few seconds, Brendan points, "Look mom."

Everyone looks to see what Brendan is pointing at and they see the message bird Prince Brian sent.

Jody holds up his right hand, "A message bird. I hope this is good news."

The message bird lands on Jody's hand.

Jody looks at the message bird, "What do you have for us?"

The message bird replies in it's chirpy voice, "I have a secret message."

Jody glances around with a puzzled look, "You can tell us all."

The message bird replies, "I cannot. It's a secret message for Stephanie from Prince Brian."

Sherry, Marsha and Jody look over at Stephanie. Stephanie has quite a shocked look on her face.

Jody smiles at Stephanie, "It's for you. Hold out your right hand."

Stephanie holds up her right hand. The message bird jumps from Jody's hand over to Stephanie's hand. Stephanie starts to walk away from the others.

Marsha smiles, "You go girl."

Marsha, Sherry and Jody let out a nice laugh as Stephanie walks about twenty feet away shaking her head at the others. Marsha, Sherry, Brendan and Jody watch as the bird talks to Stephanie. After a couple of minutes, they watch as Stephanie speaks to the message bird. After another couple minutes, Stephanie raises her right hand and the message bird flies off. Stephanie walks back over to the others with a huge smile on her face.

Jody shakes his head and smiles, "And just what was that all about?"

Stephanie continues to smile, "Oh nothing. He was just checking on us."

Sherry nods sarcastically, "Uh huh. By sending you a secret message, sure."

Marsha chimes in, "Passing love notes in class are we?"

Stephanie shakes her head trying not to show her embarrassment, "Shouldn't we keep going."

Marsha, Sherry and Jody all laugh at Stephanie's response.

Marsha catches her breath, "At least its not me getting picked on this time."

Jody smiles and shakes his head, "You girls kill me." He looks down at Brendan, "You ready to keep going big man?"

Brendan smiles, "Yea!"

Stephanie, Sherry and Marsha smile at Brendan. The group starts walking east along the trail again.

With the sun shining down from the noon sky, Gabriela is waiting in the magic chamber. She quietly thinks to herself about what she is planning on doing now. At that time, Choel walks into the magic chamber.

Choel bows his head, "You wanted to see me my Queen?"

Gabriela nods, "Yes. I wanted to let you know about

the plan I've come up with."

Choel questions, "What do you need me to do my Queen?"

Gabriela replies, "I want the spare provisions brought into the castle from the town. I want around the clock guards on the castle walls. We are going to keep inside the castle and force Prince Brian to attack the castle." She pauses, "He doesn't have the luxury of time to lay siege to the castle."

Choel nods and replies, "It will be done. What of the children my Queen?"

Gabriela smiles, "I have a new plan for them." She pauses, "You focus on defending the castle. I'll take care of the children."

Choel bows his head, "Yes my queen."

Choel turns and walks out. Gabriela walks over to the table where the crystal ball is at. She holds her hand over the crystal ball, closes her eyes and mumbles under her breath. The crystal ball starts to get cloudy. After a few seconds, Miclou's face appears in the crystal ball.

Miclou questions, "Yes my Queen?"

Gabriela opens her eyes and replies, "The plans have changed. I need you to return to the castle as fast as you can."

Miclou bows his head, "Yes my Queen."

Gabriela closes her eyes and starts to mumble under her breath again. After a few seconds, Stecher's face appears in the crystal ball. Gabriela opens her eyes.

Stecher questions, "Yes my Queen?"

Gabriela replies, "The plans have changed. I need you to return to the castle as fast as you can."

Stecher bows his head, "Yes my Queen."

Gabriela removes her hand from the crystal ball and Stecher's face vanishes. Gabriela grabs her staff and walks out of the magic chamber.

As the sun starts to pass into the evening sky, the warm breeze blows the clean, fresh air through Prince Brian's camp where everyone is preparing to eat their evening meal. Prince Brian is walking through his camp carrying his plate of food and cup. As he passes everyone, they all bow their heads. Prince Brian returns the gesture with a smile of gratitude for everything that his people, the dwarves and the elves have done for him. Prince Brian sees Jennifer, Rein and Ramaf sitting around a small fire eating.

Prince Brian walks up, "May I join the three of you?"

Jennifer, Rein and Ramaf look up a bit surprised to see Prince Brian. The three of them start to stand up.

Prince Brian speaks quickly, "Please, don't get up."

Prince Brian sits down next to Jennifer.

Jennifer questions, "Is everything okay my lord?"

Prince Brian smiles, "Yes, of course. I just wanted to walk around and see how everyone was doing." He pauses, "I figured we could talk about what our plans are while eating. It's such a nice evening to be sitting inside a tent."

Rein returns to eating and questions, "So, what were you thinking about doing my lord?"

Prince Brian finishes a bite, "We'll break camp tomorrow morning and continue on to the castle."

Ramaf takes a drink, "What do you think Gabriela will do?"

Prince Brian finishes another bite, "If I was going to guess, I would say that she'll keep her army inside the castle. She knows we don't have time to wait her out."

Jennifer speaks up after a bite, "She's going to force us to attack the well fortified castle. Not impossible, but definitely making things a lot harder for us."

Prince Brian nods as he finishes eating, "Our only

advantage is that we know the castle defenses and where the blind spots are that we can attack from."

Rein finishes eating, "So, are we going to go straight into an attack on the castle tomorrow?"

Prince Brian takes a drink, "No, the trip will tire us out. We'll setup camp in the town surrounding the hill." He pauses, "Hopefully we'll hear from Stefez and they'll be waiting in Mushroom Farm. The longer we wait, the harder it will be for us."

Jennifer nods, "I'm sure they'll be there."

Ramaf nods, "Me too."

Everyone finishes the meal and drinks.

Prince Brian stands up, "Well, then I'll see you all in the morning. Have a good night."

Jennifer bows her head, "Goodnight my lord."

Rein and Ramaf bow their heads. Prince Brian turns and walks back towards his tent.

Chapter 37

As the sun nears the evening horizon, Jody and the others continue walking along the trail through the swamp. The breeze has all but stopped blowing and the smell of mushrooms hangs in the air.

Jody speaks while walking, "I guess we should find a place to rest for the night."

Sherry speaks up, "Please tell me this will be the last night we have to spend in the swamp."

Jody smiles and stops as he spots a clearing on the side of the trail, "This will be it, unless something happens tomorrow."

Stephanie speaks while walking over to the clearing, "Good, cause I can't take much more of this swamp."

Marsha nods as she walks into the clearing, "I've had all I can take of it."

Jody takes off his things, "We'll have to go without a fire tonight."

Stephanie takes off her things, "Why is that?"

Jody glances around, "We're in the area of the swamp where the lizard men live. We don't want to draw their attention to us."

Marsha takes off her things and looks at Jody, "Lizard men?"

Jody nods as he sits down, "Yep. They're not very smart or powerful, but they eat any kind of meat they can find. Plus, I'm sure they're helping Gabriela."

Sherry removes her things and sits down, "Is there anything in this place that doesn't help her."

Stephanie, Brendan and Marsha sit down and start eating. Sherry and Jody also start eating.

Jody shakes his head, "Most everyone and everything fears Gabriela's magical powers and her army."

Stephanie speaks up, "I'll be so happy when we don't have to deal with her anymore."

Brendan chimes in, "Me too."

Jody smiles at Brendan, then looks over at Marsha. Marsha catches Jody's look out of the corner of her eye. Marsha looks over at Jody, smiles and winks at him. The conversation dies down as everyone finishes eating. Once everyone is done eating. Everyone lays down for one more night of rest in the disgustingly smelly swamp.

As darkness falls across the Kingdom, the glow of the torches lining the streets of North Town glow light up the night. North Town is a fairly large town, about the same size as River Fork with most of the buildings built nearly the same. The people are dressed in nicer clothes and the town favors the colors of blue and green over most others.

Stefez and the others are walking west along the road leading into North Town from the east. They walk by the huts and small farms that surround the actual town.

Stefez looks over at Anna, "Just keep your cloak wrapped around you and they shouldn't even recognize you as an outlander."

Anna nods, "Okay."

Shaun speaks up, "We should just find a place for the night. None of the supply shops will be open until the morning."

Michael nods in agreement, "Yea, get some food and some rest, then get an early start tomorrow."

Bailee chimes in, "That sounds good to me."

The group continues to walk along the road as they

start passing the stone buildings that make up the outskirts of North Town. They continue on for a couple blocks, then they spot an open tavern.

Stefez speaks to the others, "Lets try that tavern."

The group walks over to the main door. Michael opens the door and steps inside. Like the other taverns, there is a large, open room with numerous tables. A caldron hangs in the back and a bar lines the left wall. Off in the back, right corner is the stairs that lead up to the rooms. Michael looks around and notices that the tavern is nearly empty.

Michael speaks to the others, "This will work."

Everyone follows Michael into the tavern. They walk over to a table and sit down. In a couple of minutes, an older woman walks up to the table.

The older woman smiles, "What can I do for all of you?"

Stefez returns the smile, "We'll each have some stew and just some water to drink."

The older woman nods, "Okay. I'll be back shortly."

The older woman walks off.

Anna speaks up, "I hope the others are doing okay."

Shaun smiles, "I bet they're fine. They'll probably beat us to Mushroom Farm."

The older lady walks back up with a teenage girl. They place the food on the table and walk off again. A few seconds later, the lady and girl return with the drinks.

Stefez smiles, "Thank you." She pauses, "Do you have any rooms open?"

The older lady smiles, "Of course. How many?"

Stefez glances around the table, "Two."

The older lady nods, "Sure. You can take the last two rooms at the end of the hallway on the right."

Stefez smiles, "Thank you." She pauses, "We don't have much, but we'll pay you what we can."

The older lady smiles, looks around and lowers her

voice, "You're the group helping Prince Brian, aren't you? The ones trying to get the outlander children out of the Kingdom?"

Everyone stops eating and looks at the older woman, not believing what they just heard.

Stefez nods and whispers, "Yes we are."

The older woman smiles and whispers, "Its okay, your secret is safe with me." She pauses, "And everything is on the house. Just get Prince Brian back in the castle."

Michael smiles and bows his head, "Thank you very much. We are in your debt."

The older woman smiles and walks off. Everyone returns to eating.

Bailee speaks up from next to the table, "That was close. I thought we were in trouble."

Anna chuckles, "Me too."

Stefez smiles, "Things are looking up it might seem." She pauses, "When we head upstairs, Anna, Bailee and Michael will stay in a room with me. Jencent and Shaun will take the other room."

Everyone nods and continues eating. Once dinner is finished, everyone gets up and walks across the room and heads upstairs to their room for the night.

——— ——— ———

As the half moon shines in the clear night sky, the temperature has dropped as it gets closer to dawn. Gabriela walks into her magic chamber as the emerald ring on her left hand is glowing a dull green color.

Gabriela leans her staff against the table, "Someone is trying to contact me."

Gabriela holds her hand over the crystal ball, closes her eyes and mumbles under her breath. The crystal ball gets cloudy, but nothing appears. Gabriela concentrates harder and after a few more seconds, Jencent's face appears in the crystal ball.

Gabriela opens her eyes and smiles, "What do you have for me?"

Jencent glances and whispers, "We are in North Town. We are still heading to Mushroom Farm. Where are the dark riders?"

Gabriela replies, "I've changed the plan. I have them returning to the castle." She pauses, "But now that I'm able to talk to you, I think you can help me."

Jencent whispers back, "What do you want me to do?"

Gabriela smiles, "Kidnap one of the children in the middle of the night and bring them to the castle."

Jencent glances around again, "Stefez keeps a very close eye on the child. I might have more luck when we meet up with the others in Mushroom Farm."

Gabriela nods, "Very well. Just grab one of the children as soon as you can and get back here to the castle. Prince Brian is getting closer."

Jencent bows her head, "It will be done my Queen." She pauses, "I have to go."

Gabriela removes her hand from the crystal ball. Gabriela grabs her staff and smiles.

Gabriela speaks as she walks out of the magic chamber, "I bet even you didn't see this coming Stefez, my dear little sister."

———

As the morning sun breaks the horizon casting light across the once dark Kingdom, Prince Brian walks out of his tent and over to his horse. As he unties his horse, Prince Brian looks around and sees everyone working hard to breakdown the camp and pack everything up. Prince Brian climbs on his horse and starts slowly riding northwest.

As he gets a hundred yards from his tent, Prince Brian sees Jennifer, Rein and Ramaf on their horses at the front of the army. Prince Brian starts towards them when he hears a chirping bird from the air above him. Prince Brian looks up and sees the message bird he sent to Stephanie flying towards him. Prince Brian holds up his right hand and the message bird lands on his hand.

Prince Brian speaks to the message bird, "Did you find her and deliver my message?"

The message bird replies in a chirpy voice, "Yes."

Prince Brian smiles and questions, "Did she send a message back?"

The message bird replies again, "Yes."

Prince Brian swallows to clear his throat wondering what Stephanie sent to him, "May I have the message?"

The message bird delivers the message, "She says that she feels the same way. That while in Lover's Keep she looked into True Loves Mirror and saw your reflection."

Prince Brian gets the biggest smile he has ever had, "Thank you."

Prince Brian raises his hand and the message bird flies off. Prince Brian rides over to Jennifer, Rein and Ramaf. Jennifer smiles, knowing what the message bird was about.

Rein questions, "Did you receive word from Stefez my lord?"

Prince Brian replies in a very cheerful tone, "No. It was a personal message."

Prince Brian looks over at Jennifer and gives a quick nod.

Ramaf speaks up, "We're ready to move out."

Prince Brian sighs and glances around, "Then lets get going."

Jennifer raises the horn to her mouth and blows into the horn. The sound echoes all around and the soldiers prepare to move. Prince Brian, Jennifer, Rein and Ramaf start riding slowly northwest and the army follows.

Chapter 38

As the morning sun shines down on North Town, Stefez and the others are walking the streets near the center of town looking for a supply shop. The group weaves it's way through the various crowds of people as none of the townspeople notice Anna as an outlander.

Michael speaks up, "Two doors up on the left."

The others look up ahead and see the sign hanging over the door Michael spoke about. They work their way through the crowd and finally reach the door. Michael opens the door and steps inside. Stefez and the others walk in behind Michael.

Stefez whispers to the others, "We can't take long. No telling where the dark rider is at."

Stefez hands her pouch to Anna, "Here. Gather some fruit. I'm going to see what we can do to pay for the fruit."

Everyone nods and starts to gather some fruit as Stefez walks over to the shopkeeper. Bailee stays with Anna.

Bailee speaks to Anna, "Make sure you get some good carrots."

Anna looks down at Bailee and smiles, "I wouldn't think of forgetting."

As everyone finishes filling their pouches, Stefez walks back up to them. Anna hands the pouch of fruit back to Stefez.

Stefez slings the pouch over her shoulder, "Everything is set."

Shaun questions, "What about water?"

Stefez replies, "There is a lake halfway to Mushroom Farm from here. We have enough to get there. We should get going. If we travel fast enough, we'll reach Mushroom Farm tonight."

Michael nods, "Sounds good to me."

Bailee chimes in, "What are we waiting for then?"

Everyone smiles and glances around to make sure no one is watching them, then they walk out of the supply shop. The group walks along the road until they reach the western outskirts of North Town, then Stefez leads them off the road heading west.

Anna questions, "We're not going to take the road?"

Stefez shakes her head, "No. The road leads to the castle."

Anna nods, "Oh."

As the group continues west across the plush, green grasslands and rolling hills, the breeze starts to pick up drastically. The wind continues to blow harder and harder.

Anna looks at Stefez scared, "What is it?"

Stefez smiles at Anna, "It's okay. We're getting a message from the wind."

The wind continues to howl all around the group as it creates a vortex. The vortex spins around the group faster and faster until finally, the wind stops and the face appears as it did to Jody and the others.

The wind speaks in it's powerful voice, "I have a message from Jody."

Stefez bows her head, "May I have the message master wind?"

The wind replies, "Jody and the others are okay. They are traveling north and are nearly to the swamp. They will meet you in Mushroom Farm and wait if they arrive first."

Stefez bows her head, "Thank you master wind."

The face starts to disappear and the vortex returns.

After a few seconds, the vortex and strong winds disappear and the gentle breeze returns.

Stefez looks at the others, "Well, that's good news."

Anna smiles, "I'm glad they're okay."

Shaun nods, "Me too."

Michael nods in agreement, "We should get moving."

The group starts walking west across the plush, green grass and rolling hills again.

The mushroom smell hangs heavy on the warm breeze as the sun has started into the noon sky. Jody and the others continue east along the trail through the swamp.

Brendan speaks up as they walk, "Are we getting close Uncle Jody?"

Jody looks at Brendan and smiles, "We're getting real close big guy." He pauses, "Maybe a couple of miles."

Stephanie looks over at Jody, "You know this land really well."

Jody nods, "Like I said before. Shaun tried to help me get out of the Kingdom when I first got here. We spent a lot of time around this area and the castle." He pauses, "Once we decided it was hopeless, we traveled all over the Kingdom."

The talking stops for a minute as they continue on.

After a couple minutes, Sherry glances around as if she heard something, "Did anyone else hear that?"

Marsha looks over at Sherry, "Hear what?"

Sherry stops and looks around, "I'm not really sure how to explain it."

Jody stops and looks around, "Try. What did it sound like?"

Sherry shrugs, "I don't know. Kind of like someone was breathing under the water."

Stephanie stops and looks around, "What?"

Jody grabs the handle of his sword and looks around some more, "That's not good."

Marsha looks at Jody, "Why?"

At that time, Marsha's question is answered as five lizard men emerge from the pond of swamp water off on the left side of the trail. The lizard men are all around five and a half feet tall. They look human except for the solid black eyes, green scales that cover their entire body and a long tail that drags on the ground behind them. Each lizard man is carrying a very crude looking, three foot long wooden sword.

Stephanie grabs her sword, "I take it those are lizard men."

Jody draws his sword, "You got it. Brendan, get behind me."

Stephanie draws her sword as Marsha and Sherry ready their staves for the upcoming fight. The lizard men rush out of the swamp water and head straight at Jody and the others. Jody steps away from the others a few feet, trying to separate the lizard men. Two of the lizard men head for Jody. The other three lizard men head for Stephanie, Sherry and Marsha.

The first lizard man steps up to Jody and swings it's sword down at Jody's head. Jody raises his sword and blocks the wooden sword. The second lizard man steps up and thrusts it's sword in at Jody. Jody quickly steps to the side and brings his sword down, knocking the second sword away. Jody quickly kicks the second lizard man in the stomach. The second lizard man staggers back. Jody moves fast and puts himself between the two lizard men and Brendan again.

The lizard man steps up and swings it's sword at Stephanie from the left. Stephanie brings her sword over and blocks the wooden sword. Stephanie quickly pulls her sword back and swings her sword at the lizard man. The lizard man brings it's sword across and stops Stephanie's sword. The lizard man pulls it's sword back and swings it at a downward angle at Stephanie's head. Stephanie moves to her left and brings her sword across as the wooden sword just misses her head. Stephanie's sword strikes home and cuts deep across the lizard man's chest. The lizard man drops it's sword. Stephanie brings her sword back around and sends the lizard man to the ground with a blow to the upper back.

The lizard man steps up to Marsha and swings it's sword down at Marsha's head. Marsha raises her staff and blocks the sword. Marsha pushes the sword up with her staff and swings her staff around at the lizard man's head. The lizard man brings it's sword over and blocks the staff. Marsha quickly swings the other end of the staff in at the lizard man's legs. This time the staff finds the mark and smashes into the lizard man's right knee. The lizard man lowers it's sword only to leave an opening and Marsha doesn't hesitate, just like Jody told her. Marsha brings her staff across again and this time it slams into the side of the lizard man's head. The lizard man crashes to the ground.

Sherry readies herself as the lizard man gets closer. Sherry jabs her staff out as the lizard man raises it's sword. The end of the staff jabs the lizard man in the face, stopping the lizard man dead in it's tracks. Sherry brings the right end of her staff around at the lizard man's head. The lizard man moves it's sword over and blocks the staff. The lizard man steps in and swings it's sword down at Sherry. Sherry steps to the side and the sword misses. Sherry quickly brings her staff up and it finds the mark as the staff smashes into the lizard man's chin. The lizard man falls to the ground and lays motionless.

The first lizard man steps back in at Jody and swings it's sword at Jody from the left. Jody ducks under the sword and quickly spins around the first lizard man. Jody brings his sword around at the second lizard man. The second lizard man raises it's sword to block. When Jody's metal sword hits the wooden sword of the second lizard man, the wooden sword breaks off at the handle.

The second lizard man looks shocked as Jody steps in and swings the handle of his sword at the second lizard man's head. The handle slams into the second lizard man's head and the second lizard man falls to the ground. Jody quickly turns back and sees the first lizard man standing there. The first lizard man takes a step closer to Jody. Jody smiles and lowers his sword. The first lizard man thinks that Jody is defenseless and starts to take another step. Suddenly, the first lizard man is struck by a powerful blow from Marsha's staff in the back of the head. The first lizard man falls to the ground ending the short fight.

Jody smiles at Marsha, "Thanks beautiful."

Marsha smiles back, "Anytime honey."

Jody puts his sword away and looks around at the lizard men laying on the ground, "Nice work everyone."

Stephanie puts her sword away, "I think we're all getting the hang of this."

Jody smiles and laughs, "It sure looks that way to me."

Marsha, Sherry and Stephanie all get a good laugh.

Brendan bounces around a little bit, "Yea, we showed them."

Everyone laughs again at Brendan.

Jody finally catches his breath, "Lets get moving and get out of this swamp."

The others nod and the group starts off east down the trail again heading towards the edge of the swamp and Mushroom Farm.

———————

As the sun moves into the afternoon sky which is

dotted with puffy, white clouds, Gabriela walks into her magic chamber. She walks over and leans her staff against the table. She closes her eyes, places her hand over the crystal ball and starts to mumble under her breath. The crystal ball starts to get cloudy. After a few more seconds, the face of Stecher appears in the crystal ball.

Gabriela opens her eyes and questions, "Where are you?"

Stecher replies in his cold, evil tone, "I've just entered the town surrounding the castle. I'll be there very soon my Queen."

Gabriela nods her head, "Good. Come see me as soon as you and Miclou get here."

Stecher bows his head, "Yes my Queen."

Gabriela closes her eyes and mumbles under her breath some more. After a few seconds, the image in the crystal ball changes to the face of Miclou.

Gabriela opens her eyes and questions, "Where are you?"

Miclou replies in his hauntingly hollow voice, "I'm at the crossroads between North Town and the castle. I'll be there by mid-afternoon my Queen."

Gabriela smiles, "Good. Stecher will already be here. Get with him and come see me as soon as you get here."

Miclou bows his head, "Yes my Queen."

Gabriela removes her hand from the crystal ball and Miclou's face vanishes. Gabriela grabs her staff and walks out of the room to prepare for the arrival of the dark riders.

Chapter 39

With the sun crossing into the early afternoon sky and the warm breeze blowing across the emerald green rolling hills of the grassland, Stefez and the others catch the smell of fresh, crisp water. The group tops the hill they were walking up and they see the lake just ahead. The lake is about the same size as the lake near Flower Town. The sun reflects off the crystal clear water.

Stefez smiles, "The lake. This means we're halfway to Mushroom Farm."

Shaun nods, "So, we should make it there sometime after night fall."

Anna smiles, "Good, I'm ready to see Marsha again."

Michael speaks up as they continue walking towards the lake, "We'll just refill our water and get moving. We can eat while walking."

The group continues on and finally reach the shore of the lake. Michael, Shaun, Stefez and Jencent walk up by the water and start to fill their flasks. As the four of them are filling their flasks, they fail to see what is moving fast towards them in the water.

Anna points towards a large snaking motion in the water, "What's that?"

Stefez, Michael, Shaun and Jencent look up to see what Anna is talking about. Suddenly, a thirty foot long water serpent with the body of a coral snake with ten short legs with webbed feet and the head is shaped like a king cobra snake head, lunges up out of the water at the four of them.

Moving fast, Stefez, Shaun, Jencent and Michael all leap backwards as the two, long deadly fangs and razor teeth of the water serpent just barely misses them. Michael, Shaun and Jencent quickly draw their swords as Stefez moves back over by Anna. The water serpent comes up on the bank of the lake as Michael, Shaun and Jencent slowly move backwards.

Michael speaks while staring at the water serpent, "We need to get out of here."

Jencent speaks up, "I'm not turning my back on that thing. We'll never outrun it."

The water serpent lunges forward at Shaun. Shaun leaps to her right and swings her sword. The water serpent misses, but easily moves out of the way before Shaun's sword even gets close to it. The water serpent lunges again, this time at Jencent. Jencent jumps back as the water serpent narrowly misses. Jencent swings her sword upward as Michael tries to move in from the side. The water serpent is way too fast and Jencent's sword cuts nothing but air.

The water serpent sees Michael moving in with his sword. The water serpent snakes back and Michael misses. The water serpent brings it's tail around at Michael. Michael just barely sees the tail in time and ducks out of the way. The water serpent snakes around and lunges back at Jencent again as it whips it's tail around. Jencent leaps out of the way of the head as the fangs just miss. However, Shaun is not so lucky having tried to sneak up on the water serpent as the tail of the water serpent whips around. By the time Shaun sees the tail its too late and the tail slams into Shaun's legs knocking Shaun off her feet.

Anna yells as the water serpent raises up in preparation to strike down at Shaun, "Shaun!"

Michael moves fast to try and draw the water serpent's attention away from Shaun. Michael can tell he is never going to get there in time as the head of the water serpent starts down. However, during all of this, everyone including the water serpent didn't see Stefez preparing a magical spell.

Stefez is holding her staff with her left hand and mumbling under her breath. The stone on the end of the staff is glowing a dull purple. Stefez snaps out her right hand as if she was snatching something out of the air in front of her. That's when everyone sees a huge hand made of water form and come out of the lake. The water hand grabs the water serpent's head about three feet shy of it biting Shaun. Stefez jerks her right hand back and the water hand reacts the same way, jerking the water serpent back into the lake.

Michael yells, "Now, everyone run!"

Bailee takes off hopping as fast as she can heading west. Jencent takes off running right after Bailee. Stefez and Anna take off running as Shaun gets to her feet. Michael and Shaun take off running and fall in right behind the others as they keep running west towards Mushroom Farm.

With the afternoon sun beating down on the castle, the air around the royal stables should be warm, but the two undead humans standing guard at the stable look at each other as the air starts to get colder around them. The two undead humans hear the thunderous sound of a horse riding fast towards them. As the two undead humans look around, they finally see Miclou riding hard towards them. The two undead humans look at each other nervously as neither of them like the thought of the dark riders.

Miclou rides up and stops by the two undead humans, "Has Stecher arrived yet?"

The undead human slowly nods his head.

Miclou climbs off his horse, "See to my horse."
The second undead human walks over and takes the horse's reigns as Miclou walks off towards the castle.

As the soft, warm breeze blows across the open grasslands and the white clouds move slowly across the afternoon sky, Prince Brian and his army continues towards the castle. As the army continues to move, Prince Brian tops a hill and sees the town and castle in the distance. Prince Brian smiles as he slowly starts down the side of the hill.

Jennifer rides up next to Prince Brian, "Almost there my lord."

Prince Brian nods, "It's been a long time coming."

Rein rides up, "Do you think they've spotted us yet?"

Prince Brian replies as Ramaf rides up, "I'm sure they have."

Ramaf smiles, "Good. I want them shaking with fear by the time we attack."

Prince Brian, Jennifer and Rein smile at Ramaf. The army continues and closes in on the town surrounding the castle. A few people working in the fields of the farms around the town see Prince Brian and his army getting closer. A middle-aged man smiles and runs off towards his hut.

Prince Brian looks at the others, "We'll set up camp in these fields. The whole army will stand guard as the camp is being prepared." He pauses, "I want scouts riding around in every direction. I don't want any surprises."

Jennifer bows her head, "Yes my lord."

Jennifer, Rein and Ramaf turn their horses and start back towards the army and the rest of the people close behind. Prince Brian rides up to the hut that the middle-aged man ran into. Prince Brian stops by the entrance to the hut. In a few seconds, the middle-aged man walks out with his wife and teenage son next to him.

The man bows to Prince Brian, "My lord. It's an honor."

The woman and teenage boy bow their heads.

Prince Brian smiles, "I was wanting to know if we could use your fields to setup our camp?"

The man's eyes widen and he replies quickly, "Of course my lord. If there is anything we can do to help, it would be an honor."

Prince Brian nods, "Actually, there is something you can do for me and my army."

The man replies, "Name it my lord."

Prince Brian replies, "Send word through the town that we are here in your fields. See if they will bring some food for my people. It's been a long day of traveling."

The man smiles, "Of course my lord." The man looks at his teenage boy, "Son, go as fast as you can. Tell everyone you see and have them bring food."

The boy smiles and runs off as fast as he can for town as Jennifer, Rein, Ramaf and the rest of the army move into the fields.

Prince Brian nods, "Thank you sir. I shall take my leave now."

The man and woman bow their heads. Prince Brian turns his horse and rides back towards the fields where Jennifer and the others are getting the army into place.

Jennifer bows her head to Prince Brian as he rides up, "The army is nearly in place my lord. The camp will be here before long."

Prince Brian nods, "Good. I've sent word to have food brought to us from the town." He pauses, "Now I'll send a bird to Stefez to let them know we're here and ready."

Prince Brian turns and rides away a few hundred feet and holds his right hand up in the air as he whistles. A bright colored bird swoops down from the sky and lands on Prince Brian's hand.

Prince Brian speaks to the message bird, "I wish to send a message to Stefez. She should be in Mushroom Farm."

The message bird replies in it's chirpy voice, "What is the message my lord?"

Prince Brian replies, "Tell them that we are outside the castle and ready to attack. Have them let us know when they are ready for us to do so."

The message bird replies, "It will be done my lord."

Prince Brian raises his hand and the message bird flies off. Prince Brian turns his horse and starts back to the others.

As Prince Brian and his people are setting up their camp in the fields around the castle, Gabriela is waiting in the throne room. The two main doors open and the air starts to get colder in the throne room. Choel, Miclou and Stecher walk into the throne room. The doors shut behind the three of them as they walk across the room and up the stairs to where Gabriela is sitting.

Choel kneels in front of Gabriela, "You wanted to see the three of us my Queen?"

Gabriela nods, "Yes. Please stand."

Choel stands up.

Gabriela questions, "Do we know what is going on with Prince Brian?"

Choel nods, "He is in the fields just east of the town and castle. He is setting up his camp."

Gabriela nods, "Do we know how large his army is?"

Choel replies, "Just slightly larger than ours. However, the castle defenses will even things out or give us the advantage."

Gabriela smiles, "Good."

Choel questions, "What do you have planned my Queen?"

Gabriela explains, "I have contacted my spy and she is going to kidnap one of the children and bring them to the castle. When she gets here, I'll take the child to the torture room where the well is at. I have no doubt that Stefez will try to sneak into the castle while Prince Brian is attacking us." She pauses, "Choel, you and my spy will handle Prince Brian and his army. Miclou and Stecher will wait for Stefez and the others to try and sneak into the castle. I'll work on getting the magic from the child."

Choel nods, "Sounds like an excellent plan my Queen."

Gabriela smiles, "Yes it does." She pauses, "Now, you three go and make sure everything is in place."

Choel, Miclou and Stecher bow their heads, turn and walk off.

Chapter 40

As the sun starts to get lower to the evening horizon, the breeze that once was blowing the horrible smells of the swamp is starting to change. The smell is now that of fresh grown mushrooms being cooked. Jody and the others continue around a bend in the trail and they see the edge of the swamp just a hundred yards ahead.

Stephanie smiles and speaks as they continue to walk, "Finally."

Sherry nods, "You can even start to smell the difference."

Jody glances around, "It won't be long now. Mushroom Farm is only a mile or two from the edge of the swamp."

Marsha chimes in, "I'm definitely ready to stop for the night."

Brendan speaks up, "Me too."

The group continues walking and soon finds themselves walking out of the swamp and back into the green rolling hills of the grasslands. The smell of food fills the air as Jody and the others continue walking east. Before too long, they top a small hill and see the village of Mushroom Farm ahead.

Mushroom Farm is a small village about the same size as Havel. The village made of huts and a couple of barns is surrounded by fields of mushrooms. The people of Mushroom Farm are dressed in clothes made of different shades of brown and are not nearly as nice as the clothes of the larger towns.

Jody and the others continue on towards Mushroom Farm. As they walk by the fields, the people of Mushroom Farm take notice of the outlanders. Whispers start to find their way through the village as Jody and the others walk by the first few huts of the village.

Stephanie whispers, "Everyone is staring again."

Jody glances around and nods at the villagers, "Of course. Its going to be okay though. The people here like to be left alone."

Marsha questions, "So, where are we going to wait for the others at?"

Jody replies, "There is a barn on the east edge of the village like the one we just passed. We'll wait there. The others should approach from that direction and we'll be able to see them."

Sherry nods, "Sounds good to me."

As they continue to walk through town, Brendan waves at a couple small girls and a young boy. The village kids wave back which kind of makes everyone feel a little less nervous on both sides. Jody and the others finally reach the east side of the village and the barn that they are planning to wait in.

Jody stops and looks at the others, "Okay, this is it. Lets climb up in the loft and wait."

Jody walks over to the door of the barn and opens it. Jody and the others walk inside. The barn is filled with mushrooms and hay. Jody leads the others over to the ladder and everyone climbs up to the loft to wait.

Prince Brian walks into his tent as the sun sets over the Kingdom giving way to the moon and the clear night sky full of stars. Prince Brian removes his weapons and sits down to rest while he waits for the others to arrive at his tent to go over the plans for the castle. As he waits,

Prince Brian thinks about Stephanie and the message she sent him. He can't help but smile at the thought of her being his true love and him being her true love. He wonders if she would stay in the Kingdom or not. However, he hopes that Stephanie will not have to face making such a decision. He hopes that fate will intervene and show them what is meant to be.

At that time, Prince Brian hears Jennifer's voice, "My lord!"

Prince Brian blinks a couple of times and replies, "Come in!"

Jennifer, Rein and Ramaf walk into the tent. The three of them sit down.

Prince Brian looks at Jennifer, "Is the camp completed?"

Jennifer nods, "Yes it is my lord."

Prince Brian looks over to Rein, "Are the scouts and guards in place?"

Rein nods, "Yes my lord."

Prince Brian smiles and looks at Ramaf, "And is the rest of the army ready for tomorrow?"

Ramaf smiles and replies in his gruff voice, "Ready to kick Gabriela and her army into the netherworld."

Prince Brian smiles and chuckles, "Very good." He pauses, "Hopefully the message bird will reach Stefez tonight so she can send it back to us by tomorrow morning."

Jennifer questions, "How do you want to approach the castle my lord?"

Prince Brian sighs and explains, "We will use the long wooden shields we made to protect the battering ram as we try to breach the main doors. We will use the elves to also cover them with volleys of arrows."

Ramaf nods, "What of the dwarves?"

Prince Brian replies, "The dwarves and the rest of the humans will remain protected under the other shields or whatever other cover we can find until the doors are breached."

Rein nods, "They will no doubt reinforce the center of the door."

Prince Brian nods, "I'm counting on it. However, those of us that know, know that the doors are weak on the outer edges. We can break the wood around the hinges and the doors will fall."

Jennifer smiles and nods, "I guess it's a good thing your father never fixed that flaw."

Prince Brian smiles, "A very good thing."

Rein speaks up, "Then tomorrow will be the day that decides the fate of the Kingdom."

Prince Brian nods, "It would appear to be that way. Go ahead and get some rest. We'll see what comes when the sun rises in the morning."

Jennifer, Rein and Ramaf bow their heads, stand up and walk out of the tent. Prince Brian lays down. Jennifer's words makes him think about his father. He also thinks about his younger sister who vanished when his father was killed and they escaped the castle. He says a short prayer that one day he will know the fate of his sister. His last thoughts before he falls asleep are thoughts of Stephanie.

———

With the moon and stars shining bright in the clear sky, Stefez and the others can see the outskirts of Mushroom Farm as they start through the fields east of the village. As they continue to get closer, they can make out the barn on the east edge of the village.

Anna questions, "I wonder if the others are here already?"

Stefez smiles, "Mushroom Farm is not very big. It won't take us long to find them if they're here."

The group gets about a hundred feet from the barn when they hear a familiar voice yelling to them.

Jody yells down from the outer loft door of the barn, "Hey, up here!"

Stefez and the others stop and look up. They see Jody standing in the open loft door.

Stefez smiles, "Its good to see you! We'll be right up!"

Jody moves back inside as Stefez and the others make their way around to the barn door. Jody walks over to the top of the ladder as Stefez and the others walk inside the barn and look around.

Jody hollers, "Over here!"

Stefez and the others walk over to the ladder. Anna is the first up the ladder followed by Stefez. Shaun is next followed by Jencent. Michael picks up Bailee and puts her in his pouch, then climbs up the ladder. Anna reaches the top of the ladder and sees Marsha standing up. Anna runs over to Marsha and the two of them hug.

Anna speaks joyfully, "Oh my God! I'm so happy to see you Marsha!"

Marsha gets a few tears in her eyes, "I'm so happy to see you too. I thought I lost you."

Everyone else makes it up the ladder and over to the others. Everyone smiles, shakes hands and hugs are passed all around as the atmosphere is that of joy and happiness.

Jody steps over to the loft door, "Let me close this and we can sit, eat and catch up."

Then Jody hears the chirpy voice of the message bird, "Good evening."

The message bird flies into the barn. Stefez holds up her right hand and the message bird lands on it.

The message bird speaks, "I have a message from Prince Brian."

Stefez nods, "Okay."

Everyone listens as the message bird speaks, "He is at the base of the hill surrounding the castle and he waits for your signal for when you want him to attack."

Everyone smiles as they hear that the plan is going as they had hoped it would.

Stefez smiles, "Thank you. Please tell Prince Brian that we will leave at dawn. I'll send a lightning bolt into the sky when we are ready for him to attack."

The message bird replies, "It will be done."

Stefez raises her hand and the bird flies off. Jody shuts the loft door as everyone sits down and grabs something to eat. Jody walks over and sits next to Stephanie and Marsha. Michael sets Bailee down on the ground and Bailee hops over next to Anna.

Anna sets a carrot down for Bailee, then looks at the others, "Oh my God. You have to hear about the things we had to go through."

As everyone eats and drinks, they each take turns telling stories about the journeys that has brought them to Mushroom Farm. The barn is filled with laughter as everyone enjoys the stories and the various reactions to the stories. After a little bit of time has passed, everyone finishes eating.

Brendan is standing and bouncing around as he finishes his story, "And the lizard men attacked us, but we beat them up really good." He pauses and finally sits down next to Stephanie, "This place is so cool!"

Everyone laughs at Brendan. The laughing finally starts to die down after a minute or two.

Stefez speaks up, "We should probably get some rest. Tomorrow is the big day."

Everyone nods and spreads out in the loft, each finding a place to lay down. Before long, everyone drifts off to sleep except one. Jencent lays quiet pretending to be asleep and listening for her chance.

Chapter 41

In the darkness of the night, Stefez and the others are sleeping in the dark and quiet barn loft. At that time, Jencent raises up and looks around. After a few seconds, Jencent is sure everyone is asleep. Jencent gets up as quietly as possible. She gathers up her things making little to no noise as not to alert anyone else.

Jencent slowly moves around the loft until she sees Anna. Anna is sound asleep, but Marsha is laying next to Anna with her arm around her. Jencent knows that would be taking too much of a chance so she slowly walks around until she spots Stephanie and Brendan. Jencent stops next to Brendan and sees her opportunity. Brendan is laying next to Stephanie and Jody, but neither one is close enough to feel him move.

Jencent pulls out a small vile of liquid from her belt and takes off the cap. She grabs the bottom corner of her cloak and pours the liquid from the vile on the cloak. Jencent puts the vile away and holds the corner of the cloak just above Brendan's nose and mouth so he can breath in the fumes. Jencent knows it won't take the potion but a few seconds and she will be able to move Brendan without him waking up.

Jencent glances around the loft to make sure no one else is awake. Once she is sure the potion has taken effect, Jencent lets go of her cloak. Jencent scoops up Brendan in her arms and stands up. She looks around the loft again to make sure everyone is still asleep. Jencent puts Brendan over her shoulder and quietly makes her way over to the ladder. She carefully climbs down the ladder and walks over to the door of the barn.

Jencent quietly opens the barn door, steps out and closes it behind her. She makes her way over to a couple of horses. She puts Brendan on the back of one of the horses and walks the horse over to the gate. Jencent opens the gate, walks the horse out and closes the gate. She climbs on the horse with Brendan and looks around one last time. Completely sure that no one has seen her, Jencent rides off into the night heading for the castle.

As the sun breaks the morning horizon, the peaceful quiet in the loft of the barn is also broken.

Stephanie hops up in a panic, "Brendan! Brendan, where are you!?"

Jody pops up hearing Stephanie. Jody starts looking around, but doesn't see Brendan. Everyone else starts waking up to Stephanie's calls for Brendan.

Jody grabs his things, "I'll check outside."

Jody rushes over to the ladder and climbs down. He rushes over to the barn door and runs outside. As Jody looks around outside everyone gathers up their things.

Stephanie continues to yell, "Brendan! Brendan!"

Marsha starts looking around the loft with Stephanie. Michael climbs down the ladder and starts looking around the barn. Stephanie rushes around in a panic as she is unable to find Brendan. Anna and Stefez start looking through the loft as Shaun climbs down the ladder and helps Michael look around the barn.

Marsha looks over at Stephanie with a frightened look on her face, "He's not up here Steph."

Stephanie shakes her head as her face is that of complete panic.

Michael yells up from the bottom of the ladder, "He's

not down here!"

Stefez, Marsha, Anna and Stephanie climb down the ladder and join Michael and Shaun.

Marsha speaks up hoping to calm Stephanie, "Maybe Jody found him outside."

Finally, it comes to Stefez that someone else is missing also and Stefez questions, "Has anyone seen Jencent?"

Shaun looks around for a second, "Now that you mention it, I don't see her."

Michael looks at Stefez, "You don't think …"

Before Michael can finish what he is saying, Jody walks back in shaking his head.

Jody sighs, "No sign of him outside. However, a horse is missing and there are tracks leading off to the southeast."

Stefez shakes her head, "I don't believe it. I should've seen this."

Stephanie looks at Stefez in fear, "What?"

Stefez sighs, "She took him. She took Brendan to Gabriela."

Jody walks up, "Who are you talking about?"

Stefez shakes her head, "Jencent. She must have grabbed him last night and took off." She pauses, "The little signs were there. I can't believe I didn't see it."

Shaun tries to console Stefez, "It's not your fault. None of us saw it."

Stephanie questions still in fear and shock, "What do we do? I can't lose Brendan."

Jody turns and starts for the barn door, "We head for the castle. The more time we waste, the more chance Gabriela has to hurt him and I'm not going to let that happen."

Marsha hurries up after Jody. Stephanie and Anna quickly hurry up and catch up to Jody who is nearly at the barn door.

Bailee yells down from the loft, "Don't forget me!"

Michael climbs up the ladder quickly and puts Bailee in his pouch. As Michael climbs down, Jody, Marsha, Stephanie and Anna walk out of the barn. Shaun and Stefez exit the barn a few feet behind Jody and the others. Michael hops off the ladder and puts Bailee down. Michael and Bailee quickly catch up to the others as everyone starts off across the field heading southeast towards the castle.

———————

As the sun breaks the morning horizon and the cool morning breeze blows gently across the Kingdom, Prince Brian walks out of his tent and looks around. He already hears the people in his camp getting ready for the day. Prince Brian closes his eyes and breathes in the crisp morning air. At that time, Jennifer, Rein and Ramaf walk up.

Jennifer bows her head, "Good morning my lord."

Prince Brian opens his eyes and nods, "Good morning everyone."

Rein speaks up, "Everyone is having their morning meal. The army will be ready to go soon."

Prince Brian smiles, "Good."

At that time, the four of them hear the chirping of the message bird in the sky above. Prince Brian looks up and sees the message bird. Prince Brian holds up his right hand. The message bird swoops down and lands on his hand.

Prince Brian questions, "What do you have for us little bird?"

The message bird replies in it's chirpy voice, "Everyone made it to Mushroom Farm okay. They will leave for the castle this morning at dawn. Stefez said she will send a lightning bolt into the sky when they are in position."

Prince Brian smiles and nods, "Thank you."

Prince Brian holds up his hand and the message bird flies off.

Ramaf speaks up, "If they left at dawn, they should reach the castle by noon."

Prince Brian nods, "That's what I figure." He pauses, "Make sure the army is ready. We'll start moving towards the castle soon."

Jennifer, Rein and Ramaf bow their heads, turn and walk off.

———————

As the sun gets closer to the noon sky, Gabriela is sitting in the throne room. The doors open and Choel, Miclou and Stecher walk in. The doors close as the air starts to get colder. The three of them walk across the room and up the steps.

Choel kneels, "You wanted to see us my Queen?"

Gabriela nods, "Yes."

At that time, the doors open again. Choel stands up and turns around. Miclou and Stecher look back at the door.

Gabriela stands up, "What is the meaning of this interruption?"

Then, Jencent walks into the throne room carrying the still unconscious Brendan in her arms. The doors close behind Jencent. Jencent walks across the throne room.

As Jencent walks up the stairs, Gabriela smiles, "You have the child."

Jencent stops next to the others, "Yes my Queen."

Gabriela laughs, "This is turning out to be a good day. Prince Brian will never know what hit him."

Choel questions, "What do you want us to do my Queen?"

Gabriela smiles, "Stefez and the others will still try to make it into the castle and now rescue the boy." She pauses, "Choel, you and Jencent will stay with the army and defend the castle. Miclou and Stecher will join me in the torture chamber where the magical well is at."

Choel bows his head, "Yes my Queen."

Gabriela looks at Jencent, "Hand the child to Stecher, then you and Choel go."

Jencent turns and hands Brendan over to Stecher. Choel and Jencent bow their heads, turn and walk off.

Gabriela looks at the dark riders, "Lets get to the torture chamber. It will take some time to prepare the torture spells."

Miclou and Stecher bow their heads, turn and start for the doors. Gabriela grabs her staff and starts after the dark riders.

As the sun inches closer to the high noon sky, Stefez and the others see the castle in the distance as they continue to walk across the rolling green hills.

Stefez speaks while walking, "A few more hills and we'll reach the town surrounding the castle."

Stephanie looks down dejected, "I still can't believe this. I can't lose Brendan."

Jody moves over and takes Stephanie's hand, "Nothing is going to happen to him."

Marsha moves over and takes Stephanie's other hand, "It's going to be okay Steph."

Stephanie shakes her head, "I just, I can't believe I let him get taken."

Jody tries to reassure his sister, "We'll get him back." His tone changes to more anger, "I promise you that."

Stephanie tries to smile, knowing Jody would do anything to save Brendan.

Stefez speaks up, "No doubt Gabriela will have him in the torture chamber, which happens to be where the magical well is at."

Michael speaks up, "And since we haven't seen them recently, no doubt the dark riders will be with her."

Shaun questions, "Why would she risk having Brendan that close to the magical well which leads them out of the Kingdom?"

Stefez replies, "She needs the magical water from the well to complete the torture spell."

Tears come to Stephanie's eyes at the thought of Brendan being tortured and dying.

Jody squeezes Stephanie's hand, "That's not going to happen."

The group tops another hill and sees the town surrounding the base of the hill just ahead.

Chapter 42

A s the sun peaks in the noon sky, Prince Brian walks over to where Jennifer, Rein and Ramaf are standing near the army.

Prince Brian looks at Jennifer, "Are the battering rams and shields ready?"

Jennifer nods, "Yes my lord."

Prince Brian looks at Rein, "Do you have the Elvin archers ready?"

Rein nods, "Yes my lord."

Prince Brian looks at Ramaf, "Are the rest of the soldiers ready for when we break through the main doors?"

Ramaf smiles, "You better believe it. We're ready for action."

Prince Brian smiles, "Then lets go ahead and move through town and up to the castle. They should be just about to the other side of the castle. That way we're in position to launch the attack when they signal."

Jennifer, Rein and Ramaf bow their heads and rush over to the army. Jennifer breaks off the humans handling the shields and battering ram and starts through town towards the main doors of the castle. Prince Brian links up with Jennifer and the others. Rein gathers up the elves and they start through town a little behind Jennifer, Prince Brian and their part of the army. Ramaf gathers up the dwarves and remaining humans and starts through town just behind Rein and her part of the army.

As Prince Brian and Jennifer make their way through

the streets, numerous townspeople cheer them. The loud cheering carries all the way to the castle where Gabriela's army waits. The cheering continues as Rein and her elves move through the streets and the cheering continues as Ramaf and the remaining army follows.

As Prince Brian and his part of the army starts up the hill towards the castle, they can see archers lined along the castle wall, waiting for them. Standing with the archers on the castle wall is a familiar face, it is Jencent. Rein breaks away from Prince Brian and the elves move to a position halfway up the side of the hill where they can use their bows and arrows to fire upon the castle. Ramaf stops his army a third of the way up the hill and remains far enough away where they are safe from the archers on the castle walls, but close enough to charge the castle when they hear Jennifer call them with her horn.

Prince Brian and his part of the army stop as they near the top of the hill. With their long shields overhead to protect them from incoming arrows, Prince Brian, Jennifer and the humans wait. The archers along the castle wall stand ready, but hold their fire as they see Prince Brian and his army stop moving towards the castle.

Prince Brian looks at Jennifer, "Now we wait. Keep your eyes open. Hopefully we'll get the signal soon."

Both sides wait with great anticipation as they know the final battle for control of the Kingdom is just moments away.

———————

As Prince Brian moves into position to attack, Stefez and the others have made their way up the back of the hill to the back wall of the castle. Everyone has noticed that the back wall and towers are empty.

Jody speaks as they move closer to the castle, "I can't believe they don't have any lookouts at all back here."

Michael glances around, "No doubt they are all at the front of the castle focused on Prince Brian."

Shaun questions, "So, how are we going to get by the castle wall and into the castle?"

Stefez smiles, "The same way Prince Brian got out. There is a secret tunnel that leads into the back courtyard from out here." She pauses, "Only the royal family knows about it. Prince Brian told me about it when we stopped in the Dark Valley."

Michael nods, "Once we get inside the courtyard, we can get into the castle through the servant entrance near the kitchen. There might be a guard or two, but nothing to really slow us down."

The group reaches the castle wall. Stefez leads them along the castle wall as she looks at each of the bottom stones closely. Everyone follows Stefez and after a couple hundred feet, Stefez stops in front of a stone that has the royal emblem carved into it.

Stefez smiles, "Here it is. All we have to do is clear the dirt and grass off and there should be a wooden door in the ground."

Jody, Michael and Shaun start moving the loose dirt and grass out of the way. It takes only a couple of minutes for the three of them to uncover the hidden door. Michael grabs the iron ring handle and lifts the door open.

Stefez steps a couple feet away, "I'm going to send the signal. Everyone go ahead and start down the tunnel."

Michael starts in first followed by Jody. Stephanie and Sherry go next. Marsha and Anna follow them, then Shaun and Bailee go next. Stefez holds her staff up in the air and mumbles under her breath. After a couple of seconds, a twenty foot long lightning bolt flies up into the sky. The lightning bolt explodes about a hundred yards above the castle, easily seen by everyone in and around the castle. Stefez smiles, then walks over and starts into the tunnel after the others.

———————

Prince Brian and Jennifer continue to wait with their two battering ram units. Then, everyone sees and hears the bolt of lightning explode in the sky above the castle.

Jennifer looks at Prince Brian, "I believe that's it my lord."

Prince Brian smiles, "Call for the archers and sound the attack."

Jennifer raises the horn to her mouth and blows a specific sound.

Rein hears the call and yells to her elves, "Archers, ready!"

Jennifer blows into the horn again, this time the tune is a little different.

Prince Brian yells, "Charge the gates!"

Hearing the call for the attack, Rein yells, "Archers, fire!"

The first volley of arrows fly towards the castle wall as Prince Brian, Jennifer and their two units charge towards the main doors.

Ramaf hears the call for the attack and yells, "At a walk, move towards the main doors!"

Ramaf and his part of the army slowly start walking towards the main doors.

Jencent watches from the castle walls as the battering rams come charging and the first volley of arrows come their way.

Jencent yells, "Archers, fire!"

The undead elves lining the castle walls fire their arrows at Prince Brian and his people as well as firing a few arrows at Rein and her elves.

On the inside of the castle in the open courtyard, Choel looks at the main doors where he has two large pieces of wood wedged against the middle of the doors, just like Prince Brian figured they would.

As the battering rams get closer, the two units separate with Prince Brian going with the unit on the left and Jennifer with the unit on the right. The arrows from the castle walls land all around the battering rams with a few arrows sticking into the shields protecting the battering rams. A few of the arrows from the castle wall land near Rein and the elves, but no one is hit during the first volley. Some of the arrows fired from Rein and the elves hit the side of the castle wall, some fly over the wall into the courtyard and a few are on target as two undead elves are struck and fall from the castle wall.

As the archers on both sides prepare to fire again, the battering rams slam into the main doors of the castle near the hinges with thunderous force. The wood cracks and splinters from the tremendous blows of the battering rams. As the battering rams back up and prepare to run forward again, the arrows reign down. This time a couple of arrows find their mark getting by the shields and two humans fall. A few more arrows fly in at Rein and the elves and one arrow is on target as an elf is hit and falls. The arrows from Rein and the elves fly in at the castle again. Some of the arrows fly into the courtyard where two trolls are hit and drop. Once again, an undead elf is struck and falls from the wall.

The battering rams rush forward and slam into the main doors again with tremendous force. The wood breaks off in a few pieces and splinters fall everywhere from the massive blow. The archers on both sides prepare to fire again as the battering rams back up and get ready for another run.

As the battle rages on outside, Gabriela, Miclou and Stecher are in the torture chamber. Brendan is strapped down to a stone table with a piece of cloth tied over his eyes. Miclou and Stecher are standing by the door. Gabriela is using her staff to mix a potion in a small caldron next to the table where Brendan is tied up. The cool air in the chamber from the dark riders is mixed with the awful smell of the potion in the caldron. Tears run down Brendan's cheeks from under the blindfold as Gabriela pulls her staff out of the caldron and leans it against the edge of the table.

Gabriela looks over at Miclou and Stecher, "The battle has started so no doubt Stefez and the others are in the castle. Head for the back and take the most direct way. You should run into them."

Miclou and Stecher bow their heads, turn, open the door and walk out of the room, closing the door behind them. Gabriela turns to the well in the center of the room. The opening of the well is five feet around and raises up from the floor about three feet.

Gabriela throws up her hands, "I call forth the dark powers from the netherworld!"

A golden glow starts to emanate from the well.

As the battle rages in the front of the castle and Gabriela is trying to conjure the torture spells, the back courtyard is quiet and serene. Suddenly, next to a rose bush, the ground moves. A few seconds later, a wooden door like the one outside the castle raises up from the ground next to the rose bush.

Jody is the first one out followed by Michael. Stephanie, Sherry, Marsha and Anna climb out next. Shaun helps Bailee out of the tunnel, then she climbs out. Finally Stefez climbs out of the tunnel. Michael lowers the door back down.

Jody looks at Stefez, "Which way?"

Stefez points to the left, "Just around that corner will be a wooden door."

Jody draws his sword and starts slowly jogging towards where Stefez pointed. Shaun and Michael draw their swords and start after Jody. Stefez, Stephanie, Marsha, Anna, Sherry and Bailee take off after Shaun and Michael. Jody runs around the corner and sees the door about fifty feet in front of him. Two trolls are standing by the door. The trolls see Jody and pick up their swords. Jody runs at the trolls as Michael and Shaun come around the corner.

Jody closes in on the trolls obviously not wanting anything to slow him up from finding Brendan. The first troll swings it's sword at Jody as he gets close. Jody ducks under the sword and elbows the first troll in the back. The first troll staggers forward right at Michael and Shaun. Jody swings his sword in at the second troll. The second troll brings it's sword across and blocks the sword. Jody steps in and brings his knee up, striking the second troll's arm and knocking the sword out of the way. As Jody cuts in with his sword again, Stefez and the others come around the corner. Jody's second swing is true as it finds the second troll's neck, sending the troll to the ground.

The first troll staggers towards Michael and Shaun. Michael swings his sword at the first troll. The first troll raises it's sword and blocks the sword. However, Shaun is right there and thrusts her sword in at the first troll. The sword stabs into the first troll's chest. Shaun removes her sword and the first troll falls.

Jody tries the handle of the door and discovers it is lock.

Michael sees Jody trying the handle, "Move!"

Michael rushes forward and kicks his left leg at the door. With his weight and momentum behind the kick, the door flies open. Michael runs inside with everyone else right behind him. They find themselves in the kitchen.

Stefez speaks, "Through the kitchen and out the door on the far side. Then right down the hallway."

Everyone takes off running.

Chapter 43

The battering rams rush forward towards the main doors again. As the battering rams smash into the doors nearly breaking the hinges, more arrows come flying down. A couple arrows get past the shields and two humans fall. More arrows from the castle wall flies out at Rein and the elves. Three elves are struck with arrows and fall. Rein and the elves fire their arrows back. The arrows fly in at Jencent and the undead elves along the castle wall.

Jencent moves to her right as an arrow flies by. A few arrows fly into the courtyard where two trolls are struck and fall. One undead elf on the castle wall is struck and falls from the wall. The battering rams move back and prepare for another run.

Prince Brian looks over at Jennifer, "Call the charge for Ramaf! A couple more blows and we should be through!"

Jennifer nods and raises the horn to her mouth. She blows a specific tune with the horn. The battering rams run forward at the main doors. The battering rams slam into the doors with incredible force, breaking the hinges.

Ramaf is walking towards the main doors when he hears the call from Jennifer, "That's our signal! Charge the gates!"

Ramaf and the rest of the army start running towards the main gates bringing themselves into range of the undead elves. The undead elves fire another volley of arrows. This time the shields over the battering rams do their job as no one is hit. The arrows fly in at Rein and the elves and one elf is struck and falls. This time arrows fly in at Ramaf and his army. One human and two dwarves are struck with arrows and fall as everyone continues running at the main gates. The battering rams back up and prepare for the next run at the main doors. Jencent can tell that the main doors won't hold much longer.

Jencent yells to the undead elves, "Fire one more volley, then get down to the courtyard and prepare for battle!"

Jencent runs off for the stairs that lead down from the castle wall to the courtyard.

Stefez and the others are running down a long hallway. They turn a corner and start down another long hallway. The group gets nearly all the way down the hallway as they pass by a hallway going off to their left.

Stefez yells as they run, "At the end of the hallway, we'll turn right!"

As they approach the end of the hallway, they see a doorway on the right side of the hallway they're running down that leads to one of the dining areas. As the group gets to the doorway, Miclou and Stecher emerge from the doorway into the hallway and the dark riders nearly collide with Stefez and the others.

Everyone jumps out of the way as the dark riders appear amongst them and the air immediately gets colder. The dark riders appear just as shocked to have suddenly ran into Stefez and the rest of the group. Everyone hesitates for a second.

Jody yells, "Everyone run!"

Stefez takes off down the hallway in the direction the group was already heading with everyone else right behind her. Miclou and Stecher take off running after

Stefez and the others. The group turns the corner and keeps running down the hallway.

Bailee hops quickly to the lead, "Follow me, I know a shortcut!"

Stefez yells, "What?! How?!"

Bailee quickly turns into an open doorway on the left side of the hallway. Without time to discuss the answers, the rest of the group turns and runs into the open doorway right behind Bailee. They find themselves in one of the armory rooms of the castle where the weapons for the army is stored. As they group makes it's way through the room, Miclou and Stecher run into the room and continue to slowly gain on Stefez and the others.

Rein watches as Ramaf and his people run by heading for the main doors of the castle. Rein looks up and the last volley of arrows land around them, not hitting anyone this time. Rein sees the undead elves start running off of the castle wall.

Rein yells to her elves, "Get to the main doors!"

Rein and her elves take off running and fall in behind Ramaf and his people. The battering rams rush forward and smash into the main doors again. This time the main doors twist from where the hinges use to hold the doors in place. The two large wooden beams reinforcing the middle of the doors dislodge from the shifting of the weight of the main doors and the wooden beams fall to the ground. The main doors, now with nothing to hold them in place, fall back and crash to the ground inside the courtyard.

Prince Brian yells, "Attack!"

Prince Brian and Jennifer charge into the courtyard. The men with Prince Brian abandon the battering rams and shields and rush into the courtyard. At that time,

Ramaf and his people arrive and run through the main gate area quickly followed by Rein and her elves. Prince Brian, Jennifer, Ramaf and Rein see Choel and Jencent with the rest of Gabriela's army come charging at them.

In a matter of seconds, a huge battle erupts in the main courtyard of the castle as both armies fight their hardest for control of the Kingdom.

Bailee hops through an open doorway and back into another hallway. She turns right and takes off down the hallway as Stefez and the others rush into the hallway, turn right and start after Bailee. A few seconds later, Miclou and Stecher run into the hallway, turn right and take off after the group.

Bailee yells while hopping fast, "Not much further!"

Bailee quickly turns down a hallway to the left and keeps on going. Stefez and the others turn fast and keep up with Bailee. Miclou and Stecher who have made up quite a bit of the distance, turn the corner and keep after the group.

The air hangs heavy in the torture chamber as Gabriela continues to conjure the torture spell. A soft golden glow continues to emanate from the well as smoke starts to slowly roll out of the well. Gabriela smiles as she sees the smoke start to come out of the well. Gabriela walks back over to the table where Brendan is tied up. She dips her hand into the caldron, scooping out some of the magical potion. Gabriela tosses the potion in her hand on Brendan's chest, splashing the potion all over Brendan and the table.

Gabriela raises her hands into the air, "Ghost of the

netherworld, enter this child's body and bring me his magic."

A black, three foot long shadow flies out of the well, up into the air and down at Brendan. The shadow strikes Brendan in the chest and appears to enter his body. Brendan cries out in pain as he arches his back.

Gabriela smiles, "Your magic will soon be mine."

———————

As the massive battle rages on in the courtyard with both sides starting to suffer a few losses, Jencent spots Prince Brian through the confusion. With her sword in her right hand and her short sword in her left hand, Jencent runs through the mass of people towards Prince Brian. Prince Brian uses his shield to block a sword from a troll. Prince Brian thrusts his sword in and it finds home as the troll is unable to block the sword. Prince Brian pulls his sword back and the troll falls at his feet. Prince Brian looks to his right and sees Jencent only twenty feet away charging right at him. Prince Brian turns to face Jencent and prepares himself.

Jencent rushes in and swings her sword at Prince Brian from his left. Prince Brian moves his shield over and blocks the sword. Jencent moves fast, cutting her short sword in at Prince Brian from his right. Prince Brian reacts quickly, bringing his sword down and blocking the short sword. Having opened up Prince Brian's body, Jencent snaps out her right leg and kicks Prince Brian in the stomach. Prince Brian takes the kick fairly well and shuffles back a few feet.

Jencent closes in quick and brings her sword down at Prince Brian's head. Prince Brian brings his shield up and deflects the sword away. Prince Brian moves quickly into a spin and brings his sword around at Jencent's head. Jencent ducks at the last second as Prince Brian's sword just barely misses. Jencent brings her short sword across at Prince Brian's legs. Prince Brian sees the short sword and hops back out of the way as the short sword narrowly misses.

Prince Brian steps in and cuts his sword down at Jencent's head. Jencent brings her sword up and blocks Prince Brian's sword. Jencent quickly thrusts her short sword in at Prince Brian's chest. Prince Brian steps to his left and brings his shield across his body. The edge of Prince Brian's shield strikes Jencent's left wrist causing her to lose her grip on the short sword. Jencent cries out in pain as her short sword flies off and lands a few feet away.

Seeing an opportunity to take the upper hand, Prince Brian steps in and rams his shield into Jencent with all his weight. The powerful blow sends Jencent staggering backwards off-balance. Prince Brian closes in without hesitation and brings his sword down at Jencent's head. Jencent manages to bring her sword up and block the sword. Prince Brian brings his shield across and knocks Jencent's sword out of the way. Prince Brian quickly cuts his sword in under his shield. Still off-balance, Jencent doesn't have time to react and the sword cuts her deep across the stomach.

Jencent doubles over and cries out in pain, but still manages to thrust her sword in at Prince Brian. Prince Brian sidesteps the sword and brings his sword over and down striking the final blow to Jencent's back just between her shoulder blades. Jencent drops her sword, falls to the ground and lays motionless.

Prince Brian looks around and sees that his army is starting to take the upper hand. All Prince Brian can think about is Stephanie so he breaks away from the battle and starts running for the main entrance into the castle.

Bailee is hopping as fast as she can down a long hallway with Stefez and the others right behind her. Miclou and Stecher are only fifty feet behind them. Bailee and the others turn the corner to the right at the end of the hallway. They see another hallway, but they can see at the end of the hallway looks to be a staircase leading down.

Stefez smiles and yells, "There it is! The stairs to the torture chamber!"

Bailee yells as she continues to hop, "Told you I knew a shortcut!"

As the group continues towards the staircase at the end of the hallway, Miclou and Stecher come around the corner behind them. The group slows up some as they reach the top of the staircase. Bailee starts down the spiral staircase with the others right behind her as Miclou and Stecher continue to close in.

As they get closer to the bottom of the staircase, everyone can hear Brendan scream. Bailee hops around the last bend in the staircase and sees the door down the short hallway is closed.

Bailee yells, "The door is closed!"

Michael yells, "Out of the way!"

Michael runs by the others and takes the lead. In a few seconds, Michael lowers his shoulder and throws all his body weight and momentum into the door. The door crashes open and Michael stumbles into the torture chamber. Stefez and everyone else runs into the torture chamber. They see Gabriela standing across the two hundred foot chamber next to the table where Brendan is tied up. Stone columns dot the chamber and the well is in the middle of the chamber. The floor is nearly covered by the dark smoke that is still emanating from the well. The smell in the chamber is awful, but the air starts to get colder as Miclou and Stecher close in on the door.

Stephanie sees Brendan tied to the table, "Brendan!"

Jody, Michael and Shaun draw their swords. Bailee hops off to the side out of the way. Stefez starts to the left with Stephanie, Michael and Shaun behind her. Jody starts to the right with Marsha, Anna and Sherry behind him. Gabriela turns and looks at Stefez.

Gabriela speaks in an evil tone, "You should've not interfered little sister."

Stefez looks at Gabriela and shakes her head, "It ends today."

Miclou and Stecher run into the chamber behind Stefez and the others. Miclou draws his sword and starts to slowly walk towards Stefez, Michael, Shaun and Stephanie. Stecher draws his sword and starts to walk towards Jody, Marsha, Anna and Sherry.

Gabriela smiles at the arrival of the dark riders, "You're right Stefez, it does end today." She pauses, "For all of you!"

Jody yells to Stefez, "Take care of Gabriela and get Brendan, we'll handle the dark riders." He pauses, "Anna, find a safe place to hide."

Anna moves away as Jody, Marsha and Sherry turn around to face Stecher. Michael, Shaun and Stephanie who draws her sword now, turns to face Miclou. Stefez grips her staff with her left hand as she continues to walk towards Gabriela. Gabriela grabs her staff from where it is leaning against the table and turns to face Stefez. Bailee finds her way around the room and stops next to Anna.

Chapter 44

As the battle in the courtyard rages on, it's clear that Prince Brian's army has taken control. Rein, with her sword in her right hand, and Jennifer, with her sword in her right hand and her short sword in her left hand, are fighting side by side in the middle of the courtyard. Jennifer finishes off the troll she was facing and Rein finishes off the undead human she was facing. Rein and Jennifer both turn and find themselves facing Choel who is standing ten feet away with his sword in his right hand and his shield in his left hand.

Rein approaches Choel on his left and Jennifer approaches Choel on his right. Jennifer moves in fast and brings her sword around at Choel's head. Choel raises his sword and blocks Jennifer's sword. Rein moves in and swings her sword at Choel. Choel moves his shield over and blocks Rein's sword. Jennifer quickly thrusts her short sword in under her other sword. Choel spins around the short sword and brings his sword around at Jennifer's head. Jennifer brings her sword over and blocks Choel's sword. Choel quickly brings his right leg up and kicks Jennifer in the ribs. Jennifer stumbles away off-balance.

Rein moves in fast and brings her sword across at Choel's head. Choel brings his sword across his body and blocks Rein's sword. Choel continues into a spin and brings his shield around. Choel's shield slams into Rein's body sending Rein staggering back and nearly falling to the ground. Choel closes in on Rein seeing that he has an opening, but Jennifer has regained her balance and steps over between Rein and Choel.

Jennifer thrusts her sword in at Choel. Choel brings his shield over and knocks the sword away as he swings his sword around at Jennifer's head. Jennifer brings her short sword up and blocks Choel's sword. Choel steps in and using his size and strength, pushes Jennifer back and Jennifer stumbles away a few feet. By this time, Rein has regained her balance and comes back in at Choel. Rein brings her sword down at Choel's head. Choel spins to his left as the sword comes down and misses. Choel continues his spin until he is behind Rein. Choel throws his right elbow into Rein's back. Rein is knocked forward a few feet ending up next to Jennifer.

Choel turns and faces the two women. Jennifer and Rein turn back to face Choel.

Jennifer speaks to Rein, "I think we need a new plan."

Rein nods and the two women start to move towards Choel in a very slow, calculating manner.

———————

Prince Brian runs into the castle through the main door. He stops for a second to catch his breath and takes off running to the right down a long hallway. He turns left at the end of the hallway and keeps running. After another couple of turns, Prince Brian stops at the doors leading into the throne room. Expecting to be facing Gabriela on the other side, Prince Brian throws his shield and shoulder into one of the doors, knocking it open. Prince Brian runs into the throne room and stops.

Prince Brian looks around a bit puzzled, "She's not here."

Prince Brian thinks for a few seconds, then it hits him.

Prince Brian gets a look of worry, "She must be in

the torture chamber."

Prince Brian turns around and runs out of the throne room heading for the torture chamber.

As the battle rages on in the courtyard, the showdown in the torture chamber is about to begin. Michael, Shaun and Stephanie face off with Miclou as Jody, Marsha and Sherry face off with Stecher. Stefez and Gabriela are facing each other with their staves ready. Anna and Bailee are watching from the side of the chamber.

Michael moves in and thrusts his sword in at Miclou. Miclou brings his sword across and knocks Michael's sword away as Shaun cuts her sword in from the right. Miclou brings his leg up and kicks Shaun's right hand, stopping the sword. Stephanie steps in and swings her sword at Miclou's head. Miclou ducks under Stephanie's sword and spins. Michael brings his sword up and Stephanie's sword hits Michael's sword. Miclou brings his leg around as he finishes his spin and sweeps Stephanie's legs out from under her. Stephanie's feet come off the ground and she crashes to the floor on her back.

Michael steps in quick and swings his sword at Miclou who is still in a low crouch. Miclou dives forward and rolls under Michael's sword. Miclou rolls to his feet and as he stands up, Shaun thrusts her sword in at him. Miclou brings his sword across and knock's Shaun's sword away. Miclou brings his right leg up and kicks Shaun in the stomach. Shaun staggers back a few feet. Miclou spins around and brings his sword around as if he knew Michael was getting close behind him. Michael just barely manages to bring his sword up in time to block Miclou's sword. With Michael's sword locked with Miclou's sword, Shaun moves in and thrusts her sword at

Miclou's back. Miclou hears Shaun coming at him from behind and steps to his left. Michael sees Shaun's sword miss Miclou and head straight at him. Michael jumps to his left to avoid the deadly sword. Miclou shuffles away a few steps and turns to face Shaun and Michael. Stephanie is still laying on her back trying to get her breath back that was knocked out of her.

Jody steps in and brings his sword around at Stecher's head. Stecher brings his sword up and blocks Jody's sword. Marsha steps in close and swings her staff around at Stecher's knees. Stecher pulls his sword back and jumps up. Marsha's staff goes under Stecher's feet. Jody sees Marsha's staff at the last second and jumps back as Marsha's staff barely misses his legs. Sherry steps in and thrusts her staff at Stecher's head. Stecher leans his head out of the way and the staff narrowly misses. Stecher steps forward and kicks Sherry in the stomach. Sherry steps back and drops to her knees in pain.

Seeing Jody out of the corner of his eyes, Stecher brings his sword around at Jody. Jody brings his sword across and just barely blocks Stecher's sword. Stecher brings his right leg around and kicks Jody in the side of his left knee. Jody's knee buckles and he nearly falls to the floor, but keeps on his feet. Stecher hears Marsha coming at him and turns to face her. Marsha thrusts her staff in at Stecher's head. Stecher reaches up with his left hand and catches the end of the staff. Stecher brings his sword around at Marsha who is unable to get her staff away from Stecher. Marsha's eyes widen as Stecher's sword heads straight at her left ribcage. Jody quickly steps over and just barely manages to get his sword between Stecher's sword and Marsha's body, blocking the would be deadly blow.

Jody steps in and kicks at Stecher with his right leg. Stecher lets go of the staff and spins around Jody's leg, ending up behind Jody. Stecher thrusts his elbow back and it strikes Jody in the middle of his back. Jody stumbles forward a couple steps, but quickly turns back around. Sherry steps in from the right and swings her staff at Stecher as Marsha thrusts her staff at Stecher's head. Stecher, moving like lightning, brings his sword across, blocking Sherry's staff while at the same time, moving his head just enough for Marsha's staff to miss going over his left shoulder.

Stecher leaps towards Marsha and brings his knee up. Stecher's knee slams into Marsha's stomach. Marsha takes a step back, then drops to both knees. Stecher quickly spins around and sweeps Sherry's feet out from under her before she can even react. Sherry crashes to the floor landing hard on her back. Stecher comes back around and stands up as Jody closes in. Stecher brings his sword around at Jody's head. Jody brings his sword up and blocks Stecher's sword. Jody snaps his leg out fast and kicks Stecher in the stomach. Stecher steps back a couple of steps and smiles at Jody. As Jody and Stecher face off, Marsha and Sherry try to regain their breath.

Stefez steps in and brings her staff around at Gabriela's head. Gabriela brings her staff across and blocks Stefez's staff. Gabriela brings her staff up at Stefez. Stefez steps back as the staff barely misses. Stefez swings her staff around at Gabriela's legs. Gabriela hops in the air and the staff goes under her feet. When Gabriela lands on her feet, she brings the claw end of her staff down and it catches Stefez's hand and staff. Gabriela jerks her staff back and Stefez loses her staff as it goes sliding across the floor. Gabriela brings her staff around at Stefez's head. Stefez ducks under the staff, shuffles back a couple steps and draws her sword.

Stefez steps back in quickly and thrusts her sword in at Gabriela. Gabriela steps to her left and knocks the sword away with her staff. Gabriela swings her staff around at Stefez's knees. Stefez brings her right foot up and stops Gabriela's staff. Stefez quickly brings her sword down and it strikes Gabriela's staff between Gabriela's hands. Gabriela loses the grip on her staff and the staff falls to the floor. Stefez, moving fast, thrusts her sword in at Gabriela. Gabriela spins around Stefez's sword and elbows Stefez in the back. Stefez staggers forward a couple of steps, then turns back to face Gabriela. Gabriela draws her sword.

As everyone in the room is fighting, Bailee speaks to Anna, "While they're busy, we should sneak over and untie Brendan."

Anna looks down at Bailee and nods. Anna and Bailee start to slowly move around the edge of the room towards the table where Brendan is tied up.

Chapter 45

As the fight goes on in the torture chamber and the two armies continue to fight in the courtyard with Prince Brian's army clearly in control, Jennifer and Rein start moving in slowly towards Choel. Rein quickly crosses in front of Jennifer and cuts her sword in at Choel from the left. Choel brings his shield over and blocks the sword. Jennifer steps to the side and swings her sword in from the right. Choel raises his sword up and blocks Jennifer's sword. Choel pushes forward with his shield, then steps back as Jennifer thrusts her short sword in at his chest.

Choel just manages to avoid the short sword as he spins around it and brings his sword around. Rein steps over and brings her sword up, blocking Choel's sword from hitting Jennifer in the back. Jennifer turns quick and brings her short sword around at Choel from his left. Choel brings his shield up and blocks the short sword, just like Jennifer was hoping. Jennifer holds Choel's shield in place with her short sword and brings her sword over and down behind Choel's shield. With his shield and sword both engaged, Choel has no way of stopping Jennifer's sword as it strikes him on his left shoulder.

Choel's left arm drops down and he drops his shield on the ground. Jennifer steps close and brings her knee up and slams it into Choel's lower back. As Choel staggers forward, Rein steps around and brings her sword in at the back of Choel's legs. Rein's sword strikes Choel in the back of the knees. Choel drops to his knees and his right arm falls to his side leaving him completely open. Rein spins around and brings her sword around at Choel's chest as Jennifer steps in and swings her sword at Choel's back. Rein's sword slams into Choel's chest at the same time that Jennifer's sword slams into Choel's back. As Jennifer and Rein withdraw their swords and step back, Choel drops his sword to the ground, then falls face first into the courtyard ground.

The remaining trolls, undead humans and undead elves see their leader fall. The last bit of Gabriela's army stops fighting and drops their weapons after Choel falls on the battlefield. The remaining humans, elves and dwarves of Prince Brian's army surrounds the last of Gabriela's army. Jennifer and Rein look at each other and smile. Then both women get a look of concern as they start to scan around the courtyard. Jennifer and Rein smile again as they see Ramaf walking towards them.

Ramaf walks up to the two ladies, "Its over."

Jennifer sighs, "Maybe."

Rein nods, "Gabriela and the dark riders."

Ramaf motions with his head, "You two go find them. I'll take care of the prisoners."

Jennifer and Rein nod and run off towards the main entrance into the castle.

As the fighting in the torture chamber continues, Anna and Bailee reach the table where Brendan is tied up.

Anna whispers to Brendan, "Its me, Anna. Don't make a sound."

Anna quickly unties Brendan from the table and removes the blindfold. Anna helps Brendan down off the table. Anna, Brendan and Bailee hide behind the table and watch as the fighting continues.

Stecher moves in fast and brings his sword around at Jody's head. Jody raises his sword up at the last second and blocks Stecher's sword. Jody spins around and cuts his sword in at the back of Stecher's head. Stecher ducks under Jody's sword and spins bringing his sword around at Jody. At that time, Marsha steps in and thrusts her staff at Stecher. The staff strikes Stecher in the chest knocking Stecher back just far enough that his sword narrowly misses Jody.

Jody smiles, "Thanks sweetheart."

Marsha moves over next to Jody, "Anytime honey."

Jody and Marsha watch as Sherry moves up behind Stecher and swings her staff at the back of Stecher's legs. Stecher, hearing the slightest of noises behind him, jumps up in the air as Sherry's staff misses going underneath his feet. As soon as Stecher lands, he kicks his right leg back and it catches Sherry in the stomach. Sherry steps back a couple steps and drops to her knees.

Jody moves in fast and swings his sword at Stecher from the left. Stecher brings his sword across and blocks Jody's sword. As Marsha steps in and thrusts her staff, Stecher spins around causing the staff to miss. Stecher brings his leg around and kicks Marsha in the back of the knee. Marsha's knee buckles and she drops down to one knee. Stecher raises his sword, but before he can bring it down at Marsha, Jody thrusts his sword at Stecher just over Marsha's head. Stecher jumps back and Jody's sword falls short, but it gives Marsha time to get back to her feet.

Jody speaks to Marsha, "We can't keep up this pace. He'll eventually take us as we tire out."

Shaun moves in at Miclou and brings her sword in at him from his right. Miclou brings his left leg around and kicks Shaun's sword away with his left foot. Miclou continues into a spin and brings his sword around as Michael closes in. Michael sees Miclou's sword at the last second and just manages to bring his sword up and blocks Miclou's sword. Miclou quickly snaps out his right leg this time, kicking Michael in the stomach. Michael steps back a couple of steps. Miclou moves in fast and brings his sword down at Michael. Michael raises his sword just in time to block Miclou's sword. As Shaun closes in, Miclou draws his dagger with his left hand. Shaun thrusts her sword in at Miclou from his right. Miclou brings his dagger over and knocks the sword away.

Michael steps forward and snaps out his left leg. This time it works and Michael kicks Miclou in the stomach. Miclou stumbles back a few feet, then stops. As Shaun and Michael stand next to each other, Miclou looks at his stomach, then at Michael and Shaun and smiles.

Shaun speaks a little winded, "We can't keep this pace up forever."

Michael nods, "I know."

Stefez moves in fast and swings her sword at Gabriela's head. Gabriela brings her sword over and blocks Stefez's sword. Gabriela pulls her sword back and brings it around at Stefez from her left. Stefez moves fast and blocks Gabriela's sword with her sword. Stefez snaps her right leg out, but Gabriela was expecting Stefez to do just that. Gabriela moves to her right just enough for Stefez's foot to miss. Gabriela brings her right leg around and kicks Stefez in her left knee. Stefez's knee buckles and Stefez falls. As Stefez falls, her head clips one of the columns near the well. Stefez lands on her back and drops her sword. Gabriela steps over next to Stefez who is obviously dazed.

Gabriela raises her sword up, "Now it ends little sister."

Suddenly, Gabriela jumps back as Stephanie steps over and thrusts her sword at Gabriela. Stephanie's sword misses, but it makes Gabriela move away from Stefez. Stephanie steps around and places herself between Gabriela and Stefez.

Gabriela shakes her head, "You should've not

interfered outlander."

Gabriela steps in and swings her sword at Stephanie from the left. Stephanie brings her sword up and just manages to block Gabriela's sword. Gabriela quickly brings her sword back and around at Stephanie from the right. Stephanie steps back and manages to barely block the sword again. Gabriela moves too fast and brings her sword back and around at Stephanie again. Stephanie steps back again, not realizing she is only a few feet from the side of the well.

Stephanie brings her sword around and just manages to block Gabriela's sword again. This time, Gabriela quickly brings her right leg up and kicks Stephanie in the stomach. Stephanie staggers back and she hits the side of the well with her lower back. Stephanie drops her sword and falls to her knees in pain.

Gabriela raises her sword, "Its over for you outlander."

Brendan sees his mom in trouble and runs out from behind the table straight at Gabriela's back. Gabriela steps forward and starts to swing her sword down. Stephanie sees Brendan right behind Gabriela and Stephanie moves to her left. Brendan runs full speed and pushes Gabriela in the back with both hands.

Brendan yells as he pushes Gabriela, "No!"

Not expecting the shove, Gabriela stumbles forward and flips over the edge of the well. Gabriela lets out a scream as she falls into the magical well. After a couple of seconds, an explosion emanates from inside the well. Stephanie grabs Brendan, pulls him away and covers him underneath her on the floor. Everyone stops fighting as the entire chamber shakes from the explosion. However, the massive explosion causes the well to collapse, sealing the entrance of the well in a pile of rubble about fifty feet down into the well. As the shaking stops and the dust settles, everyone looks around the chamber and quickly notices that the magical well, the only portal back to their world, has been destroyed.

Chapter 46

As the shaking stops and the dust settles, Prince Brian rushes into the torture chamber. The first thing Prince Brian sees is the destroyed magical well in the middle of the chamber. Everyone is still in shock, but suddenly, a blast of artic air blows through the room. With Gabriela destroyed, the person who conjured the dark riders, the dark riders start to disappear into a cloud of black smoke. After a few seconds, Miclou and Stecher have completely vanished and the temperature in the room returns to normal.

Stephanie and Brendan get back to their feet. Jody, Marsha and Sherry walk over to Stephanie and Brendan. Anna runs up and hugs Marsha. Michael and Shaun walk over next to Stefez. Michael helps Stefez back to her feet, then Michael, Shaun and Stefez walk over to the others. They all look at each other in shock, not wanting to believe what happened to the well.

Prince Brian walks up and smiles as he sees Stephanie, "Is everyone okay?"

Stefez sighs, "Yes my lord."

Stephanie questions, "What happened?"

Stefez shakes her head, "When Gabriela fell into the well, the powerful magic in the well overcame her and caused her to explode."

Jody sighs, "The well, the way home, is destroyed."

Shaun sighs, "So, what happened to the dark riders."

Stefez explains, "They were conjured by Gabriela. When she dies, so does her remaining magical spells. The dark riders went back to their horseshoes."

About that time, Bailee hops over to the group and speaks, "That means my curse is lifted too."

Everyone looks puzzled at Bailee. Then, Bailee starts to glow a soft, golden glow. Everyone gets a surprised look as they step back a couple of feet. The glow gets brighter and brighter as everyone takes a couple more steps back. Then, the glow gets too bright and everyone looks away. Suddenly, a golden sparkling explosion occurs and the glow disappears. When everyone looks back, they are shocked at what they see.

Where there was once a fluffy, white rabbit is now a pretty, cute as a button, Caucasian woman standing there. She looks to be in her mid-twenties, standing about 5'6" tall and weighing a nice looking 165 pounds. She has short, straight blonde hair that hangs to her shoulders and enticing blue eyes. She is wearing a beautiful, lightweight, form-fitting dress in various shades of blue and blue sandals.

The young woman looks over at the group who is still shocked at what they are seeing, "This is what I couldn't tell you. If I did, the spell would have permanently made me a rabbit."

Prince Brian can't believe his eyes, "Bailee? Is that really you little sister?"

Jody, Marsha, Sherry, Anna and Stephanie look over at Prince Brian, not believing what they just heard him say. Bailee runs over to Prince Brian and the two of them embrace.

Bailee speaks with tears in her eyes, "I've missed you so much Brian."

Prince Brian squeezes Bailee, "I've missed you too Bailee."

Everyone smiles at the happy reunion. However, the realization finally sets in again.

Sherry questions, "So, what are we going to do now

with the well being destroyed?"

Stefez lets out a big sigh, "There is nothing we can do here. Lets find a better place where we can figure out what to do."

Prince Brian nods, "Lets go to the throne room. I also need to check on my army to see how the battle has gone."

Stefez nods in agreement, "The throne room sounds good." She glances around at everyone who looks shocked and saddened, "I'm so sorry, but there's nothing more we can do in here. Come on. Lets go."

Everyone nods at Stefez as they put away their weapons. Everyone follows Prince Brian and Bailee out of the chamber.

———————

With the sun in the late afternoon sky now, Prince Brian and the others walk into the throne room. Everyone is still quiet trying to come to terms with the fact that the portal home has been destroyed.

Finally, Stephanie questions, "So, is there any other way except the well?"

Stefez shakes her head, "I'm afraid not."

Sherry questions, "Is there any way to fix the well?"

Stefez nods, "Yes, but it will take quite some time." She pauses, "A long time to be exact."

Marsha chuckles and shakes her head still in shock, "So, what do we do now?"

At that time, Jennifer and Rein walk into the throne room. Everyone turns and sees the two women. Jennifer smiles when she sees that everyone is okay. Jennifer and Rein walk up to everyone else. Jennifer can't believe her eyes when she sees Bailee. Michael and Rein share a caring smile.

Jennifer bows her head, "Its finished my lord.

Gabriela's army has been defeated." She looks over at Bailee, "I can't believe it. I thought we lost you my lady."

Prince Brian nods and replies in a sad tone, "That's good."

Bailee manages a smile, "Its good to see you."

Jennifer can tell something is wrong, "What is it my lord?"

Prince Brian sighs, "The magical well is destroyed. They don't have any way of getting home."

Rein shakes her head, "I'm sorry to hear that." She pauses, "What of Gabriela and the dark riders?"

Stefez replies, "Gabriela has been destroyed and the dark riders are gone."

Jody speaks up, "It still doesn't answer the question as to what we do now."

Stefez sighs, "I hate to say this, but there isn't much we can do."

Prince Brian steps a few feet away and turns back around, "Stay with us, here in the castle. We owe you such a debt for all you've sacrificed. I'll have my people work night and day to rebuild the well." He pauses and looks over at Stephanie, "Until then, stay with us in the castle. We'll take care of everything you need."

Everyone gets quiet for a moment, then Ramaf walks into the throne room. Ramaf walks over to where everyone else is standing.

Ramaf smiles, "All the prisoners have been secured. The army is now working on putting up new castle gate doors and securing the castle."

Prince Brian nods, "Thank you my friend."

Jody finally speaks, "We really don't have much choice, but to stay here until the well is fixed."

Anna looks at Marsha, "Its not a bad place. I actually like it here."

Brendan finally smiles, "Me too."

Stephanie lets out a sigh, "I guess there are worse

places where we could've been stuck in."

Sherry nods, "Yea, like the swamp."

Finally, everyone smiles and accepts the fact that they are stuck in the fairytale land. Jody walks over, bends down and gives Brendan a big hug.

Jody squeezes Brendan, "You did great big man. You even defeated the evil Queen."

Brendan steps back and smiles, "Yea, I showed her."

Everyone laughs at Brendan, then they allow themselves to finally relax. Jody and Stephanie hug as Marsha and Anna hug. Then, Jody hugs Anna and Marsha hugs Brendan as Stephanie and Sherry hug. After that, Sherry and Marsha hug as Jody hugs Anna and Stephanie hugs Brendan. The hugging continues around the room until everyone has given everyone a hug. Finally, everyone stops and stands together in the middle of the throne room.

Stephanie is standing with her hands on Brendan's shoulders. Marsha and Jody are standing next to each other holding hands. Michael and Rein are holding hands and so is Prince Brian and Bailee.

Jennifer speaks up, "So, you know what this means now?"

Shaun questions, "What's that?"

Jennifer smiles, "We have to have a coronation ball."

Stefez nods, "That's right. The land must have a King or Queen." She looks at Prince Brian, "Or both."

Prince Brian smiles, "Tomorrow we can plan the coronation. I think that we could all use some rest."

Bailee speaks up, "I could go for some real food too."

Brendan smiles, "Yea, and ice cream."

Everyone laughs at Brendan.

Prince Brian smiles, "I bet we can manage that."

Jennifer smiles and questions, "So, what do you need me to do my lord?"

Prince Brian glances around, "Get our caretakers in

here so one of them can take our friends to some rooms where they can clean up. We'll have another caretaker gather up the cooks and get dinner ready."

Jennifer bows her head, "Yes my lord."

Jennifer turns and hurries off.

Prince Brian looks at the others, "I owe you my Kingdom. If not for all of you, I could never have accomplished all of this. You are all welcome here for as long as you wish, my castle is your castle." Prince Brian bows his head, "I thank you."

Everyone smiles, but can't find the words to say anything. Then, Jennifer walks back into the throne room with two men dressed in nice clothes.

Prince Brian nods to the men, "I need one of you to take them to some rooms. I need the other to make sure dinner is prepared."

Both men bow their heads and reply, "Yes my lord."

Prince Brian looks over at Stephanie, "They will take care of all of you. I'll see you all shortly for dinner."

The man on the left motions with his hand, turns and starts out of the throne room. Stephanie, Jody, Marsha, Anna, Brendan, Sherry and Shaun follow the man out of the room as Michael, Rein, Ramaf, Stefez and Bailee stay with Prince Brian in the throne room.

After dinner that night, everyone settles into their rooms in the castle. Each one thinking about the journey that led them to where they are now and each one thinking about what lays ahead. As night falls over the Kingdom that now belongs to Prince Brian, everyone finds that sleep is much easier to come by.

While everyone settles in and sleeps, the message birds that were sent after dinner start to arrive in every town and village in the Kingdom to spread the word that Gabriela has been destroyed and that Prince Brian has control of the Kingdom. The message birds also tell the people that Prince Brian's coronation is in two days.

Chapter 47

As the morning sun shines down from the clear blue sky, workers are busy all over the castle. People are everywhere cleaning the castle, the castle grounds and decorating for the coronation of Prince Brian which is scheduled for the next day.

Jennifer is working on making the castle safe and getting everything in place in order to make sure everything is ready as far as security for the coronation. Stefez is going over the coronation ceremony to make sure everything is done according to tradition. Stefez is also over seeing the coronation ball after the ceremony as well as the decorations and entertainment. Shaun is making sure her rangers are going to be ready for the coronation. Ramaf is making sure his dwarves will be ready for the coronation.

Rein, who is still dressed the same just without her weapons and equipment, is walking by the royal stables. Michael, who is also dressed the same just without his weapons and equipment, starts walking towards Rein. Rein sees Michael approaching and smiles at him. Michael walks up to Rein and they embrace in a caring hug, then share a brief, but very nice kiss.

Michael steps back and smiles, "I can't believe it's finally over."

Rein smiles, "I'm so happy you decided to come back."

Michael looks into Rein's eyes, "Me too."

Rein sighs, "So, what will you do after the

coronation?"

Michael shakes his head, "I'm not sure just yet." He pauses, "How about you?"

Rein shrugs, "Prince Brian is going to create four sections inside his Kingdom and have each one watched over by a local ruler that will report to him." She pauses, "I'm the Elf Queen. I will return with my people and watch over the section of the Kingdom that Prince Brian asks me too."

Michael nods slightly, "No doubt it will be somewhere in the forest."

Rein nods and smiles, "I'm pretty sure that's right." She pauses, "You know, the last time an Elf Queen took on a companion it was two Queens ago."

Michael looks at Rein, "What are you saying?"

Rein gazes at Michael, "I want you to go with me. Be my companion and help me look after the Kingdom and my people." She pauses, "I was lost when you were not around and I don't want to go through that again."

Michael is quiet for a second, then smiles, "There is nothing I would like more than to go with you."

Rein steps forward and the two of them embrace again.

Rein speaks while they hug, "We should go and start making sure that our people are ready for the coronation."

Michael smiles as they hug, "I like the sound of that, our people."

Rein and Michael step back, gaze at each other and smile. Then, the two of them head off to find the elves.

Bailee, Sherry, Brendan and Anna, who are all dressed the same just without any of the equipment or weapons that any of them might have had on the journey, are walking through the huge back courtyard. Beautiful flowers are everywhere as stone walks wind their way through the courtyard. As Bailee and the others walk by the various workers, the people stop and bow their heads to Bailee as a show of respect to the Princess.

Sherry smiles, "That's so crazy. The very first friend we had in the Kingdom was a talking rabbit who just happened to be the Princess."

Bailee smiles, "I know. When Gabriela took over the castle and killed my father, I was there. My brother had already escaped like my father ordered him too. Instead of killing me, Gabriela decided it would be more fun to change me into a rabbit."

Anna chuckles, "I guess that backfired. You were a big part of us making it to the castle and beating her."

Bailee nods, "Yea, Gabriela thought my brother was her biggest enemy when in fact, what finally brought her down was her own arrogance."

Brendan just keeps looking around, "This place is so awesome."

Bailee looks down at Brendan, "Come on, I'll show you all some even more cool things in the castle."

Brendan smiles, "Yea!"

Bailee starts to playfully and slowly run towards the castle as Brendan starts to chase after her. Sherry and Anna laugh and start after Bailee and Brendan.

Marsha and Jody, who are still dressed the same just without their weapons and equipment, are walking through the front courtyard of the castle. It looks a lot like the back courtyard, just not nearly as big. As they walk along one of the stone walkways, they take each others hand and smile at each other. The workers take notice of the two of them, but continue on with what they are doing as they work hard to get the castle ready for the coronation.

Marsha looks at Jody as they walk, "So, it looks like you're going to be a resident of the Kingdom awhile longer."

Jody chuckles, "It looks that way, but that's okay." He gazes at Marsha, "Its gotten a lot better here as of late."

Marsha smiles, "I think I'm going to like it here too."

Jody questions, "So, what did you leave behind?"

Marsha shakes her head, "A job and a few friends, but no family. Anna is here with me and that is all that matters."

Jody nods and smiles, "That's good."

Marsha adds, "Plus, you got your sister and nephew, who is absolutely adorable, back."

Jody can't help but smile at that thought, "That was the one thing I was missing while being here, Stephanie and Brendan."

Marsha questions, "So, where do we go from here?"

Jody shrugs, "I'm not sure, Prince Brian has asked to speak to me in private later today along with Rein, Ramaf and Shaun." He pauses, "As far as us, I can only pray for one outcome."

Marsha slyly looks at Jody, "Just what are you saying?"

Jody gazes at Marsha, "Well, in the Kingdom when a man and a woman are in love, they become what is called companions." He pauses, "I was hoping you would be my companion."

Marsha playfully questions, "Jody, are you saying that you are in love with me?"

Jody stops walking, steps forward, takes Marsha in his arms and kisses her. When the kiss is done, Jody steps back and smiles.

Marsha sighs and smiles, "Wow. I guess that answers that question."

Jody lovingly gazes into Marsha's eyes, "I love you with all my heart Marsha. Will you be my companion?"

Marsha returns the loving gaze, "Of course I will." She jumps back into Jody's arms, "I love you so much."

Jody and Marsha continue to embrace as they are completely oblivious to all the work going on around them.

Stephanie, who is still dressed the same just without her weapon and equipment, is standing on the balcony of her room looking out at the back courtyard of the castle. She closes her eyes and lets the soft breeze blow across her face. Prince Brian, who is still dressed the same just without his weapons or equipment, walks up behind Stephanie and stops at the balcony doors.

Prince Brian speaks, "Is everything okay Stephanie?"

Stephanie quickly opens her eyes and turns around, "Oh, Prince Brian." She bows her head, "Um, yes everything is okay."

Prince Brian starts towards Stephanie and holds up his right hand, "Please, for everything you've gone through and sacrificed, you will never have to bow to me."

Stephanie smiles as Prince Brian stops and stands next to her at the rail of the balcony. The two of them look out at the back courtyard of the castle.

Prince Brian finally breaks the silence, "So, what do you think of the Kingdom?"

Stephanie smiles as she continues to look out at the back courtyard, "It's beautiful and an absolutely amazing place."

Prince Brian looks at Stephanie, "I'm sorry you're not able to return home."

Stephanie looks at Prince Brian, "You want to hear

something strange?"

Prince Brian smiles, "Sure."

Stephanie sighs, "When the well was destroyed, I was of course shocked and sad, but a small part of me inside was actually happy."

Prince Brian gets a puzzled look, "Why was that?"

Stephanie smiles, "Ever since looking in that magical mirror in Lover's Keep, I've thought about wanting to stay here in the Kingdom. Then, after you sent me that message telling me how you felt about me, I was wanting to stay even more. I just wasn't sure if I would be able to find the strength to stay." She pauses, "When the well was destroyed, I no longer had to worry about making the decision."

Prince Brian smiles, "The decision was made for you." He pauses, "So, you want to hear what I was thinking?"

Stephanie nods, "Of course."

Prince Brian sighs, "From the moment we saw each other, you captured my heart. All the time we were traveling and fighting our battles, I was thinking of you." He pauses, "I didn't want to see anything happen to any of you, but I was hoping something would happen to keep you in the Kingdom."

Stephanie smiles and chuckles, "That's funny."

Prince Brian continues, "Yea, it's funny how fate has a way of working things out for us."

Stephanie looks back out at the courtyard, "So, are you ready for the coronation?"

Prince Brian stares at Stephanie, "For the most part. I'm meeting with Jody, Shaun, Rein and Ramaf later. Everything else is being taken care of." He pauses, "Just one thing remains."

Stephanie questions while continuing to look out from the balcony, "What's that?"

Prince Brian reaches over and takes Stephanie's

hand, "You."

Stephanie looks over at Prince Brian, "What?"

Prince Brian smiles, "I have my sister back. I have my Kingdom back. I'm going to become King tomorrow and there is peace throughout the Kingdom." He pauses, "But none of that matters to me if I can't share it with someone, and you're the only one I can see myself sharing it with."

Stephanie gets a surprised look, "What?"

Prince Brian steps a little closer still holding Stephanie's hand, "In this land when two people are together, they are known as companions. I want to share my life and my Kingdom with you, and of course, Brendan."

Stephanie just stares at Prince Brian in shock, unable to say anything.

Prince Brian gazes into Stephanie's eyes, "Will you be my companion and sit beside me on the throne?"

Stephanie is speechless at what she is hearing. Her heart is pounding and her mind is racing, unable to focus on anything. Then, Stephanie remembers something Jody told her a long time ago when he was teaching her about self-defense and philosophy. She remembers the words of the very first lesson in philosophy Jody told her about, "follow your heart".

Stephanie breaks a smile as a tear rolls down her cheek, "Yes. Oh my God, yes!"

Prince Brian gets a big smile on his face as he steps towards Stephanie. Prince Brian and Stephanie embrace each other tight. The two of them share a long, passionate kiss.

Epilogue

B anners made of beautiful and vibrant colors hang all over the huge throne room. Wooden tables line the two walls between the main doors into the room and the steps that lead up to the throne. Cups of ale sit all over the tables and the tables are decorated with bouquets of fresh flowers. The tables are full of people except for the table closest to the stairs on the right side of the room. Near the main door is a small band playing music. At the top of the ten steps on the other end of the room is four gold trimmed, purple velvet chairs. Two men in nice clothing are standing near the chairs. Both are holding purple velvet pillows. On one pillow in a golden crown encrusted with various jewels. On the other pillow is a white gold tiara encrusted with diamonds.

Humans, elves and dwarves fill the throne room. They are all dressed in very nice, formal clothing. They are drinking ale and visiting with each other while the music plays. Then, the two main doors open. The music stops playing and everyone in the room gets quiet. The humans, elves and dwarves part the way making a clear path to the throne. Jennifer walks in with Stefez.

Jennifer is wearing brown boots that come up to just below her knees. She has on form-fitting, royal blue with gold trim pants, a royal blue with gold trim, long sleeve top, a royal blue tunic that has the seal of the royal family on the front of it in gold trim and a brown leather belt. She is carrying a four foot long, gold handle with silver bladed sword on her left hip.

Stefez is wearing a beautiful, form-fitting, formal dress in various shades of red and red sandals. She is carrying her staff in her right hand. Stefez and Jennifer walk across the room. Jennifer stops at the bottom left of the stairs and waits, but Stefez walks up the stairs and stops. She turns around in front of the four chairs and faces the throne room.

Stefez taps her staff on the floor, "Bring in the honored guests." She pauses, "First, the Dwarf King, Ramaf."

Ramaf walks into the room. He is wearing brown boots, nice brown pants and a nice brown, long sleeve top. He is wearing a shiny silver plate of armor that covers his torso. Ramaf is wearing a small, shiny silver crown on his head. Ramaf walks across the room as everyone bows to show their respect. Ramaf stops next to Jennifer and waits.

Stefez taps her staff again, "Next, the Elf Queen, Rein, and her chosen companion, Michael."

Rein and Michael walk into the room. Rein is wearing a beautiful, formal dress in various shades of brown and brown sandals. She is wearing a small, shiny silver crown with an emerald stone on her head. Michael is wearing brown boots, green with brown trim pants, a white long sleeve top, a green with brown trim, long sleeve, open breasted jacket with tails and a brown leather belt. Rein and Michael walk across the room as everyone bows their head to show their respect. Rein and Michael stops next to Jennifer and Ramaf and waits.

Stefez taps her staff again, "Next, the Queen of the Ranger Clan, Shaun."

Shaun walks into the room. She is wearing a beautiful, form-fitting, formal dress in various shades of blue and blue sandals. She is wearing a small, shiny silver crown with a ruby stone on her head. Shaun walks across the room as everyone bows to show their respect. Shaun stops next to Jennifer, Ramaf, Rein and Michael and waits.

Stefez taps her staff again, "Bring in the rest of the honored guests."

Jody and Marsha walk into the room. Jody is wearing brown boots, royal blue with gold trim pants, a white, long sleeve top, a royal blue with gold trim, open breasted jacket with tails and a brown leather belt. Marsha is wearing a beautiful, form-fitting, formal dress in various shades of pink and pink sandals. Marsha is wearing a small wreath made of fresh flowers on her head and the silver necklace she was wearing when she entered the Kingdom. Jody and Marsha walk across the room and stop at the bottom right of the stairs.

Anna and Sherry walk into the room. Anna is wearing a beautiful, formal dress in various shades of yellow, yellow sandals and the necklace she was wearing when she entered the Kingdom. Sherry is wearing a beautiful, form-fitting, formal dress in various shades of green, green sandals and the necklace she was wearing when she entered the Kingdom. Anna and Sherry walk across the room and stop next to Jody and Marsha.

Stephanie and Brendan walk into the room. Brendan is wearing brown boots, royal blue pants, a white long sleeve top, a royal blue, open breasted jacket with tails and a brown leather belt. Stephanie is wearing an absolutely beautiful, formal, white and ivory colored dress, white sandals and the silver St. Jude necklace she was wearing when she entered the Kingdom. Stephanie and Brendan walk across the room and stops next to Jody, Marsha, Anna and Sherry.

Stefez taps her staff one more time, "Now, bring forth the royal family."

Prince Brian and Princess Bailee walk into the room. Princess Bailee is wearing a beautiful, form-fitting, formal dress in various shades of purple with gold trim and purple sandals. She is wearing a small, white gold with diamond encrusted tiara on her head. Prince Brian is wearing brown boots, purple with gold trim pants, a white, long sleeve top, a purple with gold trim, open breasted jacket with tails and a brown belt. As Prince Brian and Princess Bailee walk across the room, everyone bows their head to show their respect. Prince Brian and Princess Bailee walk up the stairs. Prince Brian stops in front of Stefez as Princess Bailee walks over to the fourth chair, turns and faces the room.

Stefez speaks in a powerful voice, "To all the witnesses hear, behold the coronation of Prince Brian!"

Stefez taps her staff twice. The man carrying the pillow with the gold crown walks over and stands next to Stefez.

Stefez speaks again, "The blood of the royal family flows through your veins. As the oldest child, you are the rightful heir to the throne." She pauses, "Kneel Prince Brian."

Prince Brian kneels in front of Stefez. Stefez lets go of her staff and it continues to stand on it's own. She reaches over and picks up the crown from the pillow. The man quickly returns to where he was originally standing. Stefez turns and places the crown on Prince Brian's head.

Stefez speaks once more, "May you rule with strength, courage and wisdom." She pauses, "Now rise, King Brian."

King Brian stands up. Stefez grabs her staff and walks over next to Princess Bailee. King Brian turns to face the room. Everyone in the room kneels to the newly crowned King.

King Brian speaks, "Please, everyone rise!"

Everyone in the room stands up.

King Brian speaks in a powerful voice, "Before we begin the ball, I have some things I wish to address first." He pauses, "As I may rule the entire Kingdom, it occurs to me that I cannot be everywhere to look out for the people as a good ruler should. I have decided to break the Kingdom into four smaller sections, each one governed by a very capable leader that will keep in touch with me."

King Brian takes a deep breath, "First, King Ramaf, please approach."

Ramaf smiles and walks up the stairs. He stops in front of King Brian.

King Brian smiles, "To you, I give the northeast section of the Kingdom. You will govern the snow lands and the mountains. May you and your people have peace and prosperity. I can never thank the dwarves enough for everything they have done for the Kingdom."

Ramaf bows his head, "It was our honor my King. Thank you."

King Brian nods. Ramaf returns to where he was standing.

King Brian speaks, "Next, Queen Shaun, please approach."

Shaun smiles and walks up the stairs. She stops in front of King Brian.

King Brian speaks, "To you, I give the southwest section of the Kingdom. You will govern the forest from the west and south edge of the Kingdom all the way to River Fork and South Town. I can never thank the rangers enough for everything they've done for the Kingdom."

Shaun smiles and bows her head, "It was an honor my King. Thank you."

King Brian nods. Shaun returns to where she was standing.

King Brian speaks, "Now, Queen Rein and her companion, Michael, please approach."

Rein and Michael walk up the stairs and stop in front of King Brian.

King Brian speaks, " To you, I give the southeast section of the Kingdom. You will govern from the east and south edge of the Kingdom the forest all the way to River Fork and South Town and north to the mountains to include Ghost Town." He pauses, "I am forever in debt to you and the elves for everything they've done for the Kingdom. Michael, you once served the royal family. You will be greatly missed, but may your life be full of happiness in your never endeavor."

Michael bows his head, "It's been an honor. Thank you my King."

Rein bows her head, "It was an honor to fight beside you my King. Thank you."

King Brian nods. Rein and Michael return to where they were standing.

King Brian takes a deep breath, "I would like to make a couple of announcements next. First, Jennifer will be the Captain of my army. Her courage and bravery have no limits." He looks at Jennifer, "Thank you for everything."

Jennifer bows her head, "Thank you my King."

King Brian speaks again, "Now, I would like to recognize Stefez. She has agreed to stay here as my magical advisor." He looks at Stefez, "I can never thank you enough for what you've done for this Kingdom. If not for you, this could not have happened."

Stefez bows her head, "Thank you my King."

King Brian looks back to the room, "Now, I have asked Sherry to take on the task of creating what is called a school and creating an education program. Sherry has agreed to do so." He looks over at Sherry, "What you did since arriving in the Kingdom has been amazing. You showed great courage and bravery in the face of things you have never seen before. I know you have had to leave a world behind and I only hope we can give you the life you want here in the Kingdom. I thank you."

Sherry bows her head as a tear rolls down her cheek, "Thank you my King."

King Brian smiles, "Now, would Jody, Marsha and

Anna please approach."

Jody, Marsha and Anna walk up the stairs and stop in front of King Brian.

King Brian looks at Jody, "If not for your bravery and courage, Gabriela would've surely succeeded in her plans. You have proven to be a capable leader with the qualities any one of us would be honored to have." He pauses, "Therefore, I am giving you the title of Duke. You will govern the northwest section of the Kingdom which includes the grasslands all the way from the mountains to the western edge of the Kingdom and south to the forest."

King Brian takes a breath, "I understand that Marsha is your companion?"

Jody replies with a smile, "Yes my King."

King Brian looks at Marsha, "Then, I bestow upon you the title of Duchess." He looks over at Anna and smiles, "By nature of blood relation, I bestow upon you the title of Duchess as well."

King Brian looks back out at the room, "Let all witness, from here forth, these three shall have all the rights and entitlements that are afforded any other royal family in the Kingdom."

King Brian looks back at Jody, Marsha and Anna, "Your sacrifices have been great and too many to count. Marsha and Anna, I know you've had to leave a life behind. I hope that we can help you in making a new life here in the castle and Kingdom with Jody. I can't thank the two of you enough for everything you've done and had to go through."

Jody bows his head, "Thank you my King."

Marsha bows her head as a tear rolls down her cheek, "Thank you my King."

Anna smiles and bows her head, "Thank you my King."

King Brian nods. Jody, Marsha and Anna return to

where they were standing.

King Brian gets a big smile, "Finally, would Stephanie and Brendan please approach."

Stephanie and Brendan walk up the stairs and stop in front of King Brian.

King Brian looks at Stephanie and Brendan, "You two have had to sacrifice so much and have had to leave a world behind. You've had to face challenges most people could not have imagined. If not for the two of you, none of this would be possible. You helped restore peace to the Kingdom."

Brendan smiles as a tear rolls down Stephanie's cheek.

King Brian looks back out to the room, "I have asked Stephanie to be my companion and she accepted." He looks back at Stephanie and Brendan, "Would the two of you please kneel."

Stephanie and Brendan both kneel as the man with the tiara on his pillow walks over next to King Brian. King Brian takes the tiara from the pillow and the man returns to where he was standing.

King Brian places the tiara on Stephanie's head, "Before all the witnesses here, I take you as my companion to share my life and my Kingdom with." He pauses, "Please rise, Queen Stephanie and Prince Brendan."

Stephanie and Brendan stand back up. The two of them step over next to King Brian and turn around to face the room. Everyone in the room kneels to show their respect. Stephanie looks down at Jody to see him smiling at her. Stephanie smiles at Jody as she tries to hold back the tears.

King Brian speaks in a powerful voice, "Now, let the coronation party begin!"

Everyone stands back up. The music starts to play again and it is an upbeat tune. A young woman standing with the musicians starts to sing a love song to the upbeat tune. Numerous people start dancing to the music.

King Brian looks at Queen Stephanie, "Would you like to dance?"

Queen Stephanie smiles, "I would love to."

King Brian and Queen Stephanie walk down the stairs to the dance floor area. King Brian bows to Queen Stephanie and she curtsies to King Brian. Then, the two of them come together and start dancing. Rein and Michael walk out to the dance floor area. Michael bows to Rein and she curtsies to Michael. Then, the two of them come together and start dancing.

Princess Bailee walks down the stairs and over to a handsome man in his mid-twenties. The two of them walk out onto the dance floor area. The man bows to Princess Bailee and she curtsies to the man. Then, the two of them come together and start dancing. Shaun walks out onto the dance floor area with a handsome man in his late twenties. The man bows to Shaun and she curtsies to the man. Then, the two of them come together and start dancing.

Ramaf walks over to Sherry, "May I have this dance my lady?"

Sherry smiles, "Of course."

Ramaf and Sherry walk out to the dance area. Ramaf bows to Sherry and she curtsies to Ramaf. Then, the two of them come together and start dancing. Jody looks over to Prince Brendan and motions to him. Prince Brendan runs down the stairs to Jody.

Jody looks at Brendan, "Why don't you and Anna go dance?"

Brendan makes a face, "Dance with a girl Uncle Jody?"

Jody smiles, "Sure. Marsha and I are going to dance. Just walk over to her and hold out your hand."

Brendan smiles, "Okay Uncle Jody."

Brendan walks over to Anna and holds out his right hand.

Anna smiles, "Awe, Brendan. Your so sweet." She kisses Brendan on the cheek, "I would love to dance."

Jody and Marsha watch Anna and Brendan with a smile.

Jody holds out his hand to Marsha, "May I have this dance?"

Marsha smiles and gazes at Jody, "This one and the one for the rest of my life."

Marsha takes Jody's hand and they walk out to the dance area. Anna takes Brendan's hand and they walk out to the dance area next to Jody and Marsha. Jody looks at Brendan, then looks at Marsha and bows. Brendan copies Jody and bows to Anna. Marsha curtsies to Jody and Anna curtsies to Brendan. Jody and Marsha come together and start dancing. Brendan and Anna come together and they start moving back and forth the best they can.

Jennifer and Stefez watch as everyone in the room continues to dance to the music as others drink some ale and visit. The tune changes to a slower song and everyone continues to dance. The coronation party continues as everyone across the Kingdom celebrates the new found peace.

THE END

www.ingramcontent.com/pod-product-compliance
Lightning Source LLC
Chambersburg PA
CBHW022144010726
47493CB00002B/338